HEARTS IN PERIL™

Bayou Cold Case

Robin Caroll

Annie's®
AnniesFiction.com

Books in the Hearts in Peril series

Library of Congress-in-Publication Data
Bayou Cold Case / by Robin Caroll
p. cm.
ISBN: 978-1-64025-513-5
I. Title
2022949865

AnniesFiction.com
(800) 282-6643
Hearts in Peril™
Series Creator: Shari Lohner
Series Editor: Amy Woods

10 11 12 13 14 | Printed in China | 9 8 7 6 5 4 3 2 1

1

"*W*hat's *he* doing at my crime scene?" Detective Sienna Rose Jordan gripped the disposable gloves she'd pulled from her pocket. Her grasp tightened to offset the tremble in her hands.

Officer Hazel Moncrief glanced over her shoulder at a man leaning over a recently discovered murder victim. The rookie officer let out a dreamy, exaggerated sigh, wearing a soft expression. "Special Detective Cruz? He's from New Orleans, leading a task force assigned to help us with these murders, since they seem to be connected." She smiled at Sienna Rose. "And if you ask me, he's a beautiful addition to the investigation. Fair warning, you can get lost in those eyes. It's as if he can see right into your soul."

Sienna Rose ground her teeth. She knew all too well how Legend Cruz's eyes could see right through someone. She tugged on the rubber gloves, struggling to work them over her sweaty palms. Shadows danced as the light moved closer to the horizon. She bent to slip on her shoe covers, ignoring the afternoon Louisiana sun that peaked through the tall cypress trees along the edges of the bayou. Maybe that would hide the telltale sign of heat rushing to her face. She needed a moment to compose herself and get to the job at hand. At some point, she'd have to deal with the emotions she'd buried half a decade ago, but it had to be later.

Inhaling deeply, she shut out everything but the scene around her. A row of local police vehicles, deputy cruisers, and a few state police cars snaked along the road, some with their lights flashing. A throng of officers—many she didn't recognize—gathered beside the yellow crime scene tape that fluttered in the November breeze, talking soberly as the unmistakable gloom of death permeated the air.

Already two news vans were making their way down the dirt road. Sienna Rose let out a breath and forced herself to relax and observe. Too many people. Too many opportunities to contaminate her crime scene.

Sienna Rose focused her attention on training questions that would help the rookie cop beside her, who hoped to become a detective in the Envie Police Department. "Officer Moncrief, if you are the first detective to arrive, what is your initial act after ensuring that the officers have secured the area to protect the crime scene?"

"Set up the crime scene log and make sure gloves and shoe protectors are available to every person before entering the cordoned-off area."

"Correct," Sienna Rose confirmed. "Please go find who has the log and get us both signed in. With this many people here, a log will have already been created." Sienna Rose handed the woman a box of shoe protectors she kept in the back of her SUV. "In case the patrol officers didn't have any when they set up the perimeter." She'd seen way too many cops forgoing the protectors at outside scenes, which was unacceptable. Sienna Rose knew of more than one case that had been thrown out of court because of possible corrupted evidence. She didn't intend for hers to be among them.

She shut the back door of her vehicle and continued the training information. "Make sure the officers know only essential personnel are allowed past the tape, and that no media is permitted anywhere near this area. They might need to push back the block so that there are no photos or videos using zoom lenses. I'll go check in with Special Detective Cruz. Meet me by the body as soon as you're done."

Sienna Rose struggled to keep her voice and demeanor neutral. Though the discovery marked the fourth killing in what was most likely a string of connected murders, why did Legend have to be the one leading the task force? It didn't matter. Regardless of the history she shared with Cruz, she resolved to remain professional. They were merely colleagues. No less—and certainly no more.

Anxiety flashed across Officer Moncrief's face, but she straightened her shoulders and headed off toward the circle of her fellow officers, toting the box of shoe coverings. The young woman wanted so badly to make detective someday. Sienna Rose wanted it for her too. The test was difficult and filled with obscure questions, which was why she pushed Moncrief so hard.

Sienna Rose lifted the yellow crime scene tape and walked carefully to where the body was. She inhaled deeply, willing herself to calm.

This was usually her favorite part of working a crime scene—letting her senses register every little thing whether it seemed relevant to the crime or not, allowing her mind to process every nuance, and absorbing the facts as she discovered them.

But she was too tense to even experience the moment.

And feeling that way was ridiculous. She was a grown woman, a detective for pity's sake. She was considered one of the best in the region, and she commanded respect from every cop she'd worked with over the last five years. It'd been quite a feat—a lot of long hours and hard work—but she'd earned it. No one could take that away from her, not even Special Detective Cruz and his elite task force.

She had been assigned as lead detective on the first murder, so the ones that followed and appeared to be related had become her cases too. The murderer designated his next target by leaving an index card with their name on the body of his current victim. Chief Savoie had specifically requested that she take charge of the investigation after the first murder, and she would not let him down.

Yet *he* was bent over the victim, his back to her, making notes on the small pad he held. Despite the ease and convenience of newer technology, he'd always preferred keeping his case details in those little notepads.

"Legend." That one word nearly clogged her throat with emotion.

Ever so slowly, he stood. His piercing eyes locked with hers. "Sienna Rose." His voice saying her name was as warm as she remembered.

She lost her ability to speak.

A heaviness hung between them. So much history filled the air.

He'd aged a bit over the last five years. A few lines peeked out from the tanned skin surrounding his blue eyes. Dashes of silver were visible in the thick hair over his ears. Otherwise, Legend Cruz was everything she remembered.

And that was a problem.

He cleared his throat. "What are you doing here?"

She licked her lips and squared her shoulders, every fiber of her being wishing she was anywhere but where she stood. "The question is, what are *you* doing here?" He wasn't needed, and he surely wasn't wanted. Not by Sienna Rose anyway.

"My special task force was requested." He slid his notebook into the back pocket of his jeans, then crossed his arms over his chest.

His task force. A specialized, elite group of detectives that assisted law enforcement across the state when the need arose. The task force she'd been asked to join at its inception five years before, exactly like Legend. What gave him the right to call it his?

She wished someone had warned her Legend would be there. Chief Savoie had given her no heads-up when he'd called her. Then again, it was the chief's daughter who had been found and identified as the victim. Perhaps that was why Savoie hadn't mentioned the task force. Sienna Rose could certainly understand. It was probably the last thing on his mind. The chief was most likely buried in grief.

"I've been called in to help with this string of murders." He tapped the badge hanging around his neck.

The enormity of the situation weighed on her shoulders. His jurisdiction outranked hers. Her heart sank. "Uh-huh. Taking over, right?" She hadn't worked hard enough or fast enough, so she was losing the case, and she had let the chief down by allowing the monster to murder his daughter.

He frowned at her. "No one is taking over. If I'm not mistaken, this is your case, Sienna Rose. I have every intention of working alongside you, as partners." His voice had no business being so gentle. It reminded her of what they'd once meant to each other. But that was in the past and needed to stay there, out of her way. "At least, if that's not asking too much."

"I'm able to conduct myself professionally without bias or prejudice. I won't be ousted from the case." She wasn't about to be brushed aside, especially not by him. Sienna Rose pulled herself up to her full height of five foot, six inches and stuck out her chin. "I'm the lead detective. I'm staying on."

"Fine. But given our jurisdiction, I'm head of the investigation." His tone carried more than a hint of authority. Then again, it often had. At one time, she'd found that attractive. Currently, she found it annoying. It was clear his need to be in charge hadn't mellowed much over the last five years.

There wasn't much more she could say. He was right. It was his case, much as that frustrated her.

Officer Moncrief joined them. "We're all signed in, Detective Jordan," she told Sienna Rose. Then she faced Legend, her pearly-white smile nearly splitting her face. "I see you've met Detective Jordan, Detective Cruz. She's the best on the force."

Legend's stare remained locked on Sienna Rose. He raised his left eyebrow the way she'd always found so endearing and gave a half smirk. "Is that so? I believe it."

Sienna Rose refused to squirm under the smoldering intensity. She had a job to do, and she'd do it to the best of her ability, as always. It didn't matter who else was on the case.

Ignoring Officer Moncrief and Legend, Sienna Rose moved to the body, which lay on a bed of pine needles. She closed her eyes and inhaled a very faint undertone of something. Floral. Maybe it—

A gasp from behind her made Sienna Rose spin around. Officer Moncrief's face was pale and her eyes wide with shock. Sienna Rose knew the young officer hadn't seen many murder victims, and it was a tough experience for many people.

Legend patted Moncrief's shoulder.

"Officer Moncrief, take a moment and gather yourself." She ignored Legend's glare. Moncrief's reaction was understandable, but she would need to learn to control it. No detective could afford to be too shaken up in the field. It would compromise her observation skills and judgment, causing her to miss something important that could make or break a case. The woman had to toughen up so she could be a good detective once she was promoted.

"I'm okay." Officer Moncrief straightened.

"Good." Sienna Rose pulled out her phone and began snapping wide-angle shots of the victim, noting her location about twenty feet from the edge of the bayou. "While the crime scene techs will take plenty of photos, it's always convenient to have your own set. Sometimes broader pictures can reveal things that are missed at the scene." She clicked off four or five more photos, then pulled up the weather app.

The body couldn't have been out too long, based on the physical evidence that Sienna Rose could see. It didn't appear decomposed, nor touched by area wildlife. "The temps over the last few days and nights have been highs in the upper sixties and lows in the midfifties. That would explain the lack of decay."

Officer Moncrief scrambled for her phone and began typing in notes. Legend crossed his arms over his chest and studied Sienna Rose.

She refused to let him unnerve her. Sienna Rose slid her phone into her pocket, then squatted beside the exposed body, careful not to let the soggy marsh suck her feet into the muck. Even in the fall, Louisiana bayous rarely loosened their smothering humidity.

The victim was half African American, half white. Beautiful complexion, petite build. Multiple stab wounds marred her torso. Her long black hair clung to her face, covering her eyes. Sienna Rose's heart ached for Chief Savoie. His daughter, Magdalene, had always been beautiful.

The last time Sienna Rose had seen Magdalene was at her high school graduation a few years before. Magdalene had been all smiles as valedictorian, the apple of her daddy's eye. She'd made him proud, that was for certain. Now she lay lifeless, discarded in the bayou as if she didn't matter. Nothing was promised in this life.

Sienna Rose knew that to be true.

"It's inexcusable." Legend's voice was soft beside her, almost a whisper in her ear.

"I can't imagine," Sienna Rose murmured as she straightened. It was okay to let some emotions slip in. Empathy for the family of victims usually pushed detectives to dig into the case until it was solved.

Turning her attention back to her observation of Magdalene's body, Sienna readied herself for the killer's customary calling card, naming the next target.

A yellow index card stuck to Magdalene's torso bore black capital letters that set the hairs on the back of her neck at full attention. The card read: *Sienna Rose Jordan.*

2

*W*hen he'd seen the card before Sienna Rose's arrival, the last five years dropped away from Legend.

There had been no texts, no calls, no letters—absolutely nothing for those five years. Sure, he was the one who had left Sienna Rose behind. But he'd tried to contact her many times since, and she'd never answered or returned his calls or texts. Finally, he had attempted to push her as far from his mind as possible.

Yet as soon as she'd said his name, his traitorous heart had skipped several beats.

She'd always had that effect on him, but he'd assumed that was over and done with. Apparently, five years hadn't been long enough for his heart to forget what he'd felt for her. If he were honest with himself, that was why he hadn't been back to Envie. He'd always known, deep down, that eventually she would pull his heart back to the small town he'd grown up in.

And he'd found her again—just in time to see her marked for death at the hands of a serial killer.

Sienna Rose stood and wobbled a bit.

Legend reached out to steady her. "I know. It's a shock." Despite his calm demeanor, seeing his ex's name on the killer's calling card was tearing him apart, which was exactly what he'd like to do to the murderer if—when—they caught the person.

She took a step away from him and cleared her throat, but her gaze stayed locked on the index card bearing her name.

It must have thrown her for a loop. If he knew Sienna Rose, she would force herself to behave professionally, to prove to herself and everyone else that she wasn't rattled, but he'd heard the slight gasp she probably thought she'd hidden. He'd seen the color drain from her face. He'd felt the slight trembling when he'd touched her.

"I'm fine," she said. But her voice cracked. "Let's go over what we know already."

She activated a recording app on her smartphone and met his stare. "Okay, Special Detective Cruz, what do we know about the victim?" She cleared her throat.

Sienna Rose was obviously still working to put her composure firmly back in place.

Legend pulled the notebook from his back pocket and poised his pen over the paper, even though he already knew the details by heart. "Victim is Magdalene Savoie, daughter of Chief Leon Savoie. Twenty-three years old, a senior at McNeese University. Came home for Thanksgiving break two days ago. Chief said she didn't seem any different than her usual happy, bubbly self."

Sienna Rose gestured for him to continue, so he did. "Magdalene went out shopping with her girlfriends at approximately ten thirty yesterday morning. Her plans were to spend the day with her friends and return home later that night. She said they might catch a movie."

"And?" Sienna Rose prompted.

"That was the last time Chief saw her. He woke around two this morning and discovered that Magdalene hadn't come home. Considering the prior murders and his name having shown up on the last victim's calling card, he was immediately concerned."

"I warned him after Megan Rooster was murdered and his name was left on the index card." Sienna Rose shivered slightly.

"Megan Rooster? I didn't recognize her name in the file the chief sent over." The file he'd received felt a little thin overall, although he understood that working a murder took time. He had noticed that Sienna Rose was the lead detective on the three previous murders, the first of which had occurred a little more than a month ago.

"Megan Rooster. She was starting out in the DA's office when you moved away."

Legend racked his brain until an image of Rooster came to mind. "Wasn't she known for being somewhat arrogant, as if she knew more than everybody else?"

"That's her."

"Yeah, I remember her. She was a spitfire, but not above playing dirty to suit her own needs. Never really could figure out what angle of a case she was playing."

"That about sums her up," Sienna Rose said. "She left work and stopped by the store to pick up a bottle of wine. Her fiancé wanted to surprise her by cooking dinner at her place over in Mooring Heights, so he was in the kitchen. When she got home, she was murdered in her own driveway. Her fiancé said he never heard a thing. A neighbor walking their dog saw her lying in the driveway and called it in. The chief's name was left on an index card on her body." Sienna Rose returned her attention to Magdalene Savoie's body and pinched her lips together.

Sienna Rose appeared to be lost in thought—probably about being named the murderer's next victim.

Legend shifted his weight. "What precautions did the chief take after seeing his name on the previous victim? Were there patrol officers outside his home?"

"I offered to put together a team, but the chief refused." Her tone softened. "He believed it was his job to protect his daughter. And he's the chief. When he said it wasn't needed, no one argued."

Legend understood that. He doubted he'd have made it through the academy without Chief Savoie's belief in him, and he would never have questioned the chief's judgment on a case.

Sienna Rose continued the rundown. "Chief tried calling his daughter, but got no answer, so he used her phone's location tracker app and found her here."

"The chief found her?" He hadn't been made aware of that fact. His insides burned.

"Yeah." Sienna Rose's voice was barely above a whisper.

Legend felt the punch to the gut that Sienna Rose's somber tone echoed. He tried to imagine what it would be like for a father to find his daughter like that. His stomach knotted into a tight ball. Chief was one of the best men he knew, a fill-in father figure to Legend. For him to have to go through such brutality was unthinkable.

Sienna Rose cleared her throat a little too loudly. "Okay, Officer Moncrief, as a detective, one of the most important things in your arsenal is your initial take on the scene. Your impressions can be extremely valuable. So, examine the crime scene and tell me what you see."

"The chief's daughter is lying—"

"No." Sienna Rose shook her head as she interrupted. "You're telling me what you know. Tell me what you *see*."

Hazel studied the scene. "The victim has been beaten."

"Good," Sienna Rose said. "What else?"

The young cop pinched her lips together. "She's lying on the ground and appears to have been stabbed to death."

Sienna Rose rested a hand on her hip. "The coroner's office has already inspected the body?" She asked the question in an innocent tone, even though Legend could sense the admonishment in her voice.

Her question was meant to make the young cop think and learn, especially since the coroner's office van was barely visible as it pulled up beside the row of cruisers.

Hazel's shoulders sagged. "No ma'am."

"Even though you're staring at the victim and can make out what appear to be stab wounds, you can't know if they are the actual cause of death. A medical examiner or coroner's office can make that determination, but if we assume, we can start the investigation incorrectly with inaccurate preconceived notions." Sienna Rose's tone softened a degree as she explained.

"Yes ma'am." Hazel shifted her weight from one foot to the other, then back again.

Sienna Rose was correct in her teaching, of course, but her methods could be considered a little brusque. Legend couldn't help but feel sorry for Hazel. He knew firsthand what it felt like to disappoint Sienna Rose. She could be quite intimidating.

Sienna Rose continued to push the young officer. "What else do you see? Specifically the small details."

He noticed Hazel kept her focus off of the body as she continued her assessment. "There isn't a lot of blood around the scene. At least on initial inspection. It's possible that this is a secondary crime scene."

"Very good," Sienna Rose said. "What else do you notice about the scene?"

"There are no obvious signs of a struggle." Officer Moncrief scanned the area. "That backs up the idea that this could be a secondary crime scene. It seems likely to me that the victim was killed somewhere else and then dumped here."

"Nicely done. A good detective takes notes. I use the notes app on my phone." She glanced at Legend and a little smile tugged at her lips. "Some prefer writing things down the old-fashioned way."

"Yes ma'am." Officer Hazel Moncrief pulled out her own smartphone, her eagerness to mimic Sienna Rose apparent.

"Now tell me about the body itself. Tell me what you notice about the victim herself."

Moncrief inspected the body, even though it was obvious she was more than a little uncomfortable by the way she kept shifting her weight and averting Sienna Rose's gaze. Despite the coolness of the November afternoon, Hazel's forehead glistened with a sheen of sweat.

Sienna Rose cut her eyes to Legend. He could almost read her mind. If Hazel wasn't able to look at a victim, she'd never make detective.

Legend bit his tongue and moved a few feet away from the body. At least he could help save the rookie cop more embarrassment.

He let the gentle breeze coming off the bayou cool his emotions. He'd never expected to see Sienna Rose again after she had blown him off by not taking or returning his calls or texts. He certainly hadn't planned on ever returning to Envie.

When Chief Savoie had called and asked Legend to assist—his own involvement in the case would have been a conflict of interest—Legend hadn't been able to say no. He'd known that agreeing to help would mean working alongside Sienna Rose, but he hadn't been prepared for the onslaught of conflicting emotions.

Legend crossed his arms over his chest as he watched Sienna Rose, who continued to grill the young officer. Technically it was Sienna Rose's case on the local level, but that didn't mean he wouldn't still work it as he usually did, nor would he back off for fear of stepping on any toes, even hers. The case was too important. Too close to home. Too personal. But training Officer Moncrief was all Sienna Rose's responsibility, so he would stay out of that.

Legend's cell rang, and he checked the caller ID before answering. "Cruz."

"Detective Cruz, this is Officer Moody with the Envie Police Department. I'm calling to confirm that your team has arrived and has set up outside Detective Jordan's mother's home. I've let Mrs. Jordan know that they are here and she can call if she needs anything. I didn't answer her questions about what's going on. I figured you would prefer to talk to her and give her whatever information you want her privy to."

He'd called in the request before Sienna Rose had arrived on the scene, as soon as he'd seen her name on the index card.

"Thank you, Officer." At least Sienna Rose's mother and brother would be safe.

"Yes, sir. I'm heading back to my station now."

Legend called one of the team members he'd sent to Lillian Leigh Jordan's house.

The man picked up right away. "Hey, Cruz. I was about to call you."

"All good?"

"Yes. We're in position and will be here around the clock until otherwise instructed. We'll be taking surveillance walks around the house every hour as well."

"Thank you. Keep me updated if you see anything out of the ordinary." Legend ended the call, slid the phone back into his pocket, then rejoined Officer Moncrief and Sienna Rose.

"Once CSU gets finished here, please put a rush on the results and have them call me as soon as they know anything," Sienna Rose was saying to the officer.

Her voice carried more authority than he'd ever heard before, but it didn't surprise him, given her position and the strength of character he remembered.

Moncrief walked away to carry out her orders.

He felt her move to stand beside him. Funny how, even after five long years, he could sense her movements. Would that ever go away?

Silence hung over the bayou. The sun dipped below the horizon, leaving streaks of orange to paint the late afternoon sky.

"I'm not being mean to her for the sake of it." Sienna Rose's voice was softer, the way he remembered it.

"I didn't say anything. You don't have to explain yourself to me."

"Not out loud, but you were thinking it," she said. "Sometimes the best way to learn is by being put on the spot. It teaches them. A little embarrassment cements procedure so it's retained."

"Embarrassment or humiliation?"

"It's never my intent to humiliate anyone." She pushed her bangs out of her expressive brown eyes.

Once upon a time, he'd run his fingers through her long hair. Sometime in the last five years, she'd cut it short in a pixie style. "I like the new hairstyle." The words were out before he realized.

Sienna Rose's cheeks pinked as she ducked her head. "Thanks. I got tired of always putting it up in a ponytail or back in a bun."

How could he have complimented her? He hadn't wanted to speak to her about anything on a personal level, much less compliment her hair.

She released another sigh, then faced him. "I know this is awkward for the both of us. Trust me, I never would have requested you coming back here."

On that, they agreed. "Oh, I know," he assured her. "I didn't want to come either, but it's the chief."

"Right." She used the toe of her boot to move around dried leaves. "I didn't know he had called you in." Sienna Rose swallowed loud enough for him to hear. "Did he think I wasn't handling the case well enough?"

"No, that's not it at all. He saw your name on that index card, and he knew standard protocol would be to remove you from the case. He wanted someone who would allow you to stay on."

"I'm not letting go of this case." Her tone had gone from sweet to challenging in less than a nanosecond.

"I'm not asking you to, and, like I said, I think that's why he called me in. He knew he'd be out dealing with Magdalene's death and wanted someone who would fight to keep you on."

"I won't let him down. He's been a mentor to me over the years." The edge had disappeared from her voice.

He had forgotten that the chief had been instrumental in securing her placement and opportunity to advance in the department. Even though times had changed in recent decades, Legend had to admit it was still harder for women to succeed in law enforcement. Chief Savoie had ensured that Sienna Rose could climb as high up the ladder as she wanted.

Legend stared out over the bayou that, for once, was silent. No grunts from alligators, no birds chirping. Even the tree frogs had gone quiet. The late afternoon November sun crept lower on the horizon, readying to dive toward the tree line. It was as if the sun were hurrying to usher in the night, seemingly as tired of the day as Legend was.

Maybe it was Sienna Rose's vulnerability at being named a future victim, or maybe it was his sense of owing the chief everything too. Chief Savoie was the father figure he'd never had. He'd encouraged Legend and pushed him along as soon as he'd graduated from the academy. The chief had been instrumental in both Legend's and Sienna Rose's careers, but also in Legend's life. Because of that, Legend was back in Envie, working with the woman he'd once loved and abandoned when a career opportunity arose that he'd been unable to refuse—the same opportunity Sienna Rose had felt she couldn't accept.

"We'll figure it out," he said.

But would they? Neither had been able to the last time they tried to work as partners to solve a problem. Why should this time be any different?

$\mathcal{T}$he morning sun did nothing to cheer Sienna Rose's stormy mood. Restlessness over Magdalene Savoie's death, paired with Legend's reappearance in her life, had kept her tossing and turning, making sleep nearly impossible. Her body trembled as she got out of her SUV and headed indoors. Anger punched each step harder into the tile floor as she rounded the hallway of the Envie Police Station.

"You put officers on security detail duty at my mom's house?" Sienna Rose glared at Legend, hoping with everything that looks could, in fact, kill. *Well, maim at least. Okay, hurt. But hurt really badly.*

He glanced up from the desk he'd settled at in the detectives' area. That made her even madder. No matter that nobody was using it. Simply the fact that he was there and acting as if he belonged set her teeth on edge. "I did." There was no trace of apology in his tone.

She hadn't returned her mother's calls last night—she'd been too tired and out of sorts—but when she drove by her mother's house on her way to work that morning, there was no mistaking the police cruiser sitting out front. "In case you've let the enormity of the New Orleans Police Department make you forget your humble beginnings, *Special* Detective Cruz, Envie doesn't have the manpower for security detail. Not counting the desk sergeants, we only have the chief, the captain, a lieutenant for each shift, four detectives, and four officers per shift—two of which you've pulled off patrol." Her heart raced as she clenched her hands into fists, then forced them to relax as she pulled out her chair.

"Temporarily," he said, his tone still calm. "The Envie officers are there for an hour while my team members take a break to shower and eat."

"You mean you called in officers from the special task force to watch my mother's house?" Heat burned her face with embarrassment.

"That's what our task force does, Sienna Rose. We assist with investigations and help where needed. Often that help comes in the form of manpower for smaller towns or parishes. Such as security detail for the families of someone a serial killer has publicly marked as his next target."

"I don't need security detail."

"Like the chief didn't, right?"

The nonchalant way he said it raised her hackles. "Who knew the sicko would go after Mag—"

Legend held up a hand to cut her off. "No one could have predicted that, which is why I'd rather play it safe than regret not doing enough down the road." He leveled her with his stare. "It's not really for you, Sienna Rose. It's for your mom and brother."

A lump the size of Texas clogged her throat. She opened her mouth but could think of nothing to say, so snapped it shut again. Plopping down in the chair behind her desk, she grabbed her cell to call her mother.

"Hey, honey. What's going on? There are cops here outside the house—they came yesterday. I called you, but then heard on the news about Magdalene Savoie, so figured you were busy. The poor chief."

"It's awful, and yes, we're all working the case." She chewed her bottom lip as she studied the framed picture on her desk—her with her mother and brother, Dean. "I'm sorry, Mom, I should've called earlier, but I just found out the officers are at your house. I'll explain more later, okay?"

"Okay. I'll wait to get the details."

"Thanks, Mom. Love you."

"Love you too, honey. Bye."

Sienna Rose set her phone on the desk and ran her fingers through her hair.

Legend joined her at her desk. "So, give me the scoop on the first murder."

It was odd having him back and asking the standard questions, yet also welcomingly familiar. In fact, she felt soothed by the familiarity in such a terrifying situation.

No, she refused to let her mind—or her emotions—go down that road again. She wouldn't be hurt the same way twice. She'd learned her lesson. She crossed her arms over her chest. "Didn't you get the file?" So far, they didn't have much to go on.

"I read the facts," he said. "I prefer to hear the lead detective's thoughts though. I find it much more helpful."

"Have it your way. You remember Judge Terrence Hughes, right? He was the judge who sat on the bench for our practice trials."

Part of their training at the academy had been to sit in a witness box to prepare for how they might be called to testify in cases ranging from traffic tickets to murder. Legend had excelled at giving testimony, and it had merely fed into her infatuation with him. They'd been so interesting to each other back then, a romance headed toward happily ever after—or at least that's what she'd thought.

Obviously unaware of the memories she struggled with, Legend shook his head. "I don't quite recall."

"Really?" She stared at him. The judge was a permanent fixture in her mind. "The guy with white hair and facial features like a hawk. Beady eyes behind thick glasses, never smiled."

Legend grinned. "Yeah, now I remember. He was intense, even for practice trials."

Sienna Rose tore her gaze away from the charming smile that displayed his dimples. "He retired a few years after you left. Settled on the outskirts of town with his wife and enjoyed spending time with his grandkids and even a few great-grandkids. Judge Hughes was actually a really nice guy once you got to know him."

He'd signed many warrants for her before he'd retired, and they'd come to have great mutual respect. His death had been a shock.

"Hughes was killed while checking the mail?" Legend asked.

She tried to focus on the data, not her feelings about it. "That's right. When he didn't come back inside, his wife went out to check on him. She found him in the road at the end of his driveway, stabbed to death." She swallowed hard, refusing to let herself think about the horror, grief, and shock Mrs. Hughes must have felt. "An index card that had Barney Pratt's name on it rested on top of the judge's body." If it weren't for the index card, the murder would have probably been written off as an opportunity killing, rather than a planned one.

"How long after he left the house to check the mail did his wife find him?"

"She wasn't sure. Granted, she'd had an intense emotional experience, but follow-up questioning yielded the same response—about forty-five minutes to an hour, give or take."

Legend tapped the pen on the legal pad in front of him. "That's a long time to go to the mailbox and not return."

"To be fair, their house sits quite a way back from the road. The judge isn't as spry as he was when he sat on the bench, and he wasn't that agile then. At his pace, I'd guess it'd take him maybe twenty to thirty minutes to get there and back."

Legend finished making that note. "That's logical. Say it took him fifteen minutes to get there, then another fifteen for her to walk up and find him. According to her timeline, that leaves approximately fifteen to forty-five minutes for the killer to stab him, place the index card, and leave. It's tight but doable."

Sienna Rose sat back in her chair. "That's about right."

"I'm assuming his wife didn't see a car or anybody around when she found him?"

"During both interviews, she stated she saw nothing out of the ordinary." Sienna Rose narrowed her eyes. "I *do* know how to do my job."

"I never meant to imply you didn't. Sometimes it's helpful to go over all the information again, especially with a fresh pair of eyes. I'm not questioning your work. I'm making sure I understand everything you've done thus far." Legend scanned his notepad. "Was it established that this was the judge's daily routine? To check the mail at approximately the same time?"

"His wife said he checked the mail at ten every morning."

"Why that time? Did his wife ever join him?"

Did he think she didn't know if a routine didn't vary, it wouldn't take much for anybody watching to recognize the pattern? She was good at her job, and she was coming to resent both Legend's questions and his demeanor. "According to his wife, that was the time her DIY show came on. The judge wasn't interested in the show, so it was his routine to rinse out their coffee cups and coffeepot, then empty the filter. If the trash bag was full, he'd take it out to their bin on his way to check the mail. She said he'd sometimes refill the bird feeders if they were empty."

Legend made notes as he continued with the questions. "How long is her show?"

"An hour, which is why when it was over and she didn't see him puttering around—her words, not mine—she went to find him."

"I assume you've already pulled Hughes's cases to see who has been recently released and such."

Sienna Rose's eyes narrowed. "I might not be a *Special* Detective and work cases all over the state, but you should remember they do train us around these parts."

"I have to check, Sienna Rose. It's not personal."

"I keep forgetting not much is personal with you. Everything is about your career, of course." The words were out before she could stop them, but she couldn't help how she felt. He'd chosen his career over her five years ago, and it still stung. His being back in town reminded her of the way he'd crushed her dreams, and of what could have been between them.

His eyes widened, but he said nothing. His smoldering gaze was enough.

She wished she could take back the words. They crossed into personal history and had nothing to do with the job. She was a professional, and she'd act like it, no matter how many of her buttons he pushed. "Anyway, as I said, the index card named the second victim, Barney Pratt. He's a defense attorney. He mostly handles drug charges, not including his mandated pro-bono work."

"Ambulance chaser?"

"Sometimes. Not always. Most of his recent cases are drug related."

Legend shook his head. "I don't remember him."

Sienna Rose forced herself to relax. "You wouldn't. He was a paralegal when you were here. He finished his law degree and passed the bar after you left. His wife, Amanda, was working on the rosebushes in their backyard and was stabbed to death with her own pruning shears."

"You know him?"

"Not really. I mean, you know how Envie is—everybody knows who everybody is and most of their business. But we didn't run in the same circles."

"Who did?" Legend asked. "Who were his friends?"

Sienna Rose lifted a shoulder. "According to our initial round of questioning, he mostly kept to himself. He had drinks occasionally with some of the guys from the firm where he worked. Everyone said he and his wife had a good marriage."

"Which firm did he work for?"

"Broussard, Simmons, and Abram."

"I'm assuming the index card was not only checked for prints, but also for a possible handwriting match?"

Her cheeks burned again. "We aren't some backwoods outfit, Special Detective Cruz. We did have it checked for prints, and there were none. Like there were none left on either of the bodies, nor at the crime scene." She chewed her bottom lip and willed herself to calm down before she continued. "We had the handwriting analyzed. The writing was block style and nondescript, without any identifying markers, or so the expert stated in his report."

Legend continued to make notes without addressing her outburst. "And the third victim was Megan Rooster?"

Sienna Rose toyed with the paper clips on her desk. "That's right. I gave you the details of her murder yesterday."

"You did. Any evidence uncovered at the scenes?"

"No. Not a single fingerprint, hair, or fiber. The CSU has gone over it all. Some of it twice." Sienna Rose crossed her arms over her chest and leaned back in her chair. "And before you ask, yes, all of these cases have been pulled, and we're cross-referencing them against each other, and now Magdalene's murder."

"And now you." His voice was barely audible. "That should shorten the connection list, if there even is one."

Her phone rang and she snatched it from her desk. "Detective Jordan."

"Detective, it's Anna Henry."

Thank goodness the head of the crime scene unit, or CSU, was on duty today. "What do you have for me?"

"As with the other crime scenes, no prints or anything else was left," Anna said. "We're still running DNA on the blood samples. However, I suspect it'll all belong to the victim unless we get really lucky."

They hadn't yet. Frustration threatened to choke Sienna Rose.

People were dying, and they couldn't catch a break. The killer was moving too fast. Five weeks ago, the judge had been killed. Two weeks later, Pratt's wife. Last week, Megan Rooster. Yesterday, Magdalene Savoie. They had no forensic evidence, no suspects. She hadn't thought of anyone who could tie all the murders together. And the killer had been shortening the time between victims, with Sienna Rose marked as his next target.

Anna's voice pulled her attention back to the call. "One thing we do have that we didn't from any of the previous crime scenes is a cast of a footprint taken yesterday. It indicates that your suspect wears a men's size twelve shoe, is about five-eleven to six-three, and weighs approximately 180 to 210 pounds."

"That's more than we've ever had before. Maybe it'll lead somewhere."

"I hope so," Anna said. "Also, you were right. The crime scene in the bayou is the secondary crime scene. I'll call you as soon as I have anything more."

"Thanks, Anna."

Sienna Rose hung up and briefed Legend. "Let's go to the conference room. The desk sergeant put all the requested files there." Without waiting for a reply, she headed down the hall and heard the sound of Legend following her lead.

If only he'd followed her lead five years ago, and stayed in Envie.

4

For Envie being such a small town, the case files towering in two piles on the police station conference table were exceptionally intimidating.

Legend took a seat across from Sienna Rose. "These are all the files?"

She grabbed the top folder off one of the stacks. "Each of these has some kind of connection between all four victims, going back eight years to when Barney came to town and Chief was a captain." Sienna Rose opened the folder and began flipping through papers, making it clear that she was done talking for the time being.

He'd played the scenario of him and Sienna Rose working cases side by side in his mind a million times over since he left five years before. In his imagination, however, she hadn't given him the impression that she couldn't stand him. Nor had she glared at him every chance she got. He could understand, in a way—she resented him for leaving. It wasn't *her* he'd left, but he could easily see how she might feel that way.

The opportunity had been a once-in-a-lifetime chance, and at the time he'd felt that if she'd truly loved him, she would have pushed him to go. He'd begged Sienna Rose to join him, but she'd refused due to a sense of family obligation. Her father had recently died, and she'd believed it was her duty to stay behind and help care for her mother and brother. Circumstances beyond his control.

Obviously, they hadn't been under Sienna Rose's control either. With him embarking on a new career in New Orleans and her working her way toward detective in Envie—well, it never would have worked. Neither of them believed in long-distance relationships.

Heaven knew he'd tried to convince her they were different and could make it, but she had known better. She'd been right too. The new job and responsibilities had left him little time to keep up with basic things, much less continue a relationship with someone in a different parish altogether.

But being here, working beside her, being scared for her safety—it all seemed to put things in a different perspective. Maybe—

Sienna Rose glanced up and spotted him staring. "Something wrong?" Accusation saturated her voice, almost as if she could read his thoughts.

"No." He grabbed his own folder and began flipping through the papers. The file gave details about a person who'd been arrested by Savoie for embezzlement and defended by Pratt in a case where the presiding judge had once gone out with Rooster. It met all the parameters until he got to the most current page. The man had died in prison and had no remaining family alive for the killer to target. And there was no link to Sienna Rose.

A dead end.

Legend sighed. "Where are we putting the files that aren't under consideration?"

Sienna Rose tilted her head toward the end of the conference table closest to him. "Let's put those that aren't connected to all four victims here." She set the folder she'd been going through to her right.

He set his folder on top of hers. The process could take longer than he'd thought. He left the conference room, grabbed two cups of coffee from the break room, and returned. He set one of the mugs in front of her, along with three packets of sugar, remembering how much she took to make station coffee palatable.

She gave him a brief smile. "Thanks."

Her smile revived him from the tediousness of the task.

They worked in silence, reading and rearranging the stacks. Legend noticed there were still too many files in the stack of cases that could potentially provide a lead. His head was beginning to ache, and his eyes were dry, but he rubbed them and pushed through.

The fact that Sienna Rose had been named the next victim made his chest tighten anew each time he thought about it. Of the four murders thus far, the victims hadn't been limited to the person named on the killer's calling card. In two of the cases, the victims had instead been people close to the names on the cards. It implied that, aside from Sienna Rose, her mother, Lillian Leigh, and her brother, Dean, could be in danger.

Truth be told, Dean was the main reason Sienna Rose had rejected the opportunity to go with Legend to New Orleans to train for the new task force. Dean had cerebral palsy and autism, and Sienna Rose was totally devoted to him. Especially after their father's passing. Sienna Rose felt obligated to stay and help her mother care for Dean. Not that she ever resented him. On the contrary, she loved her older brother dearly, but looking after him and her mother was a lot to carry on her own. Sienna Rose wouldn't say so, but Legend had been around the family enough to see how demanding her role could be. He'd never blamed her for staying behind when they'd both been offered jobs on the new task force in New Orleans.

Yet she blamed him for leaving.

Sienna Rose's voice yanked him back to the conference room as she handed him a folder. "Can you put this in the dead-end stack?"

"Sure." He set it down, along with the one he'd been going through.

They were down to one stack, and there were at least fifteen folders in the pile that might hold potential leads. It felt insurmountable.

Legend flipped to a new page in his notepad and began brainstorming a profile of the suspect, including the details CSU had provided, as well as what his training told him about someone who would leave calling cards naming a next victim.

"What are you doing?" Sienna Rose broke his concentration.

"I'm creating a profile of our suspect. Tell me what you know about the killer so far."

Sienna Rose drained her coffee cup. "Statistically, he'd be a male who's strong and quick enough to carry out the violence evident in these crimes. He's been watching and paying attention. He kills with intent, as shown by the index cards. Because he's not leaving evidence, he's careful, which indicates a certain level of intelligence."

She would have been amazing on the task force. He agreed with everything she'd said. "What else?"

"We know his height and weight based on the cast impressions of his footprint." Sienna Rose's mouth tightened. "He killed the chief of police's daughter right under our noses—that would indicate he's confident he won't get caught."

"Thinks he's smarter than law enforcement."

"Most likely."

Legend stood and stretched his back and shoulders. "Great profile. I think the public needs to be on alert."

"Why? The public isn't at risk. Most citizens have no link to judges, prosecutors, and cops. To go public with the information would only cause fear and panic."

"I disagree. The chief's daughter had nothing to do with the legal system. She didn't even live here full-time after graduating high school. And I'm sure Amanda Pratt didn't have a personal connection to anyone in the system besides her husband."

"But they were related to those whose names had been left on the index cards. That's the connection. To me, that indicates that unrelated people aren't at risk."

"Can you be so sure? What if this guy decides to start going after jurors in a connected case? Or people who worked in the courthouse going back eight years? I'm talking from judges to custodians. Or their families or friends."

"Don't you think that's going a little far?" she asked.

"Not at all." He ran a hand over his jaw. "Face it, Sienna Rose, this could affect anybody in Envie. People in the community need to be made aware."

Captain Arnold Brewer entered the room. His lean physique belied his forty-plus years, but the thinning of his gray hair hinted at it. "I agree with Cruz. We can't risk not informing the public. If we don't and there's another victim, God forbid, the outrage would be loud and justified."

"Any word on the chief?" Sienna Rose asked.

Captain Brewer lowered his voice. "He's taking an extended leave of absence to make arrangements, gather Magdalene's things from college, and take care of all the other little details nobody thinks about. I told him I'd cover him, and to take as long as he needs. Especially since we have members of the special task force here to back us up."

"I can't even imagine how difficult this must be for him," Sienna Rose said. "He probably hasn't even had time to begin the grieving process."

"He said he'd let me know when arrangements were made for the funeral. That will be after the body is released, of course." Captain Brewer faced Legend. "Shall we hold a press conference?"

Legend deferred to Sienna Rose. "Would you like to hold it, Detective Jordan? I can give you my profile notes. The people in this town know and trust you."

"No thanks. You should hold the press conference."

"But you stand with him, Detective." There was no mistaking that the captain's words were an order.

"Yes sir." She set her jaw.

"I'll have it set up immediately. The press will probably be here in the next fifteen minutes, so get prepared." The captain marched from the room.

"I'm sorry he asked me. That was rude," Legend told her.

Sienna Rose stood, avoiding his gaze. "It's fine, Cruz. Prepare your speech while I finish going through these files."

She used his last name like she had back when they'd started at the police academy. Back when she was the lone female and had a chip on her shoulder as big as the Atchafalaya Basin. That alone told him how irked she was. "That's not fair."

"None of this is fair. Not all these murders. Not the chief calling you in. Not you showing up here and taking over every aspect of my case. No, none of it is fair, but here we are."

It was no use arguing with her. When her feelings were hurt, she tried to hide it by lashing out, and there was no productive conversation to be had with her. Heaven forbid that anyone suspect she had normal emotions like everyone else. She hid her pain and frustration behind anger. Some things never changed.

Fifteen minutes passed quicker than he'd expected, and in no time, Captain Brewer was back. "All the local outlets are here and set up. I thought it might be best to have the press conference on the front steps."

Legend noticed the captain had put on a new tie and combed his hair.

He glanced over at Sienna Rose, who slid another folder down to his end. "Are you ready?"

"As I'll ever be." She stood and shrugged into her jacket.

He fell into step alongside her, but she remained silent and hugged the wall of the hallway, placing as much distance between herself and him as possible.

"I'll introduce you, then turn the mic over to you," Captain Brewer said as he pushed open the front doors.

The November air held a crispness but no breeze. Bright-yellow and dark-orange mums were in full bloom in the flowerbeds along the stairs, but no fragrance tickled the senses. The air felt as somber as the message he was about to give. It certainly didn't feel like Thanksgiving season. So many in the community had recently faced tragic loss.

News cameras waited in front of the little podium, along with reporters sporting badges from area newspapers and radio stations. The police station sat across from town hall in the middle of a downtown square. Parking meters lined the street, most of them empty. A collection of leaves rustled across Main Street as the wind gusted.

"Thank you, everyone, for coming," Captain Brewer began. "As many of you are aware, Envie has been hit with four murders over the past five weeks, the latest being our beloved chief's daughter. To assist in the investigation, we've called in the state's special task force. Many of you will remember Envie's own Special Detective Legend Cruz. He's here to lead the task force, and he'd like to give an update on the situation." Captain Brewer stepped back, falling in line beside Sienna Rose.

Legend took over the microphone. "I'll keep this brief. As Captain Brewer stated, there have been four murders. At this time, we are working on the theory that the cases are linked, so we do not believe this is the work of some random serial killer."

He occasionally referenced his notes as he recited the description they'd put together of the killer based on his footprint. The reporters hung onto his every word. That meant they would take the information seriously enough to get the word out, and perhaps a life could be saved. Serial killer stories were always hot, for good or bad.

He took a breath before continuing the description. "Profiling is not an exact science, but our suspect's behavior indicates he's in his late thirties to midforties and is arrogant. He believes he is above the law, meaning either that he is smarter than law enforcement, or that he won't be held accountable for his actions. We believe he has either lost a criminal court case or has a loved one who has. So far, the killer has targeted victims directly related to the Envie legal system."

No one interrupted with questions, so he went on. "We ask that the public be aware of their surroundings and remain vigilant. We encourage anyone who might have information about this suspect to contact the Envie Police Department. I will take a few questions now."

One young reporter raised her hand. "Detective Cruz, are you saying the risk to the residents of Envie is high, even if they have nothing to do with the legal system?"

"It's possible. This suspect seems to have a plan. Since we don't know what that plan is at this point, we want everyone to stay safe. The best way to do that is to ask everyone to take care, remain alert, and call the police if they see anything out of the ordinary around themselves or their neighbors. We would all prefer that our residents be too cautious rather than endanger themselves needlessly."

Another reporter called, "Detective Jordan, why did you feel like you needed to call in outside help? Is the case too big for the Envie police?"

Sienna Rose was going to have his hide. Legend stepped to the side so she could speak into the mic.

"Special Detective Cruz was called in by the Chief of Police because of his personal connection to the people of Envie, and to Chief Savoie in particular. Cruz's task force out of New Orleans has resources we don't, such as more manpower, access to the state crime lab, and those types of things."

She smiled wide at Legend, and if he didn't know how fake it was, he would have gotten lost in her eyes.

But he did know.

She faced all the reporters like a pro. "We're very thankful that Cruz has brought his connections and resources—not to mention his vast knowledge—to assist with our investigation. Now, if there are no more questions, we have a case to solve. Thank you." She headed back into the building.

Legend and Captain Brewer had to use long strides to keep up with her. Brewer ducked into his office as they passed it.

Sienna Rose glared at Legend. "Happy now? You practically taunted the killer. Was that your plan? To have the killer come after his next victim—me?"

That was her fear talking.

"Of course not. I merely wanted to make the public aware of what type of criminal we're dealing with." How could she think such a thing? He would never instigate anything that would bring harm to her. "Let's grab a bite and compare notes on the files." Had he really asked out a woman who looked as if she would love for him to drop dead on the spot?

A beat passed as she apparently tried to process the same question. Finally, she said, "You know what? Yes. But only because I'm hungry and need the help."

A small victory. He hid a smile.

"Because the quicker we figure this out, the quicker we solve the case, and the quicker you can run back to New Orleans and leave me alone."

Or maybe it wasn't a victory after all.

$\mathcal{S}$ienna Rose still couldn't believe Legend had had the nerve to ask her to lunch. Even more, she couldn't believe she'd accepted.

He followed her out the back door of the station into the parking lot. They were colleagues who needed to discuss the case—nothing more, nothing less.

Sure.

Town square was busy during the midday rush. Lawyers, clerks, and city employees bustled about on their lunch breaks, overflowing the little diners and fast food places. Some picked up to-go orders and sat on the benches lining the grounds of the square, enjoying the cool November weather and bright sunshine.

"I'll drive." Without waiting for his reply, Sienna Rose led the way to a black SUV, the door locks clicking as she pressed the button on her fob.

He sank into the luxurious leather front seat. "Wow, this baby is sweet." The widening of his eyes as his gaze raked over the cockpit-like control panel and built-in swing arm that held a computer almost made her smile. She loved her ride.

"It's fully decked out too. State-of-the-art GPS tracking, Wi-Fi, bulletproof glass, self-sealing tires. All the cool bells and whistles." Sienna Rose fired up the engine, and muted notes of soft jazz filled the vehicle. "The department received a bequest from an independently wealthy previous sheriff, designated to provide these babies to detectives on the force in four towns."

"That's a sweet deal."

"Yeah, it's been nice." She backed out of the space. "Bertrand's okay?"

"It'd be sacrilegious if I said it wasn't." He grabbed the files Sienna Rose had brought with her. "Tell me about John Harper."

"He had a case before Judge Hughes, and Pratt was his attorney," Sienna Rose explained. "Megan Rooster was the prosecutor. From what I recall, Rooster really tore into Harper. She pulled out all her cheap tricks and won. Megan Rooster had quite the reputation of hitting below the belt. Not many respected her, and even fewer liked her, but her successful track record was undeniable."

"No ties to the chief or to you?"

"Not that I recall."

He flipped to the next file and read.

From the corner of her eye, Sienna Rose glanced at him, then back to the road. Knowing she'd made the right decision not to go to New Orleans with him didn't make it any easier to see him so successful. Not that she was jealous of him. It could have been her as well. She simply had a different set of priorities.

His leaving had ripped her to shreds, but over time, she'd realized that he didn't have the same responsibilities to keep him in Envie. Naturally, he should've taken the opportunity. She shouldn't have blamed him for going. Then again, her heart should have gotten over him, and clearly it hadn't.

It still hurt to be around him and not have the relationship they'd had before.

She whipped into the parking lot of the diner and stepped out. Her boots crunched on the gravel, even as her heart skipped a beat. How was she going to sit across a table from Legend and not recall old times?

Better times.

He started to lead the way toward the back booth—the booth where they'd always sat. Sienna Rose spun and slid into a seat, three booths up. Legend noticed and took the seat across from her without comment. A waitress walked over and took their orders: two coffees, deluxe cheeseburgers, french fries, and onion rings.

The setting was all too familiar, even though it'd been five years. She remembered the first time they'd met up there. They had finished their first week at the police academy and were physically exhausted but had a procedural code test the following Monday. Every cadet planned to cram the entire weekend. She had walked into Bertrand's with a large book in her hands. Legend had called her over and they'd had coffee while studying. They'd quizzed each other until the sun came up. It was the first of their many nights spent talking and getting to know one another in the same booth at Bertrand's. She had to wonder if either of them would have done as well in the academy or in their careers without their study partnership.

Legend jerked her from her walk down memory lane by tapping the folder he was reading. "What about this Ted Poe? He had connections to the chief, Pratt, and Rooster, but not Judge Hughes."

She let out a breath as she stretched her hands. "I couldn't find anything to connect the judge to this one, and I have no connection to him either."

He flipped to the last folder. "Haven Webster, murdered. How awful."

Sienna Rose closed her eyes. Somehow, she'd known it would come down to that case. The image of the young victim still haunted her dreams.

"Her murder has connections to all four, and to me," she said quietly. "I arrested a suspect named Andy Paul as directed by the chief, who was a captain then, and both the chief and I testified at the bench trial. Megan Rooster was the new prosecutor. Barney Pratt was assigned to defend Paul by the public defender's office. I think it was Pratt's fifth or sixth assignment there. He was new to the role and maybe to the nuances of the office, but he got the job done."

"And let me guess—Hughes was the judge."

It was more of a statement than a question. "Yeah."

"What do you remember about the case?"

"I was a rookie detective, and it was my first murder. We don't usually get many of them here, remember?"

"I hate to ask this, but I have to. Did you make a mistake?"

"I don't think so." Sienna Rose balled her hands into tight fists under the table. "Listen, Legend, I know our force isn't perfect, but I assure you that we know how to do our jobs. Even back then, the chief and I went by the book to arrest Andy Paul."

"But?"

"But what?"

"There's something that doesn't sit well with you about the case." His intense stare nearly made her lose concentration.

It wasn't fair that he could still read her so easily.

She had to come clean. "Andy Paul was Haven Webster's boyfriend, and he didn't have an alibi for the time of the murder. Homer Miley, the DA at the time, pushed for an arrest. It was an election year. When the initial evidence led to Andy Paul, Miley was bound and determined to go forward with the trial, even though we were still processing evidence and the case wasn't closed. He demanded it go to court."

"Even in small towns, political ambitions can get in the way of the truth."

Sienna Rose wished she could argue with his statement, but since she couldn't, she continued her story. "But our department did everything by the book. All the i's were dotted and all the t's were crossed, even though some things were a little off, at least to me. Not enough to raise an argument, but enough that it still bothers me."

The waitress brought over their coffees and gave them a bright smile. "Your order will be up in a sec."

Legend thanked her, then watched Sienna Rose dump sugar into her cup. "I'm not trying to imply you don't know how to run an investigation. I know better. You've always been one of the best at noticing details. I'm simply asking questions so I can get a grip on what we know, not to second-guess you. You were amazing at your job five years ago, and I imagine you've only gotten better since then."

Sienna Rose cleared her throat. "Thank you."

He took a sip of coffee. "I hope you know that I would never try to step on your toes, Sienna Rose. That's not who I am."

She nodded, not trusting herself to speak. She knew that, of course, or she'd never have fallen in love with him in the first place.

"I promise, I'm going to do my job, then leave. I know it's not ideal that we have to work together in the meantime, but I can't help that."

Why did the thought of him leaving make her pause? She'd gone five years without seeing or hearing from him. It had been a clean break. He'd been back less than twenty-four hours, and the thought of him leaving again tightened her gut.

The waitress delivered their plates. "Can I get you anything else?"

"We're fine, thank you," Legend assured her, as if he knew Sienna Rose couldn't manage it at the moment.

She took a bite of her burger. Even though Bertrand's burgers were some of the best in the state, it tasted like cardboard.

He sprinkled salt over the fries and onion rings. "I'm sorry for the way things ended before. We were in different places then, and—"

"Then?" She finished swallowing. Her mind and heart quarreled. She didn't want to have the discussion, but she also wanted to get everything out in the open, even if that meant leaving herself feeling raw.

"What?" He frowned at her in confusion.

"You said we were in different places *then*. Aren't we still?" Nothing indicated to her that Legend was any less ambitious and career-focused than he'd been five years ago. She took another bite, almost unable to enjoy the food. Her mother was still the primary caregiver for her brother, Dean, but over the past year, Sienna Rose had noticed her mother slowing down somewhat. Her priorities hadn't changed either.

Legend seemed to be searching for a way to answer her. "Now that you mention it, I guess we are." He took a bite.

They ate the rest of their meal in silence. After the waitress took their plates and refilled their cups, Legend said, "I'll do my best to stay out of your way, Sienna Rose, but since you've been named the next target, I don't have much of a choice. I have to make sure you're safe."

"I don't need protection."

"Then think about your mom and Dean."

Her jaw tightened automatically. He'd lost the right to be concerned about her family when he'd left.

"Are you ready to go? It's been a long day."

He tossed some bills on the table.

"Thank you for lunch." She slid out of the booth and headed toward the door.

Legend moved around Sienna Rose to open the driver's door for her. "Hey, I didn't mean to offend or anything—"

Tink, tink!

"Get down!" She grabbed his jacket and yanked him down into a crouch.

He whipped around on his toes.

Sienna Rose's eyes widened as she pointed to the SUV's rear window. Her heart pelted against her rib cage. Little round indents circled in the glass.

She pulled her gun from its holster. "Bullet marks."

Opening the driver's side door, she grabbed the police radio and gave the dispatcher her name and badge number. "Shots fired outside of Bertrand's. Officers on scene. Requesting backup."

"Officers dispatched."

The sound of more bullets striking her vehicle filled her ears.

Sienna Rose clipped the radio to her waistband and briefly popped her head over the hood of the vehicle to see better. A dark sedan sat across the street, front windows down and back windows tinted darker than was legal. A long-sleeved arm held a gun out the driver's side window.

Thank goodness there was no one walking down the street, and no cars driving down the road.

Sienna Rose fired at the sedan.

The door to the diner opened and the cook peered out, wearing a grease-stained apron. A few minutes had passed since they had been fired upon, but it felt like a lifetime.

"Stay inside and get everyone away from the windows," Sienna Rose ordered the cook as she grabbed the radio once more. "Shots fired at Bertrand's. Suspect is in a dark sedan across the street. I can't see the plate number. ETA on backup?" She rose again and fired over the hood of her SUV.

A bombardment of shots rang out from the sedan, followed by the sounds of bullets ricocheting off the gravel.

Legend tackled her to the ground, crushing her knees against the unforgiving gravel as a barrage of bullets rained down around them. "Stay down." He jumped up and returned fire from his handgun at the vehicle across the street.

Maybe he didn't remember her as well as he thought. *Stay down, my foot!*

Sienna Rose sprang up as the vehicle's engine revved. The tires squealed, and the dark car gunned toward Main Street. A police cruiser skidded into the parking lot, sirens wailing and lights spinning. It whipped into a U-turn and tore back onto the street in the direction the sedan had gone.

Captain Brewer pulled up alongside Sienna Rose's SUV. "Detective Jordan, are you two okay?"

She holstered her weapon. "Yes sir."

He got out of his car and moved beside them. "What happened?"

"We were heading to my vehicle and shots hit the back windshield. I got to my radio and called it in. We took more fire, so I returned fire, as did Special Detective Cruz."

"Did you recognize the shooter?"

Sienna Rose shook her head. "I only caught a glimpse of a driver, and I didn't see a face. Appeared to be male. He had on what looked like a beanie cap that obscured my view of his face, and he wore a faded denim jacket." She pressed her fingers against the bridge of her nose. "He had on gloves and used what appeared to be a 9mm."

"Anything else?"

She shook her head.

"He also wore a long-sleeved gray shirt," Legend said. "His aim was terrible, for which I'm grateful. When we left Bertrand's, he would have had a clear shot to Sienna Rose or me. He fired a couple times before we even realized what was going on, and he missed us every time."

"Doubtful he was simply trying to scare you." The captain finished making notes. "Either of you remember anything else?"

Both Legend and Sienna Rose shook their heads.

"Your knees are bleeding." Captain Brewer gestured to Sienna Rose's legs.

She glanced down. Sure enough, two red stains spotted her trousers. She hadn't felt the injury in the rush of the shoot-out but her knees throbbed and stung. She swayed.

Legend steadied her.

Sienna Rose jerked away from his touch. It was his fault she was injured. "I'm fine. Special Detective Cruz tackled me to the ground. This is where the gravel dug into my knees." Not that she'd needed his interference. She'd been doing fine without it—for years, in fact. She was, after all, a trained cop.

"I'll call you an ambulance." Captain Brewer lifted his radio.

"There's no need. I'm fine. I'll wash up at home and put bandages on the scrapes. I'll be good as new by tomorrow."

Captain Brewer frowned at her. "You have to be checked out, Detective Jordan. It's department policy. You can either ride in an ambulance or let Cruz drive you, but you're going to a hospital one way or another."

She let out a sigh, then glared at Legend. "Fine. I'll drive."

"No you won't. Cruz will take you to the hospital, then deliver your SUV to the station for CSU to get what they need from the bullet marks. He can pick up his car and return to take you home from the hospital."

She opened her mouth to argue, but Captain Brewer cut in. "That, or you can choose the ambulance, and I'll arrange to have Cruz take you home after you're checked out. This isn't up for debate, Detective."

She didn't like it, but she passed her keys to Legend.

On the bright side, she'd get to tell Legend exactly what was on her mind without him being able to escape. That alone was enough to make her smile as she limped to the passenger side and climbed in.

6

"*G*ood thing your SUV is shielded. All it got was a few dings. No actual punctures that I could see. CSU can also pull bullets from the parking lot." Legend gripped the steering wheel tight enough to cramp his hand. Small talk was all he could muster at the moment. Every fiber of his being stood at full alert.

"It was a 9mm. I saw the gun." Sienna Rose leaned her head back against the seat and closed her eyes. Fear hung around her. "You know, I'm a cop and perfectly able to handle myself in those situations. You know, like you are. There was no need for you to knock me down like that."

It had been instinct. He had no argument. None that she'd accept, anyway. "You're right. I'm sorry. I shouldn't have done that."

She studied him with a raised brow, obviously a little taken aback at his apology. She let out a burst of breath before settling back against the seat and closing her eyes. "I hate that we couldn't identify the shooter."

"Hopefully the cops in pursuit will catch him." He glanced at her again, taking in the way her face had fallen with disappointment. She would replay the incident over time and again in her mind, questioning her actions.

He understood the unspoken fear. They knew she'd been named a target, but actually having someone try to take her out was a totally different animal. Legend's mouth went dry. "I caught the angle of their shots—you were definitely the intended victim."

"I figured it's the killer, trying to follow through on his threat." Sienna Rose was clearly making an effort to sound nonchalant, but he wasn't fooled. "From a distance, though? That's not the killer's MO."

"He wouldn't have been able to leave an index card. Maybe you're the last target?" If it was true, then at least no one else was in danger, but it also meant the killer would get away if they couldn't solve the case as soon as possible.

She chewed her bottom lip, probably thinking along the same lines. "I guess he considered you collateral damage."

Sienna Rose went silent, probably mulling over the range of possibilities. The case, the threats against her—he had to admit they brought up some feelings in him that he'd pushed away and ignored for so long.

"I'm sorry for leaving things the way I did." Adrenaline was making him crazy, it seemed. He was simply blurting things out without thinking.

Sienna Rose lifted her head and stared at him with the dark eyes he'd missed so much in New Orleans.

"I mean, I know I hurt you, and I never meant to. I'm really sorry for that." He truly was. He'd loved her then. Being back was forcing him to question whether such feelings ever truly died. Especially when they'd just found out how quickly and easily she could be taken from him for good.

"You don't have the right to apologize to me, Legend. Not now. Not after all this time." Her voice cracked. "When you left, you gave up that right."

"I had to go, Sienna Rose."

"Don't give me that. It was a choice, Legend. I had a choice, and you did as well. We chose differently. No need to apologize for leaving to further your career."

"I understand why you had to stay, but I didn't have family. I didn't have any ties to Envie."

"Except for me. And apparently that wasn't enough." Her voice was so low, it was barely audible.

He felt his heart crack. Words failed him.

She sighed as if the day had gone on forever, although it was still early afternoon. "There's no sense in rehashing what happened. Let's find the link between these cases, catch whoever killed Magdalene and the others, and let you get back to New Orleans. No matter why you left, you did. Sure, I got hurt, but I made my choice too." She gazed out the passenger window. "Nothing has changed, Legend. You have your life in New Orleans, and my life is still in Envie. That's the way it is. We had to accept it then, and we have to accept it now."

He wanted to tell her about the tangle of feelings that threatened to burst from his chest, but she was right. No matter how his old feelings were resurfacing with a vengeance, the impossibility of a relationship between them hadn't changed.

Legend took another right and pulled into the emergency drop-off circle at the hospital.

She snorted. "I would hardly call my skinned knees an emergency."

"You know as well as I do that if you're injured on duty, officers get to enter through the emergency room and take priority." He helped her out, then parked the SUV before returning to her side. "Hang on."

He rushed to grab a wheelchair and let a nurse know he was bringing in a detective.

"You've got to be kidding me. A wheelchair?" she demanded, giving him her fiercest glare.

"Come on, I saw you limping to the vehicle. You didn't want Captain Brewer to realize how much pain you were in, but I'm not falling for it. Nobody will judge you for accepting help."

She stopped arguing and sat down.

He pushed her through the automatic door.

The nurse he'd spoken to waited for them. "I'll take it from here, sir. You can take a seat in the waiting room. Someone will come get you when the detective is ready." She grinned at Sienna Rose. "Hi, Detective, I'm Hilary." She spun the wheelchair around, but not before he caught sight of Sienna Rose's smug smile.

If he knew her, she was gloating to herself that he'd been sent off to wait. She knew how much he hated sitting around. Instead, he went outside to move the SUV to a spot under a tree, so he could identify it to the member of his team that would bring Legend's rental to pick up the SUV for the CSU.

He'd backed into the perfect place when a familiar vibrating hum sounded.

He dug around and found Sienna Rose's cell phone. A text message had popped up on her home screen, and Legend read it before he realized what he was doing.

Heard some stuff went down. Are you okay? Update when you can—I'll distract as I can. Hugs and love.

It was sent from someone listed in her contacts as *The Man*.

Who called someone "The Man" as a name? Was this some guy she was dating? A boyfriend? Someone who sent "hugs and love"?

A raw ache of jealousy clawed the inside of his ribs.

Pulling out his cell, Legend called a team member to pick up the SUV, then dialed his office to update his boss in New Orleans.

When he finished his report, Special Detective Luxton Steele cut right to the chase. "Cruz, I don't like this at all. I'll feel much better when you wrap all of this up and are able to come home."

Home.

Funny that, for the past five years, Legend had called New Orleans home. In truth, he hadn't set up a home. He still lived in the same apartment as when he'd first arrived in the Big Easy, despite having a nice salary that would allow for nicer digs. It held nothing but the bare minimum he needed to survive.

Why hadn't he settled in yet? What was he waiting for?

"Me too. Detective Jordan and I will link the victims soon and find a suspect. I know we're getting close."

"Check in with me tomorrow. I'd like all of your team back as soon as you can manage. We're about to be assigned another case and I need all the teams I can gather." Luxton Steele was the best at handling all six of the special task force teams. He'd started the task force five years before, and showed no indication of retiring anytime soon.

"Yes sir." Legend disconnected the call, then made another to check on the protective detail he'd assigned to Lillian Leigh Jordan and her son, Dean. His team member assured Legend that the house and perimeter were secure, which offered him a degree of relief.

Special Detective John Toutte whipped into the parking lot in Legend's rental and parked next to Sienna Rose's SUV. He and Legend swapped keys, then Toutte jumped into the SUV and took off toward Envie's CSU.

Legend made his way across the hospital parking lot. A hint of coolness drifted through the quiet streets. New Orleans, while attractive to tourists and residents, was often too crowded, whereas Envie never felt like it was about to burst at the seams.

Flashing his badge, Legend checked in at the triage desk and was given permission to check on Sienna Rose in her examining room. He knocked and was allowed in.

Sienna Rose sat on a paper-lined exam table. Her jeans had been replaced with scrubs, and a nurse poured liquid over one of her knees—likely an antiseptic. Sienna Rose grimaced as the liquid ran into a silver bedpan the nurse held under her leg. Her face flushed and her jaw locked as she fixed her stare on Legend. He caught a little pooling of moisture in her eyes.

Without thinking about anything but her pain, he went to her side and took her hand.

She didn't jerk away. Instead, she squeezed it tightly as the nurse continued to treat her knees. He could feel, rather than hear, her whimper, and it twisted his insides.

"There, that should do it. You did great," the nurse told Sienna Rose. "Although you don't need stitches, you should try to avoid too much physical activity for the next day or so."

Sienna Rose tugged her hand out of his.

The nurse handed her a small tube. "Use this, and cover the wounds with gauze during the day to prevent infection. Wash with antibacterial soap, and let your skin breathe as much as possible at night. Here are some written instructions." She passed Sienna Rose a few papers. "The doctor has sent prescriptions to your pharmacy. Be sure to take all of the antibiotics. Use the pain pills tonight, then as needed starting tomorrow. Do you have any questions for me?"

Sienna Rose shook her head.

"Your discharge papers are included there, so you're good to go. Don't be afraid to follow up with your regular doctor if it starts to feel worse." She began cleaning up the space. "Hubby, you can bring the car around to the emergency room entrance. I'll bring her out."

"We aren't married."

"He's not my husband."

He and Sienna Rose spoke at the same time.

The nurse smiled at them. "My mistake. We'll meet you out front, sir."

Legend left the room with his mind and feelings in a jumbled mess. The same old feelings for Sienna Rose had rushed to the surface when he'd recognized her pain, and he had been relieved when she let him hold her hand. Yet her quick reaction to the nurse assuming they were married reminded him that she wasn't in love with him anymore.

He'd hurt her too badly.

And she had someone in her life she referred to as The Man. That clenched his jaw as he started his rental and backed out of the parking spot.

True to her word, the nurse had Sienna Rose in a wheelchair in the circle drive. He pulled up to the curb, then rushed to open the passenger door and help her into the seat.

"Good luck," the nurse said. She pushed the wheelchair into the building.

Behind the wheel once more, Legend switched off the radio, which Toutte had set on a local station.

"Where's my SUV?"

"One of my team members took it to CSU." He pulled away from the hospital entrance, then realized he had no idea where she lived. "Where to?"

"I need to see Mom and let her know what's going on. Is one of your team still outside the house?"

Legend eased his foot off the brake. "Yes."

Sienna Rose leaned her head back against the seat. "She has questions and is obviously concerned. I'd rather let her know what's going on myself. That way she can take extra steps to make sure she and Dean stay safe."

A few minutes passed as he steered toward the Jordan house.

"Captain Brewer called. The shooter got away." She let out a heavy sigh. "They have a BOLO out for the sedan. He's asked us to give a statement tomorrow morning."

"I'll go give mine after I drop you off, then I'll come back for you and take you to your place."

Sienna Rose shook her head. "I'll stay at Mom's. Since I'll be there, armed and on alert, you don't need to use resources to have a protective detail at her house. She can give me a ride to work in the morning."

He tightened his jaw and drove. He'd already planned to run by his motel for a quick shower before camping out in front of wherever Sienna Rose would sleep that night. It didn't matter if it was her place or her mom's. She wasn't going to shake him that easily.

Legend did, however, begin to mentally prepare for the battle he would surely face once she figured it out. Sienna Rose had never liked being taken care of.

But for that night, she would have to accept his help, whether she liked it or not.

7

*E*vening had snuck up on Envie while they'd been at the hospital, casting shadows over the town. Sienna Rose checked her watch, not believing the clock in Legend's rental car. Sure enough, it was already six.

"You can drop me off here, dismiss your team member, then head on to your hotel. It's been a long day." Sienna Rose didn't need him walking her to the door, which would surely cause Mom to ask more questions than she already would.

"Now what kind of gentleman would I be if I didn't see you to the door?" He flashed that smile of his, the one that showed off his dimples despite the stubble already visible on his face.

It made her traitorous heart skip a beat.

She narrowed her eyes. "This wasn't a date, and whether you're a gentleman or not has no bearing on our working together." Sienna Rose couldn't keep the snappishness from her voice, but in her defense, she was tired, hurt, and an emotional mess.

He parked in the driveway and killed the engine. "Would you like help out of the car?"

"No. I've got it." Yet, extending her legs to step down was excruciating, and she gripped the door handle until her nails dug into the soft leather. She grabbed the top folder—the one containing Haven Webster's murder case file—and tucked it under her arm. She managed to stand without shrieking in pain. "You can go ahead and leave."

"I'm going to talk to my team member, if you don't mind. Let him go for the evening."

"Right." She'd told him to do that. Sienna Rose slowly made her way to the front door, but before she even crossed in front of the car, the motion detector lights blazed on.

The front door opened, and her mom stepped outside. "Sienna Rose? Is that you, honey?" She walked farther out.

Sienna Rose ground her teeth. She'd told Mom a million times not to go outside until she knew who was there. But at the moment, Sienna Rose didn't have the strength to chastise. "It's me, Mom."

"What are you doing out here, and why has there been a police car out front all day?"

She had so much to explain, but first she needed to sit down. She limped toward the front door.

"Oh, my goodness. You're hurt!" Her mom rushed out to help her to the house. "How on earth did you drive home?"

"I drove her."

Sienna Rose froze. Why hadn't Legend and the cop already left as she'd instructed? She thought she'd been pretty clear.

"Legend, is that you?" Her mom squinted.

He stepped beside Sienna Rose. "Yes ma'am."

Her mom threw her arms around him and gave him a big hug. "What are you doing back in Envie?"

"Chief Savoie called him. He's here helping on some cases." Sienna Rose hopped up the three stairs to the ranch-style wraparound porch. "Thanks for the ride home. I'll see you tomorrow." She limped through the door her mother hadn't closed, pulling her mother in with her, and shut it behind them. She couldn't take being close to Legend anymore.

How many times had they crowded onto the couch in the living room, eating popcorn and watching a movie? The memories were everywhere. The kitchen, where she'd tried to teach him how to make crawfish étouffée, had been a mess after he'd failed miserably to make a decent roux. The flour had ended up on the counters, the floors, and both of their noses. After that incident, Legend had only been allowed to work the grill on the back patio. She had to admit the man could make a mean steak.

Except for that one time he'd accidentally put too much cayenne on the meat, not realizing he'd already spiced it. But they'd been able to stay up all night and watch the sunrise on the patio. There was something special about the orange and red streaks climbing up out of the bayou.

She shook her head as memories rolled like a movie through her mind—and over her heart.

"That wasn't very polite, Sienna Rose." Her mother helped her to the kitchen table.

Sienna Rose sank onto a chair and tried different positions to stop her knees from throbbing. "I can't be around him right now. We have too much history, and I'm too worn out to deal with him and our past right now."

"What happened, honey?"

As briefly and with as little detail as possible, Sienna Rose gave her mom a rundown of the day, emphasizing the need for her mother and Dean to stay in the house as much as possible, and to be very careful until they were out of danger.

"We'll follow your instructions to the letter," her mom assured her.

"Good. Is it okay if I spend the night here and you give me a ride to work in the morning?"

"Of course." Her mom stood. "Dinner should be finished soon. I'll fix you a plate."

Before Sienna Rose could argue that she wasn't hungry, her mom called out to her brother, "Dean, dinner's ready. Your sister's here."

Dean rushed in and wrapped Sienna Rose in a big bear hug. She clung to him. It was exactly what she needed. Her big brother's hug felt like a balm to her weary soul. She loved him so much and couldn't imagine not being able to see him whenever she wanted. He was the main reason she'd remained in Envie and had no plans to move away.

She dreaded the day when their mother wouldn't be able to care for Dean, which was why Sienna Rose had purchased a home of her own not far from the house she'd grown up in, where her mother and Dean still lived.

She was grateful that Dean's cerebral palsy wasn't as severe as it was for some. He'd endured several surgeries growing up, and was now able to wear leg braces to assist with walking. When he was tired or stressed, his mobility became more impaired.

"Are you okay? I've been waiting for an update." His grin was wide as he sat in the chair beside her.

She focused on keeping her tone light. "I'm fine. I skinned my knees at work and wanted to visit you and Mom for comfort."

He laughed. "Mom is good at comfort."

Sienna Rose smiled, already feeling better with her family around her.

Her mother walked out of the kitchen carrying two plates of steaming spaghetti and set one down in front of each of them. The enticing aroma of garlic and basil permeated the air, causing Sienna Rose's stomach to growl out loud, which made Dean laugh again. She couldn't believe she actually was hungry. Maybe it was because she hadn't finished her burger and onion rings earlier since she'd been with Legend, which had brought up a lot of memories she didn't want to address.

When their mom returned with her own plate, Dean said, "I'd better pray fast. Sienna Rose is *starving*." He ducked his head and asked a blessing over his mom and sister.

"Amen." Sienna Rose took a bite and her taste buds lit up. There was nothing like her mom's home cooking.

Dean told a funny story, and weariness slipped off Sienna Rose's shoulders as she laughed, as much from his delight as from the story itself. The evening was exactly what she needed. Home and love. No judgment, no grudges.

No complicated feelings confusing her.

A knock sounded at the door.

Sienna Rose and her mother stopped laughing. Slipping her gun from its holster, she made her way to the front door, heart pounding as she tiptoed up to peer through the peephole.

Legend stood on the doorstep.

She holstered her weapon, unlocked the door, and wrenched it open. "What are you doing here?"

He held out a pharmacy bag. "We forgot to pick up your prescriptions. I didn't want you to miss a dose."

She raised a single brow as she snatched the white bag. "How did you know what pharmacy I use?"

"I saw the address on your discharge papers."

Why did suspicion coil inside her chest when it came to him?

Because he'd hurt her before and she didn't want to open the door even a sliver to let him hurt her again. She didn't know if she could take the pain a second time.

She cleared her throat. "Did you let the officer out front go?"

"I did. If you need anything, just holler."

Her pulse kicked up a notch. "I appreciate that, but I've got this."

"I know, but if you need backup, I'll be right out front."

"What?"

"Legend!" Dean rushed to the front door and gave him a sideways hug. "I've missed you, man."

Sienna Rose sighed. "Come on inside."

Her mom beamed at him. "Hi, Legend. Would you like some spaghetti?"

"Yours? Most certainly, if you don't mind." His easy smile and compliment almost made her mom blush.

Within seconds, she and her mom were back in the kitchen while Dean and Legend carried on their conversation. She sat on a barstool and took her pills as the bottle directed. "You don't have to feed him, Mom. He's a grown man, capable of getting food for himself."

"Sienna Rose Jordan, I didn't raise you to be so unwelcoming."

"Mom, he—"

Her mom gently interrupted. "What happened in the past is in the past. It's the present I'm concerned about. He's here, Sienna Rose. When he brought you home, there was no denying the affection on his face every time he looked at you. He went and picked up your medicine for you. Those are little things people do to show they care, but you're too angry to see it."

"I'm not angry, Mom. I'm hurt. He left me. He—"

Her mom interrupted again. "Five years ago. I know. He left you and broke your heart. But he's back now."

"Temporarily. He's leaving again as soon as we solve this case."

Her mom shrugged. "Maybe. Or maybe he'll stay. Life changes people sometimes."

Sienna Rose pulled in a deep breath. "If I let myself fall for him again and he leaves again, I don't know if my heart will survive it this time, Mom. You can only be less important than someone's career so many times before it breaks you."

Her mom walked around the bar and gave her a hug, then pulled back to swipe the bangs from Sienna Rose's eyes. "Loving people can be complicated and hard at times, but it can also bring the greatest joy.

Like with Dean. I would've never wished for him to be born with CP or autism. No one ever wants their children to struggle. But he's also brought so much light into this family. He's the kindest, gentlest person. His struggles have helped shape him into the loving young man that he is. I wouldn't trade that for anything."

"I feel the same way."

"Losing your dad was hard on my heart, I'm not going to lie. But I didn't have any regrets. I loved your father with every ounce of my being, and even when we disagreed, I knew he loved me with everything in his heart. It was a risk we both chose to take—letting another person into your life." She grabbed a plate from the cabinet and scooped spaghetti noodles onto it. "Love is always a risk, honey, but it's so worth it."

"This is different, Mom. The reason we broke up hasn't changed." Which meant they were still in the same situation.

Her mom poured sauce over the noodles. "The situation hasn't changed, but have you or Legend?" She added a hunk of garlic bread to the plate, then winked at Sienna Rose. "Or both?"

Sienna Rose watched her mother carry the steaming plate to the table and set it in front of Legend, who smiled his appreciation. Through the doorway, he grinned at Sienna Rose before taking a bite around his laughter at something Dean had said.

How had her mother become so wise?

"Come on, Dean. I think it's time we both head to bed. It's been a long day." Sienna Rose's mom leaned over and planted a kiss on the top of her head. "Good night, sweetie. Legend."

Dean gave Legend a high five, and Sienna Rose a kiss on her cheek. "'Night, 'Neena Rose." Legend had forgotten Dean called her that sometimes.

"Good night, man."

Dean chuckled. "That's right, I am The Man."

"As you call yourself." Sienna Rose chuckled.

That explained the text he'd seen earlier. Legend washed his empty plate and returned to the kitchen table where Sienna Rose sat, browsing the folder she'd taken earlier.

He sat across from her. "Dean seems to be doing well. He said he had a couple more surgeries in the last few years. You can't even tell he's wearing braces. He says he has a girlfriend too?"

"He sure does. Remember Tanya White? She's about a year younger than us."

"Tall? Friendly to everybody?"

"That's her. They've been dating for a year or so and are very happy."

"I'm glad for him."

"Me too," Sienna Rose agreed. "He and Mom get along well living here together. And Dean works part-time, which allows him to take Tanya out and gives Mom some time to herself."

"I'm glad to hear that." And he meant it. "We took the forensic evidence from all four crime scenes and ran it through our CSU in New Orleans."

She raised her brows. "Come up with anything interesting?"

"They concur with what CSU here found—no fingerprints, hair, or fibers. The shoe cast information is consistent with what Envie's lab determined."

"We might be smaller, but we're every bit as good." Sienna Rose took a sip of her iced tea.

"Our handwriting analyst profiled the writer of the index card and found that the weight and stroke movements of the pen indicate that the man is over thirty and probably well-educated."

"He could tell that by index cards?"

Legend shrugged. "That's what he said, and he's the leading expert on the subject in the South."

Sienna Rose made a slight humming noise, as if she doubted that such conclusions could be drawn from block writing.

"The state coroner also concluded her autopsy on Magdalene Savoie. No DNA evidence found, but cause of death was a stab wound which left cardiac damage." Legend shook his head. "She's released the body, but the chief has said there won't be a funeral. There will be a memorial at a later date."

Sienna Rose took another sip of tea.

"So, what do you have?" He tilted his head toward the folder in her hands while pulling out his notebook.

"I've been going over the file on Haven Webster, who was barely eighteen at the time of her death. Andy Paul, with whom Haven was romantically involved, was arrested for the murder, but not convicted. After the trial, Haven's father, Steven Webster, sought out Paul and beat him to death. Webster was arrested and sent to a behavioral health unit."

"Not prison?"

She shook her head as she read. "His defense to killing Andy Paul was mental instability. His attorney claimed Webster was distraught over his daughter's murder and believed that Andy Paul was guilty despite the court's verdict. The judge in that case agreed, and Webster avoided a murder charge."

"Is Webster still in the hospital?"

"He was recently released, but his wife has given him alibis for the four murders. I wonder if he has an alibi for today? I'm sure he's plenty upset with me for failing to provide enough evidence to convict Andy Paul of his daughter's murder."

"We definitely need to talk to the Websters." Legend made a note. "Who else was charged with Haven's murder?"

"No one." Her voice was barely a whisper.

"Haven Webster's murder has never been solved?" He found it hard to believe that Sienna Rose hadn't continued actively working the case.

She shook her head. "The DA election was right around the corner, and after Andy Paul was killed and Steven Webster hospitalized, DA Miley wanted the case out of the limelight because it made him look bad."

"So, technically, the case is still open?"

"Yes. We haven't uncovered any additional leads, but the case is still open."

"To make sure we're on the same page, are you saying you believe that Haven Webster's unsolved murder may be what connects the recent index-card murders?"

"It's the only case that ties the judge and all four targets together."

"Then let's work the Webster murder. Besides Andy Paul, who were the prime suspects?"

Sienna Rose flipped a page in the folder. "Karl Robicheaux. He was in love with Haven all through their school years together, and it was suspected that he lied at Andy Paul's trial to make Andy appear guilty." Her eyes flicked back and forth as she read. "I wonder what Karl's been up to lately."

Legend studied her as she picked up her phone. Even though fatigue pulled at the corners of her eyes, they were as dark and enchanting as he remembered. With the shorter haircut, her features were more defined, and she was even more stunning than he recalled.

Sienna Rose yawned as she began tapping at the screen. "I'm going to have a report pulled on all sedans in the area matching the one driven by the shooter who targeted me at the diner. I know, I know," she said, glancing his way. "It's a long shot, but at least it's something." She yawned again. "I don't know why I'm so tired all of a sudden."

Legend smiled. "The pain medication is probably kicking in and making you drowsy. You should go to bed."

"I'm fine."

"Then let's at least move to the living room where it's more comfortable."

She let him help her, settling into an easy chair adjacent to the couch before returning her attention to the file.

He stretched out on the couch and cleared his throat. "I see a note that Haven Webster had deposited a couple thousand dollars into her account shortly before her murder, and there was no explanation of where she'd gotten the money."

Sienna Rose shifted to face him. "Right. Haven worked at a daycare, but she didn't really have friends there, just coworkers. She had no problems with anyone, and according to our interviews, no one had anything against Haven."

"You said this was your first case as a detective?" he clarified.

"Yeah. Four years ago."

It might take a cop years to make detective in a big city, but in smaller towns, fast-tracking was more common, out of necessity. Yet he detected a hint of uncertainty in her voice. She had always second-guessed herself if situations didn't turn out for the best.

"Remember how we always said we'd be the best detective team the state had ever seen?" The words came out before he could stop them.

She pinched her lips into a thin line.

He could have kicked himself for bringing up the subject, though memories of the plans they'd made, to be a team forever, had been at the forefront of his mind all day.

"Back to the Haven Webster murder," she said. "Since it was my first, the chief—who was still a captain then—went with me to question Karl Robicheaux. Karl and Haven had been best friends as children. In high school, they'd gone out a few times, but according to several of Haven's friends, she considered Karl a friend and nothing more. On the other hand, everyone questioned back then stated that Karl was wildly in love with Haven."

"You and Savoie didn't like him for a suspect?"

"There was nothing to link him forensically to the case. No fingerprints. No hair or fibers. No DNA match."

"Tell me about Andy Paul." He'd been found not guilty of Haven's murder, but Legend knew all too well that "not guilty" didn't always equal innocence.

Sienna Rose closed her eyes as she spoke. "Paul was thirty-two at the time of the trial, and by all accounts, kind of a jerk. Haven's friends reported that he often displayed controlling behavior with her and resented her spending time with any of them."

No wonder Paul had been charged.

She continued. "Andy Paul had a little brother named Baker. The two were close, and from some of Haven's friends' statements, Haven might have had a mild crush on Baker at one point. I never found any animosity between the brothers because of Haven's alleged affection toward Baker." Sienna Rose sighed. "Baker did file a wrongful death civil suit against Steven Webster that is still pending, three years later. There have been many delays, mainly because Webster was hospitalized."

"But he's been released," Legend reiterated.

"Yes. I wonder if that means he's finally going to have to answer for what he did."

Legend kicked off his shoes and stretched out his legs.

Memories assaulted him. How many movies had they watched, laughing together, in that very room?

Sienna Rose pulled the folder onto her lap and released a sigh, as if she was replaying the same memories. More likely her knees hurt.

How had he walked away from their love? He'd known how loyal she was to her family, especially at the time he left, her father having passed away mere months before. She'd needed to stay to be there for her mom and Dean. Yet Dean appeared settled and happy. Surely he didn't need much help. And her mom seemed to have adjusted after losing her husband.

Were the same things still keeping them apart?

*M*orning sun peeked around the shades in the police department's conference room during roll call.

"Would you bring Karl Robicheaux in for questioning?" Sienna Rose passed the card with his address to one of the patrol officers.

"First thing this morning, Detective."

"Thank you."

Captain Brewer called roll and gave the announcements. He also let them know that he did not have an expected date for the chief's return to work. "Our continued thoughts and prayers are with him and his family in this terrible time. Dismissed."

Sienna Rose headed toward her desk.

Legend fell into step beside her, handing her a coffee from a place two blocks away.

She took a sip. "Thanks." Her knees were sore that morning, but she wasn't about to let anyone know. No way was she sitting behind a desk and taking it easy, not while a killer was on the loose. Nor was she going to take any more of those pain pills that had made her so lethargic the previous night.

"I noticed the coffee here hasn't improved in the last five years," Legend added.

"Remember how you and I used to take turns picking up coffee on the way in so we didn't have to start our days with the sludge here?" Despite herself, she grinned and took another sip. "I think the station coffee's only gotten worse since then, so thank you."

"It's universal that all police stations have the lousiest coffee." He sat on the edge of her desk after she sank into her chair. "I'm pretty sure it's an unwritten rule."

"Even at the fancy station in New Orleans?" She froze, a little surprised the question had snuck out. She'd been determined not to probe about his life.

He blinked in surprise, then grinned. "It's the worst. Or maybe it feels that way because we have access to so much amazing coffee from cafes nearby. I'd love to take you to my favorite one sometime. You'd love the beignets. They practically melt in your mouth."

Her computer dinged with an incoming email, saving her from responding. She scanned the message. "DMV records indicate that there are four dark sedans matching our description, all registered to residents of Envie."

"That's a little surprising. Who would've thought there'd be that many in a town this size?"

"Hey, now. I'll have you know that our current population is 5,568."

"Is that counting the gators?"

She chuckled. It was an inside joke that Envie's population increased every time an alligator's eggs hatched. It was like old times.

Almost.

Her intercom buzzed and she lifted the receiver.

"Hey, Sienna Rose. It's Anna at CSU. We finished going over your SUV. We got nothing forensically except confirmation that the bullets fired were issued from a 9mm, less than two hundred feet away. You can pick up your vehicle anytime."

She hung up and filled Legend in.

Officer Hazel Moncrief joined them. "What can I do to help, Detective Jordan?"

Sienna Rose smiled at the younger woman. "We've pretty much

established that the connection between the recent murder victims—Judge Hughes, Amanda Pratt, Megan Rooster, Magdalene Savoie—and me—is the Haven Webster murder."

Officer Moncrief's eyes widened. "That's some progress."

"I sent all the evidence to the CSU in New Orleans for follow-up," Legend explained. "Seems that DNA evidence from the Haven Webster murder helped exonerate Andy Paul, as it wasn't his. And a match was never found."

Sienna Rose remembered all too well.

"The testing improves constantly. The New Orleans techs were able to isolate something very interesting about that DNA. It wasn't Andy's, but it was a familial match to his."

"So the DNA at the scene of Haven's murder was left there by a relative of Andy Paul's?"

"That's right." Legend eased into a chair beside her desk. "A male, to be more precise. How many male family members does Paul have here in town?"

"Now? I'm not sure. Back during the time of Haven's murder?" She closed her eyes to try and remember. "His brother, father, an uncle, and four or five cousins." That provided a slew of new suspects. She began to wonder if solving Haven's murder would shed light on who was behind the current ones. Maybe it would reveal someone who had been unhappy with the miscarriage of justice—unhappy enough to kill. "His father died a couple years back, of a heart attack. I think his uncle died before. Best I can recall, most of the cousins have moved off, but they were here at the time."

Officer Moncrief glanced between Sienna Rose and Legend. "I'm not following."

"Familial DNA means it's not an exact match to a specific person, but there are enough markers to verify a match to a biological family member." Sienna Rose took a sip of her coffee. "In this case, the DNA found at

Haven Webster's crime scene wasn't Andy Paul's, but it's a familial match."

"So it's a blood relative of his?" Officer Moncrief asked.

"Correct." Legend answered. "I'll have my team in New Orleans run a search for all his living biological family and see who has a record, who was still around, who had motive, all of that."

Sienna Rose wanted to object and say they could handle it but realized his team could accomplish more intel gathering than the two of them. "Who in the Paul family would have motive to kill Haven? Did someone kill her to set up Andy?"

"If that's the case, that particular someone must have been really upset when Andy was found not guilty."

"And not very upset at all when he was killed." She stood and slid her gun into her holster. "Time to go pay Mr. Webster a visit and check his alibi for yesterday when we were shot at."

Legend pushed to his feet. "Need me to sign out your SUV from CSU and bring it around to pick you up?"

"I'll do that, Detective." Officer Moncrief strode toward the side door of the police station.

"Thanks, Officer. We'll be right behind you." Sienna Rose turned back to Legend, who was adjusting his holster. "Surely Steven Webster wouldn't be stupid enough to start killing so soon after his release." She led the way to the parking lot where CSU moved vehicles after collecting evidence.

"Criminals aren't known for being the smartest, Sienna Rose. You know that. Webster already beat a man to death over his daughter's murder. In broad daylight. On the courthouse steps."

"True." She inhaled, then slowly exhaled as she struggled not to limp. "I wonder what kind of vehicle he drives."

Officer Moncrief held out the key fob, pointing it toward Sienna Rose's SUV.

"If it's a dark sedan—"

Boom!

The explosion was deafening. Sienna Rose's vehicle erupted in flames as glass and debris flew everywhere.

Officer Moncrief lay on the asphalt, unmoving.

Sienna Rose sprinted toward her young colleague, Legend at her heels. Officers spilled out of the station.

Sienna Rose pressed her fingers to Hazel's neck, searching for a pulse. "Get an ambulance here now. Officer down," she yelled to the people that had come outside. "I repeat, get an ambulance here *now*."

The young woman moaned and her hands reached for her midsection. Legend found a piece of glass protruding from her chest. He caught her hands. "Hold still. We're right here with you. We're going to take care of you."

"I didn't—" Hazel's eyes fluttered.

Sienna Rose's mouth went dry with panic as she realized how serious the young woman's wounds were. "Shh, don't try to move. An ambulance will be here before you know it. Stay still. We've got you."

"I'm sorry, Detective Jordan."

"Whatever for?" Sienna Rose brushed the young woman's hair from her face as sirens wailed, drawing closer.

"For letting you down."

"Hush now. You didn't let me down. You did nothing wrong. You're going to be okay. Don't worry about anything but hanging in there."

A fire engine parked near the burning remains of Sienna Rose's SUV, and firefighters piled out to begin damage control. An ambulance pulled up next to the fire engine, and EMTs burst out of the back doors. Within minutes, they had Hazel on a stretcher, loaded into the ambulance with an IV.

"We'll be taking her to Envie General," said an EMT before shutting the ambulance doors. The emergency vehicle sped off, its siren screaming.

The firefighters continued to spray down the SUV, though Sienna Rose couldn't see any more flames. The stench of smoke hung in the air, suffocating her.

Sienna Rose stared after the ambulance.

That could have been her. It was supposed to be her. It was her SUV.

She began to tremble.

Legend's hand appeared on her forearm, grounding her enough that she heard him when he spoke. "I've requested that my task force's forensics unit go over this mess with a fine-tooth comb and rush the results to us. They'll be here within an hour. I've notified the CSU here to expect them."

Sienna Rose stared blankly at the rubble.

"Sienna Rose?"

She couldn't move, could barely breathe.

Legend turned her to face him. "Hey, stay with me."

She swallowed hard. "This is my fault. Someone's trying to kill me, not Hazel. I didn't think about anyone else's safety, nothing but the fact that I wanted to solve this case. It's my fault she got hurt." Her vision blurred as tears filled her eyes.

"No," Legend said firmly. "None of this is your fault. It's on the person who's choosing to do these terrible things. We're going to catch them and see that they pay for everything they've done."

His words slammed against her chest. "Mom and Dean? Are they okay? They—"

"Are both fine," he interrupted before she could spiral out of control. "I spoke to the patrol officer this morning, and he will call if he sees or hears anything suspicious."

Captain Brewer joined them. "I've reached out to Officer Moncrief's emergency contact so they can meet her at the hospital. Would one of you like to tell me what happened?"

Sienna Rose filled him in, then waited for the captain's response.

He rubbed his chin. "Go question Webster, but keep your guard up. We don't need any bad PR right now. Not with four unsolved murders on our hands."

Five, Sienna Rose thought. Haven Webster's unsolved murder made it five.

"We'll take my rental." Legend helped Sienna Rose into the car, then followed her directions to the Webster home.

The midmorning sun warmed the November air as they made their way into an upscale community. The homes were older and beautiful. Some had been restored while others were in the process. All bore similar architecture on large lots.

She'd once dreamed of living in that very area, with its beauty and history. She'd often envisioned Legend by her side. Being there on a beautiful day after everything that had happened felt like an insult.

He parked the car in front of the Websters' home, and they stepped onto the driveway. Sienna Rose settled her holster as her feet hit the pavement. Her knee pain was better, but it still smarted. She climbed the front steps slowly, then used the large door knocker.

A girl much closer in age to Haven Webster than to her mother, Eleanor Webster, opened the door. "May I help you?"

Sienna Rose shifted her jacket aside to flash the detective's shield fastened to her waist. "I'm Detective Jordan, and this is Special Detective Cruz." She tilted her head toward him. "We're here to see Mr. and Mrs. Webster."

The girl—presumably a housekeeper—appeared unruffled by the badge or their presence. "I'm sorry. Mr. Webster isn't in at the moment."

"Then we'll see Mrs. Webster alone." Sienna Rose wasn't accepting any excuses.

"This way." The girl led them to a formal sitting room off of the foyer. "Wait here. I'll get Mrs. Webster." She disappeared back into the hallway.

The room boasted a sofa, two high-back chairs, a fireplace with an ornate mantel, and one of the most beautiful rugs Sienna Rose had ever seen.

The view from the big bay windows showed a gorgeously manicured flower garden. The rosebushes, while not in bloom, were tended. The chrysanthemums, however, were in full bloom, their bright golds and reds lining the pathway. A water feature drew the eye with its flowing and gentle cascades.

"This is beautiful." Legend's voice at her shoulder nearly made her jump.

She'd been so enthralled that she hadn't heard him move closer, yet he stood beside her, staring out the window into the garden as she had. "It's breathtaking." And he was too close. Close enough that she picked up a hint of his cologne, the brand she'd bought him years ago because she said it smelled the best on him.

She inhaled. It still did.

Sienna Rose moved around him to settle herself at the end of the sofa, which was much softer than it had appeared.

"I'm Eleanor Webster. How may I help you?" The woman glided into the room. Sienna Rose recalled how broken and distraught Eleanor had been the last time she'd seen her—right after Steven's sentencing, doubly broken from her daughter's murder and her husband's crime. It seemed almost impossible that the woman who stood before them was the same person. Her posture was perfect, the manner in which she carried herself flawless.

Sienna Rose stood. "Thank you for seeing us, Mrs. Webster."

Eleanor drifted into one of the wingback chairs, perching at the edge. "I didn't realize I had a choice."

"Ma'am, we're following up on some details regarding Haven's murder investigation. We have a few questions for you." Legend dropped onto the sofa opposite Eleanor.

Sienna Rose sat on the other end of the sofa and opened the note-taking app on her phone. She provided Eleanor with the date of Judge Hughes's murder. "You stated previously that, on this date, your husband was home with you, watching television between ten in the morning and noon. Is that correct?"

Eleanor's face reddened a shade. "If that's what I said, then it must be correct."

Sienna Rose provided the dates and times of the following two murders—those of Amanda Pratt and Megan Rooster. "Your statement was that your husband was with you during these times as well. Do you still stand by that information?"

"If I told an officer as much, then yes."

Sienna Rose referenced the date Magdalene Savoie was murdered. "What, exactly, were you and Mr. Webster watching on television that evening?"

"I'm not sure." Eleanor's hands twisted in her lap. Her gaze kept shooting to the arched doorway leading into the foyer.

Interesting, Sienna Rose thought. *It was only a few days ago.*

"Mrs. Webster," Legend said calmly, "was Mr. Webster with you yesterday between noon and two in the afternoon?"

Her eyes widened, and she clamped her hands together. "I believe so. I usually rest in the afternoon, but I think Steven was reading in the bedroom while I napped. Yes, I'm pretty certain he was reading then."

"Did you sleep?" Sienna Rose asked.

Eleanor shot her a condescending, tight-lipped smile. "Of course not, dear. I simply require a little lie-down, that's all."

Legend shot Eleanor an endearing smile, catching the older woman off guard. "What kind of vehicle does your husband drive, Mrs. Webster?"

"A dark blue sedan."

Legend named the make and model.

"Yes, that's right. What's this about again?"

Sienna Rose's cell phone vibrated. She read the message, then stood. "Thank you for your time, Mrs. Webster."

Eleanor stood and motioned for the girl hovering in the foyer. "Charlene will see you out."

Once outside, Sienna Rose picked her steps gingerly to Legend's rental. "I think Mrs. Webster is lying. Noncommittal statements such as, 'I don't recall,' 'I believe so,' and 'I'm not sure' are telltale indicators."

Legend started the car. "And the way she kept glancing into the foyer, like she expected someone to burst in."

"Plus confirmation that Steven Webster drives a dark sedan like the driver who shot at us. That's enough for the captain to at least allow further questioning." Sienna Rose let out a long breath. "Let's get back to the station. Karl Robicheaux is in an interrogation room."

Legend put the car in gear. "Let's go see if we can get some answers."

Answers we desperately need, Sienna Rose thought. She didn't want to think about what would happen if they didn't get those answers.

10

"*H*ow dare you bring me into the police station like some common criminal?" Karl Robicheaux sat in a metal chair in the interrogation room, glaring as Legend and Sienna Rose entered.

Sienna Rose took a seat across from him. "I apologize for any inconvenience, Mr. Robicheaux. We're simply working through some details regarding Haven Webster's case, and we'd like to ask you a few questions." She smiled, and the wattage was brighter than the overhead lights. "I remember how helpful you were before."

Legend leaned against a concrete wall in the corner, observing.

"Why would you care about an old case with all these linked murders now?" he demanded. "I thought her case was solved."

"We're just double-checking our work. After all, everyone deserves justice, don't they?" She gestured toward Robicheaux's shoes. "I like those sneakers. I might get my brother a pair for his birthday. Do they run small or large?"

He shrugged. "These are elevens and they fit fine."

"Thank you."

Sienna Rose is excellent at her job, Legend thought. *Anyone would be lucky to work with her.*

Robicheaux's shoe size helped to rule him out as a suspect in the Savoie murder. Unless he'd worn shoes too big for him on purpose, to throw them off. But he didn't seem that deliberate.

Sienna Rose gave a disarming smile. "As I said, we've been rereviewing Haven's case."

Robicheaux visibly relaxed. "I told y'all back then that Andy Paul killed her. He was too old for her and had no business hanging around her."

"Yes, I remember you telling us that. Do you have any additional information you could share with us now?"

Legend had read the case files carefully and knew that Robicheaux had lied on the stand about Andy Paul. Robicheaux had sworn that he'd seen Paul following Haven on the day of her murder. Robicheaux also testified that he'd seen Paul with blood on his shirt after the murder occurred. Both turned out to be lies.

"No. Not since Mr. Webster killed Andy."

Sienna Rose gave Legend a knowing glance. "I understand you were as angry as Mr. Webster when Andy was found not guilty."

"Yeah, I guess I was." He leaned back in the chair and spread one leg out under the table. "I was furious that he'd been allowed to get away with it. Everyone knew he was guilty, but y'all let him go. The judge, the attorneys, cops, even you." He jutted his chin out toward Sienna Rose. "At least you arrested Andy. That's more than the others did."

Legend pushed off the wall. "Furious enough that you wanted revenge?" He leaned in toward the man's face, knowing Robicheaux wouldn't be able to resist the unspoken challenge.

Robicheaux straightened, slapping his palms against the table. "Yeah, I wanted people to pay for letting that killer walk free. He needed to pay for what he did to Haven, and when you failed to make that happen, her dad had to step in." His jaw clenched.

Sienna Rose leaned forward. "And me? Do you want me to pay too, Karl? Do I deserve to die because I worked on Haven's case?"

Robicheaux simply crossed his arms over his chest and glared.

"Did you know Magdalene Savoie?" Legend asked.

Robicheaux jerked back, brows scrunching together. "Who?"

Sienna Rose's tone was as calm as if they were discussing the weather. "Would you be willing to provide us a DNA sample so we can rule you out as a suspect in Haven's murder?"

"Definitely not. I'm not some idiot, you know. I have rights."

"Can you tell us where you were three nights ago?" Legend asked. *The night Magdalene was murdered.*

"Bowling. I'm on a team in the Bayou Bros league. You can check with anybody. I'm the best on our team, and we're the best in our league."

Sienna Rose hit fast with the next question. "And yesterday afternoon—can you tell us where you were then?"

"I was at work at the plant until five thirty, then I went straight to the bowling alley. Had dinner there, then the team practiced for two games. When we were done, we had a couple of beers before we left."

"About what time was that?" Legend asked.

"I guess it was about ten thirty or so."

If his alibis were true, Robicheaux couldn't have killed Magdalene or shot at them outside the diner.

"Am I free to go now, or do I get my lawyer?"

Sienna Rose stood. "You're free to go. If you change your mind about that DNA sample, let us know. It could clear you from being a suspect in Haven's murder."

Robicheaux pushed to his feet. "Why would anybody think I'd hurt her? I loved her."

"Like I said, we're revisiting some of the facts."

"I told you already. Andy Paul killed Haven."

"It wasn't Andy's DNA we found at the crime scene."

He narrowed his eyes at Sienna Rose. "And you think it's mine?"

"I'm not at liberty to say. I have to cover all bases."

He took a step in Sienna Rose's direction. "I never would have hurt Haven."

Legend planted himself beside Sienna Rose. "That's why the detective said she wanted a sample—to rule you out as a suspect."

"Yeah, well, that ain't happening. I've heard how you cops like to say you're trying to rule someone out when you're really trying to set them up. I'm no rocket scientist, but I'm not stupid either." Robicheaux stormed out of the interrogation room into the hall.

Sienna Rose raised her eyebrows at Legend. "His alibis seem tight. I'll have someone check it out, but it sounds like he's in the clear for Magdalene's murder and our drive-by shooting." She led the way back to her desk. "I'm sure his bowling team will verify his alibi. And if his team is the best in the league, then there will be more than a dozen others who will back that up."

"Not to mention his shoe size doesn't fit the prints found at Magdalene Savoie's crime scene." He followed Sienna Rose and sat in the chair beside her desk. "I know you ruled him out as a suspect in Haven's murder, but I don't like the guy. He was in love with Haven, and she didn't return those sentiments. That's always a strong motive." Legend rubbed the stubble on his chin. "I'm guessing there's no chance he's related to Andy Paul, huh?"

Sienna Rose chuckled as she typed notes in the online case file. "Not really. I have a feeling it would make my life easier, but no."

"I'd still like to run his DNA against what was found at Haven's crime scene to be sure. Something about the guy gives me a gut feeling that he's not on the up and up."

"I'll see if I can get a court order for his DNA, but with the familial DNA not linking to his family, I don't know if it'll fly."

Legend realized something was bothering him. "You know, all the other murders were up close and personal. Stabbing, specifically."

"Because the situation is personal to the killer," Sienna Rose said. "What's your point?"

"Drive-by shooting and car-bombing are distant and impersonal. I guess I'm wondering why the killer has changed his MO with you."

"I hadn't thought about that," she admitted. "Maybe it's because I'm a cop and more likely to be able to defend myself, or be with someone who can defend me. Or he has a plan and he's running out of time. Who knows? Whatever the reason, he's clearly still got it out for me."

"Yeah." That made Legend all the more nervous. He checked his cell phone. "I got a text from my team while we were in the interrogation room. We have my CSU's report back on your vehicle."

"Wow, your team is fast. I wish we had resources like that here."

"One of the reasons our teams get called in to help—our resources are fast and accurate."

Suddenly, his stomach growled and he saw on his phone that it was two in the afternoon. Where had the day gone?

Sienna Rose's cell phone buzzed and she snatched it from its holder on her belt. "Detective Jordan. Yes. I see. That's good. Okay. Thank you. Let me know if there's any change." She returned the phone to its place. "That was the hospital."

He found himself holding his breath. What if it was bad news?

"Officer Moncrief is out of surgery. The doctor said she's handling treatment well, and her burns were less severe than they initially thought. Her prognosis is good." Sienna Rose blew out a relieved sigh. "I'm so glad she's going to be okay."

"Me too." Things could've been so much worse. Moncrief could have been more seriously injured, or even killed. Or Sienna Rose could've been killed. Legend didn't want to dwell on that. "So, about your SUV."

Sienna Rose leaned back in her chair and waited as he read from his phone.

"The bomb actually went off early. Best they can tell, it was set to explode when a driver turned on the ignition. When Officer Moncrief pushed the button, she unlocked the doors and triggered the remote start."

Sienna Rose shuddered. "If she had gotten into the car and started it, she wouldn't be alive."

Legend put a hand over hers, his fear pushing a lump up into his throat. "But that's not what happened. She's going to be okay."

"Yeah."

His phone buzzed. He squeezed her hand, then let go to answer the call. "Cruz."

"Sir, we've got the report on Baker Paul." It was his team member Michael King.

"King, I'm going to put you on speaker so Detective Jordan can hear the report too." He set down the phone and switched the call to speaker mode. "Go ahead."

"Yes sir. We did that background check on Baker Paul like you asked. He's got a few minor arrests in the past, but nothing major. Nothing he wasn't able to get out of with anything more than a slap on the wrist."

Legend was growing weary of not being able to catch a break. "Go figure."

"His background employment includes construction, a demolition crew, and minor concrete laying."

"Did you say demolition?" Legend clarified.

"Yes sir."

That was something anyway. "Anything else, King?"

"No sir, but we're still checking."

"Keep me in the loop. Thanks." Legend disconnected the call and met Sienna Rose's wide eyes. "If he did demo work, he might know how to build a bomb."

Sienna Rose was on her feet. "We need to bring in Baker Paul and see what he knows about Haven Webster's murder and the bomb in my SUV. Let's go bring Captain Brewer up to speed."

They headed to Captain Brewer's office, and she knocked on the door. When they were called in, Legend eased in behind her. Sienna Rose quickly filled the captain in, explaining how Magdalene Savoie's case was tied to Haven Webster's unsolved murder.

Captain Brewer grabbed his phone to make a call. "Officer Rucker, find Baker Paul and bring him in. Now."

"It'd be great to get a warrant for a DNA sample from Karl Robicheaux," Sienna Rose added.

"I'll do my best. Interrogate Baker Paul, and then we'll go from there. Speak to Steven Webster's wife again. You said she sounded cagey. Run with that angle. She might know more than she's saying."

"Thank you, sir. I'll keep you updated." Sienna Rose headed toward the door.

"Remember, Detective Jordan," Captain Brewer said. "When it comes to solving cases, what matters is not what you know or think you know, but what you can prove."

"Yes sir."

Legend followed her down the hall.

"Let's go talk to Mrs. Webster again. If Mr. Webster is there, we can question them both." Sienna Rose headed to her desk to retrieve her service firearm. "I'd like to get a look at Steven's car as well. If he's our shooter, I'm sure one of us hit it at least once."

And if that were the case, Legend had a few choice words for Steven Webster.

11

$\mathcal{A}$s usual, the bayou pushed a breeze across the water and onto land, lending a distinct chill and smell to the air.

Sienna Rose climbed the steps up to the Websters' front porch for the second time that day. Her knees were killing her. She wished she'd taken at least half a pain pill as she lifted the large door knocker and let it drop. It clanged loudly.

Charlene opened the door again, wearing a smile that quickly left her face. "May I help you?"

Sienna Rose knew she didn't need to flash her badge again. "We're here to see the Websters."

Charlene shook her head. "Mr. Webster still isn't home."

"Guess we'll see Mrs. Webster alone again."

Charlene pushed the door open and let them enter, showing them to the formal sitting room off of the foyer again. "Wait here." She disappeared.

Sienna Rose and Legend shared the couch as before. His knee began to bounce, just like it always had when he was antsy. He caught her noticing and grinned sheepishly.

"What is it now, detectives?" Eleanor Webster took a seat on the edge of the same chair she had chosen earlier, but she sounded tired.

Sienna Rose smiled softly. "Mrs. Webster, as we continue working to solve your daughter's murder, we have come across a few additional questions."

Eleanor's eyes flickered with an emotion Sienna Rose couldn't decipher.

"There are details from a few recent cases that may connect other murders to Haven's."

"Like what?"

Here goes nothing. "Mrs. Webster, what size shoe does Mr. Webster wear?" She was very careful not to refer to him as Eleanor's husband any longer, to avoid hinting at any loyalty due him.

"I believe a size twelve."

The right size shoe.

Legend leaned toward Eleanor. "Is there anything else you need to tell us, Eleanor?"

Eleanor stared toward the arched doorway with widened eyes before making eye contact with Sienna Rose again. "What does any of this have to do with Haven's murder?"

Sienna Rose couldn't answer the question, though her heart went out to Eleanor. The woman had lost her daughter, then her husband had brutally murdered a man and spent years in a behavioral health hospital. She couldn't imagine the pain Eleanor Webster had endured.

She softened her tone. "Are you absolutely certain that on the dates and times we discussed earlier today, your husband was, in fact, with you?" She rattled off the dates and times of Judge Hughes's murder, Barney Pratt's wife's murder, Megan Rooster's murder, Magdalene Savoie's murder, and the time the day before when she and Legend had been shot at. "Are you absolutely sure that your husband was with you during those hours?" Sienna Rose held her breath, praying she could break through Eleanor's stoniness.

Eleanor issued a short gasp, then pressed her fingers against her closed lips and shook her head.

"Did your husband instruct you to lie for him?" Sienna Rose asked.

The whites of Eleanor's eyes were visible all the way around her pupils as she glanced toward the door once more.

"It's okay, Mrs. Webster. You can tell us the truth. Did you lie about Mr. Webster's whereabouts before?" Legend spoke as gently and at as low a volume as Sienna Rose had.

Eleanor's face was pale. "I can't remember the exact times he was here, or when he was away. He told me that on the occasions you mentioned, we were watching television together. Since I can't always recall specific dates, I assumed he was correct, and that we were together."

There it was. Sienna Rose let out the breath she'd been holding. "Is there anything else you want to add?"

Eleanor bit her lip, clearly considering. When she spoke again, her voice was a raspy whisper. "He kept a journal while he was in the hospital. I don't know if they required it or if he did it on his own. I'm positive none of the doctors there read it because if they had, he certainly wouldn't have been released."

Sienna Rose tilted her head. "Why do you say that?"

Eleanor wrapped her arms around her midsection, folding herself inward. Fear crept across her delicate features. "He wrote about revenge. Vengeance. Acting as executioner to those who failed to serve justice to criminals who deserved it. To that judge, that prosecutor, the Chief of Police." She locked eyes with Sienna Rose. "To you." A tear rolled down her cheek. "I'm so sorry. I was too scared to say anything. I should have, especially after you'd been so kind to me when Haven died, but I couldn't."

"Where is this journal now?" Controlled anger etched across Legend's features. He hid it well, but not from someone who knew him as well as Sienna Rose did.

Eleanor shrugged. "I found it by accident when I was cleaning out Steven's nightstand. He caught me putting it back in the drawer and didn't say a word." She shivered. "He never asked if I read it. He never even mentioned it. The next day, it was gone."

"Any idea where he might have moved it?" Legend asked.

Eleanor shook her head. "He could have destroyed it for all I know."

Hopefully Webster hadn't destroyed the journal. It sounded like their best lead. "What else did he write in there, aside from what you've told us?"

"The entries from when he was in the hospital were violent—including plans to kill you, the judge, the chief, and the prosecutor from Haven's case." She shuddered. "It was inhumane and hard to read. I know I should have called you, but I was too frightened by what Steven might do to me."

Eleanor was displaying signs that Sienna Rose recognized from domestic violence survivors. "Eleanor, has Steven ever threatened or physically endangered you?" If the woman needed help, Sienna Rose would make sure she got it.

Eleanor shook her head. "No. It's just that since he got out of the hospital, he's different. Changed. A little scary in how cold he is toward me."

Legend's body stiffened. "What about the journal entries after he got home?"

Eleanor relaxed a little. "Those aren't nearly as horrible. Mostly mundane details. Notations about where you and the others went every day. Routines. Notes about what you were doing and who you were with."

Perhaps Webster had been planning the best times to kill everyone involved in his daughter's murder case. The journal could offer crucial evidence.

Sienna Rose straightened her spine. "Eleanor, will you grant us permission to search your house and its grounds for the journal and anything else we might find?"

"I...I don't know."

"Mrs. Webster, you gave false information to the police and withheld critical information about potential future crimes," Legend said, his voice gentle though his words weren't. "Obstruction of justice is merely one of the counts we can charge you with. It will be much better for you to assist us in any way that you can."

Her perfect posture slumped. "Oh, dear. I knew I should've brought that journal to the police."

Sienna Rose spoke softly. "You can help us now by letting us search for it."

"Okay. Yes. You may start in the bedroom. Upstairs, second door on your right."

Legend stepped into a far corner of the room, putting his cell to his ear.

"Where is Steven?" Sienna Rose asked Eleanor.

"He's supposed to be at his outpatient therapy appointment."

"Supposed to be?"

"The office called the house phone yesterday to confirm the appointment. The receptionist told me he'd missed his last three."

"Did you ask your husband about that?"

Eleanor shook her head. "I left a note on his nightstand that they'd called to remind him of the appointment."

Sienna Rose was certain they were running out of time, but she also knew that if she frightened Eleanor more than she already was, she was likely to shut down and be unable to help them at all. "What time do you expect him to return?"

"I have no idea. The appointment was two hours ago. If he kept it, they usually run about an hour long. He could be back any minute."

Legend returned to them. "My CSU team will be here as soon as they can, but let's start looking now."

Sienna Rose stood. "Make sure your team knows not to show up with their lights flashing. Steven could be on his way home. We don't want a big show of police presence to scare him off."

Legend pulled out his cell again. "On it."

"Officers are on their way to search the property," Sienna Rose told Eleanor. "They'll also gather items for DNA purposes. We will ask for a swab of your DNA for reference."

"Anything I can do to help."

Legend returned. "Captain Brewer is on his way to speak with Mrs. Webster himself."

"What does that mean?" Eleanor wrung her hands. "Do I need to call my attorney?"

"Ma'am, if you would feel more comfortable with legal counsel present, you may call your lawyer. At this time, you aren't charged with anything." Legend pulled rubber gloves from his pocket and passed a pair to Sienna Rose.

"I think I will." Eleanor moved to the door. "Charlene?"

The young woman met her in the doorway. "Yes ma'am?"

"Get Walter Oswald on the phone for me. Tell him it's urgent. Detectives, please excuse me while I make the call." Eleanor strode from the room, her perfect posture back in place.

"Let's start searching for that journal," Legend said when he and Sienna Rose were alone. "Captain Brewer is obtaining a warrant for Webster's arrest, and a BOLO has been issued."

They climbed the massive staircase and headed toward the main bedroom as Eleanor had directed. It was as pristine as the rest of the house, with large antique furniture in mint condition.

"Do you want to search the dresser or the nightstands?" Legend asked.

She scrunched up her nose. "Nightstands. I don't like digging through other people's dressers."

He laughed as he moved to the mahogany bureau. "You can stitch up a bleeding wound, but going through strangers' dressers bothers you."

Sienna Rose pulled open the first nightstand drawer and began pulling out papers. "Nothing here." She moved to the nightstand on the other side of the bed.

Legend was already through the third drawer of the bureau. "You know, I've been thinking about Haven's case."

"What about it?" Sienna Rose finished searching the second nightstand without finding the journal or anything else incriminating. She stood and glanced around the room. It didn't appear to hold many other hiding places, so she pulled open a closet door.

"I keep getting tripped up on that large deposit into Haven's account right before she died."

"Yeah? What are your thoughts?" She rummaged through the hanging clothes, feeling around for anything other than fabric.

"Your notes said she didn't make that much at the daycare, so where did the money come from?"

"I wonder if perhaps she got it from her father."

Legend moved into the adjoining bathroom. "Did you ever ask him?"

"Didn't get the chance. The DA instructed the previous chief to halt the investigation after Andy Paul was charged, and only follow up on evidence that might link him to Haven's murder. Right after Andy was acquitted, Steven Webster killed him and was taken into custody." She ran her hand along the top shelf of the closet.

"Did you ask Mrs. Webster about the money?"

"We did, but she was so distraught at the time I'm not sure she was reliable. I haven't thought to ask since." Sienna Rose's fingers touched what felt like a book. She grabbed it from the shelf—a slim volume with handwriting inside.

"We can try doing it now."

"We can." Her heart pounded as she flipped through the pages. "I've found it. Come see."

In a flash, Legend was at her side. Together they skimmed several pages of the journal. Sienna Rose gasped in horror as she read all the hatred and violence Steven Webster had inside him, directed not just toward the people he'd murdered, but also toward her. Her grasp on the book weakened.

Legend grabbed the journal. "This is almost as good as a confession." It detailed Webster's plans to murder those connected to Haven's case, as well as how he kept hoping he'd feel that justice had been served after each one, when in reality, he felt nothing of the sort. "We need to log this in as evidence as soon as my team gets here."

"Let's go talk to Eleanor while we wait," Sienna Rose said. "I want to ask her again about that money."

They descended the stairs as a knock sounded on the front door. Charlene opened it to Legend's CSU team. Legend gave them the journal and explained what it signified, speaking in quiet tones.

Sienna Rose discovered Eleanor in the sitting room, her face pale. "We found the journal. Thank you for telling us about it."

"He killed those people, didn't he? The ones I've been reading about in the paper the last couple of months?" Eleanor murmured.

Sienna Rose sat down opposite Eleanor. "We can't know that for sure without further investigation. The journal does seem to indicate as much, though."

The older woman shook her head. "I should have come forward as soon as I read that journal. I guess I didn't because I hoped my husband, the Steven I've loved all my adult life, would return to me after he came home from the hospital."

"I'm so sorry." Sienna Rose took a breath. "Mrs. Webster, I have a few more questions about Haven's case. Did you or your husband give your daughter two thousand dollars shortly before she was killed?"

Eleanor shook her head. "I didn't, and Steven didn't. At least not that I know of. There were never any unaccounted-for withdrawals from our joint account. Why?"

"Haven deposited that amount in cash into her bank account before she was killed. We haven't yet been able to figure out where it came from."

"Hmm." Eleanor's expression became distant.

"What is it, Mrs. Webster? At this point, anything could potentially help us find out who really killed your daughter and bring them to justice."

"Perhaps Haven sold her father's gun. It went missing a few months before she died. When we discovered it was gone, I thought perhaps Steven had misplaced it, but it still hasn't been found."

"Was the gun registered to your husband? Is there a record of the serial number?" Sienna Rose made a note to inquire at the local pawnshops, but most didn't keep records from that far back. The gun could be a dead end.

"I'm afraid I don't have any idea what the serial number was," Eleanor admitted.

"Do you have any reason to think Haven might have taken it?"

The older woman shrugged. "She had asked Steven for a gun to protect herself, but he told her it was too dangerous."

Legend cleared his throat from the doorway. "Captain Brewer is here to speak with you, Mrs. Webster."

Sienna Rose gave Eleanor a kind smile. "Thank you for all your help."

Legend placed his hand on Sienna Rose's back to guide her out of the Webster home. She didn't shrug off his touch.

As she filled him in on what she'd learned from Mrs. Webster, she was once again reminded that once the connected cases were wrapped up, Legend would be gone.

Sienna Rose realized that he'd slipped right back under her skin and into her heart.

Could she stand to let him go again?

12

*T*he late afternoon breeze had become more of a gust by the time Legend and Sienna Rose arrived back at the police station. She sat at her desk and began updating her files.

Legend retrieved two cups of coffee, setting one beside Sienna Rose as he took the seat next to her desk. "Sorry, it's the sludge from the pot here."

"Better than nothing." She took a sip, then made a face. "Or maybe not."

He chuckled as a uniformed officer approached.

She glanced up. "Hey, Officer Neyland."

"Detective, we have Baker Paul here in custody. Judge Orson has signed a warrant for a DNA sample. The lab tech will be here in a minute to swab him."

"Thanks." Sienna Rose secured her weapon.

Legend did the same before they headed toward the interrogation room. He pulled out his notebook as they walked down the hallway. "Confirmed alibis rule out Robicheaux for Haven's murder. Let's hope Baker Paul's DNA puts him at the scene of the crime." He slid the notebook back into his pocket.

"I'm praying for that." She grew silent as they continued. He could almost feel her thoughts. The weight of not having solved her first murder case must have been bothering her something fierce, as hard a worker as she was.

He stopped and gently turned her to face him. "Hey, are you okay?"

"My knees are healing, so the pain isn't as bad."

"That's not what I meant, and I think you know that." He could feel the tension in her shoulders. She'd always carried stress there. If only she would borrow some of his strength.

But he knew she wouldn't.

Sienna Rose straightened and flashed him a weak smile. "Guess it's been a long day. And I missed lunch."

Legend dropped his hands to his sides. "That's true. We did. After we question Baker Paul, we'll grab something to eat, okay?"

"Okay." She took a breath and opened the door to the interrogation room. Legend followed her inside.

A woman he recognized from the Envie CSU was inserting a big cotton swab into a test tube. She smiled at them. "DNA sample taken. The state forensics team will rush the results. They're much faster than we are. I'll call you with results the second I get them."

"Thanks, Anna." Sienna Rose took a seat opposite Baker Paul.

Legend leaned against the wall in the corner behind their suspect, facing Sienna Rose.

Baker Paul crossed his arms over his chest and watched Sienna Rose over the table.

She flipped through pages in a file folder, although she probably already had the details memorized. It was a tactic that subconsciously made the suspect feel as if the police already knew everything anyway, so they might as well come clean. "Aren't you curious about why we got a court order to test your DNA?"

"To tell me my daddy isn't who I thought all these years, and my real father is rich and I'm about to come into a lot of money?" He laughed at his own joke.

"Not quite. We're running your DNA against evidence found at a crime scene." Sienna Rose shut the folder and leaned back in her chair, pinning Baker Paul to his seat with a chilly gaze.

Legend loved her ability to put suspects in their place. It wasn't a surprise, of course, but she was really, really good at her job. She'd been right to stay in Envie and climb up the ranks. She'd earned her shield.

The mirth fell away from Baker's features. "What is this? I had nothing to do with the murders blasted all over the news."

"Not the recent ones."

Legend enjoyed watching emotions flit across his face as Sienna Rose toyed with him.

"Then what?"

"From Haven Webster's murder."

He opened his mouth, then clamped it shut.

"Nothing to say, Baker? That's okay. We'll have you for the murder in no time. DNA doesn't lie." She leaned back and softened her tone. "Why don't you tell me what happened with Haven? If you cooperate, I can let the DA know and maybe get you some leniency."

He shook his head.

Legend recognized fear in the man's expression. Sienna Rose had the suspect's back against the wall, and he had no idea how to escape.

Sienna Rose kept her voice calm. "There's no statute of limitations on murder, Baker. You know your DNA is going to come back as a positive match. Why not get some mercy for cooperating?"

"Can I get immunity?"

"Not for murder."

It was the moment when all cops held their breath—would the suspect talk, or lawyer up? Legend was impressed at how Sienna Rose revealed none of the anxiety she must be feeling.

"But a deal of some sort?" Baker Paul practically whined.

"There's no deal yet, Baker. I can't make any guarantees. All I can do is tell the DA that you've decided to cooperate. That's the best you're going to get for now."

She'd made her bluff. Baker Paul would either call her on it and lawyer up—or he'd give them the answers they needed.

The suspect kept quiet, likely mulling over his options. If Baker requested a lawyer, it was all over. They wouldn't be able to ask him another question.

Baker Paul ran his fingers through his already-disheveled hair. "Listen, I didn't mean to kill Haven. It was an accident."

Sienna Rose let out her breath. "What happened?"

"That greedy woman couldn't accept that my brother broke things off with her. She wasn't really interested in Andy, only his money. When she realized she couldn't get him back into a relationship with her, she started blackmailing him."

"Blackmailing him? Over what?" Legend assumed Baker was telling the truth. He couldn't imagine the guy had a good enough imagination to make up something so ridiculous.

"I guess it doesn't matter anymore, since Andy's dead." He cleared his throat. "Andy had gotten into a bind, financially. He'd been gambling down at the boats and lost several thousand dollars. He borrowed some money from the bank where he worked to try and win back his losses."

"And he lost that too?" Sienna Rose guessed.

"No. It took him several months, but Andy won back what he borrowed from the bank, and then some. He returned all the money he'd taken, but greedy little Haven knew all the details because my brother trusted her and told her everything, right down to the details of the account he'd pulled the ten thousand from."

Sienna Rose opened the file in front of her, holding it up to read. "Why didn't he simply take out a legitimate loan from the bank?"

"The bank has a policy that employees can't take out personal loans. And Andy couldn't go to another bank because he didn't have enough collateral for a loan that size."

Sienna Rose shut the folder again. "What kind of financial bind had he gotten into?"

Baker rubbed the tip of his nose. "Our father had just been diagnosed with cancer, and he needed treatment. Dad's insurance policy had a high deductible before they would start paying their eighty percent. I had a limited amount in savings, and that wouldn't even cover the deductible."

"I didn't know your father had cancer," Sienna Rose said.

Could Baker Paul be lying? All of Legend's training and gut instincts told him the man was telling the truth, but this was Envie, and everybody knew everybody else's business. Plus, Sienna Rose had actively investigated the Paul family. How had she not known?

"He wanted to keep it a secret. He didn't even tell our extended family. When we found out, Andy—as the oldest—thought it was his responsibility to make sure Dad got the treatment he needed. So Andy borrowed the money from the bank and tried to double it. He succeeded. Then he repaid the bank, and no one was ever the wiser."

"Except Haven." Sienna Rose locked eyes with Legend.

Baker's story could explain the two thousand dollars Haven had deposited. A payoff for her silence.

Baker continued. "Haven asked for the money. When Andy wouldn't give her any because he was still helping Dad with the twenty percent the insurance wouldn't cover, she resorted to blackmailing Andy."

"If Andy didn't have money left over to give Haven, how did he pay her blackmail demands?"

"He took out a small amount that he'd put into an interest-bearing account and went back to the boats."

"I'm assuming he had enough to pay Haven's blackmail demands?"

"Way more than that," Baker said. "He was able to prepay the rest of Dad's treatments. When Dad passed away, the hospital actually had to cut me a refund check."

That explained the blackmail, but not Haven's murder.

Sienna Rose practically read his mind. "You said you went to confront Haven about the blackmail the night she died?"

Legend noticed the way Sienna Rose didn't use the words *murdered* or *killed* so that Baker Paul didn't freeze up in the middle of his confession.

Baker Paul straightened in his seat and rubbed his hands together. Legend could almost feel the panic vibrating off of him. "I wanted Haven to stop. But she laughed and said she was only getting started. I knew in that moment that she'd never let Andy have a moment's peace. Nothing would ever be enough for her."

Sienna Rose kept her voice conversational. "What happened then?"

"I'm not proud of this, but I hit her. I'd never hit a woman before and haven't since. I wasn't raised that way." He shook his head. "She slapped me across the face, and I saw red. I hit her again, and the next thing I knew, she had a gun in her hand."

Legend couldn't recall anything in the file stating whether Haven Webster owned a gun. But Eleanor Webster had mentioned that her husband's gun had gone missing, and that Haven had asked for one around that time. Haven had probably taken her father's.

Baker Paul continued without prompting. "We struggled, and the gun went off. Haven fell, and I realized she was dead." He swallowed loudly. "I didn't know what to do. I panicked. All I could think of was to get rid of the gun and move the body, and hope no one would ever link me to her death."

"Why didn't you call the police?" Sienna Rose asked.

"Yeah, like they would have believed the gun went off on accident."

Legend shrugged at Sienna Rose. Baker had a point.

"If it was an accident, you'll have to plead your case to a jury." Sienna Rose stood and pulled out her handcuffs, issuing a brief nod to Captain Brewer behind the two-way mirror. "Please stand up.

Baker Paul, you're under arrest for the murder of Haven Webster."

Legend blew out a breath. At long last, perhaps Haven could rest in peace. And maybe her family could begin to find closure.

After dropping Baker Paul off at booking, Sienna Rose smiled brighter than the late afternoon sun. "I finally feel like I did my job properly. Years late, but at least it's done."

"Sometimes a detective's hands are tied, and you have to play the cards you're dealt. You should feel good about this." The lift in her mood touched every curve of his heart. "How about we get that lunch I promised you?"

"Yes please. I'm starving." She grabbed his hand and tugged him toward the door to the parking lot. "How's Italian food sound? Maybe Mamma Ricci's? I could eat everything on the menu there."

Legend's heart warmed at the touch of her hand, and he gladly followed her outside.

The wind carried a definite chill, and the sun had begun its descent toward the horizon.

He unlocked the passenger door of his rental and opened it for Sienna Rose. She paused, glancing at him. "You're going to leave again soon, aren't you?"

Her words caught him by surprise. He honestly didn't know how to respond.

"Never mind. I shouldn't have brought it up." She got into the car and shut the door.

Legend circled around to the driver's side, slipping in behind the wheel. He started the car and adjusted the temperature, still searching for the right thing to say. "I don't know, Sienna Rose. I have a job I love, but being around you these past few days, I realize how much—"

Sienna Rose's phone vibrated, interrupting him. "It's my mom. I have to get this." She answered the call. "What is it, Mom? I'm in the middle of—" Her face paled. "Mom, please try to calm down. I can't understand you. What?"

She put a hand over her mouth, and her gaze met Legend's, her eyes wide.

Legend's gut tightened with dread.

"Okay, Mom. Stay put. We'll be there in a minute."

She ended the call and faced him. Her eyes were filled with unshed tears, and her lips trembled as she spoke.

"We have to get to Mom's. Dean's been abducted."

13

*S*ienna Rose burst into the living room, her heart pounding with adrenaline. "Mom, what happened?"

Her mother sat on the couch, tears streaming down her face. "He went out to take a cup of coffee to the officer stationed by the front door. You know how Dean likes to chat with people. A few minutes passed, and I started wondering why he hadn't come back yet." Sobs overcame her, and her entire body shook as she buried her face in her hands.

Legend eased himself onto the sofa on her other side and wrapped a strong arm around her. "I know, but we're here. Take a deep breath."

Her tears subsided. Legend handed her a tissue from a box on a nearby end table, and she wiped her eyes before continuing. "I went out to check and didn't see Dean or the officer. When I got close to the police car, I saw the shattered coffee mug in the road. That's when I knew something bad had happened."

Sienna Rose swallowed hard, fighting to keep her fear from showing. She and Legend had called for backup on their way to her mom's house. The police on scene had already found the officer on duty—one of Legend's team members—in the patrol cruiser's trunk, barely breathing after being beaten. He'd been taken to the hospital and was in critical condition.

But Dean was missing. Kidnapped.

"I called for Dean, but there was no response. I came back inside and called you immediately." Her mom broke down into sobs again. "It's all my fault. I shouldn't have let him go outside alone. You told me not to."

Sienna Rose hugged her mother tighter. "It's not your fault, Mom. If it's anyone's, it's mine. I should have been here to protect you and Dean."

How could she have let this happen? She hadn't taken the threat seriously enough, assuming it was directed at her alone, rather than her family, even after seeing what had happened to Pratt's wife and the chief's daughter. She'd known the potential danger but hadn't taken enough steps to keep her mom and brother safe.

Some detective she was. She couldn't even protect the ones she loved most.

"It's not your fault either, Sienna Rose." Legend's gaze locked onto hers. "Don't blame yourself. Guilt has no place in working a case. It'll simply complicate things and inhibit clear thinking, which we need right now."

Sienna Rose blew out a breath. He was right. "Okay, where do we start?" She had fought to stay in the lead role on the linked cases, but now she recognized that she was emotionally tangled in the details. She needed Legend to take the lead.

"I've called my team in to help find Dean, and we've issued a Silver Alert."

"What is that?" Sienna Rose's mother interrupted.

Sienna Rose took her mother's hand. "It's like an Amber Alert, but for an adult, usually a senior or an adult with disabilities, like Dean."

"We have officers and volunteers going door-to-door in the neighborhood to see if anyone saw anything," Legend said. "Hopefully we'll be able to get a description of a vehicle or person."

"And if no one saw anything?" Sienna Rose couldn't keep her mind off the memory of Magdalene Savoie's lifeless body at the edge of the bayou. She felt ill.

"We'll keep working the case like we're trained to," Legend replied, his tone steady.

Sienna Rose gave her mom a final squeeze before standing. "I'm going to put on a pot of coffee. Can I get you anything, Mom?"

"I don't want anything but my son home, safe and sound." Her mother sounded so defeated.

Sienna Rose couldn't offer any promises, so she headed into the kitchen. Her hands shook as she tried to pull a coffee filter from the packet.

Legend came up behind her. "The CSU is on their way. They're going to set up call tracing on your mom's landline, in case Dean's abductor tries to contact her, which I believe they will. With this kidnapping, whoever committed the four murders—Webster or otherwise—has switched things up and will most likely reach out for attention." His voice softened. "We'll do everything we can to find your brother."

"It makes no difference, because criminals don't play by the same set of rules we do."

She placed a filter into the coffee maker and spooned in grounds, then added water and switched on the pot. "This has to be Steven's doing. He's taking revenge on everyone involved in his daughter's murder case. And as far as we know, he hasn't returned home since we left the Webster's house."

"But Steven Webster already killed the man he believed responsible. Beat Andy Paul to death. It feels like we're still missing something."

She shook her head. "What if Webster was just getting started before he was hospitalized? Sure, he killed Andy Paul, but in Webster's mind, perhaps that wasn't enough. What if Webster wants the entire justice system to pay?"

"So his retaliation is to kill everyone associated with the case?"

Sienna Rose shrugged. "It's possible. Webster lost a daughter, and it sent him over the edge. The judge's goal in hospitalizing him was to get him the treatment he needed, but maybe it wasn't enough."

If something happened to Dean, she didn't know what she would do. And she couldn't afford to think that way at the moment. "Avenging a loved one can be a very powerful motive."

"There is still a unit at Webster's house. If he returns, we'll be notified."

A call-tracing specialist from the CSU stuck his head in the kitchen. "Detectives, where would you like us to set up?"

"I'll show you." Legend squeezed her shoulder, then led the technician out of the kitchen.

Staring out the window, Sienna Rose saw the playhouse her dad had built for her and Dean when they were children. It had a door wide enough for the wheelchair Dean had used before his operations. Many happy hours had been spent out there, with Dean and Sienna Rose pretending to be astronauts, knights, and everything in between.

She tried not to think the worst, but it was growing harder by the minute.

The landline ringing made her jump.

She grabbed the handset off the kitchen wall, wondering for the hundredth time when her mother would finally decide to ditch the landline. "Hello."

The voice on the other end of the line was deep and harsh. "How does it feel to know what you value most has been taken from you and there's nothing you can do?"

Ice ran through her veins. "Steven Webster."

His laugh sent a chill up her spine. "I wondered when you'd figure it out."

She clutched the receiver, working to keep her voice calm. "If you're calling here, you must want something from me. What is it, Webster?"

Legend walked back into the kitchen and made the motion to keep Steven talking. That meant the specialist was hooked in and trying to trace the call.

Webster laughed again, the sound grating. "You always did get straight to the point, Detective Jordan. You above all are responsible for my daughter not getting justice."

"We've actually solved your daughter's murder. The killer confessed to—"

"You'll say anything to save your brother and yourself."

"No, I'm being truthful." It was so difficult to keep from begging, pleading for Webster to simply tell her where to find Dean. But she had to, for her brother's sake. "We arrested the real murderer after he confessed. We're waiting for his DNA results to confirm his presence at the crime scene."

"Oh yeah?" A hint of curiosity came through in Webster's tone. "Who?"

She shouldn't disclose that information, especially since Webster had already murdered one Paul brother. But Baker was safely in custody, and she would do or say anything to get her brother back. "Baker Paul."

"Lies," Webster snarled. "You're trying to save your own hide, like before."

"It's true," Sienna insisted.

Legend's hand found hers. His grip was firm yet gentle.

"I don't believe you. Your incompetence cost my Haven her justice. You deserve to suffer as much as she did. More. And I'm going to make sure I get to watch."

Legend fought not to squeeze Sienna Rose's hand too hard, but every muscle screamed to throttle Steven Webster.

The man's hatred came through loud and clear over the second earpiece Legend had picked up. How Sienna Rose managed any composure under the circumstances spoke to her great resolve and bravery.

"What can I do?" she asked. "Please, Steven. I'll do anything. But don't hurt my brother."

The pleading in Sienna Rose's voice nearly broke Legend's heart.

"You'd like that, wouldn't you? To be able to save your brother."

"Of course," Sienna Rose responded. "Trade him for me. It's me you want anyway."

Legend gaped at her. Was she serious? Webster would kill her on sight, then he would kill Dean too. Webster was out for revenge, and he didn't care who he hurt along the way. Didn't she know that?

"You're right. It is you I want," Webster said.

Seconds ticked by.

"All right then," Webster finally said. "I accept the trade."

Sienna Rose's shoulders sagged with relief, even as Legend's chest tightened with dread.

"I'll call you on your cell to give you directions," Webster said. "No other cops. No heroes. Just you, Detective Jordan. Alone. Got it?"

"I've got it," she said, her voice firm.

"Get in your car. I'll call you on your cell in five minutes. Once you get in the vehicle, no contact with anyone else. I'll know if you make a call out. Remember, Sienna Rose, if you don't do exactly as I say, your brother dies."

The connection dropped.

"You can't go alone," Legend said immediately after she hung up. He couldn't let her go willingly to her death.

She smiled and placed a hand on his cheek. "You heard Webster. This is the one chance I have to save Dean."

He stepped closer. "He'll kill you, Sienna Rose."

"Not if I can help it." She put her hands around his neck and pulled him toward her. Before he knew what was happening, she kissed him.

Her lips were as soft as he remembered. Softer.

She broke the kiss and stepped back. "I know what I'm doing, Legend. I have to do everything in my power to save my brother. It's a risk I'm willing to take. But I need you to promise me something."

He found it hard to speak, but finally he whispered, "What? Name it."

"Be here for Mom. She's not as tough as she'd like us to think."

Legend clenched his jaw, not trusting himself to form words. He had to do something. Had to stop her or find a way to go with her.

"I have to go now." She turned to leave, then paused, facing away from him. "I still love you, Legend. I've always loved you."

His heart pounded. "I love you too. Please don't do this." He reached for her hand.

"I have to." She squeezed his hand and then let go. Then she headed into the living room and grabbed the keys to her mother's car. "I'm going after my brother," Sienna Rose announced to the police in the room. "No one is to follow me. Understood?" She pinned Legend with a stare as he stood in the doorway. "I mean it. Not a single person."

Legend walked by the tech table and grabbed one of the micro trackers.

"Does everyone understand? And no trying to ping or call my cell. Got it?"

There were nervous glances all around, but eventually everyone nodded their agreement.

She gave her mother a quick hug. "I'm going to try and get Dean back. Stay here with Legend and the others." Despite protests, Sienna Rose hugged her mom again before leaving through the front door.

Legend followed her.

She opened her mother's car door. "I said no following me."

"I heard you." He pulled her into an embrace and kissed her forehead, slipping a micro tracker into her jacket pocket. "Please be careful."

"I will." She smiled sadly as she slid behind the wheel.

"I love you, Sienna Rose."

She shut the door and started the engine. He stood staring at her, their gazes locked, until she pressed her cell phone against her ear.

Sienna Rose slowly backed out of the driveway. With a final wave, she was gone.

And everything within him went cold.

14

Steven Webster's voice was void of any emotion as he gave her directions over the phone.

Fear had eaten at Sienna Rose for the last forty minutes of the drive. Fed up with the game, she pulled the car over to the side of the road. "I'm not going an inch farther until you let me speak to Dean." She held her breath.

"I don't think so."

Sienna Rose exhaled slowly and silently. "I've come alone. There's no backup tailing me. I've followed your instructions to the letter. I'm giving in to your demands. I think it's only fair that you let me speak to my brother."

"Fair? Nothing in life is fair," he shouted into the phone. "If it was, my sweet Haven would still be here."

She closed her eyes. "I can't imagine the loss you've suffered, or the pain you've endured."

"No, but you will."

"If you're going to kill my brother, what do you have to lose by letting me speak to him one last time?"

There was a pause over the connection.

Sienna Rose rested her forehead on the steering wheel, and did something she hadn't done in quite some time—she prayed.

"Sienna Rose?" Dean's voice shattered the silence.

"Dean, are you okay?"

"Yes. But I need you to come get me," he said. The fear in his voice went right to her heart. "This man says I can go home if you come."

She steeled herself against the tears that wanted to fall, willing her voice to stay strong for her brother. "I'm on my way. I'll be there soon. I love you, Dean."

"I love you too, 'Neena Rose."

"Very touching." Webster's gravelly voice came back on the line. "Now get back on the road. And don't try anything stupid." The connection died.

Anger replaced her fear. How dare Webster take her brother and terrify him when his real problem was with her? Her brother was completely innocent. Dean had nothing to do with Haven's death, any more than Magdalene Savoie had.

Sienna Rose gripped the steering wheel tightly as she edged back onto the road, resuming her progress in the direction Steven Webster had given. Her mind whirred as fast as the tires on the old road.

She recalled the fear etched in Legend's features as she'd driven away from him. They should have had more time together. If she hadn't been so set in her ways, they could have tried to make a long-distance relationship work, at least until things had settled for her mother. She'd been so hurt that Legend had been willing to leave her to pursue his career. At long last, she understood things weren't that simple, and it was too late. She'd never see him again.

The ache was nearly as bad as knowing how much danger Dean was in.

She thought of her mother. Caring for Dean had kept her going after Dad had died. If her mom lost Dean now, there was no telling what would happen to her.

Especially since there was almost no chance Sienna Rose would make it out of there alive.

She slowed to round the final corner Webster had given her. Almost instantly, her cell rang. It had been like this the whole trip. Had he somehow put a tracker on her car?

"Yes?"

"You're almost here," Webster growled. "Go about four more miles, then pull onto the dirt road on the left. Park by the gate and walk the rest of the way."

"Walk to where?"

"There's a cabin about a quarter of a mile in. We'll be waiting."

"I need to speak to Dean again." Her palms were so wet that she nearly lost her grip on the steering wheel.

"It's only been fifteen minutes since you talked to him. You don't need to speak to him again. You'll see him soon enough. If you've followed my directions, that is."

Maybe she could plead with Webster one final time. "Please, Steven, don't do this. Haven wouldn't want you to behave like this."

"How would you know what Haven would want? She was murdered and left near the bayou like trash. She wouldn't have wanted that." There was so much hatred in his voice. "She would have wanted to fall in love someday, have me walk her down the aisle, get to have children. She would have wanted to live a long and happy life." His voice caught on the last word.

"Yes, she would have. She would have wanted all of those things. That future was stolen from her. But she wouldn't want her father to throw away the rest of his life. She would want you to honor her life by living yours well."

He snorted. "You know nothing. Haven was my daughter, and I knew her best. Andy Paul murdered her, and the legal system failed her. As her father, it's up to me to make sure she gets justice."

"I told you, Mr. Webster. Baker Paul killed Haven. We have his confession—"

"Andy murdered my Haven," he insisted, his voice eerily calm. "You should be close to the dirt road now. You have five minutes to walk here or I'll kill Dean like I killed Andy Paul." The connection cut off again.

The early evening sky was streaked in orange and red. Nightfall would be upon them soon, hindering her ability to make a move.

Steven Webster definitely has the upper hand, she thought glumly.

Sienna Rose pulled onto the dirt road and stopped at the gate Steven had described. She parked the car and killed the engine but left the keys inside.

She hadn't considered how Dean would get back home after she surrendered herself to a madman. Maybe he could drive to the main road where, God willing, he might find a kind stranger to help. She and her mother had been teaching him to drive over the past few months, using low-traffic back roads. He wasn't ready to drive on his own yet, but he would have to try.

She stepped onto the dusty ground, her heart racing at the thought of what lay ahead.

No time for regrets.

Sienna Rose put a gun in the back of her waistband, kept her holster on with her second pistol, and checked the backup firearm fastened to her ankle. Since she'd used her mother's car instead of her SUV, she didn't have access to a bulletproof vest. If she managed to get a jump on Webster, she'd take it, as long as it didn't put Dean in danger. Webster would probably confiscate her holstered gun, but maybe she could keep one of the others hidden from him. She grabbed her high-powered flashlight, gripping the handle tightly.

She shut the car door and stepped over a single pipe gate. Her mouth grew drier with every step. Her pace sped up to match the pounding of her heart.

Despite the coolness of the air, sweat plastered her shirt to her back. She was haunted by the idea of never being able to see her mom again.

Or Legend.

Around a corner, the cabin came into view, along with a barn structure beside it. Woods lined the wide driveway. A dark-blue sedan pocked with bullet marks was parked outside the cabin.

She knew they'd hit it.

Studying the setup with her trained eye, she determined there was too much open space for her to take cover in the trees. Webster would demand she stay where he could see her, unless he planned to make the exchange inside the cabin.

She couldn't let that happen. There was no way they'd both survive if the swap didn't occur outside. At least out here, she might have a fighting chance.

"That's close enough, Detective."

Sienna Rose slowly pivoted, catching sight of an open door at the side of the barn. Dean was tied to a chair with Steven Webster crouched behind him, gun in hand, using her brother as a shield.

In that moment, she knew there was no way the situation could end well, and her heart sank.

"She's out of the car, moving on foot," Legend radioed back to Captain Brewer and his own boss, Special Detective Steele. He parked his car on the opposite side of the dirt road and walked to Sienna Rose's car.

"Then she's close. We have your coordinates," Captain Brewer said. "We're on our way."

"Don't get too close, and silence is vital. Webster is likely suspicious to begin with. We don't want him getting too jumpy and shooting Sienna Rose or Dean."

"Everyone knows to stay back. But we need to be close when it's time to move in." Steele's voice steadied Legend.

"Copy that." Legend popped open his trunk to choose a weapon, forgoing a shotgun in favor of a rifle. He knew accuracy would be more important than firepower in the upcoming situation. He added the night-vision scope, grabbed his vest, and shut the trunk.

Losing Sienna Rose had been the only thing on his mind since she'd told him she still loved him. Losing what they should have had in the past and what they could have in the present. He was determined not to let that go, even if it meant giving up his career in New Orleans. He could easily slip back into working in Envie or one of the surrounding areas. It might not be as glamorous, but it would be worth it.

Sienna Rose was worth it.

He shrugged on his bulletproof vest and secured the rental he'd been driving all week. Then he headed up the drive, keeping to the edge of the trees because he wouldn't put it past Webster to have cameras set up.

A crispness hung in the November air. The leaves had recently fallen, and piles crunched under Legend's steps. He kept his grip on the rifle loose but secure. He didn't know what to expect ahead, but one thing was sure—he was going to be ready.

The dirt road was about twenty-five feet wide and showed no signs of narrowing. Many of the rural roads in the area widened and narrowed, depending on the terrain. Louisiana was known for its bayous and waterways that often eroded the land.

Legend crept along the edge, keeping his eyes and ears on alert. The muscles in his thighs burned as he tensed, ready to run if the need arose. His heartbeat echoed in his ears.

Two buildings came into view, a cabin and a barn. Legend slowed as he caught sight of Sienna Rose standing in front of the barn. He followed her stare to Dean, who was tied to a chair, with Webster crouched behind him. Legend lifted his gun, bracing himself against a tree.

"Throw your gun to the ground and kick it toward the tractor," Webster shouted at Sienna Rose.

Legend's gut tightened even more as Dean's sobs became audible over Webster's yelling. He was clearly terrified.

Sienna Rose tossed her service handgun into the dirt and kicked it as instructed.

"Now your backup."

Legend moved a couple of steps closer to the barn but remained out of Webster's view. He reset his rifle, sighting it in.

Sienna Rose unstrapped her ankle revolver and threw it down to join her service handgun in the dirt by the tractor. She straightened, and Legend spied a flash of metal tucked into her back waistband. She looked up at Webster, hands in the air. "There. I've followed all of your instructions. Now let Dean go."

"Sienna Rose, what's happening?" Dean's face was ashen with fear.

Legend tightened his grip on the rifle. All he needed was one clear shot, and he could take Webster out.

Webster slowly lifted his gun and pressed the barrel to Dean's temple.

"Stop!" Sienna Rose's voice hit a note of panic Legend had never heard before.

His heart stuttered as he braced for whatever would come next.

15

"*P*lease stop it. I'm here. This is what you wanted." Sienna Rose's pulse thrummed in her ears.

"I'm calling the shots this time, Detective Jordan." Webster's voice was laced with venom.

Sienna Rose's fingers itched so badly to snatch the handgun from the band of her jeans and shoot, but she couldn't. Not until the time was right. Though she was a crack shot, she wouldn't risk accidentally hitting Dean.

Maybe she could distract Webster, though. "Listen, Mr. Webster, I know you don't believe me, but we are positive that Andy didn't kill Haven. His brother, Baker, did. He confessed. He's in custody as we speak."

Webster jerked further behind Dean. "I told you to stop lying." He ground the barrel of his gun against Dean's temple. "If you don't stop, I'll kill him right here, right now."

Dean cried softly. It occurred to Sienna Rose that her brother may have regressed somewhat, due to the trauma. She wished momentarily that Dean would simply punch Webster right in the nose.

Maybe, if she got close enough, she could somehow signal for Dean to hit Webster, though that wasn't her brother's nature at all. Dean didn't need to knock his kidnapper out cold. He merely needed to cause enough of a distraction for Sienna Rose to disarm him.

"I'm not lying," she called. "Hear me out."

Webster didn't reply.

Then, before she realized what he was doing, Webster yanked the barn door closed.

Sienna Rose let out a cleansing breath and scanned her surroundings for the best vantage point. Movement from the corner of her eye caught her attention.

Legend stood in the shadows, rifle at the ready.

Her heart fluttered for a myriad of reasons. First, she'd resigned herself to never seeing Legend again, and to find him there, knowing that he still loved her, set her senses reeling. On the other hand, his presence, especially with a gun, would put both her and Dean at risk if Webster found out.

"What are you doing here?" she whispered.

"No way was I going to let you come out here all by yourself."

His desire to protect her warmed her against the evening's rapidly dropping temperature. Yet—"If Webster sees you, he'll kill Dean."

"He won't see me."

She was opening her mouth to argue when Webster flung open the barn door.

He shoved forward the chair Dean was tied to, mere inches away from him. The only way Webster could be taken out was with a clear shot, and she would not risk harming her brother.

She sidestepped, moving in front of them so Legend wouldn't have a shot. She couldn't let him take unnecessary risks. Not with her brother's life.

Webster tapped the barrel of his gun against the back of the chair. "Your brother has been a thorn in my side, you know that? He's been fighting me this whole time. Absolutely refuses to cooperate."

Sienna Rose struggled to hold her tongue, not wanting to anger Webster any further.

He pressed the gun harder into Dean's flesh. "What makes you so certain that Baker Paul killed my Haven?"

"We have Baker's confession. I'm sure you'll recall that one of the reasons for a failure to convict was the lack of a DNA match to that we found at the crime scene."

"Due to your incompetency to collect the evidence at the scene."

"No, we got an accurate sample. The lack of a match was because Andy's DNA really wasn't there. However, we have since been able to run tests on the trace DNA that was."

"It can't possibly be Karl Robicheaux's. That boy would have died before he hurt Haven. He loved her. He wanted to protect her from the likes of Andy Paul, and said as much at the trial."

"His testimony was proven false," Sienna Rose corrected. "But no, I'm not referring to Karl."

"Then spit it out. You're testing my patience, Detective Jordan."

She swallowed her fear. "The DNA results showed a familial match to Andy Paul."

Webster scrunched up his face, knitting his brows together. "So it *was* Andy's DNA? Stop trying to muddy the waters."

"No, it wasn't Andy's DNA, but it matched a blood relative of his." Despite what Webster had done to hurt so many people, Sienna Rose and Legend had finally gotten justice for Haven, and her father deserved to know that. "It belonged to his brother, Baker Paul."

Webster's face blanched, and she knew she'd hit a nerve. "Haven said that sometimes he loaned Andy his car, and Andy would take her out in it." Webster waved his gun at her. "But that doesn't mean he killed her."

Out of the corner of her eye, Sienna Rose spied Legend creeping around to get a clear shot. *No.* While Webster might have relaxed a little, the risk to Dean was still too high.

She moved her body to block Legend's line of sight again, then continued to speak to Webster. "Do you have any idea where Haven might have gotten two thousand dollars the week she was killed? She deposited that amount into her account, in cash."

Webster's brows furrowed. "That can't be right. She didn't make that much at her job. She barely pulled in minimum wage over at the daycare." He loosened his grip on Dean. "She didn't have any other source of income, so coming up with two thousand dollars cash isn't possible."

As long as Webster was talking, Sienna Rose had a chance of getting them both out unscathed, but if he caught sight of Legend, it was over for Dean. "We found out where the money came from. She got it from Andy."

"So?" Webster said. "That doesn't prove anything."

Despite his words, Sienna Rose noticed a tick in his jaw. She'd piqued his curiosity.

"We were never able to figure out where the money came from back then," she said. "Now we know."

Webster snorted. "Didn't do your job correctly, so you're trying to fix it now? Surprise, surprise."

Sienna Rose straightened her shoulders. She was a big enough person to admit her shortcomings and failures. "I wanted justice for Haven. She deserved that, but my team and I made some mistakes. I can't rewind the clock, but I can make sure justice is served now. And you deserve to know who murdered your daughter. It was Baker Paul. Would you like to know why he did it?"

Webster scowled. "You wouldn't have started working her case again had I not forced your hand. It seems the only time I can get action from you people is when I take matters into my own hands." He shoved the end of the pistol against Dean's temple again. "Like now."

"Mr. Webster, I'm very sorry for your loss, and I'm sorry that we charged the wrong man. But we've solved her case now and her murderer is behind bars. If I have any say in the matter, that's where he'll spend the rest of his life."

Webster hesitated, then tapped the gun on the back of the chair. "It's a shame you want to do this now. I've made peace with the fact that nothing will bring my Haven back. Nothing you do will matter. I've accepted that. But you still have to pay for failing her."

Sienna Rose pushed on. "Don't you want to know what happened?"

"I know what happened," Webster growled. "My daughter was brutally murdered, and you and the rest of the police and legal system let her down. No more talking. It's time for you to suffer the way my wife and I have."

It was becoming less and less likely that she would be able to save both Webster and her brother, but she was running out of options. "Okay, I'm done talking. Let Dean go like you said, and you can exact your revenge on me however you want."

Webster laughed. "Stupid girl. If all I wanted was to kill you, I would've shot you as soon as you walked up. No. You will suffer by witnessing the death of your brother, knowing that there is nothing you can do about it, like I couldn't do anything to save my Haven."

Dean's eyes widened, and he struggled against his bindings.

No, this can't be happening. Not to my brother.

"Steven, please. Dean has nothing to do with this."

"That's the point, Detective Jordan. He's your brother, someone you love, like I loved Haven. She never did anything wrong either."

Tears burned her eyes as she realized she had to act. She had to do something to save Dean, even if it meant risking both their lives.

Legend's arm ached from holding the rifle. Sienna Rose had effectively blocked every shot he'd tried to zero in on. While he understood that she wanted to ensure her brother's safety, the fact that she didn't trust him stung. How could she not know that he would never do anything to endanger Dean?

The crispness of the November evening seemed fitting for that moment. Cold. Consuming. Empty.

"It's going to be okay, Dean. You're going to be okay." Sienna Rose's voice was thick with emotion.

Webster snorted. "You think so, Detective? I'm not so sure." He thumped Dean's shoulder with the side of the gun he held.

Dean cried out and slumped over, but Webster yanked him upright once more.

Legend's upper-body muscles buzzed from overuse, and he stretched out his hand before moving it back into firing position. He recognized the stance Sienna Rose had taken and knew he needed to be prepared. She would make a move soon.

"Do you want me to beg for Dean's life? I will." Her speech wobbled. "Is that what you want?"

"I don't want anything from you but the same pain I feel every day. Nothing will bring Haven back, like nothing will bring your brother back." The fury in Webster's voice filled Legend with apprehension.

Webster was likely to act against Sienna Rose or Dean any minute now. If Legend could get a clean shot . . .

"That means killing Dean or me won't bring her back either. Nothing will. You can only try to live the rest of your life in a way that will honor her memory."

"Honor? You didn't act with honor when you failed to manage her case properly. There was no honor in the way the case was tried. And if Andy was innocent, that means you made me kill an innocent man.

His blood is on your hands along with Haven's."

Legend flexed his hand again, then put his finger back on the side of the trigger guard. All he needed was one clear line of sight.

"No one forced you to take a life, Steven." Sienna Rose countered. "That was a choice you made on your own."

Webster shook the chair. Dean cried out.

Instead of Sienna Rose backing down, she pushed harder. Legend knew she was goading Webster to knock him off balance so she could make whatever move she had planned. She was doing a great job of it.

"Did you do that because you were angry that he supposedly killed Haven?" she asked. "Or were you a little angry at yourself that you let her get into a situation that cost her life? I mean, you were the parent, right? Why was she out so late that night? And why did you let her hang out with a man so much older than herself?"

"I wouldn't have if I'd known about it," Webster snapped, his face reddening.

"So you didn't even know? What kind of parent doesn't know who his daughter is dating? Especially when it's someone so much older?"

Webster's groan came from his gut. Legend watched as the man cut Dean free from the chair and jerked Dean out in front of him.

Dean cried out. "Please stop, mister. I want to go home."

Webster's face twisted into a grotesque mask. His sneer made Legend want to break him in half. He couldn't even imagine how Sienna Rose felt. Legend sent up a silent prayer for wisdom and strength. He and Sienna Rose would need both to survive if they wanted to get Dean out alive.

She took a step forward.

"Be careful, Detective Jordan," Webster snarled. "I've been known to have an itchy trigger finger, and I wasn't kidding. I have nothing left to lose now that Haven's gone, so I have no problem shooting you and your brother."

"Let him go, Steven." Sienna Rose's voice was a strange mixture of pleading and authoritative.

Webster cackled humorlessly. "What would be the fun in that?" Without further warning, Webster released Dean and raised his gun.

Sienna Rose lunged for them. She reached her brother and shoved him out of Webster's line of fire.

Legend moved his rifle, unable to get off a shot that wouldn't put Sienna Rose or Dean in danger. He kept Webster's head in the night-vision crosshairs, his finger ready to pull the trigger.

Webster wrestled with Sienna Rose. She gave the fight her all— punching, kicking, using every move from their training. But Webster didn't back down. He returned every blow without dropping his gun.

Finally, his face red with rage that made the veins stand out against his features, he slammed the butt of the gun down on Sienna Rose's neck.

She dropped to her knees, clearly stunned, but not unconscious.

Dean hadn't moved from where he'd landed, but he struggled to his feet and made a move toward Sienna Rose.

Webster lifted the gun to point it at Dean. "Eyes up, Detective. I don't want you to miss this part." He pulled back the trigger to release a bullet from the chamber.

Legend realized he would never manage a shot from his current distance. He wasn't a trained sniper. If Dean and Sienna Rose were to survive, he had to change tactics. Legend dropped his rifle and sprinted toward them.

He heard the trigger engage as clearly as if it were right beside his ear.

Legend spurred himself forward, pushing off the hard ground and flinging himself onto Dean to knock him out of the way.

The bullet bit into his right shoulder right where his vest ended.

Everything moved in slow motion. Adrenaline pushed his pain away, at least for the moment.

He felt rather than heard Sienna Rose scream his name.

Dean's whole body shook beneath him.

Legend hefted himself to his feet. Pain washed over him, gripping him in a vicious vise.

In his peripheral vision, he spied a blurred image running off into the woods.

Sienna Rose dropped to her knees beside him. She held a flashlight, running its beam over them. "Where are you hit?"

"I'm okay. Dean?"

She examined her brother, who appeared to be in shock, but otherwise physically unharmed. "He's fine, thanks to you." She took off her jacket and pressed it to the wound on Legend's shoulder.

He groaned, then fished his cell phone out of his pocket and pushed it into her hands. "Call Captain Brewer. They're close." His vision clouded. "Where's Webster?"

She answered him while she dialed with one hand, keeping the jacket in place with the other. "He ran off. We'll catch him soon enough." She spoke into the phone. "Sir, it's Detective Jordan. We need an ambulance. Special Detective Cruz has been shot. Yes sir." She set his cell back on his chest. "They're on the way. About four miles out. There's an ambulance too."

"Good. Go after Webster. Dean and I will be okay, and we'll send backup after you when it gets here."

She aimed the flashlight to where she'd seen movement in the woods. "You're hurt. I won't leave you two behind. Finding Webster can wait until the captain gets here."

"Go, Sienna Rose. If he gets away tonight, Webster will hunt you, Dean, and your mom forever. Dean and I will be okay."

"Are you sure?"

"Yes." He sensed her hesitation, mixed with her need to capture the man who had tried to kill her brother. "Help will be here soon. Go. Webster is probably rattled enough to make mistakes, so now is the time to catch him."

"Dean, stay with Legend, okay?" She squeezed her brother's shoulder and planted a quick kiss on Legend's forehead. "Keep pressure on the jacket until help arrives." She stood and gathered her guns from the dust. She handed her ankle piece to Legend, then holstered the other. "Tell the captain Webster headed due west, so that's the direction I'm going. I love you both."

"Love you too," he and Dean said in unison.

Then she was gone.

Legend closed his eyes and began to pray as sirens yowled, shattering the quiet.

16

S ienna Rose was still in shock. Legend had taken the bullet meant for her brother.

It was one thing for her to make that sacrifice. It was another thing entirely for Legend to have done so.

Sirens screeched in the near distance.

Branches slapped against her face as she made her way through the woods. She hadn't seen Webster yet, but she'd find him soon enough. Sienna Rose kept to the path, if it could be called that. She seriously doubted that Webster would have veered from it. The trees were dense, their lower limbs forming an impassible barrier. Even the beam from her flashlight had difficulty penetrating the foliage.

Sienna Rose's mind worked overtime. Had the bullet hit anything vital? Legend wasn't speaking much right before she left. Had he lost consciousness? Were EMTs working on him at that moment? What about Dean? He had a hard time communicating when he was stressed. What if they didn't realize his disability?

She should have stayed with them, but somebody had to go after Webster. They couldn't lose him. The threat was too great.

But not being there for Dean and Legend made her feel torn in two.

She tightened her grip on her handgun. She wanted payback for all Webster had put her family through. Would she be able to rely on her training when she finally found him, or would she lose control? She couldn't be certain as outrage thrummed through her.

Visibility had decreased, despite the beam from her flashlight.

Darkness blanketed the forest. Moonlight flickered through the trees, making shadows shift in a macabre dance. Sienna Rose shivered against the coolness. Without her jacket, she found the chill distracting. She reminded herself that every step brought her closer to Webster. Closer to putting an end to the nightmare.

The snap of a twig off to her right brought her up short.

She clicked off her flashlight and froze, straining her ears, hoping to hear anything over her pulse thudding in her ears. She willed her eyes to adjust to the dimness.

Another snap.

Sienna Rose crouched and peered through the thinning underbrush. Thank goodness it wasn't summer when everything was thick and green, growing overboard. She pushed aside some of the vegetation that had already lost most of its greenery.

Webster was there, less than two hundred yards away. The arm of his jacket was caught in a mess of saw brier vines.

Sienna Rose stood slowly, lifting her handgun and leveling it at Webster. She pushed her way through the brush separating them.

She clicked the flashlight back on.

Webster raised his head to face her. His eyes widened.

"Freeze!" she shouted.

The killer struggled to get out of his jacket.

"Trust me, Steven, you don't want to give me any reason to pull this trigger. I won't hesitate." She pushed through the brush, thorns dragging along her arms and drawing blood, which she ignored.

The sirens sounded farther away.

Webster stopped thrashing about. "You'd like that, wouldn't you? To be able to kill me without a reason. You could make up anything you wanted, since it's only you and me out here. No witnesses to tell the truth."

"You've already given me enough of a reason, Steven. You kidnapped my brother and assaulted him. That's the truth, plain and simple." She stumbled through the next bush, twisting against the poking and jabbing of the barbed leaves. "Not to mention that you've already committed four murders." She hesitated. "Why would you kill Barney Pratt's wife and Chief Savoie's daughter? They had nothing to do with Haven's case."

"Because I needed those two to suffer, like you were supposed to." He twisted against the vines.

Sienna Rose kept propelling herself forward until she stepped free of the bristly brambles, nearly tripping in her haste. "Why plant a car bomb or shoot at me if you planned to take my brother to make me suffer?"

He sneered. "You were my initial target. I hadn't planned on extra cops around you. That one I shot hasn't left your side. I hoped he would back off after the diner. When I realized he wouldn't, I decided to shift my focus to your loved ones, as I've done before to great effect. Chief Savoie still isn't back at work, is he? Clearly, my plans worked. He's certainly suffering. I kept watch on your mother's house and couldn't believe my luck when your brother brought that cop a cup of coffee. It was so simple to sneak up behind him and knock him out, then shove the cop into the trunk. So much easier than I'd anticipated." He jerked free from the vines.

Sienna Rose steadied her aim. "I'm sure that behind all your bravado is a desire to know the truth about why Baker Paul killed Haven."

He didn't reply, but he stopped moving.

She realized her predicament. She had no handcuffs with her. She'd have to walk Webster back to the cabin at gunpoint, where backup should be waiting.

She waved him in the direction from which they'd come. "Let's go."

"Go?"

She used the end of the gun to push him forward. "Yes. Steven Webster, you're under arrest for the murders of Judge Terrence Hughes, Magdalene Savoie, Amanda Pratt, and Megan Rooster, as well as the assault, kidnapping, and attempted murder of Dean Jordan." She rattled off the Miranda warning, thinking she would simply have to make the best of it until she reached an officer with handcuffs.

At that moment, Captain Brewer burst through the brush, Officer Rucker on his heels.

Her knees literally went weak with relief, and she swayed for a moment. "Take him, please. I don't have cuffs."

Officer Rucker turned Webster around and pulled his hands behind his back.

Webster's glare met hers. "I hope your brother never recovers from today. I hope that other detective doesn't survive my gunshot. And I hope you realize that it's all your fault."

"Get him out of here, Rucker," Captain Brewer ordered.

"No, it's okay." Sienna Rose stared at Webster. "I am very sorry for the loss of your daughter, and I'm sorry that you're unable to empathize with others and want to cause pain. I'm sure you'll wish for sympathy during your trial, but I assure you that this time your punishment will not be a hospital stay." Sienna Rose leaned closer to Webster's face. "This time it'll be prison, and I'll make it my personal goal to ensure you get the longest sentence possible."

Webster snarled at her as Officer Rucker shoved him back toward the cabin.

With shaking hands, Sienna Rose thrust her gun back into her holster.

Suddenly, the world tilted crazily.

Captain Brewer was beside her in an instant. "Whoa there." He caught her and supported her until she could stand under her own power. "Are you all right, Detective?"

"Yes. I'm sorry. I don't know what's wrong with me."

"Aftermath of an adrenaline rush. It's okay. Take a minute to breathe."

"Dean? Is he all right?"

"EMTs said he will be. I've already called to have one of the officers at your mother's house bring Lillian Leigh to the hospital."

"And Legend?"

"EMTs stabilized him enough to transport him to the ER. We haven't gotten an update on his condition yet, but I'm sure we will soon."

She released a deep breath. "I need to get to that hospital."

"Absolutely. You should probably get checked out yourself. I'll drive you."

"But my mom's car—"

"I'll have one of the officers take it to the hospital. You're in no position to drive. That's one nasty shiner under your right eye, and you'll probably need a couple of stitches for the cut on your jaw."

She'd forgotten about her fight with Webster. "I'm fine."

"No, you aren't. You will be examined, Detective. That's an order. I'll see if I can pull some strings and get you in the room next to your brother, and I'll make sure you're kept up to date regarding Special Detective Cruz's condition."

No sense arguing. Besides, there was nothing more to be done. She wanted to be at the hospital anyway. Since Captain Brewer had mentioned her injuries, she'd realized how much her face and body hurt. She gave in and let the captain lead her back to the cabin.

Representatives from all different areas of law enforcement milled about the grounds. The CSU worked in pairs to process the scene.

A man in a suit approached her. "Detective Jordan?"

"Sienna Rose, this is Special Detective Luxton Steele. He's in charge of Cruz's team." Captain Brewer made the introduction. By his tone, it was clear that Brewer was impressed with the man.

"We'll need your statement as to what happened to Detective Cruz," Steele told her.

"Special Detective," Captain Brewer cut in. "As you can see, Detective Jordan is injured herself and requires medical attention. I'm taking her to the hospital. You may take her statement there if she's up to it." The captain took her arm and led her toward his cruiser. "Where are your mother's car keys?"

"I left them on the front seat."

He instructed one of the patrol officers to drive the car to the hospital, then opened the passenger door of his vehicle.

Sienna Rose clambered inside, acutely aware of stiffness and soreness emanating from almost every part of her body. She let out a breath, closed her eyes, and rested her head against the seat.

"You okay?" Captain Brewer asked as he climbed into the driver's seat.

She opened her eyes and straightened. "Yeah. Guess everything is starting to hit me. I'm exhausted." She yawned, then issued a chuckle. "I'm not really bored, I promise."

The captain started the engine. "I didn't think you were. It's your body's way of recovering after an intense situation."

"I'm sorry for going off on my own, Captain. I couldn't risk Webster harming my brother." The protocols she'd broken could be cited as reason for her immediate dismissal from the force. How her boss reacted might give her a clue as to whether or not she'd still have a job the next day.

"I understand, but the protocols are in place for a reason, Detective Jordan. We'll talk about that later. I thought you'd like to know that Cruz's CSU team has found forensic evidence linking Webster to the bomb in your SUV. I wouldn't have guessed it, but Webster served on a bomb unit in the military a long time ago. Upon further search of the Webster home, CSU found items saved from each of the crime scenes—Judge Hughes' reading glasses, Amanda Pratt's necklace, a lock of Megan Rooster's hair, and Magdalene Savoie's pinky ring. That connects him to all four murders."

"And he confessed to me. At least to Amanda Pratt's and Magdalene Savoie's murders," Sienna Rose said.

"He'll definitely be locked up for the rest of his life."

"Good. I'm glad."

While she always tried to do her job by the book, after everything she'd gone through that day, she realized she would have done whatever it took to keep her loved ones safe.

And, she noted with a smile, that included Legend Cruz.

"Detective Cruz, the bullet went through your shoulder, and the wound isn't life-threatening. However, a ligament was damaged. To ensure that it doesn't become permanent, we advise immediate surgery to reattach the ligament and surrounding tendons. We're preparing the operating room now."

Legend gaped at the doctor who had examined him. Her words made sense, of course, but he was having a hard time accepting the fact that they applied to him.

"Detective Cruz, you do recall being shot, yes?" The doctor peered at him over wire-rimmed glasses.

He wasn't sure. Everything was a blur. Sienna Rose arguing with Webster, begging for Dean's life, Webster pointing a gun at Dean.

Legend remembered jumping in front of Dean. If Sienna Rose's brother had been hurt—or worse—it would devastate her. Legend had done the one thing he could think of to stop that from happening.

He recalled the burning pain that had spread out from his shoulder, on the edge of his vest. The wound had felt hot, like a branding iron against his flesh.

"Detective Cruz? Can you respond?" The doctor watched him with open concern.

The room spun, but he managed to answer. "Yes, Doctor. I was shot. In the shoulder."

"That's correct. I am Dr. Tao, and you require surgery. Do you understand?"

"Yes," he croaked.

"Please sign this consent form, to the best of your ability."

A nurse pushed a pen into his hand and held up a clipboard. Legend scribbled on the line she'd pointed to.

"Good. We're preparing the operating room and will take you there as soon as it's ready. Are you allergic to any medications?"

He shook his head.

"Do you have any questions?"

More than he could count, but his vocal cords appeared to be tied in knots, and he couldn't get a single word out. The dryness of his mouth stuck his lips to his teeth.

He used all his strength to try. "Sienna Rose?"

"I'm sorry, what?"

He ran his dry tongue over the sandpaper that had replaced his lips. "Sienna Rose. Is she okay?"

"I'm sorry. I don't have information about anyone else involved in today's incident, and even if I did, privacy laws would prevent me from sharing it with you. I'm sure you'll get an update on your friend after surgery, but for now we need to take care of you."

How could she be so calm? Didn't she understand that Sienna Rose could be injured or—no, he couldn't let himself think that.

Dr. Tao took the clipboard from him and passed it back to the nurse.

"Okay, then. I'll see you in the operating room."

The physician left, and the light in the room felt oppressive. He squinted. "Water, please?" he asked the nurse hoarsely.

"I'm sorry, but you can't have anything before surgery. This is the best I can do for you right now." She wet a cloth and ran it over his lips.

It was amazing how soothing that felt.

"Thank you. Can you please check to see if a Sienna Rose Jordan was brought in?" The last time he'd seen her, she was chasing down Steven Webster. What if that murderer had shot her? What if she was wounded like him, but alone out there in the woods? What if backup never found her?

Legend shoved the dark thoughts from his mind. He couldn't let himself go down that road. He wouldn't be able to take it. He'd just gotten her back. Surely he wouldn't lose her again so soon.

"I'll see what I can find out." She put a paper hat over his hair, the elastic popping against his head.

Two men in scrubs with hats and face masks appeared. "Detective Cruz? We're here to take you to the OR."

They lifted him to a gurney, and he felt himself being rolled from the room on the narrow bed where he lay. The lights above seemed to pierce his brain as the nurses pushed him down a hallway.

Legend came to a sudden stop, and the men in scrubs and masks disappeared from his sight. Another man stood over him with an electronic tablet in his hands. "Detective Cruz, I'm Dr. Reese. I'll be your anesthesiologist this evening. Have you ever had a reaction to anesthesia before?"

Legend shook his head as best as he could from his position on the bed. The paper hat shifted as he did, and he reached to straighten it, only to find he couldn't move his arms. What in the world? He struggled against the odd sensation.

Dr. Reese gripped his arms and pushed down. "It's okay. That's in place so you don't accidentally dislodge your IV or move during the surgery. We'll take it off as soon as it's safe for you, okay?"

Legend glanced at his arms. He hadn't even realized he had an IV, but, sure enough, there was one taped securely in his arm.

He must be more out of it than he'd thought. He met Dr. Reese's gaze. "Sienna Rose Jordan. Do you know if she's here?"

His need to see her swallowed him. Why couldn't anyone tell him how she was? Fear threatened to stop his heart.

"I don't know. I'll see if a nurse can check and let you know as soon as you wake up."

It wasn't good enough, but he didn't have any other options.

Dr. Reese placed a clear plastic mask over his mouth and nose. "Count backward from ten for me. Out loud."

"Ten." But what if Sienna Rose was hurt?

"Nine." A disembodied sensation flooded Legend. What had he been thinking about?

"Eight." What if Sienna Rose was in critical condition? Or worse?

"Keep counting, Detective." Dr. Reese's face hovered over him, but the physician's voice echoed off the walls.

"Seven." Legend struggled to focus. Sienna Rose. She *had* to be okay. He couldn't accept anything else.

"Six." The room tilted. Legend tried to look right, then left, but his head refused to move. A weight pressed against his chest.

"Fi—" He couldn't remember the next number, couldn't keep his eyes open. The sensation of weightlessness filled him.

And the range of emotions he felt for Sienna Rose.

Why hadn't he stayed? Why had he been so focused on fast-tracking his career? He hadn't realized how precious love was. How rare.

He remembered the day he'd told Sienna Rose he was going to New Orleans. There was so much he wished he'd said . . .

"An opportunity like this won't come around again. We have to jump on it." Excitement filled Legend. It was a true dream come true.

Sienna Rose's beautiful eyes filled. "I can't go, Legend. Dad's barely gone, and I can't leave Mom here alone to take care of Dean. She's hardly functioning as it is. She can't take care of herself, much less Dean."

"We could come back every weekend to help. I could take care of the lawn and do repairs and chores around the house. I could help with Dean." He wasn't begging, simply pointing out how they could make it work. Being in on the ground floor of a brand-new task force would jump-start their careers. The fast track to end all fast tracks, and in New Orleans, no less. It didn't get any better than that.

She shook her head, the long, silky waves of her hair caressing her shoulders. "She needs daily help, Legend. Maybe once Dean gets a couple more operations under his belt and Mom has adjusted to Dad being gone—"

"We can't defer, Sienna Rose. You heard what the chief said. There aren't many positions open."

She sniffed. "I know. But I can't go right now."

"What if we were to hire someone? A caregiver?"

Sienna Rose pressed a hand to her forehead. "Where on earth would Mom and I find the money for a service like that? And how can I trust anyone else to take care of my family?"

Deep down, he knew she was right. But he also knew he couldn't stay. It was his chance. He would never find a better one.

Ever since law enforcement had saved him from a difficult childhood, he'd known he wanted to be a detective. He wanted to solve crimes and help people, to bring peace and answers to grieving families. If he took the traditional route, it might take years to get as far as he wanted to go.

"I have to go, Sienna Rose." Even as he said the words, pain lined her face and filled her eyes. "I don't want to leave you."

She pressed her lips together so tightly that they turned white around the edges. Her heavy sigh twisted his heart. "And I have to stay," she said. "I don't want to lose you, but I can't leave my family behind."

He dared not kiss her for fear his resolve would be broken. "There has to be a way for us to make this work."

She shook her head. "I can't go, and you won't stay. There's no way to make that work, Legend."

"There's long distance. I could still come back every weekend."

Her lips trembled. "No one survives that, and you know it. I'm not going to tie you down to your schoolyard sweetheart when there are sure to be thousands of women in New Orleans whose goals make sense with yours."

"So that's it? We're done?"

Her silence was deafening.

Time stood still.

A minute passed. Two. Three. His mind spun frantically for some way to keep them together.

She stepped back and walked into the house, closing the door behind her.

That was the last time he'd seen her in five years. She'd kept the door to her heart shut until now.

He would never let her close it again.

Legend prayed, unsure whether he was dreaming or not. Either way, he prayed for Sienna Rose to be safe.

And for their love for one another to prevail at last.

*H*ow much longer would Legend be in surgery?

Sienna Rose could barely sit still long enough for the emergency room doctor to finish stitching the cuts on her face, even after the pain medication they'd given her as soon as she'd arrived. She'd been demanding updates about Legend and Dean since then. As soon as she was stitched up, she'd go find out for herself.

Captain Brewer stepped into the examining room.

She sucked in a hard breath as the doctor tied off another stitch. "What's the word on Legend? All they've told me is that he's in surgery and will be there for another couple of hours. And what about Dean?"

"If you sit still, this will go faster and hurt less, Detective." The doctor frowned at the captain as if he were to blame for Sienna Rose's unruly behavior. "Detective Jordan has sustained multiple injuries and will be admitted for observation. She has been through a serious trauma this evening and needs to rest."

"I won't stay. Finish stitching me up and I'll get out of your hair." No way was she going to laze around in a hospital bed when she didn't know if the two most important men in her life were okay.

"Absolutely not," replied Captain Brewer, his voice firm. "You'll follow the doctor's orders to the letter. Chief Savoie's orders."

He'd told the chief? "But, sir, I'm fine." Sienna Rose pleaded with her eyes, doing her best to remain still so the doctor wouldn't kick her superior out of the room. "I don't know if Dean and Legend are."

"I thought that might be the problem. Your brother is being treated for minor physical injuries. Your mother is with him. His counselor is on her way to assess the trauma and begin therapy. As I'm sure you know, he's experienced some regression, and they want him to get back on track as soon as possible. I've prevented everyone from trying to obtain Dean's statement until his counselor gets here. You'll know more once she's had a chance to evaluate him, but he's going to be fine."

There was no way Dean was in any shape to give a statement. As it was, Sienna Rose guessed her brother would need extensive therapy to even begin to process the traumatic event. "Thank you." She flinched as the physician tied off another stitch. "And Legend?"

"From what the doctor said, the bullet nicked a ligament in his shoulder. They say it's all repairable with the surgery he's undergoing now. That's the latest update I have. Nothing life-threatening."

She let out a long breath. No matter what, Captain Brewer wouldn't lie to her. At least Legend wasn't dead or in critical condition. That was something to be thankful for.

The doctor put a bandage over her stitches. "All done. They'll take you up to a room as soon as one is ready." He stood, and a nurse swooped in to dispose of the used materials. "You really need to get some rest."

"She will, Doctor," Captain Brewer assured him with a stern glare at Sienna Rose.

The physician glanced at his watch. "You can stay until they move her into a room, Captain. After that, she'll need rest. The medication will hit her soon, and she'll likely fall asleep. I'm informing the nurses that she is to be left in peace." He laid a hand on Sienna Rose's arm. "I mean it. Get some sleep."

"Yes sir."

The doctor left.

Moments later, a knock sounded at the door.

"Yes?" Sienna Rose answered hesitantly.

Legend's boss stepped into the room.

"She's not ready to give a statement yet, Steele," Captain Brewer announced.

"I wouldn't dream of it," Steele assured him. "The doctor said I could see her for a moment to give a quick update on Special Detective Cruz."

She scooted forward eagerly. "What is it? Is he all right?"

"He's out of surgery and in recovery, and the nurse said the operation went very well."

Relief washed over her. "Thank you for letting me know." The smile pulled at her stitches and made her face hurt all over again, but she didn't care. Both Dean and Legend were going to be okay. They'd all survived the worst day ever.

Steele smiled. "Of course."

"Sienna Rose Jordan?" A nurse pushing a wheelchair entered. "I'm here to take you to your room."

"You get some rest, Detective Jordan. You've had a long day." Special Detective Steele turned to Captain Brewer. "Just to let you know, we've filed a request to interrogate Steven Webster."

Sienna Rose bolted upright. "I need to be there when he's questioned."

"Don't worry. No one is talking to Webster tonight. We'll take care of it in the morning." Captain Brewer patted her shoulder. "You concentrate on resting and healing."

As if she could simply put Webster out of her mind.

Once both men were gone, the nurse smiled at her. "Let's get you up to your room, shall we?"

In less than thirty minutes, Sienna Rose was settled on a bed in a private room on the third floor. The floor nurse on duty, Tori, fluttered around fluffing her pillows, filling her mug with ice water, and putting an extra blanket at the foot of the bed.

"Are you hungry? I see you were given a few meds, but there's no notation of the last time you ate. Do you remember when that was?"

"Um." Sienna Rose tried to think. She hadn't had dinner because she'd gotten the call from Mom that Dean was missing. Before that—

Tori chuckled. "If you have to think that hard, then it's been too long. What kind of sandwich do you like? We have turkey, ham, and tuna."

None sounded good at the moment. "I'm not really hungry. I'd like to know when Legend Cruz moves out of recovery." Her stomach growled loudly.

Tori laughed again. "Your body says otherwise. How about this? I'll get you a sandwich, and while you eat, I'll try to find out that patient's status. Deal?"

"Ham, please."

Tori bustled out the door. She returned moments later with a boxed lunch. "Ham and Swiss on a croissant, with potato chips and a chocolate chip cookie." She sat it on the tray and pushed it over the bed. "Eat up while I go make a few calls regarding that update."

Sienna Rose slathered the contents of a mayo packet onto the sandwich and took a bite. It was the best sandwich she'd ever had. She'd devoured it and half the bag of chips by the time Tori returned.

"Good job." She moved Sienna Rose's lunch trash to a can on the opposite side of the bed. "Now, I spoke with my friend Deena, who works in the OR. She stepped into the recovery room your friend Legend is in. She says he's doing well and they'll start waking him up in the next ten minutes." Tori patted her leg. "Deena says his vitals haven't dropped once, so that's really good. As soon as he's out, or if there's any change, she'll let me know."

Relief washed through her. "Thank you. Please let me know as soon as you hear anything. I don't care if I'm asleep. Wake me up. Please."

Tori cocked her head. "You really care about this guy, don't you?"

"I have for years," Sienna Rose confessed. "He's in here because he took a bullet for my brother."

Tori's eyebrows rose. "I'm sure there's a story here, but you must be tired. I'll be sure to wake you up as soon as I hear anything." She strode out of the room, shutting the door behind her.

Sienna Rose rested her head back against the pillows for a moment, then she heard her mother's voice. "Sienna Rose?"

She straightened in time for her mother to gather her in a tight hug. Sienna Rose avoided flinching against the soreness because it was her mom, and being held felt good.

"My sweet baby girl." Her mother planted a flurry of kisses on the crown of her head. "I was so scared for you." She inched back and sat on the bed beside Sienna Rose. "They said you were okay, but I couldn't rest until I saw you for myself."

"How's Dean?"

"The doctor said his physical wounds were minor and have been treated. His counselor is with him. They're keeping him at least overnight to make sure he's stable.

"Mom, I'm so sorry I put him in that position." Tears burned her already aching eyes. "And you. It was all my fault."

"Shh." Her mom took Sienna Rose's hand in hers. "Don't be silly. That man chose to do all of this, so it's his fault, not yours. I know that. Dean knows that too. He asked about you nonstop until a nurse dropped by to reassure him that you were fine."

"But the trauma could leave a mark on him."

"If it does, they'll work with him until he's back on track. Don't you fret. He actually pouted when the nurse told him you had to get stitches.

He said he'd always wanted a little scar." Mom smiled. "He's a little jealous that you'll have one and he won't. I can't imagine any residual trauma being too bad."

That made her feel a lot better.

The smile slipped from her mother's face. "I guess you've heard about Legend's surgery?"

"My nurse, Tori, filled me in."

"That's good she's going to keep you updated. There are a lot of cops I don't recognize in the waiting room, and they seem concerned. Captain Brewer told me they were all part of Legend's team from New Orleans."

"They're probably as worried about him as I am."

"And he's probably every bit as worried about you. That man's head over heels in love with you, you know." Her mother shook her head. "Always has been. I'm guessing even if he took off for another five years, he'd still be in love with you."

Sienna Rose took a sip of her water. She didn't have the energy to explain to her mom that she'd decided she didn't want to be without Legend ever again.

If he asked, she'd follow him to New Orleans this time.

And she hoped he would.

Cold.

Legend couldn't remember the last time he'd felt cold so deep into his bones. He shivered, and agony stretched its icy fingers around his body.

He tried to move, but couldn't. Pain splintered his focus, his concentration, everything. His whole body hurt. Even breathing was difficult. The smell of disinfectant mixed with something else permeated the space and burnt Legend's nostrils.

What had happened to him? Legend couldn't recall. What was the last thing he remembered? Counting. He had been counting down to something.

The light nearly blinded him. He squeezed his eyes closed. A groan escaped his lips before he could stop it.

"Shh. You're doing great. Try to breathe normally. Dr. Reese gave you some medication in your IV before he left, so it should take the edge off the pain soon." The woman's voice was familiar. He couldn't place it, but it brought comfort. Her touch on his uninjured shoulder reassured him. "It's normal to be disoriented, Detective Cruz. The surgery went well, and you're doing great. We're going to move you to your room in a bit." Her presence put his mind at ease.

A weight settled over his torso and warmth seeped into his body. Despite the ache, he sighed.

"I'll be right back."

He sensed the woman had moved away, leaving him alone in his confusion.

He would try to remember things one at a time.

Slowly, as if through a haze, images began to form in his mind. Memories returned.

He'd watched Sienna Rose struggle with Steven Webster. Webster aimed a gun at Dean. Legend had sprinted toward them with everything he had.

He'd been shot.

The ambulance ride to the hospital. The surgery, which certainly explained the pain.

"We're going to move you to your room now, Detective Cruz." The woman's soothing voice returned.

He sensed the hospital bed being rolled along. Legend blinked as overhead lights bore into his retinas. He felt every bump and jostle.

An eternity later, there was a final, wide turn and then different voices. "Let me dim these lights for you, Detective Cruz." He could hear curtains being drawn, the metal rings scraping against a rod.

He chanced opening his eyes again. The light was less blinding. He blinked several times. Three nurses worked as if performing a finely choreographed dance while they connected his IV bag to a rod, pushed buttons on the machine next to the hospital bed, and tapped on a tablet.

One of the nurses smiled down at him. "You're in good hands. Take care, Detective Cruz."

"Thank you." Somehow, he managed to get the words out past the scratchiness in his throat.

One of the other nurses held a stethoscope to his chest. "Deep breaths for me, Detective."

He tried as best he could, but it felt as if a twelve-foot gator sprawled across his chest, crushing his ribs into his lungs.

"Sounds good." She draped the stethoscope around her neck, then wrapped a blood pressure cuff around his arm. Other wires were attached to his limbs, connecting him to the machine at his side. The machine tightened the cuff until he thought he would burst, then it began to loosen again.

"Your blood pressure is a little elevated, but that's normal considering your surgery and the events before it." She glanced at the machine. "Temp is in normal range."

As nice as the nurse was, Legend still hadn't gotten the details he needed. How severe were his injuries, and when would he be able to return to work? He was right-handed, so he'd need that shoulder healed in order to qualify on the shooting range. "My surgery—how bad?" It hurt to speak.

"Don't try to talk." The nurse patted his good shoulder as she adjusted the hospital gown for him, making sure his arm with the IV was outside the blankets covering him. "The doctor will be by to check on you before long. You can ask him all your questions. For now, don't worry about anything but waking up and staying calm."

Patience had never been Legend's strong suit.

Legend's mind replayed the horror of Steven Webster's assault on Dean and Sienna Rose, and he felt his stomach lurch. "Dean and Sienna Rose Jordan. I think they may have come in right after me. How are they?" Despite the pain talking caused, he had to ask. He needed to know if they were okay. He reached out with his left hand to grab the nurse's arm, but his grip was weak. "Please. I need to know."

Maybe it was because his voice was so hoarse, or maybe he appeared really pitiful, or maybe the nurse simply had a kind heart, but she smiled when she responded. "Let me see if I can find out anything for you, okay?"

"Thank you." Two little words, but they were all he could manage to express his gratitude.

Sienna Rose had been so fierce. Legend had always known she wasn't one to back down, but she'd given Webster a run for his money. It took a brave woman to engage in hand-to-hand combat with a repeat murderer. And she'd done it all to save her brother.

And, Legend knew, to save him.

A different nurse brought him a cup filled with ice chips. "Try sucking on these. It will ease the sore throat." She helped him sit up a little in the bed, supporting him with extra pillows.

The frozen chips felt amazing. He was parched.

Legend realized he couldn't feel the fingertips of his right hand. It was the oddest sensation. Come to think of it, he couldn't feel his lips either.

He didn't think he'd ever felt so helpless. He wanted to get up and go find Dean and Sienna Rose for himself and make sure they were okay. Legend needed to tell Sienna Rose how shortsighted he'd been to ever leave Envie, to leave her. There was so much he wanted to tell her, but first he needed to make sure she was okay.

A quick knock sounded at the door and a man walked in, carrying a tablet. "Hi there, Detective. Remember me?"

After a moment, Legend recalled his name. "Dr. Tao."

"That's right." He stood at the foot of Legend's bed, his white coat bright against the gray walls. "Your surgery was a bit more involved than we'd initially anticipated. There was extensive damage to one of the supporting tendons in your shoulder. You're a very lucky man, Detective. We were able to repair everything. I don't believe you'll have any long-term complications."

"When will I be back on my feet and able to get back to work?"

"Hard to say for certain, but if you take it easy and follow my discharge instructions, I'd estimate about eight weeks with physical therapy."

Eight weeks? Seriously? "Couldn't I go back to work a little earlier than that?"

"If you would be comfortable staying on desk duty for a while, then sure." Dr. Tao shook his head. "But that's what concerns me. I'm very familiar with your type. You'll throw caution and my instructions to the wind because you think you need to and try to do too much too soon, which will impede your recovery. Most law enforcement professionals are the same."

Legend recognized the expression in Dr. Tao's eyes. He sensed that arguing with the physician would be futile. And to be fair, the doctor was right.

"For now, we'll concentrate on your recovery following surgery, then set you up with a physical therapist. I've ordered pain medication for you, and the nurses will dispense it as prescribed until your release."

"Okay," Legend said meekly.

"I'll check in on you during morning rounds. If you need anything tonight or before I see you tomorrow, you can buzz the nurses' station." Dr. Tao gave him a stern gaze. "As I said, get some rest, Detective. The more you rest now, the sooner you'll be able to get back to work." The doctor left.

The thought of being off for eight weeks filled him with despair. But he supposed he would have to accept it, as the outcome was so much better than it could have been.

Another knock sounded on his door, and Sienna Rose's mother appeared. "May I come in?"

"Of course." He hitched himself up into a sitting position as she came to stand beside his bed. "How are Sienna Rose and Dean?" He couldn't get the question out quickly enough.

"Dean has been admitted for observation. His doctor and counselor are working with him already. He went through a lot of trauma, and he may have more challenges than some, but Dean is a determined guy. He won't let this get him down."

She leaned over and hugged Legend's left side, but not too tightly. "Thank you," she whispered in his ear before releasing him.

"For what?"

"Taking that bullet for Dean. Words are not enough, but I'll be forever grateful that you saved my son's life." Tears filled her eyes. "You're a wonderful man, Legend Cruz."

"Don't start spreading that around, Lillian Leigh. I've worked hard to earn a reputation as a hardnose, so don't go ruining it." He grinned, but inside, he was a little overwhelmed by her show of gratitude. After all, he'd merely done his job. "Now, tell me how Sienna Rose is."

Before I go out of my mind with worry.

"She's got twenty or so stitches on her face where her cheek was busted. The beginnings of what will be a wicked shiner. A cut or two here and there. Other than that, and a great deal of muscle soreness, she seems no worse for wear."

He let out a breath. Sienna Rose's mother wouldn't lie to him or downplay her daughter's injuries. Relief wrapped around Legend like a comfortable old flannel shirt.

"Of course, you know Sienna Rose," Lillian Leigh went on. "She wasn't happy about having to stay overnight for observation, but since Chief Savoie ordered her to follow the doctor's instruction, she didn't have a choice. Everyone understands why Sienna Rose went out there to meet that man. He had Dean, and she needed to save him. Even Captain Brewer told me that while she broke protocol, he would do everything in his power to make sure she doesn't lose her job over it."

"Of course." Sienna Rose had caught Webster and solved multiple murders, so Legend had no doubt in his mind that her career wasn't in jeopardy.

"And anybody can see why you followed her."

He tilted his head. "And why's that?"

"Because it's obvious you love her and you wanted to protect her. Her and Dean both. And you did. You saved my boy and made sure my daughter came safely out of a bad situation."

His motive might be admirable to Lillian Leigh, but Legend had never had a choice—not when his heart belonged to Sienna Rose.

"You know I'd do it again if the situation ever arose," he said quietly.

Sienna Rose's mother nodded, her eyes filling with tears as she squeezed his hand.

"With one caveat, though. I'd figure out a way not to get shot next time," he said, and they both laughed.

18

*S*unlight snuck through a crack in the curtains and rinsed the drab hospital room in cheery brightness. It chased the dark shadows until they disappeared like a bad dream.

Sienna Rose stretched, then made her way to the bathroom. She splashed water on her face, being careful to avoid the area where she'd gotten stitches, and studied her reflection in the mirror. She looked rough, and it was more than the bandage over her stitches. Her whole face reminded her of someone who'd gone ten rounds in a boxing match.

Brushing her teeth hurt more than she'd imagined it could. When she sat down on the bed again, her ribs protested, and a gasp escaped. Where was all that pain coming from? Her scuffle with Steven Webster hadn't seemed so intense at the time. Maybe adrenaline had blocked the initial pain.

She'd barely gotten back into bed when a nurse entered, a different one from the woman who'd awoken Sienna Rose to let her know that Legend was resting comfortably in his room. The older woman pushed a cart with a blood pressure machine, thermometer, and other various implements to check Sienna Rose's vital signs.

"Good morning, Detective. My name is Sally, and I'll be your nurse until this afternoon." Sally wrapped a blood pressure cuff around Sienna Rose's arm. "How are we feeling this morning?"

Really? We *are hurting in more ways than one.* Sienna Rose swallowed the uncalled-for sarcasm as Sally secured the cuff. It wasn't her fault Sienna Rose was in so much pain. It was all her own doing. "Pretty sore."

The older woman gave her a sympathetic smile as the cuff tightened. "I'm sure you are, sweetie. I hear you're quite the hero." Sally scanned Sienna Rose's chart. "You're allowed a little more pain medication this morning, if you'd like."

"No thank you. I'll be okay." She didn't want anything clouding her mind. "What time does the doctor usually make rounds? He said he'd check in and release me sometime today."

Sally finished her duties and patted Sienna Rose's foot. "I'll check his schedule and let you know." She pushed her little cart around the bed. "If you decide you want any meds, hit your button and I'll come as quick as I can." With a squeak of the wheels, she trundled out of the room.

A brisk knock sounded on the door.

"Come in."

Special Detective Steele entered. "Is it okay to ask a few questions now?"

"Of course." Anything to pass the time until she was released.

"Why don't you tell me what happened back at the cabin?" Luxton sank into the chair beside her bed and pulled out his cell phone to record the conversation.

"When, specifically?" She shifted in the bed, facing him.

"Let's start with the preliminaries. As a detective, you knew the odds of a successful outcome if you went to meet Steven Webster alone, yes?"

Sienna Rose wondered if she could get that pain medication after all. Instead, she stared Legend's boss straight in the eye. "Yes. However, having seen the rapid decline of Steven Webster's mental state, I knew I had to act, even though that meant going outside proper protocol."

"Did you hide the information that you were going alone from other law enforcement?"

"No. I told my colleagues not to follow me. I made it clear to everyone that going after Webster alone was my choice. I didn't want to endanger any of my fellow officers." Sienna Rose took a sip of water from the cup beside her bed, wondering how Steele would frame her statement. Her hand trembled slightly with anxiety as she set the water back down. She would be honest, even if it meant her job.

"Was there any discussion between you and Special Detective Cruz regarding Cruz tracking and following you?"

"Nothing beyond that I told him not to, and he seemed to agree. But I think he said that so I wouldn't suspect he was following me." She frowned. "How would he have tracked me? My cell?"

Steele couldn't quite hide the smile tugging at the corners of his mouth. "He slipped a tracking device into your jacket. You were unaware?"

Legend hadn't been willing to lose her out in the middle of nowhere. The thought warmed her more than the two blankets on her hospital bed. "I was totally unaware. This is the first I'm hearing of it."

"So, this is something Special Detective Cruz did on his own?"

Sienna Rose swallowed. Steele was Legend's boss and could probably determine the trajectory of his career. She couldn't afford a single misstep. Had she already said something that would hurt Legend? "If he discussed this with my captain, it was without my knowledge."

Steele peered at her. "Is it your true statement, then, that you had no idea Special Detective Legend Cruz intended to follow you when you went after Webster, even knowing that you acted in conflict with your training?"

"No, I did not. In fact, as I said, I thought he'd agreed to stay at my mother's house."

"Can you think of any reason why he would have followed you?"

Because he loves me. But how could she tell Legend's boss that he'd gone against direct orders because of his feelings for her? "It's possible that he spoke with my captain, and they formed a plan to ensure my safety. I have no idea. You'd have to ask one of them."

"And you can think of no other reason Special Detective Cruz would have followed you when you went to meet Steven Webster?"

Before Sienna Rose could answer, Sally re-entered the hospital room with a filled syringe. "I'm back with your medication." The nurse injected clear liquid into Sienna Rose's IV bag before she could object.

Coldness spread up Sienna Rose's arm and throughout her body. It was strange but better than the nagging pain. She relaxed back against the pillows and released a sigh.

"I hate to interrupt, but the doctor will be here soon. I'll have to ask you to leave now," Sally told Steele.

"I understand." He stood and pocketed his cell phone. "Thank you for speaking with me, Detective Jordan. We'll finish up later."

The nurse refilled Sienna Rose's ice water and moved the tray out of her way.

"Thank you, Sally."

"You just get some rest, sweetie. The doctor will be around as soon as he can." Sally drew the curtains, pitching the room into semidarkness. The door swung shut behind her.

Sienna Rose knew she should try to find Legend. They needed to talk. She needed to apologize for endangering his job. To say nothing of how she'd endangered his life the previous day.

But that conversation would have to wait. She could barely keep her eyes open. Nurse Sally must've given her more pain medication or some kind of sedative.

Burrowing under the covers, Sienna Rose let her mind drift.

If Legend lost his job, would he blame her? If he did, even subconsciously, there was no chance that they could make a relationship work. That resentment would build under the surface. What if she lost her job? What would she do instead? How would she support herself? What if Legend didn't lose his job and went back to New Orleans? Could they figure out a way to make it work?

Five years ago, Legend had put his career over her, breaking her trust.

Then again, what if his priorities had changed since then? He wouldn't have followed her into the wilderness, risking his job and safety, if he didn't have feelings for her. When she'd admitted that she still loved him, he had said the same.

Maybe it was time to let go of the past, to put her faith in the one she loved, and give him a second chance to be the partner she knew he could be.

Legend felt like he'd been run over by an eighteen-wheeler carrying a full load.

Everything hurt, and there was no position he could shift himself into that helped. The one thing that offered any relief was the pain medication the nurses dutifully delivered via his IV every four hours.

"Good morning, Detective Cruz." A nurse with a long braid hanging down the middle of her back smiled at him as she entered and began taking his vitals. "They're bringing your breakfast in a few minutes."

"I'm not hungry." With every bone in his body screaming in agony, food was the last thing on his mind.

The blood pressure cuff tightened on his arm. "I'm sure, but the doctor requested that you eat something. You don't want to disobey orders, do you?"

As if he hadn't done enough of that already. "Detective Sienna Rose Jordan. She came in after me. Do you have any updates on her?"

"I'll see what I can find out." She studied his vitals from the machine at his side, entering the data into a tablet. "Now, about not eating—you can't have any more pain medication without something in your stomach."

The thought of going a minute longer than necessary without pain medication was definitely a deal breaker. "All right. I'll try."

She finished recording his information on her tablet, then smiled down at him. "Good. I'll go check on your breakfast tray and see what I can find out about your friend."

When a knock sounded on the door, he expected it to be the nurse returning with a tray of bland food that wouldn't upset his stomach, and maybe an update on Sienna Rose.

Instead, he got his boss, Special Detective Luxton Steele.

Legend pushed himself into a sitting position, although he immediately regretted it as agony shot through the entire right side of his body. "Sir."

"How're you feeling, Cruz?"

"Sore as can be, all over, but ready to get out of here. One of the nurses said I'd probably be released today."

Steel's expression was unreadable. "I heard you were in pretty bad shape before they patched you up."

He might as well get the bad news out of the way. "The doctor says I'll need about eight weeks of physical therapy before I can return to my regular duties."

"I understand. We want you to make a full recovery. You can't rush the process."

"Yes sir."

"Can you tell me what happened yesterday? I need to confirm for the paperwork."

Legend met his boss's steely eyes—true to the namesake—and lifted his chin. He couldn't straighten anything else as the pain had become almost unbearable. "A criminal's behavior can be unpredictable. Webster's actions couldn't have been foreseen. No one could have predicted that he would abduct an innocent man and take him hostage. His MO up until that point was to kill people where they were."

"Yet you were able to locate him when he lured Detective Jordan to offer herself in exchange for her brother, correct?" Steele's gaze pinned Legend in place in the hospital bed, which had suddenly become uncomfortably warm.

"Yes."

"You followed Detective Jordan into the woods, carrying a rifle. You attempted to provide backup for the detective and rescue her brother from Webster. Not once did you have a clean shot, even with the rifle?"

"No sir. Not without risking Dean Jordan's safety."

"I know for a fact that you're a pretty good shot, Cruz."

"Yes sir."

"But you couldn't get one clean shot?"

"As I said, not one that didn't put the civilian at risk. Webster stuck close to him the whole time."

"Hmm."

"What does that mean?" Legend was in too much pain to deal with sarcasm, internal affairs or not.

"I heard you never got off a single shot." Steele crossed his arms over his chest.

"That's correct."

"Please tell me how you took a bullet, then. Your lack of fire would normally indicate that Webster shouldn't have known you were there to shoot you. I mean, I have the general sequence of events, as I spoke to Captain Brewer, but I want to hear it from you."

"Webster and Detective Jordan engaged in combat. Webster pointed his gun at Dean Jordan. I had very little time to react. I knew he was going to fire, and I couldn't make a shot without risking Dean's safety. I dropped the rifle and dove for Detective Jordan's brother to knock him to safety. The bullet hit my side as I took Dean to the ground."

"You intentionally shielded Dean Jordan from a bullet?" Steele's tone was filled with incredulity.

"It wasn't a conscious decision. We are charged to serve and protect, and in that moment, that's what I did. I wouldn't have been able to get a clean shot on Webster, so I did the next best thing to ensure the safety of an innocent man."

"You were the lead on the Webster case, were you not, Special Detective Cruz?" Steele's eyes penetrated to the pit of his stomach.

"I was. However, I also believe that part of our job is to maintain good rapport with other departments. I might have been able to take out Webster, had I gotten a clear shot. That opportunity never came. I can't say what anyone else would have done, but I kept an innocent civilian safe. Detective Jordan was able to apprehend Webster with minor injuries."

Steele studied him for a long time while Legend's stomach did an anxious dance. Finally he said, "You did a good job, Cruz, and that's how I'll write it up. Understand that I have to send the report to the task force's review board because you were shot. They will determine whether you acted within the confines of your position. They can decide to pin a medal on your chest, or let you go."

Legend felt sick, and it had nothing to do with being shot.

Let him go?

Sienna Rose hadn't meant to eavesdrop. But as she neared Legend's hospital room, she'd heard voices inside and didn't want to interrupt. She considered walking in but realized that would probably do more harm than good.

Legend might face disciplinary action, or possibly even termination? She couldn't let that happen. He loved his job too much to lose it because of her.

"I'll put in my own recommendations," Steele was saying.

"Which will be what?" Legend sounded desperate.

"I'll recommend you for a medal, but I have to list alternative ideas in case the review board goes a different way."

"What are you going to recommend as an alternative?"

"You're going to have to sit at a desk after you return from sick leave anyway. I'll most likely recommend you be assigned desk duty until you're fully recovered."

Sienna Rose chewed her bottom lip.

"If I hadn't gotten shot, would I still be facing the review board?"

"I can't say, Cruz, because you *did* get shot." Steele sounded almost apologetic.

Legend took a deep breath, and when he spoke again, his voice was firm. "It wouldn't matter. I'd take the same course of action, every single time."

Sienna Rose could picture Legend's stance—chin jutted out, muscles above his jaw twitching, eyes narrowed. Defiance.

"If you truly believe you did the right thing in the situation, be sure to state that in your report."

"If the review board goes against your recommendation and chooses to bench me, the mark on my record will cost me a promotion, won't it?"

There was a long pause. "Most likely. At least for a couple of years."

It was wrong to continue eavesdropping. Taking a deep breath, Sienna Rose knocked on the open door, then stepped inside. "Hey there, hero." She beamed at Legend, even though her heart was doing a full gymnastic floor routine at the sight of him.

He was paler than she'd ever seen him. Gauze taped down his right shoulder and peeked through a small gap in his hospital gown. His face split into a smile as she entered the room.

"I'll check back with you later, Cruz." Steele patted her shoulder on his way out the door. "I'm glad to see you're okay, Detective Jordan."

"Only because of this guy here." Mentally, she added, *So give him a break and don't let them consider him anything less than a hero, because that's what he is.*

Steele nodded and left. If she had to guess, he'd understood exactly what she'd left unsaid.

Sienna Rose approached Legend's bed and lifted his left hand. "I can't thank you enough." Tears burned her battered face. "If you hadn't shielded Dean . . ."

He squeezed her hand. "Don't think about it. I'd make that same decision again and again. I hate that you got hurt, though." He ran gentle fingers over the gauze over her stitches.

She waved off his concerns. "This is nothing. You got *shot*." She ran her fingers through his hair, straightening it. "How are you feeling?"

"It hurts, but it's not unbearable. The pain meds help."

"They do," Sienna Rose agreed. "Except I don't like how groggy they made me, so I'm on regular over-the-counter pain relief now. What does the doctor say?"

"The doctor said the surgery went well. He said I should be released today."

"That's great, Legend." She'd been afraid he might have more damage that would prolong his recovery. "I can't thank you enough for what you did."

He took her hand again. "No more of that. You would've done the same thing in my shoes."

"Maybe." The whole thing had made her reevaluate her commitment to the job. While she knew she'd definitely step in front of a bullet for her family or Legend, she wasn't sure she'd do it for many others. That made her wonder if she should stay on the job.

"I know you, Sienna Rose. You'd do what you had to, like you did last night."

"I'd like to think so."

"I know so." He smiled, then changed the subject. "How's Dean?"

"His doctor and therapist kept him overnight for observation. They were concerned that he might have severe nightmares, so they wanted him to have access to immediate medication and sedation in a controlled setting. Mom is going to see him this morning before she comes to get me once I'm discharged."

"So they haven't released you yet?" he asked.

"Not yet." She glanced at the clock. "I should get back. My doctor is supposed to be making rounds now."

He shook his head. "You snuck up here. I knew it."

She chuckled. "I had to come see you as soon as I could." Sienna Rose gave him a quick kiss on the forehead. "I'll be back."

He met her gaze seriously. "Good. We have a lot to talk about."

Sienna Rose rushed from the room.

They did have a lot to talk about.

She only hoped he hadn't changed his mind about still being in love with her.

*L*egend finished packing his suitcase as well as he could using one hand in the dreariness of his room. He'd been released that morning. Steele had picked him up and driven him to the team's motel. He was packing to go back to New Orleans with his boss.

He knew Sienna Rose had been discharged as well a few days earlier, but he'd had to stay longer than he'd hoped, and she hadn't come by to see him again.

Worry gnawed at him that she might have changed her mind about what she'd said. Her words echoed in his mind—*she still loved him*. And he'd already decided that, no matter what, he wasn't going to lose her again. Every passing hour away from her without settling things between them felt like an eternity.

"We'll grab an early dinner on the way back," Steele had said when he'd helped Legend to his room. "I can't wait to be in the city again."

Legend couldn't have cared less about New Orleans at the moment. He had to see Sienna Rose, to tell her that he loved her and would do whatever it took to be with her. He'd even move back to Envie. If he lost his job, it might very well be a blessing in disguise, and he felt a strange sort of peace about it. The idea of losing the job that had broken them up because he'd saved her brother felt poetic in a way. As if he were righting a wrong.

"I've got to go finish up some paperwork with Captain Brewer. Will you be okay here on your own for a while?" Steele asked.

"Of course."

"It shouldn't take more than a couple of hours, so don't overdo it while you're packing. If you get tired, rest. I can finish everything else when I get back."

"Thanks."

Legend tried to call Sienna Rose but got her voicemail. He decided that a shower would both pass the time and do him a world of good.

An hour later, he was clean, had rebandaged his wound, and was eating a piece of leftover pizza when there was a knock on his door.

"It's propped open," he called. "Come on in."

He was surprised when Lillian Leigh stepped inside. "Is this a good time?"

"This is a perfect time. Have a seat. Have a piece of pizza."

She sat, grinning at the takeout box. "You always did love that place."

"And I've missed it. I mean, New Orleans has amazing food, but sometimes I miss the familiar."

Lillian Leigh's smile melted away. "That's what I'm here to talk to you about."

Legend wiped his mouth with a napkin and took a drink of water. His gut told him he was about to hear something he didn't want to.

"I know that you and Sienna Rose have reconnected. You know I've always loved you, and I'll never be able to thank you enough for saving Dean. You will always have my undying gratitude for that."

He sensed it. "But?"

"But—and please know I'm not trying to be one of those overbearing mothers—I want you to ask yourself if you're truly interested in Sienna Rose, and not merely the fact that being in a relationship with her is familiar."

Wow. He hadn't seen that coming. He supposed it was natural for Lillian Leigh to be cautious about him with her daughter, especially considering the way he'd left five years ago. The pizza sat heavily in his stomach. He hadn't realized how the situation might appear to her. "I can certainly understand your concern about my intentions, Lillian Leigh. But I assure you, my interest in Sienna Rose is not about familiarity."

She stared at him so intently that he had to struggle not to squirm, which would probably have hurt a great deal, given his current physical condition. "Good, because she isn't the same person she was five years ago. She's built a life for herself that doesn't require a man to provide happiness."

"I don't intend to repeat what happened five years ago. It was the biggest mistake of my life to give up what I had with Sienna Rose for a mere job." He had clearly hurt Sienna Rose even more deeply than he had realized for her mother to be so protective now, especially after what had happened with Dean.

She studied him as the moment stretched out. Finally, she smiled. "Okay then. That's what I needed to know."

"I hope I've put your mind at ease."

"You have. At least for the time being."

He chuckled. "How's Dean? Is he back home yet?"

"He is. It's a struggle at times, but since Sienna Rose is home with us, Dean is getting better by the day. I think he relived the trauma in his nightmares for a few nights, but those have decreased."

"I'm so sorry he went through all of that."

"I am too, but we didn't cause it. Neither did Sienna Rose, but she's carrying that guilt anyway."

"I'm not surprised." He was certain that if he were in her place, he'd feel guilty too.

Lillian Leigh stood. "I'd best be going. It's almost time to pick up Dean from his therapy appointment." She leaned over and kissed Legend's cheek. "I'm sorry I had to ask about you and Sienna Rose. I wanted you to really think about what you want for your future."

"I understand. Thank you."

She gave a little wave and disappeared. She'd asked hard questions, but they weren't much different from the ones already bouncing around in his head. Good thing he'd already decided that Sienna Rose was the woman for him.

All he had to do was convince her of that.

Half an hour later, he slowly made his way back to the motel room from the ice machine. Despite the crispness of the November afternoon, a bead of sweat formed on his upper lip. The short walk wore him out. He didn't even have the energy to shut the motel door. He sank onto the end of the bed, fighting against the pain shooting down his arm.

"May I come in?" Sienna Rose peeked around the open door.

Legend's heart skipped a beat. "Please do. I was starting to think you were avoiding me."

"No. I simply wanted to give you space to heal." She smiled and sat in a chair by the little round table. He felt himself grinning from ear to ear. Seeing her made him feel better. Even the pain shooting down his arm lessened at the sight of her.

"How're you feeling?"

"Good. The doctor says I'm healing wonderfully and that he's transferring all my records to my doctor back home."

Sienna Rose's smile vanished. "Oh. That's great news." Her disappointed tone belied the words.

He swallowed, feeling awkwardness settle in. The mention of his home in New Orleans brought their complicated relationship, with all its past and present baggage, to the forefront.

She went quiet, obviously feeling the same.

Might as well get everything out in the open.

"Sienna Rose, I know that we went through an intense situation, but I meant what I said. I love you. I never stopped. I was just too stupid to realize it. I should never have left five years ago. I want us to be together, and I'm willing to do whatever it takes to make that happen. I won't lose you again."

Her hesitation made him more nervous than he'd ever been. "Legend, I need to be honest with you. I know you're facing a review board that may jeopardize your job. I'm sorry you got caught up in this case and took a bullet to save my brother. I'll always be thankful you did, but I never would have wanted you to risk your job. I know how much you love it. That aside, I don't want to be your backup plan."

How could she think such a thing? The idea that she had ever thought of herself that way crushed him. "You aren't now, nor have you ever been, my backup plan." He frowned. "Wait, did my boss talk to you?"

"He did, but that's not how I know about the possible outcome." Sienna Rose ducked her head and stared at the floor. "I was on my way in to see you and I heard voices from inside the room. I didn't want to interrupt, so I was going to wait outside. I couldn't help but overhear your conversation with Steele."

She'd heard that his career might be in jeopardy. No wonder she thought she could end up as his backup plan if he didn't have a choice about whether to keep his career, which he'd established to her as his priority—wrongfully so. He was certain that if he could hold her, he would be able to assuage that fear, but his shoulder prevented it.

"Sienna Rose, all of that may be true, but it doesn't matter. Maybe losing my job would be a blessing. At least it would ensure that we could be together here in Envie. Or maybe I'm able to keep my job, and then you and I can decide how to make it work. No matter what the outcome with the review board, *you* are my priority. I love you, and I mean that with every beat of my heart."

Her eyes glistened. "I love you too, and I want to figure this all out as well." She reached out and took his left hand. "I need us both to be sure, before we go any further and either of us winds up getting hurt."

Guilt washed over him like a cold waterfall. He would do anything to undo what he'd done to her five years ago.

"That's completely understandable, Sienna Rose. My track record isn't so great. I get it, but I love you. I've changed. Tell me what I need to do to prove that I'm not going to hurt you again." He *had* to make her understand.

"Sometimes love involves risks. I'm not afraid of that. I simply need to know that we're both committed to the same thing—us."

"We are. I am." He tightened his hold on her hand. "How can I earn your trust?"

"It'll take time." She squeezed his hand in return. "I think a good start would be sorting out where we hope our career paths will lead."

"I'd love to show you New Orleans." He smiled, dreaming about their future together. "The French Quarter is a popular vacation spot, but there's so much more. Like Jackson Square, where the Louisiana Territory was turned over to the United States from France in 1803. Or The Fly, a strip of frontage land along the Mississippi River behind the Audubon Zoo. On weekends, people go for grilling, crawfish boils, sunning, and sports. I'd love to show you what it's like at dusk too. It's the perfect time to visit, as the sun sets right over the river—truly a spectacular sight."

Her hand had gone slack in his. She still smiled, but it didn't quite meet her eyes.

"What's wrong?"

"You light up when you talk about New Orleans. If you lost your job there and decided to move back to Envie, would it ever really be enough for you?"

He had to admit her question was fair. "You know, I've been thinking about that very thing off and on each night since Steele and I had our talk."

"And?"

He laced his fingers with hers. "Honestly, I would hate to not be able to work in law enforcement, but I could be happy doing anything." He paused, willing the sincerity in his words to sink into her heart. "As long as I'm with you."

He still held her hand, hoping she wouldn't pull away from him. He needed her to see how much she meant to him, how he longed to build a life with her.

She didn't reply at first.

"I'm serious, Sienna Rose." He gently tugged her hand until she moved closer. "I've had time to consider every scenario, and to search my heart. The question is, are you willing to work with me if I keep my job in New Orleans?"

Sienna Rose chewed her bottom lip. "I've tried to imagine how that might work. I just don't know. I'm not sure we have the same goals."

"What are your goals, Sienna Rose?"

"I'd like to take the captain's test the next time it's offered, which is in the middle of December."

"You'd be a great captain. You're fair, honest, and dedicated."

Her smile took on a wistful air, not shining quite as brightly as it had before. "Thanks, but what if you get a promotion and can't leave New Orleans? I'm trying to envision myself living in that city. I think Mom and Dean would be fine on their own once he's recovered from the trauma Webster caused, so I could go then. I'd try to make a name for myself with the New Orleans police, but would that be a conflict, considering our involvement?"

"I don't know." That she'd even begun to consider giving up her entire life in Envie to join him meant more to him than he could say.

"That's the point—we'd have to figure it out as we go." He resented the sorrow that slipped into his voice, but he couldn't let her go. "Please say you're willing to try. I love you, Sienna Rose. Nothing is going to change that."

"I love you too."

Lillian Leigh's voice broke into the moment. "Sorry to interrupt, but you have a visitor."

"Hi, Mom." Sienna Rose straightened and smiled. "And Dean."

Her brother's smile was so pure and open. She ran to wrap him in an embrace.

"Sienna Rose, you're squishing me," Dean said, laughing.

Legend sat up straighter, not willing to let Dean think he'd been hurt badly by taking a bullet that had been meant for him. It was good to see Dean up and about. "Hey, Sienna Rose, lighten up on the guy."

She stepped away, and Dean approached Legend's side. "Hey, Legend."

"Hey, my man, how are you?"

Dean reached out and hugged him. Legend didn't squirm, though the embrace caused his wounded side to smart.

"Thank you, Legend." Dean's voice was so thick with emotion. "You saved my life."

Legend clapped Dean's back. "I couldn't let anything happen to my main man, now could I?" He kept his tone light.

But Dean understood the enormity of what had transpired. "You took a bullet for me."

"Hey, I'd do it again in a heartbeat, if it meant you'd be okay." Legend meant every single word.

"I love you, Legend."

"I love you too, buddy." Legend noticed tears in both Lillian Leigh's and Sienna Rose's eyes. He felt a little moisture starting in his own.

"Are you really going back to New Orleans today? Mom said that's what your boss told her." Dean still clutched Legend's side.

"Yeah. I've got to get back to the city. We can't hang out here all the time." Legend grinned at Dean to lighten the emotional moment.

"You'll come back, right?" He glanced over his shoulder at Sienna Rose, who dropped her gaze.

Legend sensed she wouldn't encourage her brother to believe in a promise that even she wasn't yet certain Legend could keep.

Dean looked back at Legend, his expression hopeful.

Who knew how long it would take for Dean to fully recover from the trauma he'd endured? The nightmares alone could last for a while, or fade for a time only to return. Legend hoped Steven Webster would never see the outside of a jail cell again.

"I'll make plans to return as soon as I can."

"Promise?"

Legend met Sienna Rose's eyes over her brother's shoulder. "I promise." He hoped she understood that the words were meant for her as well, on the chance she wouldn't join him.

"Okay." Dean finally smiled.

"All right, Dean. We need to get to your appointment." Lillian Leigh motioned for Dean to join her.

"Okay," Dean said. "My last physical exam is today. Goodbye, Legend. See you soon."

"Bye for now, bud."

Sienna Rose snatched another hug from her brother. Lillian Leigh kissed Sienna Rose on the cheek, then left with her son.

Sienna Rose resumed her seat. "I forgot to tell you. I got a confession out of Steven Webster, out there in the woods. At least for two of the four murders." Her eyes lit up as she talked about the confession and arrest, and it was easy for Legend to picture her in the role of captain.

He could even envision her as Chief Jordan one day. No way could he ask her to give up on her dream.

Five years ago, he'd followed his career.

He realized with a sinking heart that it was her turn to do the same.

Sienna Rose checked the clock on the police station wall, which read a few minutes after three, and wondered what Legend was doing. It had been five long days since he returned to New Orleans, and their nightly video chats merely left her missing him more.

"Detective Jordan?" Officer Rucker drew her attention.

"Yes?"

"Steven Webster is about to meet with his wife."

"Thanks, Rucker." It was her chance to talk to the Websters together, to tell them why their daughter had been killed. They deserved an explanation.

Sienna Rose hurried to Chief Savoie's office. The chief had recently returned to work. His office door was ajar, and he stood in front of his desk. Everyone seemed to be tiptoeing around him after the horror his family had gone through.

"I need a few minutes with him, Chief." Sienna Rose refused to walk on eggshells around Savoie. She treated him the same as she always had—with honesty and respect. "I need to tell him who really killed his daughter, and why."

"The man wanted to kill you, Sienna Rose. He almost killed your brother. And I don't need to remind you that he did shoot a special detective from the task force." The chief crossed his arms over his chest and sat on the edge of his desk. "I don't think talking with Webster is the best idea you've had."

"Sir, with all due respect, as a father, you needed answers when Magdalene was killed. It's been five years, and Steven Webster still doesn't know what really happened to his daughter." She watched his face pale as he stood. "I don't mean to dredge up hard feelings for you. Trust me, this man tormented me and those I love. I want nothing more than to see him spend the rest of his life in a jail cell. But this was my case back then, and I'd like to tell Mr. Webster that justice will finally be served for his daughter. If nothing else, Mrs. Webster deserves the truth. She's been an innocent victim in all of this from the beginning."

Chief Savoie remained silent, watching her thoughtfully.

She softened her tone. "I know this is hard because he took Magdalene from you. I can understand that, and as someone who can't stand the man, I agree. But as a detective, I owe him and his wife the information I was able to get from Baker Paul."

The chief stilled, then slowly nodded. "Put Webster in the inter-rogation room, fully shackled. His wife can sit at the table with him. I'm seriously considering discussing an obstruction of justice charge against her with the DA. She had that journal and didn't contact us. Lives might have been saved if she had."

Lives like Magdalene's. Sienna Rose heard the unspoken words. "Yes sir."

He released a heavy sigh. "I'm getting too old for this job. I've thought about retiring before. I probably should have so I could spend more time with my family, but now—well, I've got a lot of things to consider." He moved behind his desk. "Go ahead."

"Thank you, sir." Sienna Rose put in the order with the officer who oversaw the holding cells, then went to secure her weapon in her desk safe.

The application to take the captain's test sat, completed, on her desk. She fingered the edge of the paper. What would it hurt to take the test? She didn't have to do anything with the results, right? If she went to New Orleans, maybe it could make a difference.

She took the application and dropped it in the chief's box, then headed back to her desk. If he didn't think she was ready, he'd be quick to tell her. He always had been one to shoot straight with her.

Her desk phone rang, and she snatched up the receiver.

"Detective Jordan," said the holding cell officer. "Steven Webster is in the box, as instructed."

"Thank you. I'm on my way." She picked up Haven Webster's file and glanced through it. Officer Rucker had verified all the details of Baker Paul's confession. She closed the folder and set it back on her desk, then headed off down the hall.

Sienna Rose paused, her hand resting on the knob of the interrogation room. She prayed for words that would bring comfort to the mother and father inside, even though anger still burned inside her for what Webster had done to Dean.

With a deep breath, she squared her shoulders and opened the door.

Both of the Websters looked up as she entered.

A slow, crooked sneer crept over Steven's face. "Why, hello, Detective. Have you come to gloat?" His shackles rattled as he stretched out his legs under the table. The chains between his feet clanked across the tiled floor. "You got your man. Good for you. You're such a great cop. Getting a promotion because you caught me, I presume? I don't suppose they're considering that if you'd done your job in the first place and protected my Haven, all those other lives would have been spared. To me, that merits a demotion, don't you think?"

She pulled out a chair across the table from them, ignoring him. "I wanted to let you both know that we obtained a confession from the person who killed Haven, and he's been arrested."

Eleanor's features blanched. Her lips formed a tight line. "Who was it?"

Obviously, Steven hadn't shared that important fact with his wife. "Baker Paul."

"Andy Paul's brother?" Eleanor's eyes widened in shock.

"That's right."

Steven snorted. "Nonsense. We've been over this, Detective Jordan. Or don't you remember our little discussion in the woods?"

She focused on Eleanor. Her responsibility was to share the facts, not convince him to believe them. "It's true. Baker was a match for the DNA found at Haven's crime scene."

Anguish flooded Eleanor's expression as tears pooled in her eyes. "But why?"

Though it was clear Steven tried to hide his emotions, Sienna Rose caught a hint of sorrow behind his eyes.

"Did either of you know that Andy and Baker's father had cancer?"

"You know, I think I heard mention of it once, but no one really said much after that." Eleanor's brows knit together. "But what does that have to do with Haven?"

"Baker said that the treatment costs were astounding. We did confirm that the family had to pay quite a large sum of money to the hospital. To secure funding for his dad's treatment, Andy embezzled money from the bank he worked for."

It was always difficult to tell a family that their murdered loved one had been involved in a crime that had led to their death. It wasn't fair, but the truth was the truth, and Sienna Rose believed that family members deserved to know the whole of it.

She took a deep breath before continuing. "Andy told Haven about his embezzlement. After they broke up, she—"

"I had no idea they'd broken up." Eleanor's voice cracked.

"His brother claims they did. After the breakup, Haven began to blackmail Andy, using the information about his embezzlement as leverage."

Steven scowled. "As I've said, that's absurd. Haven wouldn't blackmail anyone. We raised her better than that."

Sienna Rose closed her eyes as images of Dean, bound and terrified, filled her memory. It took all her effort to separate those moments from the present, to ground herself in the fact that, despite what Steven had done to her brother, she faced grieving parents who were in denial. "I'm sorry you don't believe me, Mr. Webster, but this has been verified. There were thousands deposited into her account, without any other plausible explanation regarding the source of the money."

"I won't believe it." Steven Webster clenched his fists, and an edge tinged his words, pulling Sienna Rose back to that dark day. "She made her money by working an honest job, and if she needed more, she knew she could come to her mother and me."

Sienna Rose shook her head. "I'm sorry, but she did blackmail Andy. Baker found out about it and confronted her." She watched the range of emotions shift in both Eleanor's and Steven's facial expressions. "Baker said they argued, and Haven hit him. Baker hit her in response."

Eleanor's eyes squeezed shut.

Sienna Rose sat quietly, giving the Websters a moment to process the information. "Baker said Haven pulled a gun on him during the struggle, and the next thing he knew, the gun went off and she was dead."

Eleanor covered her mouth, and her husband's eyes widened. "My missing gun."

"That's right."

Steven's face paled, then gradually reddened. "That monster."

Sienna Rose hadn't considered how the detail about his gun might affect Steven. "Baker was frightened about the way things appeared, so, as you know, he took Haven down to the bayou and attempted to hide her body, hoping that if she were ever found, no one would connect him to her death. I believe you were trying to mimic that with Magdalene Savoie, weren't you?"

"Chief Savoie deserved to know how it felt to have his daughter treated like trash," Steven snarled.

Eleanor buried her face in her hands.

Despite how much Sienna Rose loathed the man, she did feel sorry for him as a father. But she wouldn't offer sympathy.

Sienna Rose pushed back her chair and stood. "Baker's in custody and has been charged with Haven's murder. We're confident that we'll get a conviction, given our forensic evidence and his confession. I know it's not enough to bring back your daughter, but at least now you know."

"Better late than never," Steven snarled, but it lacked his usual venom. Sienna Rose knew grief had sunk in.

She didn't bother with a reply. She opened the interrogation room door and stepped into the hall, motioning to an officer next to the holding area. "Take him back to his cell. I'm done with him."

And she was. For good.

20

"Special Detective Legend Cruz, your presence at the Special Task Force review board is required on Monday at nine at the city municipal building, room four," Inspector Heath Lancaster informed Legend in his most official tone.

Legend leaned back in his desk chair and stared up at the guy. "Thanks for letting me know." He turned back to the file on his last open case.

Having returned to New Orleans the week before without Sienna Rose had cemented in his mind what he had to do. Phone calls during their breaks, nightly video calls, and nonstop texting weren't enough. The job he'd thought was so important was meaningless—had always been meaningless—without her.

He grabbed the file and headed to his supervisor's office. "Got a second?"

Steele waved him inside, and Legend shut the door behind him.

Steele raised a brow. "Must be serious. Lancaster stopped by and gave me the hearing details. Have you been in touch with your union rep?"

"No sir, but it's not really necessary."

Steele leaned back in his chair, lacing his fingers behind his head. "Cruz, you have to talk to your rep. You may need someone backing you at the hearing. I have no idea what direction the board is going to take."

"I'm not going to the hearing."

Steele popped upright and put his palms on his desk. "What do you mean you aren't going? It's not optional."

Legend sat down in the chair across from his boss. "I'm not going to the hearing, sir, because I'm quitting." He laid the file on Steele's desktop. "This was my last case. All the reports are there, and all the loose ends are tied up in a neat little bow."

"You're serious?" Steele raised a brow.

"Yes sir." Legend was surprised at how peaceful he felt speaking his intentions out loud.

"Son, you need to think long and hard about this. I don't know what you've got up your sleeve, but a move like this could kill your career."

"Sir, I *have* thought long and hard about this. I appreciate the opportunities I've been given and the training I've received, but I've come to realize my home isn't in New Orleans."

Steele leaned back in his chair again. A minute passed. "Am I to assume this has something to do with Detective Jordan?"

Legend couldn't stop the smile that spread across his face. "It has everything to do with Sienna Rose."

"I often wondered why she didn't come five years ago when you did. Chief Savoie had put in for both of you to join the task force. She'd been accepted, same as you, so we were a little surprised when she didn't accept the offer." He tapped his fingers on the edge of his desk. "Then when I showed up in Envie and met her mother and brother, I understood."

"Yes sir. She'd just lost her father, so you can imagine the adjustment it was for her family. Sienna Rose felt like she needed to stay at home to care for them."

"Admirable." Steele sat up and tented his fingers over his desk. "But are you sure you fit in there? I assume you're going to try and get on with the Envie police? You know I can't give you a recommendation without the board's approval. There may be consequences if you don't show up at the hearing."

"I know, and I understand your position. I'm hoping that Chief Savoie, who knows what happened, will hire me anyway." Legend shrugged, shocking himself with his lack of worry about what might become of his career. "If not, I'll try a security firm. I hear they pay better anyway." He grinned at his supervisor.

Steele chuckled. "Does Detective Jordan know what you're doing?"

"No sir. I wanted to make the decision independently, so that I'll always know it was my choice. I don't think she'd accept me any other way."

For the first time in the conversation, uncertainty knotted inside Legend's chest. Sienna Rose might not accept his decision anyway. He hadn't mentioned his plans to her, hoping it would be a surprise.

"I'm assuming you want to leave immediately?" Steele stood.

Legend pushed to his feet. "I'm sorry, sir. I hate to leave you shorthanded."

"Don't worry about it. I'm going to put out a call soon for new recruits to expand the task force anyway." Steele held out his hand to shake Legend's. "I hate to lose such a talented detective, but I understand why you're doing it. I wish you the best of luck, and I hope our paths cross again. You're a good man, Legend Cruz."

"Thank you, and thanks again for everything, sir. It's been a true honor to work under your direction."

Legend laid his shield on Steele's desk, then headed back to his own. He collected a few personal items, shrugged into his jacket, and strode out to the parking lot. He climbed into his truck. He'd already given notice to his landlord and hired a service to pack up his belongings. His truck was loaded and ready to go, and he'd already returned his apartment's key, so he didn't even need to stop by the space he'd never felt at home in.

He was ready to get back to Envie and to Sienna Rose, but his last stop couldn't wait.

His doctor had checked him out the day before and said he was ready for physical therapy. Legend had set his appointment for the following week—with a therapist in Envie.

One final stop and he'd be on his way to his real home, the home where his heart had always been.

It was a beautiful night.

Sienna Rose stood on her patio, gazing across the bayou. Christmas lights in the distance cast beautiful halo effects over the gently rippling water.

She sat back on a chaise longue, curling her stocking feet underneath her. She put earbuds in and restarted the latest audiobook from her favorite suspense author. She loved such nights. The air wasn't too cold, but chilly enough for sweats and a hoodie. Maybe a soft fleece blanket and a cup of tea. A cool breeze lifted her hair.

It was her favorite time of year.

Leaning her head back against the plush cushion, she closed her eyes. She couldn't help wondering what Legend was doing at that moment. Was he working late? He hadn't called or texted yet that evening, so most likely he'd been caught up with work.

She stopped the audiobook. Try as she might, she couldn't concentrate, even though the story was really good. Her mind refused to be pulled from thoughts of Legend. Was he being careful? Was he okay?

Tossing the earbuds on a side table, Sienna Rose sat up. She couldn't stand worrying about him. In their line of work, danger was commonplace. She'd never really considered how it felt to worry about someone in law enforcement, instead of being the one who might face danger.

They had been partnered at the academy, so they'd always been aware of what was happening with each other. No wonder her mom wanted her to check in regularly. Sienna Rose made a mental note to call her mother more often, to let her know that she was okay.

According to her watch, it was eight o'clock. *He really is late calling tonight.*

A number of scenarios filled her mind. Had his surgery site gotten infected? Had he been in a vehicle accident? Was he simply stuck in traffic?

Whispering a twofold prayer—one for Legend's safety and well-being, and another for her own peace of mind—Sienna Rose hugged her legs to her chest and rested her chin on her knees.

She'd missed Legend so much that week. She loved him with her whole heart. They were supposed to be together. They'd wasted enough time and needed to make the most of that which lay ahead.

She exhaled and stretched back out on the chaise, unable to get comfortable. Even if it meant giving up her job here and leaving her mom and Dean, she'd move to New Orleans. She could always come home for weekends and holidays. It'd break her heart to give up her beloved house that she'd finally finished tweaking to her liking, but maybe she could figure out a way to keep it. It'd been a fixer-upper, and she'd enjoyed doing the DIY repairs. That, along with work, had kept her busy and sane after Legend had left five years before.

Then there was the captain's test. She'd received her notice in the mail to report for the exam the following week. She'd been studying every night. It helped to pass the time while Legend was gone. She felt ready, but she wasn't sure. Her nerves bunched. Was she making a mistake, giving herself something else that would lock her in Envie? She loved the town and always would, but she loved Legend more.

"Hey, what are you doing out here?" came a familiar voice.

Sienna Rose jumped up to see Legend leaning against the patio gate, grinning. "I could ask you the same question." She ran over to unlock the gate. She barely got it open before she was in his arms, careful of his right shoulder.

She'd never had such a sensation of being at home. Not like this all-consuming feeling of wholeness. Sienna Rose exhaled from the depths of her soul and breathed in the earthy scent of his cologne. She'd always loved the smell. It was uniquely Legend.

"You aren't supposed to be back until tomorrow." She led him to the patio.

"I can leave and come back tomorrow evening if you'd rather."

She pulled him down on the chaise beside her. "Don't you even think about it." She kissed his cheek, then leaned back. "But seriously, what are you doing here? Not that I'm complaining."

She could barely believe he was there with her.

He caressed her cheek. "I couldn't wait to see you."

"How did you know where I live?"

"I'm a detective, remember?" He chuckled as he glanced around the patio. "This is really nice. I don't know that I'd ever leave this patio, given the choice."

"It's my favorite place. Close enough to see the bayou, but far enough away to deter the gators and snakes."

"That's always a good thing." He laughed. "Do you remember that call we had to take where a woman reported an intruder knocking over her trash can and lawn furniture?"

"And it turned out to be an alligator who'd caused havoc with its tail?" She laughed with him, and it felt really good. "I would've preferred to face an intruder."

"Me too."

The night wrapped around them. She noticed him shiver and offered the blanket.

He shook his head. "I'm good."

"Then why are you shivering?" She grinned.

He looked down at his hands and then back up, meeting her gaze. "Actually, I need to tell you something, and I'm nervous about it. I don't know how you'll react." His voice had grown serious.

Her heart skipped a beat, with worry or anticipation, or maybe a little of both.

Surely he wasn't leaving her a second time. She could handle anything except that. "Okay." She instructed her pulse to slow down so she could hear him over the sound in her ears.

Legend shifted to face her, taking her other hand so that he held both. "I quit my job today."

"You what?" She didn't know what she'd been expecting, but it wasn't that.

"I quit my job," he repeated. "I packed up my apartment, loaded everything into my truck, and came home."

Sienna Rose forced herself to breathe normally. "Care to explain?"

"When I got back to New Orleans, I walked around my little apartment, going over the details of my life there. Mementos, pictures, anything like that. Things that prove you're really living. I found nothing. I realized how empty my life was there, and I was reminded of how full it once was, here with you. I realized I had very few personal things in the apartment. A couple of pieces of art that I'd bought, books, dishes, and linens, but it was all generic stuff. Nothing personal that should fill a home."

Her mouth was as dry as sandpaper. She swallowed, but couldn't think of anything to say.

"I realized that my entire life in New Orleans was focused solely on my career. Is that any way to live?" Legend shook his head. "I went into work on Monday, hoping to find my groove again. But it didn't happen. All I could think about was coming back to you."

Her heart pounded, as if it would explode out of her chest, but she wanted him to be certain. To be sure of his choices, so he wouldn't have regrets later and eventually come to resent her.

She wouldn't be able to take that.

"That night, as I walked into my apartment, I realized how lonely I was. I couldn't even enjoy watching my usual sports because the sound echoed off empty walls. The steak I grilled tasted bland, despite all the seasonings I put on. I counted the minutes until I could call you. Seeing you on my computer screen made me realize how much I wanted to be able to hug you and snuggle up in front of the television. I didn't even care what we'd watch as long as I was with you."

All the things she had been feeling since he'd left, but had been too afraid to speak out loud.

"On Tuesday, I felt like I was just going through the motions, and for what? My life wasn't a life. It was an existence, a shell. Then and there I knew I'd be coming back to Envie. Coming home to you. I can't have a real life without you." He paused and searched her face in the dim patio light. "That is, if you'll have me."

She nodded and pulled him into her arms. She could feel his heartbeat, and it danced in time with hers.

"I've missed you so much. I didn't want to tell you how miserable I've been since you left." Sienna Rose smiled at him.

"Why didn't you say anything? Maybe I would have been able to figure it out quicker if you had." He went back to holding her hand. It warmed and comforted her.

"Because we hadn't talked about who would move where, or what to do about our jobs, or if that was even on the table for discussion yet," she explained. "I didn't know how to ask either of us to give up our goals."

"You offered to move to New Orleans. Do you want that?"

"I don't," she admitted. "I mean, I'd like to visit there with you sometime, so you could show me the city, but I really, really don't want to leave Envie. I'm incredibly grateful that you've made the decision." Sienna Rose would have left the small town that had always been her home if that was what it took to be with Legend, but ultimately she was glad she didn't have to.

"Do you think I have a shot of getting hired with the Envie Police?"

She laughed. "Like Chief Savoie wouldn't hire you without a moment's hesitation." Behind the joy, a troubling thought niggled in her brain. "Did you ever hear anything from the review board?"

He shrugged. "Lancaster came by today to tell me that my hearing is scheduled for next week, but I'd already made up my mind that I was leaving. I even had my apartment all packed up, what there was of it anyway. Steele understood my decision. He didn't even seem that surprised. I think he knew before I did."

"That's good that he understood." It made her feel a lot better that he'd already packed up his apartment before the hearing notification.

"Yeah." He let out a heavy sigh, as if the weight of the world sat on his broad shoulders.

"Hey, what's wrong?" Had saying everything out loud made him regret his decision? "Don't shut me out."

Legend smiled. "I'm not shutting you out. I'm trying to figure out how to ask this."

"Whatever it is, just ask." She couldn't remember ever seeing him so stressed over asking her something.

"Okay then. Here goes."

He slid to the ground on one knee and held out an open box. A diamond ring sparkled at her from inside.

"Sienna Rose Jordan, I have loved you for so many years, and I didn't know how deeply until I came back to Envie. You are my home, my everything, the keeper of my heart. Will you do me the honor of becoming my wife?"

Everything inside her trembled with joy. She found that her ability to speak had disappeared, along with any coherent thought. She stood, pulled him up with her, and stepped into his arms. *Home.* And she would never have to leave it again.

He rested his forehead against hers. "I'm going to take that as a yes."

"Good. That's what it is." Sienna Rose's heart pounded against her ribs.

Legend grinned, then kissed the tip of her nose. "Did you even see the ring?"

"It doesn't matter. What's important is you picked it out for me."

"Hold out your hand."

She did, and he slipped it onto her finger. The platinum metal was cool against her skin. On closer inspection, she recognized the design. It was almost an exact replica of her grandmother's wedding set, except the diamond was bigger and the surrounding stones were sapphires instead of diamonds. "How did you manage this?"

"I snuck a photo of your grandmother's wedding that showed her ring. I made a change or two that I thought would suit you better. Do you like it?"

"I love it, and I love you." She reached up and pulled his head down to kiss him.

He was perfect. The ring was perfect.

Everything was perfect.

21

"*M*om, I really don't want a big to-do. It doesn't need to be anything more than you and Dean, Chief Savoie, Captain Brewer, and the rest of the squad. Really small and intimate."

Sienna Rose should have known a lunch out with her mother was a strategic ploy to get wedding information. Her mother was nothing if not sneaky.

The date had been set, the caterer reserved, the flowers ordered, and the DJ contracted. Her few friends, all people from work, had been invited. Almost everything was in place.

Except for what she was going to wear.

Her mom folded her arms over her chest, wearing a no-nonsense expression. "You still have to have a wedding dress, Sienna Rose. Every bride needs a special dress on her big day."

Sienna Rose sighed. "Okay, but nothing fancy. I want something simple. Our wedding is a celebration of starting our life together, not a reason to show off how fancy a party we can put together. I don't want anything to take focus from the meaning of the day."

"I'm sure we can make that work. Let's go to the dress shop now. Dean is with the therapist for another hour. We can at least get an idea of what you might like."

Her mother wouldn't let up until Sienna Rose agreed, so she did. They paid and headed out to her mom's car.

Once her mom had started the engine and pointed them in the direction of the dress shop, she asked, "How's Legend liking the new job?"

His eight weeks of physical therapy were flying by, and then he'd be released to full duty.

"He loves being a deputy. He said it's a lot different than what he's used to, but he really likes his coworkers and he said the sheriff is a good boss."

He'd even told Sienna Rose that he'd like to run for the role himself one day.

Her mother pulled into the boutique's parking lot and claimed a spot. "That's good to hear."

Twenty minutes later, Sienna Rose walked out with a white A-line gown that was soft, timeless, and beautiful. She loved the way it felt on her. She would be able to dance and eat in comfort, and it was exactly what she'd wanted.

After picking up Dean, her mother dropped her off at her house. She loved her days off. It was something she and Legend would have to start coordinating so that they could spend time together. They'd already agreed that they would live in her house.

She glanced around her living room. Soon, her home would hold Legend's belongings as well. They would combine their stuff and their lives. Sienna Rose couldn't wait. Good thing the wedding was mere weeks away.

Flipping through the mail she'd brought in, her heart nearly stopped. The results from her captain's test were there in an envelope, staring her right in the face. Chief Savoie had made it very clear that he was retiring soon and that Captain Brewer would take his place. That would leave a lead captain spot open. If she scored high enough, it would be another dream accomplished.

She set the rest of the mail down and held that one piece very tightly.

Her hands trembled.

Please let me have passed.

Three weeks later

Legend stood at the altar beside Dean. He'd never thought the day would come, and he stood with shaking legs, overwhelmed by emotion. On one hand, he wanted Sienna Rose to hurry down the aisle so they could be married. On the other, he wanted to savor every moment of their special day.

The music changed, and there she was, at the other end of the aisle, walking slowly toward him on her mother's arm. Her beauty took his breath away. The way she smiled at him took his breath away. His heart did backflips.

"She's beautiful," Dean whispered at his side.

"Yes she is," Legend whispered back. He'd never seen anyone more beautiful.

He took her hand as she reached the altar.

How did I get so lucky?

Legend kept his gaze locked onto Sienna Rose's. He was aware that the preacher was talking, but he couldn't concentrate on anything but his soon-to-be-wife. To think, she was going to be his. Forever.

Dean nudged him.

Legend looked at the preacher, who said, "Do you take this woman to love, honor, and respect, for all the days of your life, until death do you part?"

"I do."

The preacher repeated the question to Sienna Rose, who replied with the same vow.

"Do you have the rings?"

Legend turned to Dean, who handed Sienna Rose's ring to Legend, then to Legend's ring to Sienna Rose.

"Please place the ring on her finger."

With shaking hands, Legend slipped the platinum band on his fiancée's petite finger and repeated the vow the preacher recited. "With this ring, I pledge to you all my love, in every way, for the rest of my life."

"Sienna Rose, please place the ring on Legend's finger."

She obeyed, echoing the vow.

The preacher smiled. "By the power invested in me by the state of Louisiana, I hereby pronounce you husband and wife. Legend, you may kiss your bride."

Legend kissed her, putting all his love and promise into it.

Their friends clapped from the pews.

He hated to end the kiss, but there would be more kisses to come. A lifetime of kisses. They were bound together forever.

Legend helped Dean down the stairs from the altar, then took Sienna Rose's hand and walked down with her.

Lillian Leigh met the couple in the aisle, hugging them both. "Come on. Everything's ready at the reception." She led the way out.

Legend wanted nothing more than a few minutes alone with Sienna Rose, to hold her and make sure it wasn't all a dream. But the photographer was waiting.

Once dinner was over, the cake cut and consumed, the band played their favorite song for their first dance. At last, he could hold his new wife in his arms.

"How does it feel to be Mrs. Cruz?" he asked.

She beamed at him, her dark eyes sparkling. "Like I've been gifted a little slice of heaven, right here on earth."

He kissed her, excited to spend the rest of his life with her.

As they had always been meant to do.

PRAISE FOR

❧ The Daniel Fast ❧
for Spiritual Breakthrough

Elmer Towns has taught all the students at Liberty University and Liberty Baptist Theological Seminary to fast the way the Bible teaches. I fully recommend *The Daniel Fast for Spiritual Breakthrough* when you need God to answer a specific prayer.

Dr. Ergun Caner
President, Liberty Baptist Theological Seminary and Graduate School
Lynchburg, Virginia

When we were building our new facility in 2007, our staff committed to a 21-day Daniel Fast. We had a target date of March 2008 to be in our building. We knew that was a stretch, but we believed God for that date. During our fast, we discovered that the building crews were well ahead of schedule and we would actually celebrate Christmas 2007 in our new facility. God showed up in a big way, and 1,000 people were added to our services when we moved in. We believe it was a direct result of our focused prayer and fasting that God was able to do what even the construction crews could not explain. We have since made it a practice to do an annual fast, and we encourage our congregation to join with us.

Matt Fry
Lead Pastor of C3 Church, Clayton, North Carolina

This book is meant for this moment! The Holy Spirit is calling each believer to lay hold of the *power of fasting with prayer!* Daniel's prayer and fasting literally affected a shaping of history at a desperate time in the ancient world. Today, we are at a profound, prophetic intersection in time—one calling us to lay hold of the practical guidelines unfolded in this book. *The Daniel Fast for Spiritual Breakthrough* shows how God's people can see the same results in our generation but on Jesus' terms: "This kind can come out by nothing but prayer and fasting" (Mark 9:29).

Dr. Jack W. Hayford
Chancellor, The King's College and Seminary
Founding Pastor, The Church On The Way

When our church was having difficulty getting a building permit for its present worship sanctuary, Dr. Towns came and taught a seminar on fasting. Then we as a congregation fasted to intervene in what seemed like an "immovable mountain." God turned around an impossible situation, and we now are using that building to reach our community with the love and message of Jesus Christ. *The Daniel Fast for Spiritual Breakthrough* is a great spiritual tool for the work of the Kingdom.

Tom Mullins
Senior Pastor, Christ Fellowship, Palm Beach Gardens, Florida

Elmer Towns has been a friend of mine since the early 1970s and has made a contribution to my church both in Sunday school growth and the enrichment of prayer ministry. I've had him preach at pastoral conferences at my church on fasting and, in my opinion, he is a modern-day expert on fasting. The stories he tells in this book about how I led my church in a Daniel Fast indicate our commitment to fasting and prayer. Fasting remains a regular discipline among many of our people . . . and is part of my life.

Ron Phillips
Senior Pastor, Abba's House, Chattanooga, Tennessee

About two years after entering full-time ministry, I heard Dr. Towns speak on the power of fasting. Sadly, fasting was not part of my "Christian discipleship" process until that point. Since then, I have sought to incorporate fasting in my regular disciplines and into my church leadership, and I have experienced the spiritual power of fasting each time. This book is perfect for a personal or church-wide fast, and the daily readings will be an ever-present encouragement to you as you experience God's blessings through a planned season of fasting.

Nelson Searcy
Lead Pastor, The Journey Church (New York City)
Founder, ChurchLeaderInsights.com

Elmer Towns is a man who breathes with God! His insights come as if from heaven itself. Every ounce of this book is as powerful as a pound of dynamite! Elmer previously wrote a bestselling book on fasting, and now he has added even more to our spiritual arsenal. This book taught me something I did not know: targeted fasting, and how to aim for and hit a bull's eye in the spirit. Ready! Aim! Fast!

Tommy Tenney
Founder and CEO of GodChasers.network
Pineville, Louisiana

The
DANIEL
FAST
for Spiritual Breakthrough

ELMER L. TOWNS

BETHANYHOUSE

a division of Baker Publishing Group
Minneapolis, Minnesota

© 2010 by Elmer L. Towns

Published by Bethany House Publishers
11400 Hampshire Avenue South
Bloomington, Minnesota 55438
www.bethanyhouse.com

Bethany House Publishers is a division of
Baker Publishing Group, Grand Rapids, Michigan

Bethany House edition published 2014
ISBN 978-0-7642-1596-4

Previously published by Regal Books

Printed in the United States of America

Library of Congress Control Number: 2014955386

Unless otherwise indicated, Scripture quotations are from the New King James Version. Copyright © 1982 by Thomas Nelson, Inc. Used by permission. All rights reserved.

Scripture quotations labeled CEV are from the Contemporary English Version © 1991, 1992, 1995 by American Bible Society. Used by permission.

Scripture quotations labeled CJB are from the *Complete Jewish Bible*, copyright © 1998 by David H. Stern. Published by Jewish New Testament Publications, Inc. www.messianicjewish.net/jntp. Distributed by Messianic Jewish Resources. www.messianicjewish.net. All rights reserved. Used by permission.

Scripture quotations labeled CSB are from the Holman Christian Standard Bible, copyright 1999, 2000, 2002, 2003 by Holman Bible Publishers. Used by permission.

Scripture quotations labeled ELT represent the author's paraphrase of Scripture.

Scripture quotations labeled KJV are from the King James Version of the Bible.

Scripture quotations labeled THE MESSAGE are from *The Message* by Eugene H. Peterson, copyright © 1993, 1994, 1995, 2000, 2001, 2002. Used by permission of NavPress Publishing Group. All rights reserved.

Scripture quotations labeled NASB are from the New American Standard Bible®, copyright © 1960, 1962, 1963, 1968, 1971, 1972, 1973, 1975, 1977, 1995 by The Lockman Foundation. Used by permission.

Scripture quotations labeled NET are from the NET BIBLE®, copyright © 2003 by Biblical Studies Press, L.L.C. www.netbible.com. Used by permission. All rights reserved.

Scripture quotations labeled NIV are from the Holy Bible, New International Version®. NIV®. Copyright © 1973, 1978, 1984, 2011 by Biblica, Inc.™ Used by permission of Zondervan. All rights reserved worldwide. www.zondervan.com

Scripture quotations labeled NLT are from the *Holy Bible*, New Living Translation, copyright © 1996, 2004, 2007 by Tyndale House Foundation. Used by permission of Tyndale House Publishers, Inc., Carol Stream, Illinois 60188. All rights reserved.

Scripture quotations labeled *Phillips* are from The New Testament in Modern English, revised edition—J. B. Phillips, translator. © J. B. Phillips 1958, 1960, 1972. Used by permission of Macmillan Publishing Co., Inc.

Scripture quotations labeled TEV are from the Good News Translation—Second Edition. Copyright © 1992 by American Bible Society. Used by permission.

Scripture quotations labeled TLB are from *The Living Bible*, copyright © 1971. Used by permission of Tyndale House Publishers, Inc., Wheaton, Illinois 60189. All rights reserved.

Note: The fasts suggested in this book are not for everyone. Consult your physician before beginning. Expectant mothers, diabetics, and others with a history of medical problems can enter the spirit of fasting while remaining on essential diets. While fasting is healthful to many, the nature of God would not command a physical exercise that would harm people physically or emotionally.

green press INITIATIVE

Dedicated to the memory of Jerry Falwell, my pastor,
who challenged me to my first day of fasting; and to Bill Bright,
who motivated me to my first 40-day fast. Also dedicated to
David Yonggi Cho, pastor of the world's largest church,
who challenged me to teach the ministerial students at Liberty
University to fast before seeking their first pastorate.

❦ Contents ❧

SECTION 3

APPENDICES

Is this not the fast that I have chosen: To loose the bonds of wickedness, to undo the heavy burdens, to let the oppressed go free, and that you break every yoke? Is it not to share your bread with the hungry, and that you bring to your house the poor who are cast out; when you see the naked, that you cover him, and not hide yourself from your own flesh? Then your light shall break forth like the morning, your healing shall spring forth speedily, and your righteousness shall go before you; the glory of the LORD *shall be your rear guard.*

ISAIAH 58:6-8

The Impact of a Daniel Fast

In January 1998, our church entered into our Daniel Fast in the first three weeks of January. We had begun this practice several years before and had begun a cycle of harvest and multiplication in small groups.

It was on the fifteenth day of this fast that my wife and I were leaving Baton Rouge on the way to San Antonio to minister. As we drove around the curve where the governor's mansion is visible, in my spirit I saw a wind blow the door open (a brief mental image of this flashed across my mind as I looked over at the mansion). I told Melanie, my wife, "I believe God is about to open a door to the governor's mansion for a Bible study."

We ended the twenty-first day of the fast in San Antonio and returned to Baton Rouge. There, on my desk, was a note that the governor's secretary had called. When we returned her call, she told us that the governor had been exercising on his treadmill one week before when a daily 90-second program I have done for years came on the local affiliate. A voice inside of the governor said to him, "Call and ask this man to come teach you the entire Bible in four lessons."

This invitation was especially amazing because I had never met the governor before. On the appointed day, he was gathered with 15 of his top staff for the occasion. I taught them four Bible lessons: "creation," "chosen people," "Christ" and "the Church." At the end of the month, the governor asked that I continue. The Bible study continued through the remainder of his term and four additional years after his re-election! Many times I was able to pray with this group for miracles that stopped hurricanes, broke drought over the state, and brought great favor to this governor. He became the most popular governor our state has had in recent times before his retirement in 2004.

I am persuaded that this mighty open door came through the power of prayer and fasting. Even as Daniel himself prayed and fasted, God opened the doors to the highest levels of government and authority. After Paul's fast in Antioch (see Acts 13), God opened the door to the highest official in Cyprus, Sergius Paulus. Only the power of the Daniel Fast can bring a breakthrough in the United States and state governments, and my experience with the Governor of Louisiana is living proof of that reality.

Larry Stockstill
Senior Pastor, Bethany World Prayer Center
Baker, Louisiana

❧ INVITATION ❧

Welcome to *The Daniel Fast for Spiritual Breakthrough*. This book was written as a guide for your fast. You'll read an explanation of how the Daniel Fast was named, why it's either 10 or 21 days, what you should eat and how you should discipline yourself in a fast.

This book will also examine some of your prayer experiences while fasting. Perhaps you've committed to pray throughout the 10 or 21 days of your fast and, at the same time, fast for a prayer goal. You'll learn many practical tips on prayer. You'll learn how to encounter God, worship God and pray specifically for answers. You'll look at the role of weeping, repenting and what it means to crucify yourself. Then you'll learn some principles of warfare prayer and what it means to pray desperately.

If this is your first time ever to fast, this book will relieve some of your fears and explain some of the things you are experiencing while fasting. So read to get confidence in prayer and overcome anxiety; but most of all, read to get answers to your prayers.

As I wrote this book, I fasted several times, in several different ways. I was fasting and praying that God would show me what to write and help me prepare this book so that you would touch God as you read and fast; but more importantly, that God would touch you.

Written from my home at the
foot of the Blue Ridge Mountains,
Elmer L. Towns, 2009

❧ SECTION 1 ❧

About the Daniel Fast

What Is Fasting?

I was told that no one had written a bestselling book on fasting in 100 years, so when I wrote *Fasting for Spiritual Breakthrough* in 1996, I wanted some feedback. I mailed a typed copy of the manuscript to Pastor Ron Phillips of Central Baptist Church in greater Chattanooga, Tennessee. A few days later, I received a strange phone call.

"You're a dirty dog," the voice on the line said.

"Who's calling me a dirty dog?" I asked.

"This is Ron Phillips," he said with a laugh. Ron was a friend of mine; I had been to his church two or three times to hold Sunday School growth campaigns. "I'm at the Southern Baptist Convention," he went on, explaining his joking remark. "I should be attending meetings . . . and voting . . . and talking to my buddies down in the hallways, but I'm glued to this hotel room reading your book. This book is so good that it will change my life."

Before the phone call was over, Ron convinced me to come to his church to teach a Saturday seminar on the principles of fasting. So we set a date, and Ron sent out the invitations. He expected that 800 people would attend, but only 157 showed up. The reason for the lower attendance was because Ron had asked them to come and *fast* that day. Many people were scared away because they didn't know how to fast or didn't understand what God could do for them if they fasted. That convinced me that more needed to be written on fasting—whether it was a bestseller or not.

So, what does it mean to "fast"?

Definition

*Fast (fa:st, -æ-): To abstain from food, or to restrict oneself to
a meager diet, either as a religious observance or as a ceremonial
expression of grief; to go without food; also (contextually)
to go without drink; to pass (time) fasting; to keep or observe
(a day, etc.) as a time of abstinence.*[1]

God created the human body to require food to keep it operating. To make sure the body gets fuel, God created within us an
appetite for food, called hunger. Eating satisfies our appetite and
gives us the strength to do the activities we need to do throughout
our day. So why would a person choose to fast—to go without food
for a period of time?

From God's perspective, the reason is simple. Fasting can be
used to accomplish a spiritual purpose. In the Old Testament, the
Israelites were commanded to fast once each year: "In the seventh
month, on the tenth day, you shall go without eating" (Lev. 16:29,
CEV). This fast took place on the Day of Atonement (Yom Kippur). On this day, the high priest would conduct special sacrifices
to atone for the sins of the people. During the service, the high
priest entered into the Holy of Holies in the center of the Temple—
the only time of the year that he was allowed inside. God wanted
His people to fast on this day in order to remember the experience
of their salvation. Eveyone fasted in order to identify with the high
priest, who sacrificed a lamb for the forgiveness of their sins.

Today, as Christians we live under grace, so we are no longer *required* to fast. However, Jesus makes it clear in Matthew 6:16 that
we are *allowed* to fast for certain reasons: "Moreover, when you fast,
do not be like the hypocrites, with a sad countenance. For they dis-
figure their faces that they may appear to men to be fasting. Assuredly, I say to you, they have their reward." Likewise, in Matthew
9:15, He states, "Can the friends of the bridegroom mourn as long
as the bridegroom is with them? But the days will come when the
bridegroom will be taken away from them, and then they will fast."
We also see the apostles in the Early Church fasting for a spiritual
purpose: "As they ministered to the Lord and fasted, the Holy

Spirit said, 'Now separate to Me Barnabas and Saul for the work to which I have called them.' Then, having fasted and prayed, and laid hands on them, they sent them away" (Acts 13:2-3). Many people who have never fasted before get nervous about the prospects of abstaining from food. They wonder if they will get hungry and if the hunger pains will make it too difficult for them to continue. They anticipate that it will be an unpleasant experience—probably many of the same concerns that the members of Central Baptist Church felt when Ron Phillips asked them to fast. However, keep in mind that fasting will not hurt any more than dieting to get thinner. It will also not harm you; in fact, some studies show fasting is actually good for the body, as it eliminates toxins from the body.

The purpose of fasting is not to make an outward show of your religious dedication to God, but rather to make a personal commitment between you and God. It's not always easy—like any spiritual discipline, you will undoubtedly encounter resistance and opposition. So embark on your Daniel Fast—or any fast you undertake—with the full understanding of what you are doing. Know also that although the path may be difficult, the rewards will be great.[2]

My Time to Pray

Lord, I pray that You will guide me as I begin this time of fasting.
AMEN.

Notes

1. See http://dictionary.oed.com/cgi/entry/50082578?query_type=word&queryword=fast&first=1&max_to_show=10&sort_type=alpha&search_id=ydSC-7mmrRh-7573&result_place=1, s.v. "fast" (accessed July 1, 2009).
2. For a further explanation of the purpose of fasting, see *The Beginner's Guide to Fasting* (Ventura, CA: Regal, 2001), pp. 9-15.

❧ 2 ❧

What Is a Daniel Fast?

Jentezen Franklin, pastor of the Free Chapel in Gainesville, Georgia—a congregation with 10,000 in attendance—begins each year with a 21-day Daniel Fast. Everyone participates in some measure. Some people in the church fast for one day, others for three days, some for one week, and many for the full 21 days. Jentezen has said, "I've had people testify that only three days into a fast for a loved one suffering from cancer, the cancer was completely cured at this point. Another lady's son was dying from 107-degree fever, associated with his leukemia. The very first day of the fast the boy's fever broke and he didn't suffer a trace of brain damage!"[1]

Jentezen believes it is important in the spiritual growth of the congregation at Free Chapel to fast and sacrifice for God at the beginning of every new year. Some fast to break their addiction to junk food, some fast to break the power of an uncontrollable appetite, and some fast to break addiction to nicotine, alcohol or drugs, but most fast to know God intimately. Jentezen Franklin has said, "Each year I encourage all the members of Free Chapel to join us in our 21-day fast. If in 21 days you can be a new person, why go the rest of your life feeling sick, weak, overweight, and run down? Why not take a radical step of faith? We have only one life to give God—let's get control of our bodies and go for God with the best we have!"[2]

So, how did Daniel get a fast named after him? In other words, why did Daniel fast? Daniel was 16 years old when the Babylonians took him captive. At that time, the king of Babylon was Nebuchadnezzar. Daniel had served in the king's court in Jerusalem, so he was being prepared for some type of government service in Babylon. Nebuchadnezzar chose Daniel because he wanted "young men in whom *there was* no blemish, but good-looking, gifted in all wisdom, possessing knowledge and quick to understand" (Dan. 1:4, emphasis added).

Nebuchadnezzar wanted Daniel "to serve in the king's palace" (v. 4) and help him administer his rule over the Jews, God's people. But he wanted Daniel to be "Babylonian." So, "the king appointed for them [Daniel and three of his friends] a daily provision of the king's delicacies and of the wine which he drank" (v. 5).

To a teenager today, the word "delicacies" means foods like pizza or ice cream . . . and he or she might also include beer and alcohol—and even drugs—to the list. But Daniel didn't choose luxuries; rather, "Daniel purposed in his heart that he would not defile himself with the portion of the king's delicacies, nor with the wine" (v. 8). Notice the word "purposed" in this passage. The secret to a Daniel Fast is to *purpose* in your heart; that is, to make a vow as you enter the fast that you will purpose to follow the Lord in what you eat and drink.

What did Daniel choose to eat? The *King James Version* of the Bible says that Daniel told his supervisor, "Prove thy servants, I beseech thee, ten days; and let them give us *pulse* to eat, and water to drink" (v. 12, emphasis added). The newer translations use the word "vegetables" for "pulse," which were probably leafy vegetables such as lettuce, turnip greens, cabbage, spinach and collard greens. So, Daniel ate a "salad" diet. What were the results? "At the end of ten days their features appeared better and fatter in flesh than all the young men who ate the portion of the king's delicacies" (v. 15).

The test that Daniel proposed to his supervisor appears to be a simple one, and as you enter the Daniel Fast, you may choose to eat only vegetables for 10 days. However, you may also choose to partake in a longer version of the Daniel Fast, as recorded in chapter 10: "I ate no pleasant food, no meat or wine came into my mouth" (v. 3). Daniel continued with this fast for 21 days, "till three whole weeks were fulfilled" (v. 3).

The phrase "pleasant food" is interesting in this passage. "Pleasant food" means food that you would consider pleasant to your taste, such as steak, clam chowder, fried shrimp, escargot, veal cutlets with provolone, and so on. The *NIV* translates it "choice food," the *CEV* calls it "fancy food," the *CSB* and *TLB* translate it "rich food," the *Complete Jewish Bible* translates the phrase "only food that satisfies me," and *The Companion Bible* translates it "bread of desires." All of these definitions point to the same issue: During a Daniel Fast, you give up the things you enjoy eating and eat only what is necessary. Therefore, the Daniel Fast is an expression of abstinence for purposes of self-discipline.

My Time to Pray
Lord, I purpose to follow You in what I eat and drink.
A M E N .

Notes

1. Jentezen Franklin, *Fasting: Opening the Door to a Deeper, More Intimate, More Powerful Relationship with God* (Lake Mary, FL: Charisma House, 2008), p. 55.
2. Ibid., p. 42.

Why Choose to Fast?

Daniel and his three friends were put through a Babylonian "training program" to prepare them to become managers of programs for a foreign government. Part of the Babylonians' religion was a special diet, so the young men were immersed in Babylonian customs, laws, values and beliefs.

Daniel and his friends asked to be excused from eating the meat and drinking the wine. Perhaps this was because the food was offered to idols, and eating it would have compromised their separation from false gods. Perhaps the wine was intoxicating, which would have violated their Jewish practice. Or perhaps the food included non-kosher meat, which would have violated the Jewish dietary laws. Whatever the cause, Daniel knew the king's food was off limits to him and his three friends.

So Daniel purposed in his heart that he would not defile himself with the portion of the king's delicacies (see Dan. 1:8). Was this a choice for good health, or to keep his body separated to God? It was both! Daniel wanted God's will for his body. And isn't that what you want for your body, too, during your Daniel Fast?

The Daniel Fast is not primarily a dietary choice; it is a *spiritual vow* to God. You may lose weight during your fast, or you may lower your blood pressure or cholesterol, and while these results are good, they are not the primary focus of the fast. Instead, you are fasting for a *spiritual focus*. Improved health is always a *secondary* result of doing the Daniel Fast. Look at what happens when you begin a Daniel Fast. First, you reevaluate your life in light of

God's perspective. Second, you break some bad eating habits, which will begin to restore you to better health. If you join with your church or other Christian group as you do the Daniel Fast to pray for a spiritual goal, you also build up your self-control. The outward accountability you gain in doing the fast with others will strengthen your self-discipline.

When you begin a Daniel Fast, you also begin the process of purifying your body from fats and perhaps other negative side effects that come from eating meat. You repent of sin (probably not the sin of eating meat, but other sins associated with the flesh) and are drawn closer to God through the experience. In fact, many people who participate in a Daniel Fast testify that they are closer to God when they fast than any other time in their life. Why? Because they are obeying God *every minute of the day*. When you're fasting, you're aware of your stomach all the time, which makes you aware of the reason you are abstaining from food—intimacy with God—as you fast.

A final reason to choose to fast is that it leads to worshiping God. When you fast and pray, you honor the Lord with your body *and* soul.

My Time to Pray

Lord, be glorified in my body during my Daniel Fast.
AMEN.

❖ 4 ❖

Why Vow?

The Daniel Fast is a *lengthy vow*; it is longer than a one-day fast (such as the Yom Kippur Fast, in which Jewish people traditionally fast for a 24-hour period). As we previously noted, Daniel and his young friends fasted for 10 days (see Dan. 1), and then later, Daniel fasted for 21 days (see Dan. 11).

Regardless of whether you are fasting for 10 days or for 21 days, the two questions you should be asking yourself are the same: (1) *Why am I fasting?* and (2) *What do I want to accomplish with this fast?* Technically, you should be fasting for focus and commitment to a project or for an answer to prayer. In this Daniel Fast, you've made a vow of abstinence to get the answer from God you seek. You've vowed to fast and pray for an answer from God.

The Daniel Fast is a *time vow*, so you need to decide ahead of time how long you will fast and then be firm to that commitment to the end. Because I've written several books on fasting, I receive letters from people who tell me about their experiences with fasting. On occasion, some individuals will tell me that they are on the forty-second day of a 40-day fast and are enjoying the experience so much that they don't want to stop. They ask, "What should I do?" I write back and tell them to stop immediately. Their fast was a *time vow*. They should begin on time, keep the promise to fast the entire time, and end on time.

The Daniel Fast is also a *discipline vow*. You strengthen your character in every area of your life when you fulfill your Daniel Fast. When you take control of your body—your outer self—you begin to take control of your inner character. You discipline your body to glorify the Lord.

The Daniel Fast is a *spiritual commitment*. You pray while fasting for a *spiritual goal*. Remember, fasting will not accomplish much without serious, sacrificial prayer. As you discipline your body, you are disciplining your prayer life.

The Daniel Fast is a *faith vow*. In Mark 11:22, Jesus exhorted His disciples, "Have faith in God." To explain how they could express their faith, He directed them, "Whoever says to this mountain [problem or goal], 'Be removed and be cast into the sea,' and does not doubt in his heart, but believes that those things he says will be done, he will have whatever he says" (v. 23). When Daniel began his fast, he made a statement of faith to eat only vegetables and drink water. Likewise, your fast is a verbal statement of what you want God to do.

The Daniel Fast is a *partial vow*. You don't give up all food (an absolute fast), nor do you go on just a juice fast (a normal fast). Instead, you omit certain foods that you would typically eat or eliminate certain meals for a specified period of time. This may include omitting one or two meals a day for a certain length of time, or it may involve omitting other practices.

The Daniel Fast is a *healthy vow*. You abstain from "party" food, or junk food. Usually, you don't eat between meals, and you only eat healthy foods.

Finally, the Daniel Fast is a *lifestyle vow*. When Daniel asked permission to avoid the king's delicacies for 10 days, he put his whole life into his chosen diet. Then, if he continued to look "healthy," he could continue following his own diet.

Some who take a vow against alcoholic beverages take a life-long vow—they commit to never taste alcoholic drinks again. They may make this vow for health reasons, because alcohol consumption can lead to cirrhosis of the liver and premature death. Some people make the vow because of addiction to alcohol—they have been a slave to it. Still others vow not to taste alcohol for spiritual reasons, because they believe drinking alcohol is wrong. (My father died an alcoholic, and my family suffered poverty and other problems because of his addiction. I have read the Scriptures closely and personally I conclude that drinking in any form is wrong.) In the Bible, John the Baptist, the prophet Samuel, and Samson made lifelong vows to avoid alcohol. If we want to honor the Lord as they did, we should follow their example in their Nazirite vow (see Num. 6:1-8).

Take note that nowhere in the Bible are believers commanded to observe a Daniel Fast. We have been given freedom to eat; and we eat healthy to stay healthy. God told Peter, "Rise, Peter; kill and eat" (Acts 10:13), thereby discontinuing ceremonial laws. So whenever you eat good food, eat with a good conscience to the glory of God. "Whatever you do, do it heartily, as to the Lord" (Col. 3:23). But still, some will feel guilty when they end their Daniel Fast and return to their normal eating habits. But remember, in the Old Testament, God prescribed only one day for fasting (Yom Kippur or the Day of Atonement) but seven feast days. So God likes for His people to eat, enjoy their food and be happy.

Some food, however, is not good for you. America seems to be living in a day of epidemic obesity because some eat too much while others continually eat the wrong foods. This is why believers should pledge themselves to a lifelong Daniel lifestyle, not just a Daniel Fast. For the Daniel lifestyle is a healthy lifestyle: "At the end of ten days their features [Daniel and his three friends] appeared better and fatter in the flesh than all the young men who ate the portion of the King's delicacies" (Dan. 1:15). And this lifestyle leads to a clearer mind and better thinking: "The king interviewed them, and among them none was found like Daniel . . . and in all manners of wisdom *and* understanding about which the king examined them, he found them ten times better than all the magicians *and* astrologists" (Dan. 1:19-20).

My Time to Pray

Lord, I will fast for the entire length of my fast. I will keep the time period of my vow. I will discipline my physical body, and I will discipline my prayer life.

Lord, I will fast and pray for my goal. I give up pleasure to seek Your presence and pray for my goal. Strengthen my body as I fast.

Lord, I want You to be glorified in my body. I fast to obey Your Word, and I pray to worship You with my fast.

Lord, I will eat healthy food so that I will be healthy. Give me wisdom to choose healthy food and the discipline to stick to my choice. Protect me from germs, bacteria, poisons and toxins that could damage my health. Protect me when I can't protect myself.
AMEN.

What Can I Withhold?

In the first chapter, I told the story of how Ron Phillips, pastor of Central Baptist Church in greater Chattanooga, Tennessee, invited me to come to his church to teach a seminar on fasting. I taught the Saturday seminar from 9:00 A.M. to 3:00 P.M. When I finished, Ron jumped up in front of the people and excitedly said to them, "We've got to organize ourselves to pray. We are a typical Southern Baptist church that organizes everything but prayer."

Ron asked everyone to take a visitor's card out of the pew, fill it out, and promise to fast one day each month for the church. People reached into the pew rack to make a written vow. At least 123 members signed up.

Ron continued his motivation. "We just had a revival meeting this week—Sunday through Wednesday—but not much happened. There were 12 decisions at the altar, and some of those were just children getting ready to be baptized." Ron spoke of desiring a congregation-shaking revival that came by prayer and fasting. He appointed a lady on the spot to be the prayer coordinator to organize the people so there would be one person "covering the church" every day of each month by fasting and prayer. He also assigned several people to cover the church each Sunday with fasting and prayer.

Ron's preaching took on a decidedly "spiritual" nature as a result of that conference. He called the church to sincere prayer and fasting. A few months later, another evangelistic campaign was held, and there were 998 decisions at the altar. Sunday School attendance jumped to 258, Sunday worship attendance jumped to 401, and the church received approximately $500,000 more that month than in the same month the previous year. Fasting and prayer works.

God honored the church's spiritual commitment. Two years later, the church was bulging at the seams. They now had three worship services and needed desperately to build larger facilities. So during one service, Ron passed out a card and asked the people to enter a 40-day fast with him, the deacons and the church staff. The idea of a 40-day fast scared most of the congregation. Ron smiled and told them it was a different kind of fast. He was suggesting a Daniel Fast.

Ron held up a card and asked each member to read the four prayer requests printed on the front. The first request was to pray for the size of the new auditorium. The present sanctuary seated 600, so Ron asked the people to pray whether they should build 1,200 seats, 2,400 seats, 3,600 seats, or 4,800 seats. "The decision is not ours; it's God's decision," he said. "Let's find His will by fasting and prayer."

The second request was about the type of sanctuary they should build. Ron asked them to fast and pray about whether they should build a traditional Southern Baptist sanctuary or a performing arts auditorium like those found in a civic center, so the church could have television productions, musicals and various activities.

The third request was about the location of their property. God had given the church a large piece of property that stretched from one major highway to another, around the back of businesses. He challenged the congregation, "Let's make the decision where to locate the new bulding by prayer and fasting."

The fourth request was for finances. They would need money equal to the size of their vision.

Ron then turned the card over to reveal several ways the people could fast for the items they wanted from God. "I'm going to explain the importance of each activity," he announced, "and then ask you to make a 40-day vow to fast and pray in just one of these ways for the spiritual future of the church." These are the guidelines he explained to his congregation:

- *One meal each day.* The fast is not about only giving up food, but also includes praying during a mealtime. Jesus said, "Could you not watch with Me one hour?" (Matt. 26:40). It takes about an hour to prepare a meal or travel to a restaurant or get ready to eat, so this time is a perfect opportunity to pray. Those who work in hot, exhausting jobs cannot fast completely because they need their strength and stamina for physical exertion, but they can sacrifice one meal a day for God.

- *Two meals each day.* Some people can pray for two hours each day, sacrificing two meals to God.

- *Eat only vegetables.* The Daniel Fast involves giving up meats, desserts and snacks, eating only the food that Daniel ate. While the fast doesn't give extra time to pray, it is a commitment of the heart that, when joined with prayer, moves the heart of God.

- *Give up television.* Secular folks might laugh at "fasting television"—sacrificing television—but it is a commitment to God to put Christ first. This is a spiritual choice in response to Christ, who promised, "Seek first the kingdom of God and His righteousness, and all these things shall be added to you" (Matt. 6:33).

- *Give up sports.* Giving up bowling, golfing, fishing, jogging or any other activity for 40 days to pray during that time is a choice to put spiritual exercise above physical exercise. "Bodily exercise profits little, but godliness is profitable for all things" (1 Tim. 4:8).

- *Give up pleasure reading.* Beyond required reading for a job or preparing Sunday School lessons at church, pleasure reading can be turned into prayer time. You could also give up newspaper reading for prayer.

- *Other.* This is a flexible area. Individuals can fast from anything that God brings to mind.

- *Vow.* This "faith commitment" requires the person to sign a card as a commitment to God, not to the church or to the pastor.

- *Restrict cell phone and text messaging activities.* While some use of these communication devices may be necessary, they are serious time-consuming factors to curtail during a Daniel Fast. (In the fourth quarter of 2008, teens text-messaged approximately an average of 2,272 text messages per month—almost 80 messages a day.[1])

- *Use of iPhone or MP3 players.* Some have restricted their listening of music to only Christian music during a Daniel Fast (praise worship music that prepares the heart for prayer). That means listening to no secular music during a Daniel Fast.

I was at the Metropolitan Church of God in Birmingham, Alabama, where Raymond Culpepper was pastor. (Today he is the head overseer of the Church of God, Cleveland, Tennessee.) His church was attempting to raise $5 million for a youth activity building. The audience of 2,000 people was asked to sign a vow card similar to the one used by Ron Phillips at Central Baptist Church. Pastor Culpepper said, "We will not collect the cards as we collect an offering each Sunday. I want you to come to the church altar, bow in prayer to commit yourself to the vow you are making, and then leave your card on the altar." So many people came to the altar that there was no space left. They knelt in the aisles, and then sailed their cards onto the platform. These people took their vows to pray literally.

What can be learned from these churches? Little things become big in God's sight when they are an expression of one's dedication to God. God takes note of small acts of our love: "Whenever you did this for one of the least important . . . you did it for me" (Matt. 25:40, *TEV*). So, remember, you are not primarily fasting for your church nor primarily to get an answer to prayer or for anything else. You are fasting to God, for you made your vow to Him. "God is not unjust to forget your work and labor of love which you have shown toward His name" (Heb. 6:10).

Daniel Fast Suggestions

Eliminate one meal a day and pray during that mealtime.

Eliminate two meals a day, and pray during their times.

Eliminate all desserts.

Eliminate all rich, superfluous foods eaten only for pleasure.

Eat only necessities, and only during mealtime (no snacks).

Eliminate all drinks except water
(no coffee, tea, soda or purchased drinks).

Contemporary Interpretations of the Daniel Fast

No text messaging or Facebook or Twitter communications that take your thoughts away from God.

No secular music; only praise and worship music.

No newspaper or pleasure reading; give that time to prayer.

No television; give that time to prayer.

No recreational sports; give that time to prayer.

No sex. "Both husband and wife to refrain from sexual intimacy for a limited time, so they can give themselves completely to prayer" (1 Cor. 7:5, *NLT*).

My Time to Pray

*Lord, I dedicate small things to express the greatness of
Your supremacy in all of life.*

*Lord, I will be faithful in little expressions of my faith for
great answers to prayer.*

*Lord, I vow to fulfill these small expressions
of my love to You.*
A M E N .

Note

1. Katie Hafner, "Texting May Be Taking a Toll," *New York Times*, May 26, 2009, sec. Health. http://www.nytimes.com/2009/05/26/health/26teen.html?_r=2&em> (accessed June 10, 2009).

❦ 6 ❦

What Is the Primary Focus of the Daniel Fast?

As you enter the Daniel Fast, it is easy to focus on the food you give up or the activities you surrender. It's easy to focus on your abstinence and not on the basic purpose for which you are fasting. But remember that God is not impressed just because you stop eating altogether or you stop eating certain foods, even if you do it for your health. God is not impressed with the outward actions of your fast. The secret of any fast is not what you keep from entering the stomach but what comes out of the heart. God is primarily concerned with your inner person, not your outer body.

In Mark 9:29, Jesus described the spiritual energy needed to remove spiritual barriers: "This kind can come out by nothing but prayer and fasting." So, you must give yourself completely to prayer *and* to fasting. The commitment of your outer body to fasting reflects your inner commitment to prayer. Notice also that the phrase "prayer and fasting" in this verse emphasizes continuous action. This means that you should fast more than once or make fasting a continuous practice. During your Daniel Fast, your decision of what you eat or what you withhold will have more influence on your prayer life than most other spiritual exercises. If you're flippant with the Daniel Fast, you're likely to be flippant with your prayer dedication.

The basic principles of discipleship were not *denial* or *self-discipline*, but following Jesus Christ. Jesus said, "If any one desires to come after Me, let him deny himself, and take up his cross daily, and follow Me" (Luke 9:23). This involves turning to the Lord and putting Him first in your life, and then turning away from anything that keeps you from following Him.

There are three words in this verse that should influence your Daniel Fast. First, the word "deny" means that you should get rid of anything that hinders your relationship with Christ. You must get off of the throne of your heart, and Jesus must sit there and control what you eat and drink. The second word is "daily." Following Jesus means 24-7 dedication, so your Daniel Fast requires a 10-day or 21-day vow accompanied with continuous prayer. The third word is "follow." Just as Jesus fasted in preparation for His spiritual work, so must you follow Jesus' example with a Daniel Fast for your spiritual vow.

My Time to Pray

Lord, I will deny myself enjoyment during my Daniel Fast so that I can seek Your will in my life. I count it a privilege to give up my "pleasant food" for Your glory and as a commitment of my prayer.

Lord, I have made a spiritual vow to You that I will faithfully fast and pray for 10 days or 21 days.

Lord, give me strong outer discipline to keep my outer vow to You, and give me strong inner commitment to pray faithfully for the answer I seek.
AMEN.

How Can I Prepare for My Fast?

In 1971, when I moved to Lynchburg, Virginia, from Greater Chicago, Illinois, there was a downturn in the Chicago real estate market. So I continued to own my home there and make monthly payments on it. I moved into a house in Lynchburg and made monthly payments on that house as well. Each month I prayed for the sale of the Illinois house, but I wasn't praying with a lot of faith. I found it hard to be optimistic when the bottom had dropped out of the market. My eyes were on circumstances, not on God's ability to do the miraculous.

At one point, I said to my wife, "Let's fast together on the fifteenth day of the month for God to sell the Chicago house." The mortgage was due on the fifteenth, while my Lynchburg house payment was due on the first of the month. I had arranged it that way long before thinking about praying for God's intervention. That first month we fasted and prayed, but nothing happened. No word from Chicago. Then I completely forgot about fasting, even though I continued to pray each day for the house to sell.

As I got ready to write the next month's payment, I again said to my wife, "Let's fast together on the fifteenth for God to sell the house." We did, and again nothing happened. No word from Chicago.

I continued praying daily, and Ruth and I fasted on the fifteenth day of each succeeding month, even though nothing was happening. Then, after six months, our realtor called and said,

"Pray . . . I've got a hot one." He was a Christian friend, but I didn't tell him that we were fasting.

At the end of a year, I went to Chicago to sign closing papers for the sale. I was talking casually with the buyer when he mentioned that he had been looking at our house for about a year. He then gave me the exact date that he had first looked at our house, stating, "It was on my wife's birthday." It was the sixteenth day of the month after Ruth and I first prayed—the day after we fasted! The hair on my arms and the back of my neck bristled. *This is God's work,* I thought.

I learned three lessons about fasting and prayer from my first successful fast. First, *when daily prayer is not enough, fasting takes prayer to a higher level.* God knows your heart, but when you demonstrate your sincerity with fasting, God listens attentively and responds.

Second, *there is power in two or more people agreeing to pray and fast together.* Jesus taught, "Again I say to you that if two of you agree on earth concerning anything that they ask, it will be done for them by my Father in Heaven" (Matt. 18:19). So, there is power when you join together with your spouse, your church or with any other group of God's people to pray—especially when you set a goal and make a vow to fast together for that goal.

Third, *persistence is key.* Once you begin fasting, don't quit. I am afraid to think what would have happened if Ruth and I had quit when the house didn't sell the first time we fasted. Continuing to fast demonstrates your faithfulness to God and your belief that He will do something mighty—and that He will do it in answer to your prayer.

Now let's talk in more detail about your fast. As you approach fasting and prayer, there are three items to put in place. First, you need to have a *goal.* In my case, my goal was to sell a house. Second, you need to develop a *plan.* My plan was to fast each month on the fifteenth day of the month. Third, you need to make a *vow*—a promise to complete the fast.

You probably already have a project or goal in mind, but let me suggest that you use a Fasting Checklist similar to the one on the following page. Just as an airplane pilot will go through a checklist to make sure everything is perfect before he starts down the runway—knowing that if even one little item is overlooked, it could cause a

FASTING CHECKLIST

Aim: To sell my house in Greater Chicago.

Affirmation: I believe that God answers my prayer when I ask specifically in Jesus' name and when I meet the conditions of intercession. Therefore, I enter this Daniel Fast asking God to answer prayers for the vow for which I have committed myself.

What I will withhold: This will be a Yom Kippur Fast (i.e., a one-day fast).

Begin: Sundown on the 14th.

End: Sundown on the 15th.

When I will pray: The 15th day of each month.

Biblical basis: Matthew 18:19.

Bible promise: "Again, I tell you that if two of you on earth agree about anything you ask for, it will be done for you by my Father in heaven. For where two or three come together in my name, there am I with them" (Matt. 18:19, *NIV*).

Resources needed: I will write in my prayer journal what God tells me.

Prayer partner: My wife, Ruth.

Steps after fast: Prepare for a fast next month.

crash—so you should be equally diligent when you prepare for your journey. After all, your fast is just as important, if not more important. A pilot is dealing with temporal life, but you are dealing with *spiritual* life. So use the checklist, or make up your own checklist, to ensure that you have thought of everything and that you have all you need to begin your fast, and make copies so that you will have the checklist each time you fast. (The sample checklist on the previous page is based on my experience of fasting and praying for the house in 1972 and will give you an idea of what you can do to record your faith project.)

As you fill out your Fasting Checklist, there are six attitude preparations that will help you accomplish your faith goal. These are:

1. *Focus on your need.* You are going to do something that is not in your normal routine or inclination. You are choosing to not eat (or not participate in other activities) for a purpose. Focus on what you want God to do for you. Write the need exactly; it will help you focus what you are doing in your mind and bring out your sincerity to follow through.

2. *Focus on what you will do.* You are going to do something about the need. You are going to bring the problem to the Lord God of the universe. Focus on your prayer relationship with God to solve the problem.

3. *Begin and end with a purpose.* Some people find they have missed a meal and decide to call it a "fast." Just missing a meal because of circumstances is not a fast unless you purposed beforehand to pray and use the time of not eating for a spiritual purpose. God knows your heart. Also, don't enter into a fast with the idea of seeing how far you can go or how far you can hold out before you have to eat. Begin with purpose and end at the assigned time. Then begin on a specific date and end on a specific date. Finish strong! Then break your fast and eat in victory, with rejoicing.

4. *Gather the needed resources.* Before you begin your fast, gather resources that will be needed during the fast. If you're fasting for a person, get a picture of that person to hold during prayer and to heighten your memory. If you're fasting over bills, spread them out before you as you pray over them. Do the same if you're fasting about hiring or firing someone. Spread out the person's personnel records before you as you pray. Sometimes I select a spiritual book I want to read while fasting. Or it could be some DVD that I want to see or a CD that I want to hear.

5. *Remember the "inner journey principle."* Just as a person never takes a journey without first planning the journey within, so you must prepare yourself inwardly for a fast before you can be successful outwardly. In the same way that inner rings on a tree trunk tell of its growth, you will develop inner character as you control your outward diet.

6. *Make a vow.* Again, remember that fasting is a private vow that you make to God. Even if you are joining with others in your church in doing the fast (or even joining just one other person, such as your spouse), you must deal with the issue privately with God before you join with others.

Filling out a Fasting Checklist will help you think through all the aspects of what you are about to do. Note that you don't have to sign the vow, but I urge you to do so. When you sign a contract with the world, you are pledging yourself to others and what you will do along with them. When you fast with others, they are expecting you to do your part. So sign the checklist as a promise to God and to yourself. The vow says, "God, this is what I will do."

Now it's your turn. As you fill out your checklist for the fasting and prayer project that you are now doing or are considering doing, you may also want to refer to the appendices, as they provide helpful information about reasons for fasting, the various kinds of biblical fasts and practical help for your health in fasting. I recommend that you permanently keep your Fasting Checklist—a record of your faith journey. Hopefully, you will start a notebook of collecting many such documents as you continue to trust God and seek intimacy with Him throughout your lifetime.

My Time to Pray

Lord, I have a great need that I bring to You. Help me fast and pray for this need.

Lord, my faith is not always strong and does not always prevail. "I believe, help my unbelief" (Mark 9:24).

Lord, I vow to fast according to the Fasting Checklist. Help me keep to my vow, and please answer my prayer.
AMEN.

SECTION 2

Daily Readings

Day 1 to Day 7 Overview

Learning About Fasting

A journey of 1,000 miles begins with the first step, and a 10- or 21-day fast begins on Day One. So approach the first day with obedience—praying as sincerely as you will on the last day.

Enter the first day with hope that God will answer and give you the faith project for which you pray.

Don't forget commitment. Determine that you will keep your vow to fast and pray until the end of your committed time. These daily readings are written to instruct you more fully in a Daniel Fast, as well as to motivate you daily to continue to the end.

This Daniel Fast may be the greatest step of faith you've ever taken in your life. May Christ be magnified in your prayer life, and may you experience deep spiritual growth through this fast.

Daily Readings

Day 1: Your Private Prayer in a Daniel Fast
Day 2: Joining Others in a Daniel Fast
Day 3: Daily Commitment During Your Fast
Day 4: Praying and Fasting for a Project
Day 5: Benefits of a Lengthy Fast
Day 6: Saying No in Prayer
Day 7: The Persistence of a Daniel Fast

DAY 1

Your Private Prayer in a Daniel Fast

But you, when you fast, anoint your head and wash your face, so that you do not appear to men to be fasting, but to your Father who is in the secret place; and your Father who sees in secret will reward you openly.

MATTHEW 6:17-18

My granddaughter Beth heard me talking about fasting to the family. She knew I had a bestseller book—*Fasting for Spiritual Breakthrough*—that won the Silver Medallion (second place) for the Evangelical Christian Publishers Association. But I never asked her to fast, nor did I ever carry on a private conversation with her about fasting.

Need is what usually drives us to fasting, and that happened to Beth, a 12-year-old middle school student. Her youth group had a puppet team of which she was a member (she activated one puppet into life). They planned a trip to the juvenile detention center in our city to entertain and present the gospel through singing and puppet-enacted stories to young boys who had gotten into trouble.

No one told Beth to fast, but God put a burden on her heart to see God work through her group's presentation. Beth and her team members prayed together, but she decided to fast alone. She didn't even tell the others what she planned to do.

Beth decided on a one-day fast to pray that some of the detainees in the center would pray to receive Christ. She didn't tell me or tell her parents until she was already in the fast. She said, "Mother, I'm not going to eat this evening; I'm fasting for some guys to get saved when Power Source goes to the juvenile center."

How did Jesus describe a child's faith? He sat a child in the middle of His quarrelling disciples and said, "Of such is the kingdom of heaven" (Matt. 19:14). Read on to find how God honored Beth's faith.

On the afternoon of her fast, Beth ate a snack in her bedroom when she got home from school. She began her fast at sundown and only drank something for the evening meal in her room. She spent some time praying for the puppet presentation, and specifically for her part.

The next morning Beth didn't eat breakfast; she only drank a glass of orange juice (because her grandfather drinks orange juice in the morning when he's fasting). She prayed especially before going to school.

During lunch she got permission to remain in her homeroom and didn't go to the lunchroom. She told me, "All I could think about all afternoon was food."

Then in her youthful innocence she said, "I was glad when the sun went down so I could eat a snack before dinner."

God in heaven sees all the "simple" things we do for Him. While Beth's experience may sound simple to us, this was a huge step of faith for her. And doesn't God measure our step of faith by the maturing of our faith and then reward us accordingly?

So what was the result? Several of the boys prayed to receive Christ at the program. Beth told me later, "I know that God honored my faith, but I did something that was really hard." Then she explained the working of God and how it was reflected in her prayers and the prayers of the other kids. "They didn't seem to pray as hard as I prayed, and when God answered, they didn't seem to rejoice as much as I did."

Praying Alone or with Others?

Sometimes we enjoy praying with other people who can really pray. Their voice is strong and they get through when they talk to God.

They strengthen our faith because we know God will hear them, and He will answer. It's good to pray with others because you can experience their faith, and they strengthen your faith to pray stronger.

But it's also good to pray alone. Someone said, "One intercessor alone with God can move any mountain by moving heaven." Didn't Jesus tell us to enter our prayer closet—alone—and to shut the door behind us (see Matt. 6:6)? Jesus promises, "Your Father who sees in secret will reward you openly" (Matt. 6:6).

Which way is the best way to pray? Privately, or with a group? Both are best at different times. You must walk on both your left leg and your right leg to get anywhere. Those who hobble along on one leg don't get very far, nor do they go very fast, nor is their journey enjoyable and efficient.

Left, right . . . left, right . . . left, right . . . left, right . . . it takes both legs to get anywhere. You must learn to pray both with groups and by yourself.

Because prayer is *relationship*, i.e., talking with God, you can talk to God alone or with a group. You can talk to God in the cab of your pick-up, or you can pray inwardly riding the subway in a crowd or waiting in line for a cashier to check out your purchases at a store.

Private prayer reaches God; so learn to pray inwardly by yourself, or pray silently when standing in a crowd. But also learn to agree in prayer with one other person or with many other persons. You can enjoy being lifted on the wings of a prayer with one or when joined with many.

Solo Prayer

As you read this book, you are on a solo journey of faith. No one has joined you and you are symbolically in your private "prayer closet" praying alone, like Beth. Perhaps you are part of a group fast. Many are fasting and praying for a faith project; but even in the middle of a group effort, this is a private journey for you.

Why? Because it's the first time you've fasted, or you have a hard time opening up to pray with others. That's all right! God can hear your solo prayer, because God responds to anyone who prays in sincerity and faith.

I mentioned the prayer closet earlier. *The Living Bible* translates it as "Go away by yourself . . . pray to your Father secretly" (Matt. 6:6). The *Christian Standard Bible* says, "Go into your private room" (Matt. 6:6). Because prayer is an intimate conversation with God, find your personal, usually quiet, place to do it.

Look at the Bible's illustration of Jesus praying: "As He was praying alone" (Luke 9:18), and again, "He departed again to the mountain by Himself alone" (John 6:15). The Gospel of Mark describes this situation: "After saying good-bye to them, he went to the mountain to pray" (Mark 6:46, *NET*).

When you're talking to God, you may be alone, but you're never lonely. The Lord will be there with you to hear you and encourage you.

My Time to Pray

Lord, I come to the private place alone to seek Your presence.
I am fasting and praying for my vow that I've made to You.
Even when others are praying for the same request, my prayer is private
and personal. I bring it to You.
Lord, grant my request I make to You alone. Amen.

My Answers Today

_____

_____

_____

_____

_____

_____

_____

_____

_____

_____

For suggested recipes, see pages 180-192.

❧ DAY 2 ❧

Joining Others in a Daniel Fast

*Our ability to perceive God's direction in life is directly related
to our ability to sense the inner promptings of His Spirit. God provides
a specific activity to assist us in doing this. . . . Men through whom God
has worked greatly have emphasized the significance of prayer with
fasting. . . . In an extended fast of over three days, one quickly
experiences a great decrease in sensual desires and soon has a
great new alertness to spiritual things.*

BILL GOTHARD

Asking for specific things from God is a rule of His kingdom. Jesus told us, "Ask, and it will be given to you; seek, and you will find; knock, and it will be opened to you" (Matt. 7:7).

Specifically asking is one of the reasons I was converted, and it was motivated by a group of prayer intercessors who prayed throughout most of the summer of 1950. I had just graduated from high school and was accepted into Armstrong Junior College in Savannah, Georgia, with a full scholarship. But prayer was offered for me.

Two twin brothers from Columbia Bible College—Bill and Burt Harding—came to be summer pastors at Bonna Bella Presbyterian Church, about 10 miles from downtown Savannah, and about 5 miles from my home. There was nothing exciting about Bonna Bella, located on a fishing creek with two stores, where streetcar tracks crossed LaRoacha Avenue; but the young twin brothers made Bonna Bella the talk of all Savannah.

I attended a Presbyterian church, and I thought I was saved; I even talked about becoming a minister. But my plans were fluid. I also had won a work scholarship to Georgia Tech University because of some futuristic architectural plans I submitted in a contest.

Little Bonna Bella Presbyterian Church grew from about 20 attendees to more than 50 people under the ministry of Bill and Burt Harding. Groups of teens from different Presbyterian churches around Savannah went to visit the Bonna Bella church because of the excitement going on there.

Bill and Burt Harding lived in a garage apartment over a two-car garage that had a small, screened porch with small wooden stairs leading to the second floor. They held a prayer meeting every morning from 5:00 A.M. to 8:00 A.M. If I had heard about this prayer meeting, I wouldn't have gone. I had never heard of people individually or as a group praying that long.

Bill told the small congregation, "Come and pray on your way to work. You don't need to stay the whole time, nor do you need to come every day."

The brothers convinced the believers in that community that they could change the world by prayer. "You can pray for a young person who'll become a missionary who will take the gospel around the world."

They had a list of about 60 names of young people that they left on the porch to guide the intercessors to pray for each one.

I never went to the prayer meeting, and I only heard about it after I got saved. But that prayer meeting did influence the world.

The brothers would divide the morning prayer shift: one brother would meet prayer warriors from 5:00 A.M. to 6:30 A.M., and the other brother from 6:30 A.M. to 8:00 A.M. The next day they did the reverse.

The porch was small—long and narrow—not more than four or five people could fit on this screened porch, six at the max. There was a big flat grassy yard in front of the garage apartment for parking, which accommodated more cars than people.

The people of Bonna Bella were all blue-collar mill workers, but they were real people. No rich folk there, no millionaires or anyone trying to be a millionaire. They just worked for a paycheck, took care of their families and tried to do right. But they believed Bill and Burt, and they tried to influence the world by praying for revival and for the 60 names on that sheet of paper.

It was still dark at 5:00 A.M. when the first car drove up to the front of the garage apartment and cut off the lights. A solitary figure climbed the stairs in the moonlight and knelt by the springs of an old rusty Army cot. One of the twins knelt by the squeaking old glider, the kind they don't make anymore. He could barely read the names by the yellow insect repellent light bulb in the ceiling. Then he would begin to bang on the windows of heaven:

Lord, save Elmer Towns . . .
Lord, save Arthur Winn . . .
Lord, save L. J. McEwen . . .
Lord, save Ann Perry . . .
Lord, save . . .

Then the prayer intercessor would pray for the names on that list, as well as for their little church and for revival, and finally for the world. "Lord, may one of these young persons get saved and influence the world."

In July 1950, the twins invited Joel Ortendahl, their friend from Columbia Bible College, to come preach a week of revival. The first day, Mr. and Mrs. Ernie Miller went forward to get saved. The next night Mrs. Miller stood in the church to give a testimony. "I was a Jehovah's Witness and went all over this neighborhood witnessing for Jehovah. Now I've found Jesus as my Savior, and He is my Jehovah."

"AMEN!" and shouts of "PRAISE THE LORD!" rang over the Presbyterian congregation that was not used to shouting. Then Mrs. Miller continued testifying.

"My husband, Ernest, was born Jewish. He also got saved last night; now he knows Jesus is his Messiah."

"AMEN . . . AMEN!" the shouts lasted twice as long.

That news spread quickly through the teen community. All the young people from our church began visiting the Bonna Bella church: Art Winn, Ann Perry, L. J. McEwen, and me, plus about 20 others from our church.

When Rev. Brian Nicholson wrote a doctoral project from Reformed Theological Seminary, he noted that 19 young people from Eastern Heights Presbyterian Church went into full-time ministry.[1] These 19 were saved at the Bonna Bella revival. That only represented one congregation of young people on that list of 60 for which the Harding brothers and their group of early morning intercessors prayed.

About the third or fourth night of the revival, a middle-aged man went forward for salvation. After the service, all the new converts stood in front of the church and were introduced to the audience. He said, "You don't need to introduce me, you all know me; I'm your mailman." He told of driving down LaRoacha Avenue toward the church when he felt heat coming from the Presbyterian church building. As he drove past the building, the heat went away. This happened every day the revival was going on.

Later in life, I understood this to be the *atmospheric presence* of God. You can walk into a church where God is working and feel His presence, just as you can feel wet atmosphere outside on an overcast day when it's not raining.

The mailman said he had to come to the revival meeting to find out what was going on. He testified, "I was baptized in a Baptist church as a teenager and since have become a Baptist Sunday School teacher and a Baptist deacon; but tonight I got born again . . . Hallelujah, I'm saved!" More Presbyterian shouts of "AMEN!" and "HALLELUJAH!"

On July 25, 1950, I received Christ as Savior. I refused to go forward, thinking I was saved. But under tremendous conviction of sin, I had to do something. No one went forward that Thursday night. Bill Harding walked to the Communion table and said, "Someone is supposed to come forward tonight and give your heart to Christ, but you say no!'"

I knew Bill was talking to me. He said, "Go home, kneel by your bed, look up into heaven and say, 'Jesus, come into my heart and save me.'"

I made that prayer about 11:15 that evening and I knew instantly that I was born again. My life has never been the same.

You can pray just like those people gathered in the garage apartment screened porch. You can change the world through your Daniel Prayer. Maybe you've taken a vow to fast for a particular answer to prayer, or you've joined with others to trust God for a particular goal.

God loves unity, that's why Jesus told His disciples, "Tarry in the city of Jerusalem until you are endued with power" (Luke 24:49). What did they do? "These all continued with one accord in prayer" (Acts 1:14). They followed the instruction of the Lord, and the Holy Spirit filled each one on the day of Pentecost (see Acts 2:1-4).

Notice how the church in the book of Acts came together in prayer: "When they had prayed, the place where they were assembled together was shaken" (Acts 4:31). Again, "But while Peter was kept in the prison, the church prayed very earnestly for him" (Acts 12:5, *NLT*).

The same results can happen when you separately pledge yourself to a prayer goal and when you unite with others in unity to see God work in your midst. When many agree on a Daniel Fast, God honors their faith. "If two [or more] of you agree on earth concerning anything that they ask, it will be done for them by My Father in heaven" (Matt. 18:19).

My Time to Pray

Lord, I join myself to others to fast and intercede for a prayer goal;
give me the request I ask.

May I strengthen the faith of others as they reciprocate to strengthen my
faith; together we fast and intercede for our prayer goal.

Lord, I come privately to You, even when I am in the prayer company
of others, to ask for the prayer goal for which I vowed. Amen.

My Answers Today

_____

_____

_____

_____

_____

_____

_____

_____

_____

_____

_____

_____

_____

_____

_____

_____

_____

_____

Note

1. Brian Nicholson, "History of Providence Presbyterian Church, Savannah Georgia,"
a theology project for Reformed Theological Seminary, Jackson, Mississippi.

For suggested recipes, see pages 180-192.

❧ DAY 3 ❧

Daily Commitment During Your Fast

Fasting can strengthen your faith and draw you closer to God, helping you to be a true overcomer in Christ. Fasting is a true gift to Christians who desire to be more effective in prayer.

ELMER TOWNS

The decision you make to God as you enter the Daniel Fast is much more important than what food you choose to stop eating or what other activity you sacrifice to God.

The original fast by Daniel is described in *The New Living Translation* as follows: "Daniel made up his mind not to defile himself by eating the food and wine given to them by the king" (Dan. 1:8). The *New International Version* says, "Daniel resolved," while the *New King James Version* says, "Daniel purposed," and the *CSB* says, "Daniel determined." All of these synonyms point to a life-changing decision of the will. Your Daniel Fast will be effective when you make a life-changing commitment—throughout this book I call it a vow—that you will modify your food or activities while you intercede for your prayer goal.

You have made an original vow to fast and pray for a faith project. Now you must make a daily choice to continue your fast.

Remember, a choice involves all of your personality: your intellect, emotions and will. You first know with your mind, but knowledge by itself is not enough to change your life, nor will it get the prayer goal you seek. Your emotions can be stirred for this fast, but getting excited may only change the surface things. You may change a few things—while you're excited—but what about the long haul? Your life will be transformed when your will makes a choice based on what your mind knows, and when your emotions are stirred toward the prayer goal.

> *You don't have the power to obey until you make a choice to obey.*

I learned the power of choice from my junior Sunday School teacher growing up in Eastern Heights Presbyterian Church of Savannah, Georgia. My teacher, Jimmy Breland, saturated our minds with the Bible. We memorized and repeated a Bible verse every Sunday, plus I memorized the Westminster Children's Catechism (a summary of basic theology). It seemed I learned every list in the Bible: the 12 disciples, the 12 tribes of Israel, the days of creation, the plagues on the Egyptians, the 22 kings of Judah, and so on. But knowing the Bible didn't change my life.

Next, Jimmy Breland told stories to stir our emotions—stories to make us laugh, cry and some that scared me about sin and hell. But stirring my emotions didn't change my life.

After telling a story of how Jacob disobeyed his parents, Jimmy said to us, "Raise your right hand and repeat after me . . ." I did as he requested, and repeated the following:

I promise . . .
to always obey my mother,
so help me, God.

As I lowered my hand, I asked myself, *What have I just said?* I struggled with obedience, as do most small boys. I examined my heart, asking, *Will I always obey my mother no matter what?*

On successive Sundays in Jimmy Breland's class, I raised my right hand and promised not to shoplift, not to lie, not to smoke, not to drink beer, and so on.

Jimmy Breland was the most influential teacher I ever had because he filled my mind with Scripture, stirred my emotions with stories and made me pledge to do right by raising my right hand with a promise to God.

When I was about 10 years old, I went to hang out in a corner store about a block from my house. My hand brushed across a box of Milky Ways on a low counter. The thought crossed my mind, *I could have stolen that candy car, and the lady behind the counter would have never seen me do it.*

That night I lay in my bed and thought about stealing a Milky Way. It was extremely tempting if you were as poor as my family was. We almost never had money for candy bars.

The next day I made a trial run. I picked up a Milky Way when the lady clerk wasn't looking. I held that chocolate nougat prize in my hand almost like a drunk fingering a glass of whisky. I put it back and walked out the store without stealing, thinking, *I can do this.*

The following Sunday, Jimmy Breland taught a lesson on stealing and casually said, "I don't want any of you stealing a Milky Way from a store."

Who told him . . . ? I immediately panicked. I felt as caught as if I had completed the crime.

Then it came to me, *I didn't tell anyone.* So I asked myself, *How did he know?* The realization came to me.

God told him.

Even in my 10-year-old mind, I had a God-consciousness that brought great guilt. I realized God knew the thoughts of our hearts. So Jimmy Breland made us lift our hands and say:

I promise . . .
I will never steal . . .
From a store . . .
So help me, God.

Unknown to Jimmy Breland or the other members of the class, I added, *I will never steal a Milky Way.* I purposed in my heart, just as Daniel purposed in his heart.

There are five things you need to commit to God in this fast. If you haven't done it yet, you should give to God the following five things: time, temple, talent, testimony and treasure.

First, you should commit your fast *time* to God. Pledge to begin and end according to the time limit you set in the checklist. If you are following the Daniel Fast with a group, promise to stay on your fast as long as the group fasts. *Lord, I promise to withhold food or other activities as long as my fast lasts.*

The second aspect of your Daniel Fast is your *temple*. You have pledged to eat healthy during this fast. You must commit your bodily temple to God. *Lord, I give my physical body to You. I will not eat or drink anything that will harm my body. I will refrain from alcohol, drugs, addiction and gluttony.*

The third part of your life to commit to God is your *talent*, or your abilities. In the Daniel Fast, this is committing your prayer ability to God. You must go beyond everything you have known about God and prayer in the past. You must pray many ways[1] and at many times. *Lord, I promise to keep my prayer time during this fast. Help me learn to pray more effectively, and help me learn the intimacy of Your presence.*

The fourth aspect of your commitment is your *testimony*. Those who have joined you in your prayer goal will be watching you. You can be an encouragement to them as they are an encouragement to you. Be strong for all your friends who are watching you. *Lord, fill my life with Your presence. Help me keep my fast strong to the end. Use my fast as a testimony to encourage others. May others see Christ in me.*

The fifth area is your *treasure*, or your money. Obviously, you are giving tithes and offerings to God, and usually through your church. If you're not, remember the challenge of God, " 'Bring all the tithes into the storehouse . . . and try Me now in this,' says the Lord of hosts, 'If I will not open for you the windows of heaven And pour out for you *such* blessing' " (Mal. 3:10). Remember, when you give all your money to God, He lets you use 90 percent for your needs. The 10 percent is used for His work. *Lord, I give all my treasures to You. Use them in Your work.*

As you continue your Daniel Fast, you will face many temptations to quit. Remember, quitting is a decision just as beginning was a decision. However, the greatness of your decision to begin will outweigh any temptation to decide to quit. There's a lot to lose by quitting, and there is everything to gain by continuing to the end. You'll never know the completeness of what God will do if you give up too soon. You'll never know the joy of a job well done if you are not firm to the end.

My Time to Pray

Lord, I have purposed in my heart to intercede for a prayer goal;
I will not give up.

Lord, I will not give in to my appetite to break my Daniel Fast.
I will be strong to the end.

Lord, I need Your strength to empower me. Help me realize, "I can do all
things through Christ who strengthens me" (Phil. 4:13). Amen.

My Answers Today

_____
_____
_____
_____
_____
_____
_____
_____
_____

Note

1. To learn many ways to pray, read *How to Pray When You Don't Know What to Say* by Elmer Towns, Regal Books, Ventura, California, 2006.

For suggested recipes, see pages 180-192.

❦ DAY 4 ❦

Praying and Fasting for a Project

Fasting has gone almost completely out of the life of the ordinary person. Jesus condemned the wrong kind of fasting, but He never meant that fasting should be completely eliminated from life and living. We would do well to practice it in our own way and according to our own need.
WILLIAM BARCLAY

Have you joined the Daniel Fast because you are praying for a project? If so, you need to know that you are not the first to fast and pray for a project. Many others have done the same thing. We will look at Ezra because he fasted and prayed to solve a particular problem facing him. We will learn some helpful principles from him to make fasting more effective.

As I write this chapter, I am fasting and asking God to lead me. I did not eat dinner last night, nor am I eating breakfast or lunch today. I'm spending my meal times in prayer for this project.

The book of Ezra tells how the Jews returned to the Promised Land after 70 years of captivity. God had used Nebuchadnezzar, king of Babylon, to punish God's people, primarily because of their idolatry, but other sins also sent them into captivity. Nebuchadnezzar destroyed Jerusalem and sent the majority of Jews to Babylon.

Almost 100 years later, the nations of Media-Persia defeated Babylon, and their King Cyrus of Persia gave a decree for Jews to return to their homeland and rebuild their Temple. Zerubbabel led the first wave of refugees back and began work on the Temple. The surrounding nations caused trouble, and the rebuilding went slowly but was finished in 515 B.C.

Then Ezra, a priest, attempted to lead a group back, and he gathered some Levites to accompany him. They gathered on the banks of the Ahava River (see Ezra 8:15) near the Euphrates River. To return to Israel, they had to cross the unrelenting desert and leave civilization along the mighty Euphrates.

Ezra faced a problem that seemed insurmountable. The desert was inhabited with savage nomadic tribes; many were gangs of thieves who attacked caravans for their treasure. Ezra confessed, "I was ashamed to ask the king to send soldiers and cavalry to protect us against enemies along the way" (Ezra 8:22, CEV).

This was similar to wagon trains of American settlers that needed the protection of the U.S. Cavalry when they crossed Indian Territory in the nineteenth century. But Ezra had compounded the problem by boasting, "After all, we had told the king that our God takes care of everyone who truly worships him" (Ezra 8:22, CEV). This set up their need to fast for safety.

Ezra had approximately 4,000 people he was leading back home. These Jews had gone to their relatives and friends who were not returning to receive an offering of money or valuables to rebuild the Temple. It was a huge offering: "In all there were: 25 tons of silver; 100 silver articles weighing 150 pounds; 7,500 pounds of gold; 20 gold bowls weighing 270 ounces; and 2 polished bronze articles as valuable as gold" (Ezra 8:26, CEV).

What would you do if faced with this threatening problem? "So we went without food and asked God Himself to protect us" (Ezra 8:23, CEV). This was not an individual problem, but involved a large scope of national significance. Also, the house of God was at stake. Remember, a private problem involves a private fast; a family problem involves a family fast; and a national problem involves a national fast.

How large is the Daniel Fast for which you are praying? Is the progress of God's work at stake? Is personal spiritual growth at stake? Is there danger of loss if the fast is not successful? Is God's honor at stake?

Principles for Fasting for a Project

Step 1: Find those who will fast for the project. Most likely, you are already in a Daniel Fast and you are already committed to the project. So the first thing is to find those who are also burdened for the project. You should fast and pray with others.

Step 2: Share the problem. If people are going to fast for a problem, they must either know about it or be involved in the project. Ezra said, "I proclaimed a fast . . . that we might humble ourselves before our God, to seek from Him the right way for us and our little ones and all our possessions" (Ezra 8:21). They fasted because they had a legitimate reason to be scared. The greater the number of people who feel the problem, the more likely they will be to fast for the project.

Step 3: Fast seriously. Ezra communicated the seriousness of the problem to the people. So when they understood their danger, they willingly fasted and prayed for protection. Ezra challenged them, "that we might afflict ourselves before our God" (Ezra 8:21, *KJV*). The word "afflicted" in this verse contains the idea of sorrow, mourning and repentance. When Israel fasted, they usually faced a life-threatening danger or a drought or pestilence. It was then the people fasted seriously. Then fasting was not a burden but their only means of deliverance.

FASTING PRODUCES
Spiritual introspection
Spiritual examination
Spiritual confession
Spiritual intercession

Step 4: Fast before attempting a solution. Often we wait until we get into a problem, then we try to get out of it any way possible. We borrow money, ask a friend to help, work overtime or cut back on expenses. After these don't work, we pray about the problem.

Finally, when prayer doesn't seem to be working, we fast, taking prayer to its higher level.

Fasting shouldn't be the last thing we try in desperation. No! We ought to fast about a problem before it becomes a problem. We need to try *defensive fasting*. Ezra did something before even trying to solve the problem: "I gathered them by the river that flows to Ahava, and we camped there three days" (Ezra 8:15). Notice what he didn't do:

He did not fast as he traveled.
He did not fast alone before gathering the people.
He did not try to solve the problem before fasting.

This suggests that you must recognize the spiritual nature of your problem before you begin to solve it. Actually, we ought to develop a "fasting mentality," which means we develop an attitude of dependence on God for all the times we do not fast.

Step 5: Fast on-site with insight. A new movement called "prayer walking" has developed in modern Christianity. This is praying on-site with insight. This means you will pray more seriously when you actually see your problem with your eyes than when you think about it or even when you try to see it in your mind.

> *When you stand in a place of need,*
> *you will pray with more heed.*

Actually, prayer walking was practiced in Scripture. God told Abraham to walk through the land that He—the LORD God—was going to give him (see Gen. 13:17). Also, God instructed Joshua to walk around the city of Jericho once each day for seven days, then seven times on the seventh day. Also, Joshua was told to walk throughout the land that he was going to conquer (see Josh. 1:3-9).

Ezra brought the people face to face with their problems, that is, to the banks of the Ahava River, before they launched out into the desert. Perhaps after staring at the desert for three days, the people were more challenged to fast and pray. "Beside the Ahava

River, I asked the people to go without eating and to pray" (Ezra 8:21, *CEV*).

Step 6: Fast and pray for a step-by-step guidance. They fasted before entering the problem where they could think and plan more intelligently. In the midst of a problem we usually don't think accurately or predicatively.

If you can break down a large problem into smaller issues, you usually can solve the smaller problems easier and faster than the larger problem. So do that before a problem surrounds you or you're drowning in a sea of red ink.

Before the problem hits you, pray not only for a final solution to the whole problem but also for God's guidance through the step-by-step solutions to the smaller problems along the way. There were many routes Ezra could have taken to Jerusalem, just as there is usually more than one way to solve your problem. Probably some roads were more traveled than others; some roads were more frequently traveled by soldiers or fierce tribes that could help fight back against thieves. As a result, some roads were safer than others.

Ezra called a fast, "to seek from Him the right way for us" (Ezra 8:21). The Bible teaches that God's sovereignty guides our ways, but we should use common sense along the way. "We draw our maps to the destination, but God directs each step along the road" (Prov. 16:9, *ELT*).

So why did Ezra and his entourage fast? "We went without food and asked God himself to protect us" (Ezra 8:23, *CEV*).

Step 7: Use common sense. Ezra had a tremendous amount of money to deliver to Jerusalem. It was not his money, nor did it belong to the travelers with him. It was God's money. So Ezra used his ingenuity. He divided up the money among the travelers so that everyone carried some of the money. If they were attacked, he reasoned, at least those who got through safely could deliver God's money to Jerusalem. "[I] weighed out to them the silver, the gold, and the articles, the offering for the house of our God which the king and his counselors and his princes, and all Israel who were present, had offered. I weighed into their hand six hundred and fifty talents of silver, silver articles weighing one hundred talents, one hundred talents of gold, twenty gold basins worth a thousand drachmas, and two vessels of fine polished bronze, precious as gold" (Ezra 8:25-27).

Ezra charged those with God's money, "You are holy to the LORD; the articles are holy also" (Ezra 8:28). He reminded them the money belonged to God, and so did they.

Ezra's common sense applied to the accountability of each one who was carrying God's money. It's so easy for those handling God's money to use it wrongly or use it for their own purpose, or even let a little stick to sticky fingers. (The stickiness is found in the heart, not on the fingers.) When they arrived in Jerusalem, they counted the money, "A receipt was given for each item, and the weight of the gold and silver was noted" (Ezra 8:34, *TLB*).

Just because Ezra was a spiritual man doesn't mean he was naïve. A cash register causes employees to be honest. Two or more counting the church offering makes people accountable to the other persons and ultimately accountable to God. What happened to Ezra and the people? "So we fasted and entreated our God for this, and He answered our prayer" (Ezra 8:23).

My Time to Pray

Lord, I will fast for big projects before I attempt to solve them.

Lord, I will examine all facts and try to understand a problem, then I'll ask You to give me insight how to solve my problems.

Lord, I will seek to break big problems down into smaller ones, then work on them one at a time. Help me use my common sense to solve my problems.

Lord, I will love all people; but when it comes to money, I'll make them accountable because I want them to be honest.

Lord, I will fast, and I will rejoice in Your goodness after You have honored my fast and answered my prayer. Amen.

My Answers Today

_____

_____

_____

_____

_____

_____

_____

_____

_____

_____

_____

_____

_____

_____

_____

_____

_____

For suggested recipes, see pages 180-192.

❧ DAY 5 ❧

The Benefits of a Lengthy Fast

In those days I, Daniel, was mourning three full weeks. I didn't eat any rich food, no meat or wine entered my mouth, and I didn't put any oil on my body until the three weeks were over.

DANIEL 10:2-3, *CSB*

How long should you fast? Some people fast for one day; some fast for 10 days; others fast for 21 days; a few fast for 40 days.

I fast on a regular basis, following the Old Testament sequence of fasting, i.e., from sundown to sundown. This is called the Yom Kippur fast, for all Jews were commanded to fast on that day. "On the tenth day of the seventh month of each year, you must go without eating to show sorrow for your sins" (Lev. 16:29, *CEV*). The Jews got their lead from God Himself who said the days of creation began, "The evening and the morning were the first day" (Gen. 1:5).

Usually, the more pressing a problem, the longer I fast. When I have a serious need, I fast longer than one day. My one-day fast is just to know God more intimately.

The Daniel Fast is usually 10 or 21 days. On both occasions he faced a great challenge, so he answered with a great commitment to prayer.

For the first fast, Daniel challenged the Babylonian official over him, "Please test your servants . . . ten days, and let them give us vegetables to eat and water to drink" (Dan. 1:12).

Later in life (probably in his nineties) Daniel described a 21-day fast: "I, Daniel, was mourning three full weeks. I ate no pleasant food, no meat or wine came into my mouth, nor did I anoint myself at all, till three whole weeks were fulfilled" (Dan. 10:2-3).

It seems that the first time Daniel fasted for 10 days, it was a time preset by him. The second fast seems to reflect a period of time given to prayer, mourning and seeking God for an answer. An angel was sent to Daniel on the twenty-first day, saying, "Do not fear, Daniel, for from the first day that you set your heart to understand, and to humble yourself before your God, your words were heard; and I have come because of your words" (Dan. 10:12).

Probably you are fasting with a group from your church or, perhaps, another organization. Someone else has set the time for this Daniel Fast, either 10 or 21 days. (God will not measure the success of your fast just because you fast for 10 or 21 days. God looks at the quality time you spend in His presence and then rewards you by the biblical nature of your intercession.)

For whatever the length of your Daniel Fast, join in willingly and submit to your spiritual leadership (see Heb. 13:17). Never complain about the length, or about any other aspect of what your group is practicing in this fast. *Lord, I will fast strong to the end.*

The Benefits of a Lengthy Fast

First of all, ask how serious is the fasting goal for which you are praying. If it is an extremely imperative goal, then obviously you want to spend as much time in prayer as possible to make sure God hears and God answers. Sometimes God doesn't respond to a quickly breathed prayer when we squeeze Him into our otherwise busy schedule.

Yes, God heard the desperate prayer of Peter who began to sink beneath the storm's waves. His prayer for help was filled with panic because the situation was life threatening. Obviously, a quickly breathed prayer is effective, but we probably need to pray longer over hard-to-solve problems. Why? Because it takes a longer time to solve some problems. So ask yourself, *How serious is this prayer goal?* If it's serious and imperative, then commit yourself to a 10- or 21-day time limit, and determine to stay with it to the end.

Second, your prayer will grow in intensity as the fast time unrolls. You'll develop more faith with time. Fasting for 10 or 21 days is like running a race; the closer to the finish line, the more your adrenaline begins to flow and you give it a "kick" to finish the race.

As you pray through your Daniel Fast, you'll probably keep up with the prayers toward the beginning. Usually, we lag in the middle of a fast. But toward the end, our prayer intensity kicks in. Maybe it's because money is being raised, or a sick person begins to recover, or progress is made toward completion of a goal. With any success, you will be motivated to pray deeper or to pray with more urgency toward the end of your fast.

Sometimes there is little or no progress toward the faith goal. This is the time some get discouraged and quit. If nothing is happening, some people dial down their prayer intensity. Human nature being what it is, some need outward stimulation to keep praying or even to continue their Daniel Fast to the end.

But remember, you didn't vow a pledge to a group or to a church. Your faith pledge for the Daniel Fast was made to God. Don't you think God knew the success of the project before you made your pledge or before the goal was set? Then fast to the end of your pledge to please God.

Then there's another factor: Be true to yourself. If you've pledged for 10 or 21 days, then you owe it to your integrity to keep your word. If you quit too soon, your self-perception is blurred and your self-determination is weakened. You might not keep your word on another promise completely unrelated to fasting.

There's a third reason you need time to fast: It takes time for your faith to grow. The more you pray about a project, the sharper your faith will become.

Look at Abraham! When God first called him and promised to build a nation through his children, the Bible describes him as "weak in faith" (Rom. 4:19). Didn't he go to Egypt and allow his wife to be taken into Pharaoh's harem? Didn't he compromise with Hagar, an Egyptian concubine?

But God patiently strengthened Abraham's faith so that he believed God could do what God promised. "And not being weak in faith . . . he did not waver at the promise of God through unbelief, but was strengthened in faith, giving glory to God" (Rom. 4:19-20).

Perhaps you have weak faith as you begin your Daniel Fast. But as you continue fasting—day after day—you'll find your faith being strengthened as you learn how to pray.

At another place, Paul reminds us our faith should be moving from one kind of faith to a stronger kind of faith. Paul tells us, "From faith to faith; as it is written, 'The just shall live by faith'" (Rom. 1:17).

So why fast for 10 days, or even for 21 days? You probably will begin your fast with immature faith. Maybe all you know for sure is that Jesus has saved you, God is your Father and the Holy Spirit guides you. But you can grow to intercession-faith so that you can get through to God as you fast and pray. You can grow "from faith to faith" in this Daniel Fast. It may take the total of 21 days until you have strong enough faith to pray boldly.

If your faith is weak faith (see Rom. 14:1), then begin praying daily, as the father who didn't have enough faith to heal his son but wanted his son healed. He prayed, "Lord, I believe; help thou mine unbelief" (Mark 9:24, KJV).

A fourth reason to fast a long time is so the project can grow in your mind. If someone else has set your fast goal, maybe you're not as burdened as the leader of your group, or your pastor. Maybe you are fasting for a new sanctuary at church or an evangelistic project, or some other goal. When other people set a goal, it's not felt as deeply as if you set it yourself—especially if it's for your personal ministry.

So a lengthy time of fasting and prayer will focus the goal in your heart. You will probably feel a growing burden as you continue to fast for your goal. It may take time for God to speak to your heart and show you the importance of the goal.

The longer you pray for the fast goal, the clearer you will see how God will use the goal to expand His kingdom and glorify Himself.

Keep your physical eyes open as you look at the documents of your goal. If you can, go to the place—walk around the area for which you are praying. I call this geographical praying. God may use circumstances at the place of your faith goal to intensify your prayer urgency for the goal.

There's another thing that geographical praying does for you. It revives your recessive memory. Many memories will be revived when you pray at the place for which you are praying. You may have been saved at that prayer altar, or God may have redirected your life at that location.

The fifth benefit of a lengthy fast is that it usually takes time to find sin in your life and deal with it by the blood of Christ. There may be a sin hidden in your heart, or you may be blinded to an otherwise obvious sin. Remember, "If I regard iniquity in my heart, The Lord will not hear" (Ps. 66:18). Because we justify some of our sin, we don't see the hidden sin in our heart that hinders answers to prayer.

As you tarry in God's presence, realize, "God does not hear sinners" (John 9:31) and "Your iniquities have separated you from your God; And your sins have hidden His face from you, So that He will not hear" (Isa. 59:2).

Remember, you have an enemy who opposes you. Satan doesn't want you to be holy and separated from sin. He doesn't want you to get answers to prayers. He doesn't want you to enjoy intimacy with God. Satan blinds you to sin in your life so that you will not repent of sin. He uses satanic blindness to keep you in his grasp: "The god of this age has blinded, [those] who do not believe, lest the light of the gospel of the glory of Christ, who is the image of God, should shine on them" (2 Cor. 4:4).

So, you need to pray with David, "Search me, O God . . . And see if there is any wicked way in me" (Ps. 139:23-24). It may take time for God to reveal to you the one hidden sin that blocks His blessing in your life.

You can be sure that if you ask God to show you your sin, He will do it: "There is nothing covered that will not be revealed, and hidden that will not be known" (Matt. 10:26). Therefore, don't be impatient if God doesn't answer your prayer (accompanied with fasting) the first time you pray, or even the first day of your fast. It may take 10 days, or even 21 days.

Finally, the sixth reason why you have a lengthy fast is that it takes time to search for God and find Him. When you search for something, it's because you've lost it and you need it. Searching suggests a deep desire on our part.

At times, God doesn't immediately disclose Himself. The psalmist exclaims, "Why do You hide Your face?" (Ps. 44:24). Perhaps God hides to see if we really want to find Him.

My Time to Pray

Lord, open my spiritual eyes progressively throughout this fast so that I may know You better at the end than I did at the beginning.

Lord, as I wait in Your presence, reveal to me any sin lurking in my heart that would hinder my prayers.

Lord, give me a resolute heart to pray continually, to pray sincerely and to pray in faith.

Lord, I vow not to give up until the end of this fast. Amen.

My Answers Today

_____
_____
_____
_____
_____
_____
_____
_____
_____

For suggested recipes, see pages 180-192.

❧ DAY 6 ❧

Saying No in Prayer

Fasting is the most powerful spiritual discipline of all the Christian disciplines. Through fasting and prayer, the Holy Spirit can transform your life. Fasting and prayer can also work on a much grander scale. According to Scripture, personal experience and observation, I am convinced that when God's people fast with a proper biblical motive—seeking God's face not His hand— with a broken, repentant and contrite spirit, God will hear from heaven and heal our lives, our churches, our communities, our nation and world. Fasting and prayer can bring about revival—a change in the direction of our nation, the nations of earth and the fulfillment of the Great Commission.

BILL BRIGHT

The word "afflict" is tied to fasting on several occasions. The first time a believer is told to fast is in Leviticus 16:29. The old *King James* says, "Ye shall afflict your souls." *The Living Bible* says, "Spend the day in self-examination and humility." The *Holman Christian Standard Bible* translates it, "You are to practice self-denial." The word "afflict" is constantly tied to fasting (see Lev. 16:29,34; Num. 29:7; Isa. 58:3,5).

The word "afflict" in the dictionary means "to cause distress, to cause anguish or suffering."[1] Therefore, when you give up something pleasurable, you bring some discomfort or distress upon yourself.

Why do we do this? It's not that we love pain. We do it for a spiritual reason. We do it to pray more earnestly for a faith project.

When we afflict ourselves, it's none of the masochistic things some extremists have done. It's not whipping ourselves with whips, or punishing the flesh to keep it submitted to God.

When we afflict ourselves, we say no to the sinful flesh. This is another way to express repentance. To afflict yourself expresses the desire to rid your life of sinful things. It's a way of dealing with sinful attitudes.

Why "afflict"? Sometimes we love doing sin more than serving God. We love thinking about our sin more than meditating on God. So we must repent of our actions. After all, the word "repentance" means "to turn from."

So when we fast, pray and afflict ourselves, we say no to our previous sins, and we say yes to God and His will for our lives.

Sometimes we are blind to our sin. A wrong attitude creeps into our thought life, and we don't immediately recognize it as sin. That's the way termites get into a house—unnoticed.

A neighbor of mine, about 15 years ago, discovered that some snakes had crawled inside the walls of his house into the attic. He killed one or two with traps but discovered more. So he had to deal severely with the problem. He moved out for almost a week, had a large tent placed over the house and gassed the snakes (and every other insect). It took severe action to deal with a severe problem.

Hidden sin secretly slips into our life. Sin destroys our walk with God and eats away our Christian character. So when we "afflict" ourselves by fasting, we give God an opportunity to expose sin for what it really is.

We also afflict ourselves of good things. You have made a vow to give up certain things for the Daniel Fast. Maybe you've given up one or two meals a day. Maybe you're eating just vegetables, or you've given up some other practices. The things you've given up are probably all good things. You haven't given them up because they are sinful; and probably these good things don't have a sinful hold on your life.

So, why do we give up good things? We "afflict" ourselves so that we can put God first in our life. We say no to good things so that we can say yes to the best things.

Technically, the Hebrew word for fast is *tsom,* which means to lose one's appetite for food. Suppose you got an emergency phone call that your spouse was in the emergency room at the hospital.

As you begin to rush there, you realize it is past your lunchtime. Would you drive through the pick-up window to grab a hamburger and cold drink? No! The emergency would overwhelm your appetite and you wouldn't even think of eating. That's the true meaning of afflicting yourself for a spiritual burden. You don't even think about eating. In this passage the word "afflict" is translated "weeping and mourning."

Fasting is also identified in Scripture with a solemn assembly. When hurting people come together in a meeting called "a solemn assembly," this is not a time to praise God or worship Him. Nor is it a time to sing psalms of the greatness of God, nor to be instructed in God's Word. A solemn assembly is a time to search the heart for hidden sin and to confess sins and repent of them. These types of meetings go on for hours with people begging God to forgive and restore them to His favor. The book of Joel explains the seriousness of a solemn assembly: "Now, therefore," says the LORD, "Turn to Me with all your heart, With fasting, with weeping, and with mourning . . . So rend your heart, and not your garments" (Joel 2:12-13).

Before we can establish any credible basis for God answering our prayers, we must establish inward character. We do that by examining our hearts as we fast before God.

Also, we must deal with our pride. When we fast for the glory of God, we can say no to our selfish desire to be number one. Jesus said, "But seek first the kingdom of God and His righteousness, and all these things shall be added to you" (Matt. 6:33). So the good things He gives us may be the things we give up for only a season.

When you take control of your outward body by fasting,
you begin to take control of your inward person.

There are two things that should happen when you say no. The negative repentance is what you abstain. You turn from sin. Christ gives you the power to say no whether you say no to a sinful thing or whether you say no to something as good as one or two meals a day. But there is a positive action. Remember, "I can do all things through Christ who strengthens me" (Phil. 4:13).

Christ is in your heart because of salvation. So you yield to His inward strength and let Him give you strength to complete your Daniel Fast. "Thanks be to God who always leads us in triumph in Christ" (2 Cor. 2:14). When you say no to some good things, it's a reminder who's the boss in your life. Sometimes we go through life thinking, *I've got to eat three square meals a day*, or *I deserve that entertainment* or *Everyone else is doing it; why can't I?* While these are good things, and there's nothing wrong with them, the issue is, who's running your life? This is another way of asking, Who's sitting on the throne of your heart? Make sure that:

> *When you give up some good things in life,*
> *you replace them with God who is best for your life.*

My Time to Pray

Lord, I will give up good things to seek Your best in my life.

Lord, as I fast, show me any sinful attitude or action that's hiding in my life. I will say no to it and repent of it.

Lord, the good things I give up cannot be compared with the wonderful privilege of enjoying Your presence. Amen.

My Answers Today

_____

_____

_____

_____

_____

_____

Note

1. See http://www.merriam-webster.com/dictionary/AFFLICT, s.v. "afflict" (accessed July 17, 2009).

For suggested recipes, see pages 180-192.

❧ DAY 7 ❧

The Persistence of a Daniel Fast

There are those who think that fasting belongs to the old dispensation; but when we look at Acts 14:23 and Acts 13:2-3, we find that it was practiced by the earnest men of the apostolic day. If we would pray with power, we should pray with fasting. This, of course, does not mean that we should fast every time we pray; but there are times of emergency or special crisis in work or in our individual lives, when men of downright earnestness will withdraw themselves even from the gratification of natural appetites that would be perfectly proper under other circumstances, that they may give themselves wholly to prayer. There is a peculiar power in such prayer. Every great crisis in life and work should be met that way. There is nothing pleasing to God in our giving up in a purely Pharisaic and legal way things which are pleasant, but there is power in that downright earnestness and determination to obtain in prayer the things of which we sorely feel our need, that leads us to put away everything, even things in themselves most right and necessary, that we may set our faces to find God, and obtain blessings from Him.

R. A. TORREY

There are so many distractions in modern life to keep us from praying. Sometimes it's just good things that make us stop praying. There seems to be a television set always telling us of a news disaster or selling us something or demanding our attention. Everywhere we go the cell phone interrupts us or we hear a loudspeaker in the background interrupting our thoughts. When do we ever get a little time to meditate on God? How can we listen to God when there are so many voices competing for our attention? How can we keep on praying when it seems as if everything is competing for our mind?

When you fast, you "come apart" from the bustle of life to commune with God. You seek quietness during the three meal times each day to first listen to God's Word and to His inner voice. Your fast project is a perfect time to seek God for the prayer project you seek.

Jesus tells the story of a man sleeping when his neighbor knocked frantically at his door to borrow some bread in the middle of the night. He replied, "Leave me alone, I'm sleeping and so is my family."

The neighbor kept pounding until he got the bread he sought. Jesus concluded, "Though he will not rise and give to him because he is his friend, yet because of his persistence he will rise and give him as many as he needs. So I say to you, ask, and it will be given to you; seek, and you will find; knock, and it will be opened to you" (Luke 11:8-9).

Many years ago, I learned this verse by remembering the first letters of Ask, Seek and Knock in the acronym ASK, which is another biblical term for praying.

Notice that Jesus commanded us to ask, seek, knock. All three involve persistence expressed in different ways. To ask is to use words to get what you want. To seek is to use your feet to go to where the prize is located. To knock is the idea of using all your body and mind to locate what has been hidden from you.

Think of why we parents hide things from our children. We hide Easter eggs so they will have the thrill of discovery. Maybe that's why God wants you to fast and pray for 10 or 21 days.

Parents hide Christmas gifts till the right moment because they know the kids will appreciate the gift that is appropriately given. So you may have to pray for the entire 21 days to receive and appreciate your faith project.

God may want you to pray for a project for 10 days or even 21 days. Why? The Lord honors persistent prayer. Regardless of fatigue, obstacles, discouragement or doubt, keep praying. When you enter God's presence with an iron will, determine to pray to the end. God will honor your determination and faith.

Wesley L. Duwel, in his book *Prevailing Prayer*, gives us insight into the heart of persistent prayer:

> To prevail is to be successful in the face of difficulty, to completely dominate, to overcome and tie up. Prevailing prayer is prayer that pushes right through all difficulties and obstacles and drives back all the opposing forces of Satan, and secures the will of God. Its purpose is to accomplish God's will on earth. Prevailing prayer not only takes the initiative, but continues on the offence for God until spiritual victory is won.[1]

Why must we prevail? Because God knows the flesh is weak and it's human to give up. The night before Jesus died, He took His disciples into the garden of Gethsemane to pray. He told them to "watch with Me" (Matt. 26:38). What did He say when He found them asleep?

> Then He came to the disciples and found them sleeping, and said to Peter, "What! Could you not watch with Me one hour? Watch and pray, lest you enter into temptation. The spirit indeed is willing, but the flesh is weak" (Matt. 26:40-41).

Jesus knows that your physical body is not trained to keep a 10- or 21-day fast. He will help you do it if you pray and ask Him to strengthen you: "I can do all things through Christ who strengthens me" (Phil. 4:13). So begin this fast with a commitment to complete it.

God may not immediately answer your prayer, because if He gave you a quick answer, you might not continue praying for a project in the future. Quick answers might lead to superficial praying. Instead, God waits to test our resolve. The success of persistent prayer teaches us to be persistent the next time we pray.

We must pray long and we must pray with all our heart, because we are in spiritual warfare. The Christian life is not a coffee break; it's a wrestling match or a battlefield. Life's a struggle to the grave. There is an enemy, Satan, who opposes God's work; and when you are fasting and praying for a faith project, Satan opposes you. So keep praying. The issue is, "Who will win—God or Satan?" So you must pray through obstacles and pray through discouragement. Jesus encourages us, "Keep on praying and never give up" (Luke 18:1, *CEV*).

Paul reminds us, "For we do not wrestle against flesh and blood, but against principalities, against powers, against the rulers of the darkness of this age, against spiritual hosts of wickedness in the heavenly places" (Eph. 6:12). Therefore, severe, life-changing issues demand our complete dedication until the completion of our fast deadline. Remember, these are the vows you've made:

Abstinence-vow
Time-vow
Mental-vow
Prayer-vow
Faith-vow

Sometimes you pray long to undo the work of the enemy. Sometimes you pray long to give God time to put the pieces together so the answer can happen. If you're praying long for rain (see Jas. 5:17-18), it takes time for a weather front to come together and move through your area. If you're praying for money, it takes time to move a giver's heart to give and then write the check; and everyone laughs about the slow mail system.

Then again, remember that the *principle of learning* is tied to the *principle of time*. It takes time to learn some lessons, and the harder the lesson, the longer it takes to get ready for the exam. Have you ever studied almost all night to get ready for a final exam? Therefore, as you are praying through a 10- or 21-day fast, God may be trying to teach you an important lesson. It may take a whole 21 days to learn what God is teaching. And the lesson God wants to teach you may be something entirely different from the faith project.

Prevailing prayer is an attitude God teaches, so when you learn this lesson, determine to never give up. Make a vow now that you will keep your Daniel Fast to the end. Pray till you complete the vow you've made. Pray till you finish your Daniel Fast. Pray till you get an answer.

My Time to Pray

Lord, I confess my weakness; help me to be strong in this fast.

Lord, I've completed seven days; help me to keep my vow about not eating to the end, and help me pray persistently till the answer comes.

Lord, I commit the next days of my fast to You. Be glorified by my commitment and help me keep my promise. Amen.

My Answers Today

_____

_____

_____

_____

_____

_____

_____

_____

_____

_____

Note
1. Wesley L. Duwel, *Prevailing Prayer* (Grand Rapids, MI: Zondervan: 1990).

For suggested recipes, see pages 180-192.

Day 8 to Day 14 Overview

Learning About Prayer

These seven devotionals are written to teach you some basic lessons about prayer. In one sense, you don't need to learn to pray, for it's as basic as talking. But remember, you're talking to someone; prayer is relationship with God.

So, it's not always how you talk to God, or what you say to God; the key is relationship. Spend time with God, get to know Him and learn to worship Him.

This Daniel Fast could bring you closer to God than you've ever been in your life. Wouldn't you like that? Use prayer opportunities to get to know God intimately. Paul's great passion was, "That I may know Him and the power of His resurrection" (Phil. 3:10).

So don't forget to keep your fast vow, but more importantly, keep your prayer commitment. Jesus said, "Always pray and not lose heart" (Luke 18:1, *Phillips*).

Daily Readings

Day 8: Intimacy with God
Day 9: Giving Thanks in Prayer
Day 10: Fasting to Hunger After God
Day 11: Prayer Is Asking
Day 12: Fasting to Worship God
Day 13: Fasting to Locate Sin
Day 14: Don't Violate Your Fast

DAY 8

Intimacy with God

We tend to think of fasting as going without food. But we can fast from anything. If we love music and decide to miss a concert in order to spend time with God, that is fasting. It is helpful to think of the parallel of human friendship. When friends need to be together, they will cancel all other activities in order to make that possible. There's nothing illogical about fasting. It's just one way of telling God that your priority at that moment is to be alone with Him, sorting out whatever is necessary, and you have cancelled the meal, party, concert or whatever else you had planned to do in order to fulfill that priority.

J. I. PACKER

There are many ways to define prayer. Prayer is asking, and prayer is worshiping or praising God. Also, prayer is resting in God; or prayer is spiritual warfare against our enemy. But today, let's focus on intimacy in prayer. How intimate with God are you?

Look at the model of Jesus' life. He taught us to pray beginning with the words, "Our Father in heaven" (Matt. 6:9). Jesus invites us to enter into an intimate relationship with the heavenly Father, an intimacy that He shared with the Father.

The first recorded spoken words of Jesus occurred when He was 12 years old. Mary and Joseph had brought the family to Jerusalem for a feast. They had probably traveled in a large group and assumed Jesus was with them as they began returning home. But He was not. Mary and Joseph searched for a couple of days until they found Him in the Temple. When asked why, Jesus answered, "Did you not know that I must be about My Father's business?" (Luke 2:49).

Many people read that story and emphasize that Jesus was in the house of God. As good as that point is, the emphasis is that Jesus sought intimacy with God in His house. Jesus called God His Father, a term of intimacy.

Look at Jesus' baptism. The Father showed up because it was the inauguration of His Son into ministry. Don't fathers show up for important days in the lives of their children? The heavenly Father said, "You are My beloved Son; in You I am well pleased" (Luke 3:22).

Again when Jesus was transformed in front of three of His disciples on the Mount of Transfiguration, the Father spoke from heaven, "This is My beloved Son, in whom I am well pleased" (Matt. 17:5).

There is a difference between the relationship of a father with his child and the reverence between a worshiper and God.

Relationship binds children to their father;
reverence binds worshipers to their God.

In the Old Testament, God revealed Himself by three names. First, He revealed Himself as Elohim, God the powerful Creator who called the world into existence. Second, He revealed Himself as Yahweh (Jehovah), the personal LORD who told Moses, "I AM WHO I AM" (Exod. 3:14). Third, He was Adonai, our master and owner, and we are but slaves.

Not once in the Old Testament is God given the name Father (seven times in the Gospel of John, Jesus says His name is Father). In the Old Testament, God is likened to many things; for example, He is likened to a rock (see Ps. 61:2; 2 Sam. 22:3), an eagle (see Deut. 32:18; Ps. 139:8), a mother (see Pss. 17:8; 36:7; 57:1; 91:1,4) and a father (see Eph. 3:15; Acts 17:24; Ps. 34:15-22). And here's another example: "But now, O LORD, You are our Father; We are the clay, and You our potter" (Isa. 64:8). Those are all metaphors to help the people understand God.

Jesus taught His disciples that they had a new relationship with God. He taught them to pray, "Our Father in heaven" (Matt. 6:9). Because of Jesus, we have a new relationship with God, our heavenly Father.

The relationship between the Father and Jesus was revealed in a deeper intimacy when Jesus prayed in Gethsemane, "Abba, Father, all things are possible for You. Take this cup away from Me; nevertheless, not what I will, but what You will" (Mark 14:36). When Jesus called the Father, "Abba," it's like an American calling his father, "Papa."

The strength that Jesus got from that intimate relationship with His heavenly Father gave Him the ability to face the physical sufferings and the spiritual struggles on the cross when He became sin for us (see 2 Cor. 5:21).

What's satisfying about this relationship between Jesus and His heavenly Father? It reminds us of the intimate relationship between an earthly father and a child. The child runs to the arms of his father when returning from a trip and asks, "What did you bring me?" Is that a picture of you praying for your Daniel Fast project? For what are you asking?

Look at an exhausted child sitting in the lap of his father at a picnic. The child sleeps or rests quietly in his father's lap to regain strength to go play again. They don't need to say anything to each other; they just enjoy the moment. Dad's presence is good enough.

Can we pray without words? Yes! Remember, the most used word for prayer in the New Testament is *proseuchomai* (*pros* means "toward" and *euchomai* is "the face"). Prayer is like a face-to-face relationship with God that is pictured by two lovers sitting face to face, looking into one another's eyes; they don't need to say anything; their intimacy says, "I love you."

Intimacy is enjoying the presence of God. "David . . . sat before the LORD" (2 Sam. 7:18). When you come to your time of prayer, remember that you, too, can sit in the presence of the heavenly Father. Enjoy Him.

Because you are God's child, begin your prayers the way Paul taught us to approach the Father: "And because you are sons, God has sent forth the Spirit of His Son into your hearts, crying out, 'Abba, Father!'" (Gal. 4:6). What intimate name do you use for your heavenly Father?

In another Scripture, Paul taught us, "We are children of God, and if children, then heirs—heirs of God and joint heirs with Christ" (Rom. 8:16-17). Who is an heir? The one who has the right to the assets and property of the Father. So pray confidently in your Daniel Fast project. Ask as a child seeking assets from your heavenly Father.

Intimacy with God can seem mysterious. How can you be confident in your attempts to know God as you would your earthly father? There are several ways to define intimacy and the actions that lead to experiencing it with your heavenly Father.

First, intimacy is being there. You don't get intimacy with God by methods, techniques or even correct formulas in prayer. You get intimacy by drawing close to your heavenly Father. "How lovely is Your tabernacle, O LORD of hosts! My soul longs, yes, even faints For the courts of the LORD; My heart and my flesh cry out for the living God. For a day in Your courts is better than a thousand. I would rather be a doorkeeper in the house of my God than dwell in the tents of wickedness" (Ps. 84:1-2,10).

Second, intimacy is seeking the Father's presence. The Father is sitting on the throne of heaven. Why don't you go crawl up onto His lap? Just as a child on earth goes to sit with his or her earthly father, you can do the same with your heavenly Father.

And why does a child desire to sit on his father's lap? Maybe he wants to ask for something, or he wants his father to read to him. Maybe he needs help with homework. Perhaps the child just wants to sit in his father's lap because he enjoys it. Isn't intimacy wonderful? "One thing I have desired of the LORD, that will I seek: That I may dwell in the house of the LORD All the days of my life, To behold the beauty of the LORD, And to inquire in His temple" (Ps. 27:4).

Third, to experience intimacy with God, you don't need to learn anything. Kids don't need to take a course to learn how to be children. They just are. It comes with birth. When they are born into a family, they experience a father's love. That makes them know they are family. Love teaches them how to act and how to respond to their father. Love opens the door for them to ask.

Isn't it the role of a father to provide necessities—food, shelter, clothing—to his children? Yes. Isn't it the role of children to ask for necessities from their human father? Yes. So today, ask for your Daniel Fast project.

A kid sitting on his dad's lap doesn't need to take a course in how to be a kid. He just sits there and does what's natural. What's natural for you to do in your heavenly Father's presence?

Fourth, intimacy is a privilege to enjoy. I love the picture of President John F. Kennedy sitting for an important staff meeting when his son—John-John—bursts into the room and interrupts him. What happened? President Kennedy stopped what he was doing to set his son on his lap. At that moment, the request of his son was more important than any business of the United States.

When you burst into the throne room of heaven, God will stop what He's doing to listen to your request. At that moment, your request will be more important than God running the affairs of the universe.

Fifth, intimacy is learned from heaven, not earth. While I have discussed the intimacy between an earthly father and his children, that is not our model. Remember, some children had poor human role models in their fathers. Some fathers have been drunks, gamblers, and were lazy and abusive. So some people on earth have no good memory of a positive relationship with an earthly father.

In creation, God built the concept of fatherhood into men, and if they follow the inner directive, they'll become good fathers. But when earthly fathers give themselves to sin, they destroy the positive relationship they could have with their children and their children with them.

If your earthly experience makes prayers of intimacy with God difficult, ask God to heal your memories. Then ask God to heal your inclinations; and finally, ask Him to heal your lack of desire for intimacy with Him.

You must forgive any family members that have destroyed any idea of intimacy. Pray, "Forgive us our sins, just as we have forgiven those who have sinned against us" (Matt. 6:12, *TLB*).

Sixth, let intimacy develop. Some people just don't feel connected to God. How can they get past the "asking" phase of prayer to intimacy prayer? The simple answer is to give it time. Go into God's presence and wait.

The psalmist tells us, "Wait on the LORD" (Ps. 27:14). But make sure you are waiting in God's presence. "My soul, wait silently for God alone" (Ps. 62:5).

What happens when you wait on God? "Those who wait on the LORD shall renew their strength; They shall mount up with wings like eagles, They shall run and not be weary, They shall walk and not faint" (Isa. 40:31). So waiting on God gets results.

Seventh, expect to grow the art of intimacy. What do we know about babies? They are selfish. They expect everything from their parents, and if they don't get what they want when they want it, and in the way they want it, they will cry, scream and demand attention until they are satisfied. It's natural for babies to cry. Are you a baby in your relationship with God?

They cry for food until the bottle comes. They cry when a diaper is wet until they are changed. Some even cry when they feel ignored. Are you a spiritual baby? If so, cry to God for whatever you need.

Crying babies are not concerned if it's the middle of the night and their parents are sound asleep. They're not concerned if the pastor is preaching the Word of God and they disrupt a church service. No, babies are utterly selfish. Be careful that doesn't describe your prayer life.

But babies are not irreversibly selfish. As they grow, they learn better ways to express their needs. They learn to respect others and their needs. God has given a family to teach babies how to share, receive, give and love. The password to growth is love. "We love Him because He first loved us" (1 John 4:19).

Babies grow into mature adults in an atmosphere of love. With time they learn to give Dad a tie on Father's Day; and as they grow older, they give him respect and grow in relational intimacy with him.

Eighth, true intimacy balances the tension between reverence and relationship. God is the Creator of the universe; we reverence Him.

Because God is the omnipotent I AM WHO I AM, we bow in His presence to cry out, "Holy, Holy, Holy." That is the almighty side of the door.

But when we step through the door, we find ourselves in the presence of our heavenly Father—Abba Father—Papa. We can enter close up and metaphorically throw our arms around His neck and tell Him, "I love You."

My Time to Pray

Lord, I will wait in Your presence, not asking for anything.
I wait in Your presence to know You better.

Lord, I want to know You intimately, more intimately than
I know anyone on earth.

Lord, I reverence You as my sovereign Lord and the God of the universe.
I worship, adore and bow before You.

Lord, teach me when to reverence You and when to seek
Your intimacy. Amen.

My Answers Today

_____
_____
_____
_____
_____
_____
_____
_____
_____
_____
_____
_____

For suggested recipes, see pages 180-192.

❄ · DAY 9 · ❄

Giving Thanks in Prayer

A spiritually awake person would see everything as gift, even suffering. We deserve nothing and yet we so often act as though we deserve everything. Nothing should be taken for granted. We should say thank you every day to God and to each other for all that is provided for us.
This is one reason why fasting is such an important spiritual discipline. Not just fasting from food, but also fasting from cars, shopping centres, the new—whatever we have an inordinate attachment to. Fasting can help rekindle our gratitude for all that we have been given.

GLEN ARGAN

I meet with a group of about 12 people for prayer every Sunday morning. This is my most important meeting each week because I get more spiritual power and emotional energy from these people than from any other gathering.

Recently one person asked me, "Why do you always begin praying by thanking God for answers to your prayers?"

I had never thought about it; I didn't realize I began my prayers that way. So I asked, "How long have I been doing it?"

"Forever," he said.

Then I began to analyze why I did it that way. Maybe it's because my mother taught me to say thank you when someone gave me something or did something for me. But I think it is more than a habit.

Then I realized that I often repeat the statement, "Gratitude is the least remembered of all virtues and is the acid test of your character." Those who give thanks develop one of the greatest Christian virtues of all. Maybe I give thanks because it's part of my nature. Maybe I give thanks because I know God deserves my appreciation. And yes, maybe I give thanks for past answers because that's a foundation for future answers.

The word "thanksgiving" comes from *eucharisteo*. At the root of this word is *charis*, which is "grace." When you give someone thanks, you communicate "grace"; and in the process, you acquire grace.

The message of the New Testament is grace—it's God doing for you the exact opposite of what you deserve. You deserve hell, but you get heaven. You deserve alienation, but you get intimacy with God. You deserve punishment for your sins (we all do), but you get forgiveness and you get God's love.

To know God loves you is the greatest gift of grace. That knowledge demands thankfulness. When you experience grace, you can do nothing but give thanks to the Giver of grace.

Why Give Thanks?

First, a thankful heart to God puts you on praying ground. So approach God with a grateful heart for everything He's given you. Then He will recognize your sincerity and listen. God will realize you are not bragging, nor are you self-centered. A thankful heart makes you focus on God, and that puts you on praying ground next to the heart of God.

Paul gives us the example of approaching God with a thankful heart: "Now thanks be to God who always leads us in triumph in Christ, and through us diffuses the fragrance of His knowledge in every place" (2 Cor. 2:14).

Then Paul instructs us to attach thanksgiving to our prayers. "In everything by prayer and supplication, with thanksgiving, let your requests be made known to God" (Phil. 4:6). Did you notice that "thanksgiving" comes before making "your requests known to God"?

Second, a thankful heart is an obedient heart. We are commanded to give thanks to God in the psalms: "Give thanks to the LORD!" (see Pss. 30:4; 97:12; 105:1; 106:1,47; 107:1; 118:1,29; 136:1,2,3,26).

Paul also instructed us to tie thanksgiving to our prayers: "Continue earnestly in prayer, being vigilant in it with thanksgiving" (Col. 4:2). He probably told us to give thanks because it was his habit in prayer (see Rom. 1:8; 1 Cor. 1:4; Phil. 1:3; 1 Thess. 2:13; 2 Thess. 1:3; 1 Tim. 1:12; 2 Tim. 1:3; Philem. v. 4).

Since you are instructed to give God thanks, why not do it? And if you obediently give thanks, don't you think God will realize what you're doing and listen to your request?

Third, a thankful heart stimulates your faith to trust God again for another answer to prayer and for even greater answers to prayer. When Daniel was persecuted for his faith, and a civic law was passed that prohibited his prayer life, Daniel didn't quit praying. But he began his prayer with thanksgiving:

"Now when Daniel knew that the writing was signed, he went home. And in his upper room, with his windows open toward Jerusalem, he knelt down on his knees three times that day, and prayed and gave thanks before his God, as was his custom since early days" (Dan. 6:10). Because Daniel knew God had answered his prayers in the past, he began praying—perhaps the most important prayer of his life—with thanksgiving.

Fourth, a thankful prayer or attitude will be a testimony to others. When Paul was instructing the Colossians on how to live for Christ, he told them, "And let the peace of God rule in your hearts, to which also you were called in one body; and be thankful" (Col. 3:15).

It appears that inward peace of the heart and outward thanksgiving are tied together. If we are thankful for our spouse and children, we don't criticize and desire better. If we are thankful for all the "stuff" in our life, we won't break the tenth commandment, "You shall not covet . . ." (Exod. 20:17).

Fifth, thanksgiving is a synonym for praise and blessing. It's one of the ways to worship God. When you thank God for all that you are and all you have and all that God's done for you, you put Him first. Your life centers on God, and not on yourself.

We are instructed, "Enter into His gates with thanksgiving, And into His courts with praise. Be thankful to Him, and bless

His name" (Ps. 100:4). So, what must be our attitude when we appreciate God with worship?

We give Him thanks!

How can we offer praise to God?

We give Him thanks!

How is the best way to bless God?

We give Him thanks!

Sixth, the example of Jesus. The one person who didn't need to give thanks to the heavenly Father was His Son, Jesus Christ. The Father and Son are equal in nature, so the Son didn't need to give thanks; but He did.

Notice what Jesus did before feeding 5,000 with five fishes and two barley loaves. He gave thanks: "And Jesus took the loaves, and when He had given thanks He distributed them to the disciples, and the disciples to those sitting down; and likewise of the fish, as much as they wanted" (John 6:11).

Inasmuch as Jesus came to earth as a Jew and lived a perfect life, He would have given thanks as did those Jews who wanted to be perfect in God's sight.

We should be thankful because of Jesus' example of thankfulness. Remember, Peter said that you "should follow His steps" (1 Pet. 2:21). Since Jesus continually gave thanks, how could we do otherwise?

Seventh, thanksgiving stirs our memory of Christ's death. Some Christian groups call the Communion service the Eucharist. That word comes from *eucharisteo*, which means "giving thanks." The focus of the Lord's Table is that the partakers give thanks for all that Christ did on the cross.

In looking forward to His death, Jesus initiated giving thanks: "And He took bread, gave thanks and broke it, and gave it to them, saying, 'This is My body which is given for you; do this in remembrance of Me'" (Luke 22:19). So we eat with thanksgiving.

Then Jesus took the cup and repeated the same formula: "Then He took the cup, and gave thanks, and gave it to them, saying, 'Drink from it, all of you'" (Matt. 26:27).

I was pastor of Faith Bible Church in Dallas, Texas, from 1956 to 1958. They celebrated the Communion service after the pattern of the old Moravians or the Plymouth Brethren Assemblies. The entire service was spent around the Communion service.

I would ask one of the brethren, "Would you thank God for the broken body of Jesus for your sins?" I would follow by asking several more brethren to pray the same prayer. Then the bread was passed and we all ate together.

Then we followed the same pattern for the cup. Several were asked, "Would you thank God for that spilt blood of Jesus for your sins?"

We are as close to God as we can get when we come to Him in thanksgiving for His broken body and spilt blood.

My Time to Pray

Lord, for all the "great things You have done" (Ps. 126:2, ELT), thank You.

Lord, for answered prayers in the past, thank You.

Lord, for protection from known and unknown dangers, thank You.
Lord, for guidance to do Your will, and Your patience with me when I haven't done Your will, thank You.

Lord, for saving me and giving me Your assurance in dark days, thank You.

Lord, for all Christ did for me on Calvary, thank You.

Lord, I thank You for Your awesome majesty and lovingkindness to me. Amen.

My Answers Today

_____
_____
_____
_____
_____
_____
_____
_____

For suggested recipes, see pages 180-192.

❧ DAY 10 ❧

Fasting to Hunger After God

Bear up the hands that hang down, by faith and prayer; support the tottering knees. Have you any days of fasting and prayer? Storm the throne of grace and persevere therein, and mercy will come down.

JOHN WESLEY

I had been fasting for several days, and it was going well. Bill Greig, Jr., the president of Gospel Light Publishing, asked me, "What great answer to prayer have you gotten because of your fast?"

"I'm not fasting to get an answer to prayer," was my immediate response.

"Then why are you putting yourself through all this torture if you're not fasting to get an answer to prayer?"

"I'm fasting to know God intimately," I said. "My fast is not about getting things from God. I'm fasting to experience God more intimately."

"Oh . . . write that for Regal Books. That's an enticing topic for a book."

I went straight up to my hotel room and began writing what was eventually to be published with the title *God Encounters*.[1]

Even though Bill was right in saying "knowing God" is a worthy topic for a book, Bill was wrong on two other things: First, he asked why I was putting myself through all this trouble. A lot of non-fasters think fasting is difficult or hurtful, or those fasting suffer misery and mental torture. Bill, just like a lot of people facing a fast, thought it was "no fun" or a "torturous experience."

When you spend time with God, it's a satisfying experience. Those who are meeting God experience deep joy. It's an intimacy that's hard to describe or put into words. (More about that later in this chapter.)

Bill was also wrong in thinking that fasting is only about getting answers to prayer. Oh yes, fasting does get answers to prayer. Remember, Jesus told us, "However, this kind does not go out except by prayer and fasting" (Matt. 17:21). But fasting is more than a physical activity of withholding food; we fast *and* pray to get God's attention.

Now, you're on a Daniel Fast and you may be praying for a project at your church, or some personal goal. You're probably following a modified diet and you're spending time in prayer. But in this chapter, let's turn our attention away from the project or goal of your Daniel Fast. Let's examine what happens to your fellowship with God when you fast.

Stay in the Moment

The body is a great big engine. We know that all engines need fuel, whether the fuel is gas, coal, wood or some other type of energy-producing fuel. So our body also needs food to produce the tremendous amount of energy we expend each day. Sometimes, the more energy we expend, the more fuel (calories—carbohydrates, fats and protein) we need to keep going.

When your car is almost out of gas, it begins to skip and cough to tell you it's about to stall. In the same way, if you are used to eating three meals a day—then you miss three meals—your stomach will let you know it's time for a refill.

I don't want to worry you, but during the first 20 days of a fast, you live off the fat in your body by burning it away. (Your fat is the energy to run your body.) That's good because disease is circulated in your body by the blood but finally is deposited in your fat. In a fast, you get rid of potential disease. Maybe that's why God told the

Jews in the Old Testament not to eat the fat or drink the blood (see Lev. 6:26; 7:24-25). Maybe God's instructions were *preventative health* to keep Israel physically free from physical disease and physical weaknesses. So fasting is good—not harmful—because you purge your physical body from potential sickness and disease.

So when you don't eat—because you're fasting—you get signals from your body on a regular basis, "feed me." Every signal should remind you of the purpose of your Daniel Fast. Every time your stomach "growls" or "gurgles," you are reminded that "this fast is for God."

---

*Hunger pangs should keep you in a
God-inspired moment.*

But it's not just your stomach that sends you messages. Every billboard on the highway seems to advertise hamburgers, pizza or some snack. I never remembered seeing so many of these signals until I fasted for 40 days.

Also the TV screen is your enemy. Commercials fill the screen with juicy steaks or luscious cooked lobster prepared to perfection and seasoned perfectly. And it's never a random camera shot of a plate of food; the steak or lobster fills the screen to the edges.

When these mental images of food come, that's a great time to apply spiritual discipline and pray. Rather than thinking about food, or lusting for food, I pray for my project and the goal for which I'm fasting. It's one thing to hunger for food; it's a greater thing to hunger for God's presence in your life.

Jesus said that God would bless—add value—to the one who hungered for God, because the word "bless" means "to add value." Jesus promised, "Blessed are those who hunger and thirst for righteousness, for they shall be filled" (Matt. 5:6). Did you take note of the promise "They shall be filled"? When you're really hungry for a hot, juicy hamburger from your favorite place, there's no satisfaction like sitting down to slowly munch it down.

In the same way, there are times when you really want God to manifest Himself to you. You need God, and You want Him with all your heart. Fasting from earthly food is one way to find God's presence.

The longer you fast, the more keen your thinking becomes. You're not consumed with feeding your body. God begins to consume your thinking—all your experiences. You focus on Him alone. You cry out, "That I may know Him" (Phil. 3:10).

It's not just your mental processes that focus on God when you fast. The brain thinks more clearly and you remember more when fasting. Perhaps it's because your heart is not pumping extra blood to your stomach to digest food. There is extra blood available to the brain, and more blood means the brain functions better.

That's why ginkgo biloba stimulates your mind and helps you remember. It's an herb that increases blood to the brain. So you think clearer when fasting. Therefore, focus your mind on Jesus.

The psalmist exhorts us, "Oh, taste and see that the LORD is good" (Ps. 34:8). When you refrain from earthly food, you can enjoy heavenly food; you fill yourself with Christ alone.

Jesus called Himself bread: "I am the bread of life. He who comes to Me shall never hunger" (John 6:35). We eat for strength and for life; but God also gave us the gift of food to enjoy. Doesn't food satisfy us? Cool, crispy watermelon on a hot humid day! Hot, steaming pizza on a cool evening! Sizzling steak when we're extra hungry! So think of the satisfaction we get from Jesus when we bring our empty heart to Him.

Jesus gives satisfying life, for He promised, "He who comes to Me shall never hunger" (John 6:35). As we fast, we find that Jesus fills every yearning of the heart.

Many have misunderstood Jesus' sermon on the bread of life. He promised, "Unless you eat the flesh of the Son of Man and drink His blood, you have no life in you. Whoever eats My flesh and drinks My blood has eternal life, and I will raise him up at the last day" (John 6:53-54). Some have wrongly thought Christians were cannibals who stole the body of Jesus and ate it. Others have said they must eat and drink of the Lord's Table to be saved. Both ideas are wrong.

When Jesus told us to eat and drink of Himself, it had to do with our union with Christ. When we got saved, we invited Jesus to live in our hearts, and He entered our earthly life to give us eternal life. It's a picture of eating a sandwich that enters our body to give us strength to continue living.

Yes, when we fast, we focus on Jesus who lives within. As we read the Scriptures, we take Christ into our life anew, for Jesus is "the Word [of God]" (John 1:1). So read much Scripture when you are fasting. The Bible—Jesus' words—renews our will to live for God and sharpens our mind to think on God.

That leads us to the second step; if the first step is *union*, then the second step is *communion*. You will have deeper fellowship, or communion, with Christ during a fast than at any other time. Your fast ought to produce union *and* communion.

Let's look at another verse where Jesus tells us to eat of Himself. This one promises us *union and communion*: "He who eats My flesh and drinks My blood abides in Me, and I in him" (John 6:56).

When Jesus says, "I in Him," that's when we have union with Christ. This is the union that begins at salvation because we take Christ into our heart (see John 7:12; Eph. 5:17). We are united to Christ by salvation. So where is Christ when you fast? He's living in your heart.

The other part of that verse, "abides in me," means that we have fellowship, or communion, with Christ. So when you are fasting, you ought to be closer to God than any other time during your Christian experience.

I remember once during a fast attending my church's evening candlelight Communion service. I had not eaten for more than 20 days and was not at all hungry. I hadn't even thought that the Communion service involved eating the bread. I didn't realize I had a problem until the deacon took the white covering off the elements. Then the question hit me, "Shall I eat the Communion bread?"

I was at day 20, heading to a 40-day fast. I was fasting to God and wanted Him to be glorified in all I did.

I rationalized, *I can drink the cup because I'm drinking orange juice every morning.* But no solid food had entered my mouth. Then I thought, *I won't eat the bread. I don't care what others think if I don't eat the bread; this is private between God and me.*

I decided not to eat the bread and drink the cup. I would keep my fast "perfectly" to God. I would pray and meditate as others took Communion. I even wrongly thought, *It would be better if I hadn't come to church tonight so I could honor my fast in private.* Then it dawned on me: *Eating the bread is a picture of communion with Christ; so is fasting when I don't eat.*

So I ate the bread wafer that evening as I fellowshipped with Christ who dwelt in my heart. From that moment on I didn't feel as if I was violating my fast. If anything, I was enhancing my fast because I was communing with Christ, which was one of the purposes of the fast.

My Time to Pray

Lord, I want to know You more intimately as I proceed in this Daniel Fast.

Lord, reveal Yourself to me as I seek to know You.

Lord, I confess my carnality and lack of love to You. Forgive me for being shallow; take me deep with You.

Lord, I commit myself in this Daniel Fast to know You better than I've ever known You in my life. Amen.

My Answers Today

_____
_____
_____
_____
_____
_____
_____

Note
1. Elmer L. Towns, *God Encounters* (Ventura, CA: Regal Books, 2000).

For suggested recipes, see pages 180-192.

DAY 11

Prayer Is Asking

*Fasting is not confined to abstinence from eating and drinking.
Fasting really means voluntary abstinence for a time from various necessities
of life such as food, drink, sleep, rest, association with people and so forth. The
purpose of such abstinence for a longer period or shorter period of time is to
loosen to some degree the ties which bind us to the world or material things
and our surroundings as a whole, in order that we may concentrate all our
spiritual powers upon the unseen and eternal things.*

O. HALLESBY

We come to an interesting question: Why does God want His children to ask Him for things? Isn't God all-knowing? Doesn't He already know our needs? And didn't Jesus say, "Your Father knows the things you have need of before you ask Him" (Matt. 6:8)? So why go without eating as you pray?

Because prayer is relationship with God, have you ever thought of the possibility that God wants to spend time with you? Perhaps that's the reason God gives us the opportunity to ask Him questions. He wants us to spend time with Him.

The fourteen-time Grammy Award winner Ricky Skaggs read my book *Fasting for Spiritual Breakthrough* and sent word he wanted to spend the day with me just to learn about fasting and prayer. So I spent a Wednesday in September 2007 with him.

Sir Edmund Hillary, the first man to climb Mount Everest, read the same book and sent word he wanted to chat with me about fasting. I was making plans to travel to New Zealand to have tea with him, but he died before I could meet with him.

If famous people want to talk to you about fasting, you would probably rearrange your calendar to make it happen. But God is greater than any famous person. Now you've rearranged your schedule to talk with God as you fast. Your Daniel Fast could produce your greatest conversation in history; you're going to talk with the LORD of the universe.

But you're doing more than talking to God about your prayer project. You're altering your diet for 10 or 21 days so that you can ask God for something that's special, and to you, probably very necessary.

Asking is an elementary form of dependence on God. When you ask your mother-in-law for advice, doesn't that show you trust her, and doesn't that draw the two of you closer together? Now you've honored God by asking for answers to your prayer. It shows you believe He can do the thing for which you are asking.

Asking puts you in partnership with God. When you ask someone to help you with a project, doesn't that mean the two of you will work together? Then think of how close you get to a friend when you ask him or her to pray with you about a need (see Matt. 18:19). How close does it put you with God when you ask for His help?

One more thing: You should ask because God likes to be asked. That's why Jesus told us to ask (see Matt. 7:7-8). Don't parents enjoy it when their children ask them for something? Sure! Parents probably already know what their kids need—and maybe even what their kids are wishing to get. And doesn't it make a parent feel good to know their children think they can get anything for them? Love grows in a relationship of asking and getting.

I take my grandchildren—and their parents—out to eat on Sundays after church at an Italian restaurant we all love. Nearby is a Dollar Store where everything costs $1. I take the children there after eating and say, "You can have anything you want!"

They go wild running the aisles, trying to find what they want most. Two of my grandchildren, whose mother is a strict disciplinarian, will only ask for one thing a week. Another grandchild lives only with his mother, who doesn't have much. He at first wanted two or three items. Then, five or six. Finally, it got up to 10 to 12.

What's a couple of dollars, I thought, *compared to the joy we both get out of this experience?*

So that leads to fellowship. When we ask something of God, it enriches our fellowship with our Father. We tell Him what we want, and we get as close to Him as possible to deepen our relationship so we'll get what we need.

And don't forget memories. I take my grandchildren to the Dollar Store to create pleasant memories about their grandfather. So every time you get something from God, you remember a previous answer to prayer and it motivates you to ask again and again; and of course you keep in good relationship with God so you'll get it again and again.

I can still see this little fella who gets 10 or 12 items. He'll come and stand by my chair as I finish my spaghetti and meatballs or Philly cheese steak sandwich. He doesn't say anything; he just stands there. I know what he wants, so I quickly finish and we go to the Dollar Store. You know I love it! So go stand near your heavenly Father and wait for the answer you seek.

Asking in Jesus' Name

Jesus told His disciples, "Until now you have asked nothing in My name" (John 16:24). He was introducing them to a new relationship of asking-prayer from the Father. After Jesus died and went to heaven, His followers would have a new and different prayer relationship with Him.

What was that new prayer relationship? "Ask, and you will receive, that your joy may be full" (John 16:24). That part about joy means Jesus was saying, "You're going to be happy when I answer your prayers" (John 16:24, *ELT*).

Jesus was not using His name as some sort of mantra, nor was it a secret code that opened locked things, or a magical key to open doors. When Jesus said to "[ask] in My name," He wasn't even telling us to add His name to the end of our prayers to get things from the Father, although we do end our prayers in Jesus' name.

To pray in Jesus' name is to take full advantage of His death to take away our sins (see John 1:29). Because His blood cleanses us from every sin in our life (see 1 John 1:7), His death sealed our eternal relationship with the Father. So every time we pray in Jesus' name, we take advantage of what He did on the cross to connect us to our heavenly Father.

But there's also a present relationship. When we pray in Jesus' name, we identify with Jesus' new life in heaven. More than 172 times in the New Testament we are said to be "in Christ." We are as close to the Father's heart as Jesus. So ask what you need "in Jesus' name"; He has promised to hear and answer. Paul tells us about this new relationship:

> But God, who is rich in mercy, because of His great love with which He loved us, even when we were dead in trespasses, made us alive together with Christ (by grace you have been saved), and raised us up together, and made us sit together in the heavenly places in Christ Jesus (Eph. 2:4-6).

One more thing about praying in Jesus' name: He's in your heart! You asked Him to come into your life when you got saved. Paul prayed for the Ephesians to understand their new relationship that "Christ may dwell in your heart through faith" (Eph. 3:17). So ask in Jesus' name because He's in your heart.

Conditions

Obviously, you can't ask for just anything, nor will you get everything you ask for in prayer. God doesn't do impossible things like making the past never happen. You can't ask God to take away the abortion that you wish you had never had.

God won't give you something that will hurt you, or something you shouldn't have. Take for example my little grandson who likes to get a lot of things at the Dollar Store. I wouldn't buy him a new motorcycle or a new pair of $200 wingtip shoes. He can't use them, and he's not ready for them.

In the same vein, I wouldn't buy something that would hurt him—marijuana or a beer or a pack of cigarettes.

One Sunday the little guy wanted a pack of poker chips wrapped in a tube of cellophane—I wouldn't buy them, maybe because poker chips are a symbol for gambling. I walked him over to the cookie shelf and said, "I've got something better for you." Instead of a cellophane pack of poker chips, it was a cellophane pack of chocolate cookies. He smiled and was happy.

I thought of Elijah in the desert, sitting under a willow tree, weeping. He prayed to die, "LORD, take my life" (1 Kings 19:4). But God was smiling out on the darkness because He had something better for Elijah. I can hear God say, "How about a chariot and horses of fire? How about not dying at all?"

Next time you ask for something, and God says no, maybe He has got some chocolate cookies wrapped in cellophane, instead of poker chips.

The first condition of prayer in Jesus' name is to *ask*. That's it! Prayer is as simple as asking. You can keep your prayers on the lofty heights of worship and praise—ways to pray that are necessary—but if you don't ask, you may not get what you need.

Didn't James reinforce that method of praying? "You do not have because you do not ask" (Jas. 4:2). So maybe you haven't got the things(s) for which you are fasting because you haven't asked in the right way or with the right attitude or at the right time.

The second condition is to ask repeatedly or continually. Remember, Jesus said, "Keep on asking and it will be given you; keep on seeking and you will find; keep on knocking fervently and the door will be opened to you. For everyone who keeps on asking receives; and he who keeps on seeking finds; and to him who keeps on knocking, the door will be opened" (Matt. 7:7-8, *ELT*).

Is God telling you to pester Him? No! When God tells us to continually ask, He is telling us to keep our faith in Him strong. Sometimes God waits to see if we are sincere. At other times He begins to answer, but it takes time to get the answer to you. Maybe God wants you to keep on praying because He's going to slowly unfold the answer to you. Sometimes, the longer you pray the more of the answer you get.

If prayer is like the gasoline that runs the motor, maybe you need to pray often, like when I had to fill a very small gas tank on a small green lawnmower that I bought at a garage sale. I've never seen another lawn mower like that little thing. It would take four or five tanks of fuel to cut my lawn. Sometimes you have to keep putting prayer in to continue to get answers out.

A third condition is abiding in Christ, the living Word of God. He said, "If you abide in Me, and My words abide in you, you will ask what you desire, and it shall be done for you" (John 15:7). Usually, people think abiding means meditating on Christ or communing with Christ. It means that, but it also has a more elementary meaning. Abiding means obeying His commandments or rules. "He who keeps His commandments abides in Him" (1 John 3:24).

So the third condition deals with obedience. At another place in Scripture, John tells us, "Whatever we ask we receive from Him, because we keep His commandments" (1 John 3:22). As a kid, I knew I had to obey my mother if I wanted her to make some chocolate fudge or a churn of ice cream.

Why is it that we think we can curse with the Lord's name or fulfill our lust, or have illegal sex, or disobey our parents and still expect God to answer our prayers? Those who are the most obedient get the most answers.

What does it mean to let the words of Jesus, or the Bible, abide in you? It means you fill your life with Scripture. You go to church to hear the Bible preached and taught. You read it privately; you memorize it and meditate on it (see Ps. 1:1-3). You fill your life with the written Word of God, which is like filling your life with Jesus, the living Word of God.

When you live by the Scriptures, you are living a life that qualifies for answers to prayer. When the Bible controls your life, you don't ask for selfish things. You don't arbitrarily ask for $1,000,000 to make you happier or to fulfill any wish list you may conceive. When you are filled with the Bible, it controls your desires so that you want what God wants. Those who are controlled by the Bible will more likely pray according to the will of God.

That leads us to the fourth condition. We must pray according to God's will. John promised, "Now this is the confidence that we have in Christ, that when we ask for anything according to His will,

He hears us, and we know that we will get the petitions we ask of Him" (1 John 5:14-15, *ELT*).

Notice the progression in God's promises in 1 John 5:14-15. First, we ask according to God's will; second, we know that God hears us when we ask in His will; and third, we know we will receive the petitions we request from Him.

Remember the rock song of the 1960s sung by Janis Joplin? "Lord, won't you buy me a Mercedes, all my friends have Porsches."[1] Can we really think the will of God is a mansion in Beverly Hills or the most expensive luxury car or winning the lottery? No! You must pray within God's will to get answers.

God keeps many of His children on short financial leashes because if they had all the money they desired, or asked, they would winter in Palm Springs and summer on the French Riviera. Fulfilling the lust of the flesh (physical satisfaction) or the lust of the eye (things) or the pride of life (position or fame) would destroy them (see 1 John 2:15-17).

The fifth condition is faith. "But without faith it is impossible to please Him, for he who comes to God must believe that He is, and that He is a rewarder of those who diligently seek Him" (Heb. 11:6). To get your reward you must believe that God exists, then diligently seek Him for the petitions you want. Isn't that why you are fasting for 10 or 21 days?

Jesus told us to "have faith in God" (Mark 11:22). Then He told us we can exercise our faith by speaking words. This is what we do in prayer, "For assuredly, I say to you, whoever says to this mountain, 'Be removed and be cast into the sea,' and does not doubt in his heart, but believes that those things he says will be done, he will have whatever he says" (Mark 11:23). Did you see the word "says" three times in that verse? That means you are to *say* in faith what you want to receive in prayer. So tell God right now about the faith project for which you are fasting.

So, the fifth secret to getting answers to prayer is faith. After Jesus directed us to exercise faith, He told us how to do it: "Therefore I say to you, whatever things you ask when you pray, believe that you receive them, and you will have them" (Mark 11:24).

Aren't you diligently seeking God by fasting and prayer for an extended period of time? Didn't you begin the Daniel Fast as a statement of faith that you believe God could give you the faith project for which you pray? The more time you spend in prayer, and the longer you fast, the stronger your faith becomes.

Faith is believing God will hear you and that He will answer. Faith is a growing experience: "From faith to faith . . . the just shall live by faith" (Rom. 1:17). If you have beginning faith to start a fast, then the more you pray, the stronger your faith becomes.

The sixth condition deals with your life's fruit. The prayers we seek from God are tied to the fruit in our lives. We are told to abide in Jesus to have fruit: "He who abides in Me, and I in him, bears much fruit" (John 15:5).

Then Jesus promises, "I chose you and appointed you that you should go and bear fruit, and that your fruit should remain, that whatever you ask the Father in My name He may give you" (John 15:16). Here Jesus ties answers to prayer with fruit-bearing in our lives.

We have discussed six conditions to pray in Jesus' name. We can get our prayers answered because of the *friendship factor*. Don't we enjoy giving things to our friends when they ask? Jesus said, "You are My friends if you do whatever I command you" (John 15:14). When we are in fellowship with Jesus, and we walk with Him in friendship, isn't that the place where prayers get answered?

My Time to Pray

Lord, I believe You exist; You've saved me, and You answer prayer;
so come answer the prayer for which I'm fasting.

Lord, I know Jesus came into my heart and He lives in my life;
now I come through Jesus for the prayer project for which I'm fasting.

Lord, Jesus is sitting at Your right hand in glory, and I am positionally
"in Him." Now I come through Christ to get answers for which I am fasting.

Lord, give me faith to believe You for the answer for which I am fasting.
"I believe, help Thou my unbelief." Amen.

My Answers Today

_____

_____

_____

_____

_____

_____

_____

_____

_____

_____

_____

_____

_____

_____

_____

_____

_____

Note

1. See Janis Joplin Lyrics, http://www.google.com/search?hl=en&q=Lord%2C+won%27t
+you+buy+me+a+Mercedes&rlz=1W1GZEZ_en&aq=f&oq=&aqi=g4 (accessed June 18,
2009).

For suggested recipes, see pages 180-192.

❦ DAY 12 ❦

Fasting to Worship God

It is not wrong to fast, if we do it in the right way and with the right motive. Jesus fasted (Matt. 4:3); so did the members of the early church (Acts 13:2). Fasting helps to discipline the appetites of the body (Luke 21:34) and keep our spiritual priorities straight. But fasting must never become an opportunity for temptation (1 Cor. 7:7). Simply to deprive ourselves of a natural benefit (such as food or sleep) is not of itself fasting. We must devote ourselves to God and worship Him. Unless there is the devotion of heart (see Zech. 7) there is not lasting benefit.

WARREN W. WIERSBE

Have you ever asked yourself why you should worship God when He has all the angels of heaven worshiping Him? After all, they cry continually, "Holy, holy, holy is the LORD of hosts; the whole earth is full of His glory!" (Isa. 6:3).

It would seem that the praise they offer to God is far better than any praise that we could give Him. Why? Because angels can't sin, so they worship Him with a pure heart. Also, they are not influenced by selfishness and duplicity; nor do their thoughts tend to wander when they're praying. That means angels are not influenced by earthly desires, as we are, when they worship.

Another thing, angels worship God constantly: "They do not rest day or night, saying: 'Holy, holy, holy, Lord God Almighty, Who was and is and is to come!'" (Rev. 4:8). But we don't worship God continually, because we are busy earning money or looking after our family or doing 101 other things that crowd into our schedule.

And don't angels know more about God than we know about God? They stand in God's presence as ministering spirits for Him (see Heb. 1:14).

So this brings up an interesting question: Since God has a multitude of angels to worship Him continually, and they are more pure than we are, and they know more about God than we will know on this earth, why does He need our worship at all?

Technically, worship is the only thing that God can't do for Himself. If I write my own press release, brag about my accomplishments and boast to everyone how great I am, who would believe me? Doesn't Scripture say, "And a man is valued by what others say of him" (Prov. 27:21)?

But doesn't God already know His greatness and what He can do? So if God were to praise Himself, would it accomplish any heavenly good? God can't worship Himself; He wants us to be authentic worshipers. So from a sincere heart, Jesus told us, "The Father seeks worship" (John 4:23, *ELT*). So God seeks worship from His people to manifest all the things that He is and that He can do.

In Psalm 103, David wrote, "Bless the LORD, O my soul; And all that is within me, bless His holy name!" (Ps. 103:1). First, this teaches us to approach God with all our heart; that means nothing is held back or nothing is hidden from His view. Shouldn't we be openhearted in worshiping God? He knows all that we are and do, so we should be honest in our worship of Him.

Second, when we bless God, we add value to Him just as when we bless someone on this earth we add value to him or her. The word "bless" means "to add value" to something. I can bless my grandson financially by giving him money. I can bless my wife emotionally by serving her coffee in bed every morning when she wakes. We bless people spiritually when we help them learn the Bible or follow God's commandments.

So how can we bless God? He doesn't need our money; He doesn't need any of the stuff that we can give Him; we can't do anything to make His life easier. We can't give God anything He doesn't have. God needs absolutely nothing.

But when we bless the Lord, we give Him something He does not already have. We are adding value to God's kingdom by praising Him for redeeming our soul and transforming our life. We recognize God's goodness for saving us, and His greatness for giving us eternal life.

When we worship God, we move out of ourselves and get closer to Him, perhaps closer than ever before. We move away from our prayers and our petitions, and we focus on Him and His glory. When we worship God, we are not asking for something for ourselves, nor are we asking to get out of trouble or for Him to protect us. Our worship has nothing to do with ourselves; it has everything to do with God.

Why Praise God?

Have you ever noticed that we are commanded to worship God? The writer of Hebrews says, "Let us continually offer the sacrifice of praise to God, that is, the fruit of our lips, giving thanks to His name" (Heb. 13:15). Just as a peach tree produces peaches, so our mouths must produce the words of gratitude that come from our hearts because we are thankful that God has saved us.

But there's another reason to worship God. Let's think about what worship does for us. Each of us needs hope in this life for something outside ourselves. When we praise God for His protection over our life, we are lifted higher and closer to God than ever before. And isn't thankfulness great, because it keeps us from being pessimistic where we expect failure.

Worship keeps us from becoming bogged down in the depressing circumstances of life. Worship focuses our life on something greater than our present limitations. Praise keeps us from being self-centered and negative.

Think about what worship teaches us. Every time we praise God, we begin to learn something more about God—what He has done for us, and what He has promised He will do for us in the future. And as we learn more and more of what He has done for us, it deepens our relationship with Him.

Maybe this is why the disciples "were continually in the temple praising and blessing God" (Luke 24:53), and why Paul dedicated the book of Ephesians "to the praise and glory of His grace" (Eph. 1:6).

Practicing Worship

We can never achieve the highest level of praise like the angels worship God, yet we can pray with David, "Let the words of my mouth and the meditation of my heart be acceptable in Your sight" (Ps. 19:14). Although we can't pray in the words of angels, we can pray in the words of David and ask God to accept our daily praise.

Think of all the great things God does for you. It wouldn't hurt to make a list of all the things God has done for you and audibly repeat them in appreciation to God. Paul told us, "In everything by prayer and supplication, with thanksgiving, let your requests be made known to God" (Phil. 4:6); so we ought to use thanksgiving as a tool to help us pray better in the future.

Then we should do as David suggests: "Magnify the LORD . . . And let us exalt His name together" (Ps. 34:3). Look at that word "magnify"; it's impossible to magnify God because He can't get any bigger or any more awesome. So how do we magnify God? Think of your reading glasses. I need "cheaters" to read the gray newspaper and telephone book. When I use my "cheaters," the words are not magnified on the paper. We all know the words don't get any bigger. The words are magnified in my eyes to read better.

So when you magnify God, He becomes larger in your head and heart. And what do you do when that happens? You respond to God in a bigger or better way. You become absorbed into God and now you are ready to add prayers to your Daniel Fast.

Practice the continual presence of God in your life. David said, "I will bless the LORD at all times; His praise shall continually be in my mouth" (Ps. 34:1). As you go through this day, consciously look for the little ways that you see God in your life. Say a short prayer of thanksgiving for everything He does. The more you thank God for what He is doing in your life, the more His presence will be manifested in your life.

My Time to Pray

Lord, I will worship You from the bottom of my heart and I will not hold back any part of myself in my worship.

Lord, I will continually bless Your name and worship You in the big and little things of my life.

Lord, forgive me when I haven't seen Your presence in my life; when I am unaware of Your working in my life. Help me see more clearly as You develop Your will for my life, and teach me to be thankful for what You are doing.

Lord, thank You for revealing Yourself to me. Amen.

My Answers Today

_____

_____

_____

_____

_____

_____

_____

_____

_____

_____

_____

_____

_____

_____

_____

_____

_____

_____

For suggested recipes, see pages 180-192.

❧ DAY 13 ❧

Fasting to Locate Sin

Although there are many different kinds of fasts, the most common, and the one I recommend for starting, is to abstain from food, but not drink, for a given period of time. So far as drink is concerned, all agree that water is basic. Some add coffee or tea; some add fruit juices. All also agree that something like a milkshake goes too far and is not in the spirit of fasting. Whatever, the fast involves an intentional practice of self-denial, and this spiritual discipline has been known through the centuries as a means for opening ourselves to God and drawing closer to Him. . . . To the degree that fasting becomes more of a norm in our day-to-day Christian life as individuals and congregations, we will become more effective in spiritual warfare.

C. PETER WAGNER

In October 1973, the students of Liberty University experienced the presence of God in a revival that resulted in a fast for 60 hours. The usual Wednesday night prayer meeting ended a little after 9:00 P.M., and the revival that transformed many lives began about 10:30 P.M.

The main auditorium of Thomas Road Baptist Church was the students' main place to "hang out" because this infant university didn't have many facilities, and most students were living in small houses around the church.

About 35 students were scattered in small groups throughout the auditorium when a weeping young man stood behind the pulpit to announce, "You all think I'm saved, but I'm not. . . ." He confessed his sins of lying, cheating on tests, being an egotist, and several other sins.

The shocked students listened intently until he went down to the pulpit stairs to pray. Some went to pray with him; others prayed for him in small groups. A reverential spirit gripped the room. Then over the sound of whispered prayers, another boy stood behind the pulpit. He, too, began, "You think I'm saved, but I've never received Christ. . . ." He too confessed his sins and went down the other side of the pulpit to pray. Several joined him.

Then the sound of the piano playing "Sweet Hour of Prayer" filled the prayer vacancies. A young lady had a key and had unlocked the piano cover and had begun playing. The background hymns didn't stop for approximately 60 hours. Other pianists sat on the front row waiting their turn to play. It's almost as if everyone agreed, "If the music stopped, the revival would end." Within a few minutes, melodious organ music joined the piano. There were also many willing organists to keep the revival going.

Next a girl gave the same testimony: "All of you think I'm saved because I was baptized as a young girl . . . but I'm not. . . ."

Around midnight, someone phoned Pastor Jerry Falwell and told him, "You'd better get down to church; revival's breaking out." He came in casual clothing without tie and suit. There was a sense of urgency. Throughout the night other students and church members felt a sudden urge to "come down to the church." Some received a phone call from friends; others were awakened by the Holy Spirit. By 6:00 A.M. more than 2,000 people filled the auditorium.

The university was shut down for two days; high-schoolers didn't go to school; those who owned businesses shut their doors. God's presence was in the church and no one wanted to leave. When students got so tired they couldn't stay awake, they slept under the pews; some even slept on the floor in the back foyer. When Jesus was there, who could leave? The crowd swelled to more than 4,000.

There was no formal preaching, but people formed a long line off to the left of the pulpit. When it came their time to speak, some confessed their sins; some announced that they had just prayed to receive Christ; others testified of their faith; others just requested a song to be sung by all or for some soloist to sing a favorite.

For 60 hours the mood of the audience swayed back and forth between reverential times of meditation to loud shouting of "Hallelujah!" or "AMEN."

The great revivals of Wheaton College and Asbury University were explosive. When the Holy Spirit came like a bombshell, people went everywhere spreading the revival spirit. The Liberty University revival was implosive. People were drawn into God's presence, and they dared not leave; they couldn't leave; they were like people being sucked into a whirlpool.

Many who had previously professed salvation were truly born again because they had only made an outward confession that wasn't of the heart. God showed many the hidden sin of their hearts. The proud had been boastful but now saw it as a sin of arrogance against God. Those who had many small sins that didn't hurt anyone repented when they realized their sin was against God. And of course there were some sensational testimonies of those who were hiding besetting sins.

Here's where the fasting comes in: Almost no one left the church to go out for a meal. Christ was the Bread of Life, and fellowshipping with Him satisfied any hunger that one may have had. People were so busy meeting with God that they didn't take the time to eat; no, they didn't want to eat.

One student who phoned out to have pizza delivered felt so guilty that most of the pizza ended up in the trash, even though there were multitudes who had not eaten for a day. Sometimes fasting becomes a struggle, but there are other times—like the revival at Liberty—when the Lord is so manifest that people forget about food: "Oh, taste and see that the LORD is good" (Ps. 34:8).

When God blessed the Liberty students with His presence, it was what I call the "atmospheric presence of God." Just as you can feel moisture on a cloudy day when there is no rain, so you can experience God's presence. Revival is defined when God pours out His presence on His people, as seen in the promise of the Lord: "I will pour out My Spirit on all flesh" (Joel 2:28).

In that 60-hour revival, God blessed the students of Liberty University because they fulfilled Scripture: "Blessed are those who hunger and thirst for righteousness, for they shall be filled" (Matt. 5:6).

The revival was broken about 7:00 P.M. on Saturday morning. A young man stood behind the pulpit to "confess" his sins. He included some sexual conduct in high school, but it seemed more like bragging. People didn't sense a sorrow for sin, nor was there brokenness. It's as though the Holy Spirit said, "I'll have no part of this," and He removed His presence.

Many students left for Christian service assignments, and the leader struggled to keep the meeting going. But around 9:00 A.M., everyone realized it was over; so a benediction was prayed and everyone went home.[1]

Now What?

This revival was about the Holy Spirit showing people their sin when they sought God's face and fasted and repented of their sin. You are now in a 10- or 21-day Daniel Fast, praying for a particular project or for a reason that God has put upon your heart. What does this event say to you?

Perhaps God led you into this 10- or 21-day Daniel Fast to show you some sin of attitude, actions or contemplation. Perhaps God wants you to deal with a sin before He gives you the big breakout you seek.

Let's look at reasons why there may be a barrier to your spiritual victory. Sin could be a small, insidious thing that's hindering your spiritual progress, but you might not be aware of it. Why?

Sometimes we're blinded to our sin. It's there, but we don't see it. We're like a man with cancer who has a hidden growth in his colon that's sapping his strength, but he doesn't know it. He used to walk 18 holes of golf and carry his clubs. But slowly he lost his strength, so he rode in a cart. Then he cut the game to 9 holes because he got so tired. Finally, cancer cut his stamina so he didn't even want to play. Then a colonoscopy revealed cancer; he had an operation and now he's back to 18 holes of golf.

Sin—like cancer—cuts into our spiritual strength so we can't do the things for God we used to do. Then sin kills our stamina. We don't want to pray or read our Bibles or even go to church where we praise and worship God.

Before sins binds up our strength, it blinds us. "Satan, the god of this evil world, has blinded the minds of those who don't believe, so they are unable to see the glorious light of the Good News that is shining upon them. They don't understand the message we preach about the glory of Christ, who is the exact likeness of God" (2 Cor. 4:4, *NLT*).

The longer you remain in the light, the more you realize what God is trying to tell you. In the Daniel Fast, God begins to show you the hidden sins that block the flow of His blessings. Like trash in the fuel line, the engine is poking along with half power. When you get rid of the trash, the flow of energy-producing gasoline will give new life to the engine.

But just knowing about your hidden sin is not enough. You must confess it to God to get forgiveness. "If we confess our sins, He is faithful and just to forgive our sins and cleanse us" (1 John 1:9).

Remember, confession means more than just recognition of its presence in your life. When you *confess*, you say the same thing about your sin that God says. When God says it's hideous, you must agree with Him and put it out of your sight.

Take cursing for an illustration. Some Christians treat cursing as a bad habit; or they excuse it with a bad temper or an emotional outbreak. But note what God thinks: "The Lord will not hold him guiltless who takes His name in vain" (Exod. 20:7).

When you fast for a long time, you begin to see things as God sees them. When you see how terrible your sin is, you don't have to "make" yourself repent. You don't have to make yourself give up a sin that's hard to give up. Fasting in God's presence gives you strength, and you say, "I can do all things through Christ who strengthens me" (Phil. 4:13).

My Time to Pray

Lord, I seek Your presence in my life. You have said, "You will seek Me and find Me, when you search for Me with all your heart" (Jer. 29:13).

Lord, I yield my whole life to You, including my mind, my attitude and the things I like to do. I take my control off these things.

Lord, fill me with Your Holy Spirit to study Your Word, to pray and to serve You.

Lord, take away my blindness and show me any sin that blocks Your blessing in my life.

Lord, I confess my sin (by name), and I ask You to forgive me and cleanse me. Amen.

My Answers Today

_____
_____
_____
_____
_____
_____
_____
_____
_____
_____
_____
_____

Note

1. Elmer Towns, *What's Right with the Church* (Ventura, CA: Regal Books, 2009), pp. 84-86. See also Elmer Towns, *The Ten Greatest Revivals Ever* (Ann Arbor, MI: Servant Publications, 2000), pp. 13-14.

For suggested recipes, see pages 180-192.

❀ DAY 14 ❀

Don't Violate Your Fast

One obvious value of fasting lies in the fact that its discipline helps us keep the body in its place. It is a practical acknowledgment of the supremacy of the spiritual. But in addition to this relaxing value, fasting has direct benefits in relation to prayer as well. Many who practice it from right motives and in order to give themselves more unreservedly to prayer testify that the mind becomes unusually clear and vigorous. There are a noticeable spiritual quickening and increased power of concentration on the things of the Spirit.

J. OSWALD SANDERS

What happens when you slip and eat—when you eat something that you vowed that you wouldn't eat? That's a tough question. Tough, because the slip is against God; you violated your promise to God. Tough, because the slip is also against yourself; you promised yourself to pray and fast.

Let's start with an unintentional violation of your fast. You ask how eating something can be unintentional. Isn't eating a choice? Not always.

I walked out to the receptionist in the School of Religion where my office is located. It was the Halloween season and the receptionist had a dish of "friendly" candy corn on her desk. It was her way of saying hello to those who come to Liberty University's School of Religion.

I began talking to her about a project and without thinking I popped a couple of candy corn pieces into my mouth and began chewing them. Before I could swallow, the impact of food—just a little—in my mouth dawned on me.

DEFINITIONS

To violate a fast is to breach the limits of your diet or the length of your vow that you made to God.

To break a fast is to come to the completion of the time and commitment of the fast and begin eating a normal diet.

"Ohh!" I smacked my forehead, realizing what a foolish act I had just committed.

"Ohh . . ." I continued to moan as though I had cut my finger with a knife or slammed a car door on my finger. I was thinking of the fingers holding more candy corn, like the original candy corn that committed the infraction.

"Ohh . . ." I agonized when I realized I'd just lost three days of a 10-day fast. Three days lost, and I'd have to begin again for another whole 10 days. I couldn't just say "whoops!" and keep going.

What do you do if you unintentionally violate your Daniel Fast? That's easy to answer. You do what I did. First, I immediately prayed and asked God to forgive my "ignorant" sin. That's when you are not aware of what you are doing. You presumably are innocent because you didn't know what you were doing. But try telling that to the cop who pulled you over for speeding 60 miles per hour in a 35-mile-per-hour speed zone.

In the Old Testament there was a severe penalty for presumptuous sin (intentionally sinning) and less penalty for sins of ignorance (not realizing you were breaking God's law; see Num. 15:29-31). So what do you do if you ignorantly violate your Daniel Fast, like I did? First I began eating a regular meal because I had violated my fast. Second, I asked God to forgive me of an ignorant sin. "If we confess our sins, He . . . forgives" (1 John 1:9). Third, I asked God to keep me from doing it again, "Keep me from hidden faults" (Ps. 19:12, *ELT*).

Since the reason for my fast had not been accomplished, I waited some time and began my 10-day fast a second time.

I'd like to tell you that God answered my prayer and I never ignorantly broke my fast again. But the second time was just as ignorant as the first. It was the Valentine season and I walked out to the same receptionist again with a task for her to do. This time she had chocolate kisses wrapped in silver paper. Whereas the first time I "popped" candy corn into my mouth without any effort, this time I had to unwrap the silver paper, all the time not realizing what I was doing until I was chewing chocolate.

"Should I spit it out?" I quickly asked. But realizing what had happened, I swallowed the rest of the candy kiss. I stopped my fast; I didn't begin again for another week. I followed the same procedure as before.

The Daniel Fast is a partial fast, so you are eating something. It should be easy to discipline your food intake concerning certain items. But suppose you violate your fast because you give in to temptation. The Bible calls that a presumptuous sin, and instructs you to pray, "Keep back your servant from presumptuous sins" (Ps. 19:13).

There are several layers to this problem. First, you scandalized will. You have hurt your willpower by doing the thing you vowed not to do. This impacts your self-perception and weakens your self-esteem. By violating your vow, you might build a negative self-image. This is the person who hates himself and perhaps violates his conscience to punish himself.

So how do you soothe your self-esteem and begin again to build self-discipline? You can't do it in yourself. Even Paul said, "The evil I will not to do, that I practice" (Rom. 7:19). Paul was frustrated because of this: "For what I am doing, I do not understand" (Rom. 7:15).

The answer to Paul's broken vows and unfulfilled commitments was the Lord. "I thank God—through Jesus Christ our Lord" (Rom. 7:25). You need the power of Christ to help you.

If you've violated your vow, remember that it's not just against yourself and your standards; you have sinned against God. "When you make a vow to God, do not delay to pay it" (Eccles. 5:4). Why? Because "Your mouth is making you sin" (Eccles. 5:6, *TLB*).

Don't try to fool God by saying you didn't understand how hard a Daniel Fast would be, or you didn't really understand when you made a vow. "Don't try to defend yourself by telling . . . that it was all a mistake [to make the vow]. That would make God very angry" (Eccles. 5:6, *TLB*).

Only in your private audience with God will you understand how serious it is to break your vow to God. When you pray privately, your words will choke you. When you pray out loud, the ceiling will turn to lead and your prayers will bounce back to you. Your heart will condemn you and you will realize you can't pray for the spiritual good for which you intended to fast.

But you've also let others down. If you formed a prayer bond by "agreeing" with them, will God answer them because you've broken the circle of agreement? Only you can determine that answer as you wait before God.

The depths of your conviction will determine the depth of your confession. You should cry out to be restored to God's presence, "Why do You hide Your face from me?" (Ps. 88:14). You haven't lost your relationship with God; you've only lost your fellowship with Him. Again David prayed, "Sometimes I ask God . . . why am I walking around in tears, harassed by enemies" (Ps. 42:9, *THE MESSAGE*).

Don't get down on yourself, because "The blood of Jesus Christ His Son cleanses us from all sin" (1 John 1:7). The word "all" means that God forgives deep sins like murder and theft, but He also forgives things like broken promises.

Then realize that God deals with you in mercy, just as He dealt with Paul who confessed his many sins but recognized, "God had mercy on me" (1 Tim. 1:13, *TLB*).

Then begin your Daniel Fast again, not where you left off. Begin again from the beginning, whether it's for 3 days, 10 days or 21 days. Enter the Daniel Fast with joy because you were forgiven all past violation. Begin again with all the faith that you exercised the first time.

My Time to Pray

Lord, I enter a Daniel Fast with all my integrity, and I will keep it to the end.

Lord, if I ignorantly violate my fast, forgive me for my unintended mistake.

Lord, if I presumptuously violate my Daniel Fast, forgive me and strengthen my will. I will begin again to keep the original vow I made to You.

Lord, deal with me in mercy, and give me strength to pray and fast; hear the intercessions of my heart for the spiritual goal I've set. Amen.

My Answers Today

_____

_____

_____

_____

_____

_____

_____

_____

_____

_____

_____

_____

_____

_____

_____

_____

For suggested recipes, see pages 180-192.

Day 15 to Day 21 Overview

Learn About Specific Prayers

In the final week of your fast, you'll learn how to receive the crucifixion of Jesus into your prayer life (Day 15) and you'll learn the role of weeping when you fast and pray (Day 16).

You have been fasting for at least two weeks, so you've spent some extra time in God's presence. Day 17 will tell you the strengths of introspective prayers and, most importantly, how to come out of the desert of introspection or discouragement and pray for your faith goal. Also, you need to be reminded that there is a time to rest in prayer (Day 18).

Then you'll read about urgent prayers (Day 19) and warfare prayers (Day 20). Because Satan is your enemy, be vigilant in prayer.

The last day's reading will challenge you to stay in each moment and pray to the end of your fast.

Daily Readings

Day 15: The Prayer of Crucifixion
Day 16: Weeping While Praying
Day 17: Introspective Prayer
Day 18: Resting in Prayer
Day 19: Urgent Prayer
Day 20: Spiritual Warfare Prayer
Day 21: Stay in the Moment

❧ DAY 15 ❧

The Prayer of Crucifixion

As a Boomer, I have been conditioned to enjoy the best the world has to offer. Fasting speaks boldly to consumerism, one of my generational core values. To set aside what I want so that I encourage personal spiritual growth is what it means to deny myself and take up my cross daily in this present age. I suspect it would be difficult for me to rise to the challenge of discipleship and live a consistently Christian lifestyle without practicing the discipline of fasting.
DOUGLAS PORTER

During your Daniel Fast, you will be tempted to quit in many different ways; most of the temptations will be very subtle, so that you may not even recognize them as temptations. Whether temptations are subtle or blatant calls to gross immorality, you must successfully face them and triumph over them.

Perhaps fasting is something you've never done, so be careful. Satan may probably not tempt you to overt outward sin, but he may tempt you to do less, like tempting you to quit fasting before you reach the conclusion. You may be tempted to eat just a little "bite" of the thing you promised to give up for Christ. Or, Satan may tempt you to end your fast one or two days early.

I was saved on July 25, 1950, and six weeks later I went off to Bible College. Satan couldn't trip me up with outward sin, so he pushed me to excesses, i.e., to being fanatical.

I was greatly motivated by a sermon on self-crucifixion in chapel that was preached from Romans: "Knowing this, that our old man is crucified with him, that the body of sin might be destroyed, that henceforth we should not serve sin" (Rom. 6:6, *KJV*). The speaker emphasized "is crucified," which told us it was something we students must do.

Next, the speaker challenged us from Galatians: "And those who are Christ's have crucified the flesh with its passions and desires" (Gal. 5:24). He asked, "What have you crucified today?"

Nothing, I thought. So I decided to find something to crucify. I decided to give up Ping-Pong—something I liked doing—for a week. Then I quickly added, *No softball with the guys.* That was hard, but I did it!

All the men's dorms were heated from a central furnace, and all the heat was turned off around 9:00 P.M. each evening. The room was getting colder as I began praying around 10:30 P.M. I only wore underwear to sleep in, so I began to shiver as I continued kneeling by my bed. I was tempted to jump under a warm blanket but rationalized, *No . . . I crucified my desire for physical warmth.*

I felt that praying in the cold was a way to "crucify the flesh with its affections and lusts." I kept telling myself, *If you love Jesus, you'll crucify the flesh and keep praying in the cold.* After 10 or 15 minutes, I was shivering so hard I couldn't keep my mind on my request; I was struggling inwardly against jumping into the bed. I couldn't pray out loud to focus my thoughts because my jaw shivered too much.

Finally, I rationalized, *God looks at my heart; He doesn't pay attention to my body.* I jumped under the covers, but not to go to sleep. I hunkered down on my hands and head on the bed, with my knees pulled under my body. I went back to praying. I justified myself by saying that prayer came easier as I enjoyed the warmth of the protective blanket.

Then guilt set in. I began to rationalize, *If you really love Jesus, you'd suffer the cold as you pray.* So, to "crucify" any selfish urges for warmth, I got out from under the blanket and knelt in the cold. For two or three minutes, I "felt" victorious over temptation. I felt

I was "crucifying" the bodily urge for warmth. So I prayed with ease when I was only chilly.

After about five to seven minutes, I really got cold and my jaw started shaking again. I couldn't keep my thoughts on what I was praying. Finally, I concluded, *This is stupid,* so I hunkered down again under the covers and began praying. As I got warmer, prayer got easier. Then after five to seven minutes, guilt again set in and I rationalized, *If you love Jesus, you'd pray in the cold.* I thought of how much Jesus suffered for me in His crucifixion. So again I decided to "crucify" myself.

You would have laughed if you had been in that dark dorm room to see me get in and out of bed several times. As a matter of fact, I think God probably laughed at the naïve freshman who was filled with both love and guilt, trying to demonstrate something by jumping in and out of bed.

The problem is that the chapel speaker wrongly applied the idea of crucifixion. Jesus did it all and cried, "It is finished!" (John 19:30). My crucifixion of my flesh can't add anything to Jesus' crucifixion. My crucifixion was just plain old works. The Bible teaches, "Not of works, lest anyone should boast" (Eph. 2:9).

I didn't understand that "crucifixion" is something I *receive* from God, not something I *do* for God. I think the chapel speaker had wrongly applied crucifixion because the old *King James* translates it, "Our old man *is* crucified" (Rom. 6:6, *KJV,* emphasis added), suggesting a present tense verb action. But look carefully at the *New King James Version*: "Our old man was crucified with Him." The verb "crucified" is past action in the original language.

Our crucifixion is a past action; our old nature was crucified when Christ died. We are not to *do* it, but *receive* it. Paul explains it as follows: "I have been crucified [past tense] with Christ" (Gal. 2:20). Christ was crucified in the past, and Paul identified with the cross in his life that he lived after the crucifixion.

When Jesus died, He died all the way. No life was left. When we try to "crucify" ourselves (like praying when it's too cold), we don't die all the way. The old sin nature will tempt us as long as there's life left in this body. However, when we properly "crucify" ourselves, we receive what Christ has done and we apply His death to our sin. Paul said, "I through the law died to the law that I might live to God" (Gal. 2:19). That means we yield ourselves to God and receive His life to triumph over temptation and sin.

This type of life is more about completely yielding ourselves (the inner person) to God rather than doing something to get victory. It's not about us being victorious but Christ being victorious through us. Some call this the "crucified life," while others call it the "transformed life" or the "victorious life." Some refer to it as the "exchanged life"; i.e., "I was in Christ when He died, and now I yield for Him to come into my life."

Paul told us how this exchanged life takes place: "God forbid that I should boast except in the cross of our Lord Jesus Christ, by whom the world has been crucified to me, and I to the world" (Gal. 6:14). When we are "crucified" to the world, we take up all that the cross symbolizes. It means humiliation, degradation and an end to sin. So when we take up the cross, we yield ourselves to God and determine to sin no more.

That doesn't mean we lose our sin nature. No, we still have an old nature that will tempt us to sin (see 1 John 1:8). But we surrender ourselves to God to get His victory over it. Nor does it mean that we will never sin again. We will sin, for John teaches that the one who thinks he has stopped sinning is deceived: "If we say that we have not sinned, we make Him a liar, and His word is not in us" (1 John 1:10). What it does mean is that when we "crucify" ourselves—or take up our cross—we also take on the victory of Christ who triumphed over sin in His death. His death gave us life, so we get the energy of Christ's life when we receive His crucifixion.

Dying to Self-Effort

Jesus challenged, "If anyone desires to come after Me, let him deny himself, and take up his cross daily, and follow Me" (Luke 9:23). That doesn't mean we carry a large, heavy cross, as some have done. It doesn't mean we wear a cross as jewelry, or even erect a cross in front of our home.

Jesus was describing our death to self-effort and earthly desire. Jesus continued this thought in the next verse: "For whoever desires to save his life will lose it, but whoever loses his life for My sake will save it" (Luke 9:24). To lose your life is to do only the will of Christ, not your own selfish will. We lose our life by giving up our earthly desires in order to pursue what Jesus deserves.

Notice the next verse, which tells us we gain nothing by pursuing our desires: "What profit is it to a man if he gains the whole world, and is himself destroyed or lost?" (Luke 9:25). Everything the world has to offer will not compare to the inner life that Jesus gives.

According to Jesus, the issue is that we quit (we yield) thinking what the world cares about or what the world has or what the world promises. In the next verse Jesus says, "For whoever is ashamed of Me and My words, of him the Son of Man will be ashamed when He comes in His own glory" (Luke 9:26).

Crucifying yourself does not mean doing something "religious" or following "good works" to prove yourself to God. You completely surrender yourself to God, allowing Jesus to act within you, by allowing His life to be your energy or power over sin.

Not Physical Death, but Our Inward Death

There are a group of men in the Philippines who allow themselves to be nailed to a cross each year on Good Friday. That's because Jesus died on Good Friday. Wealthy tourists, journalists and a large crowd watch these Filipino men attempt to identify with Christ by being nailed to a cross. One man, a commercial sign maker in his forties, has gone through this "penitence" ritual 21 times.[1]

Self-crucifixion is one of the most abused phenomena of Christianity. Those who do it misinterpret Paul's statement, "And those who are Christ's have crucified the flesh with its passions and desires" (Gal. 5:24). As a result, monks have starved themselves, prayed in snow, beaten themselves with whips (as Christ was beaten), gnashed themselves, placed crude crowns of thorns on their heads, and done all forms of torture. Others have lived in isolation; still others have gone without talking for seven years or longer. Still others have refused marriage, or any of the other good gifts God has given to us (see Jas. 1:17).

God did not intend any of these things when He asked us to become crucified with Christ. We simply receive what Christ has done for us in His crucifixion. We receive His death for the forgiveness of sins; we receive His life for the power to live above our selfish desires. His life gives us strength to overcome temptation.

The problem is that we like to make ourselves look good because we suffer when people criticize us or laugh at us or reject us. So we go through life trying to make ourselves look good, or we play a role. We usually play several roles to make us appealing to the different groups of people we live around.

When we "crucify" ourselves, we yield to Christ so that what He thinks of us matters more than what others think of us. We no longer live to look good to others. Oh yes, we are good neighbors and good testimonies; and we don't want to do stupid things or look weird. But we quit the hypocrite's role to make people think we are something we're not.

So to crucify yourself, you please God first, family second and others third. We live for a new purpose, one suggested by John the Baptist: "He must increase, but I must decrease" (John 3:30).

When we crucify ourselves, we live by a new value system. We give up our inner compulsions for self-power, self-protection, self-success, and gathering "stuff." We give everything to God for His control, and we use what He lets us use.

We no longer have to "win" for selfish reasons. We learn that losing everything to God is much more satisfying than winning the world. For when we lose to God, we win the most important thing in life—being in the center of God's will.

No one likes the idea of dying. All normal people struggle to stay alive. But what if you were to die today? Would life go on without you? Yes! Did life get along fairly well before you were born? Yes! So our life is not necessarily needed.

However, when we die to self, we live to God. When we die, we become important to God, and He uses us. When we die to self, we become necessary to God.

To crucify our self is another way of dealing with our pride. In the act of yielding completely to God, we become more humble. Didn't James tell us, "Humble yourselves in the sight of the Lord, and He will lift you up" (Jas. 4:10)? So our humility is important to God if He's going to use us.

Humility is an interesting word. *Webster* says it means, "to reduce oneself to the lowest position in one's own eyes, and, or the eyes of another."[2] It comes from the word *humus*, which means "from the earth." Humus is that rich organic soil that is formed from the partial decomposition of plant or animal matter. Look deeply: the rich soil that produces new life comes from the death of other matter. So when you "crucify" yourself—or you die—you produce an experience that gives new life from God.

Doesn't our life represent a seed that can be planted by God to give life to others? Remember, Jesus said, "Except a seed is planted in the ground and dies, it abides alone: but if it dies, it brings forth much fruit" (John 12:24, *ELT*). So when we crucify ourselves, others prosper and live.

So our life must be open to the renewing rain and the richness of the soil and the energy of the sun to produce new life in us and others. But that new life is brought forth with *humus*, or the death of self.

Trying to become humble is like trying to go to sleep. The harder you try, the more difficult it becomes. But when we surrender to sleep, like surrendering to the Lord, what we seek will happen. You can't deliberately pray for humility, nor can you work it up; it's a gift from God.

Fasting and Self-Crucifixion

You are on a Daniel Fast that will last 10 or 21 days. Don't be deceived. You will not become more spiritual just because you fast. Refraining from food will not get you any merit before God. Fasting is a discipline whereby you control your body to give more attention to God. When you fast, you meditate more on God, and you pray more often and more deeply. Fasting is simply a means to the end; the result is that you form a deeper relationship with God. It is God who gives the results you seek.

Fasting may drive another nail in the cross of self-crucifixion, but it doesn't make you more holy or a better prayer intercessor. And there are other acts of self-crucifixion that are effective, such as breaking up with a steady who doesn't know Christ, or when you turn down a job because it would compromise your faith, or when you sacrifice some of your money you were saving for a luxury item to give it to the cause of Christ. There are acts of self-crucifixion—when properly yielded—that will cause you to grow in Christ.

Most likely, self-crucifixion comes in small, intentional acts when we give part of our life to God. Doing without food will not gain you merit, but when you put Christ first to intercede for a prayer project instead of eating, that will be honored by Christ.

Small, unrecognizable victories over self-pleasure or self-promotion or satisfying your lust will often not be seen by others, but they will lead to the greatest amount of spiritual growth in our lives.

My Time to Pray

Lord, I acknowledge that I have a big "ego." Please teach me to put Christ first in all I do. Teach me humility.

Lord, I can't crucify myself by anything I pray or do; I receive the benefit of Christ's death to forgive my sin.

Lord, I can't become more spiritual by spending more time in prayer. I receive the life of Jesus that comes from His triumph over death. I yield to Christ and will be strong against temptation in His indwelling presence.

Lord, I will give up little things that hinder my spiritual life and big lusts that would destroy my life. I claim Your victory over temptation. I want to grow in continual steps that bring me closer to You. Amen.

My Answers Today

_____

_____

_____

_____

_____

_____

_____

_____

_____

_____

_____

_____

_____

_____

_____

_____

Notes

1. See http://www.msnbc.msn.com/id/17978154/ (accessed June 4, 2009).
2. *Webster's Dictionary, 11th edition,* s.v. "humble."

For suggested recipes, see pages 180-192.

❧ DAY 16 ❧

Weeping While Praying

"Now, therefore," says the Lord, "Turn to Me with all your heart,
With fasting, with weeping, and with mourning."

JOEL 2:12

Have you ever prayed so hard that you began to weep? Maybe when you got saved you were so convicted of your sin that you wept before God. Today, let's talk about weeping as you pray. Will tears help your prayers get answered?

The Bible teaches that there is "A time to weep, And a time to laugh" (Eccles. 3:4). So when should we weep with our prayers? Also, is there a time to laugh when we pray?

If our eyes are always dry, it probably means our soul is also dry. Because, like the sun that bakes the clay, something could have hardened our heart.

On the other hand, when we shed tears before God, it probably means God has touched the very center of our feelings. He has scratched away the scab that has protected a raw wound that needs healing. God can probably scratch away a hardened scab that even we ourselves couldn't remove.

Many people weep when they first come to Jesus. A woman who was broken over her sin came and stood behind Jesus as He ate at a banquet in Simon the Pharisee's house. "[She] stood at His feet behind Him weeping; and she began to wash His feet with her tears, and wiped them with the hair of her head; and she kissed His feet and anointed them with the fragrant oil" (Luke 7:38).

Simon criticized the woman, probably for her tears, and probably for creating a scene in his house. But mostly Simon criticized Jesus, thinking to himself, "This man, if He were a prophet, would know who and what manner of woman this is who is touching Him" (Luke 7:39). Jesus knew Simon's thoughts and told him a story about canceled debt; and then He defended the woman, saying, " 'Therefore I say to you, her sins, which are many, are forgiven, for she loved much. But to whom little is forgiven, the same loves little.' Then He said to her, 'Your sins are forgiven' " (Luke 7:47-48). There's nothing wrong with weeping our way to the cross for salvation. But not all people shed tears when they are saved.

In 1957, I pastored a church in West Dallas where many Mexican-Americans lived. We had prayed long for the mother of the Rodriquez family to get saved. Her three boys and husband were already converted. Mrs. Rodriquez was deeply touched at our Communion service and raised her hand to be saved at the end of the service. As she was led to Christ, she laughed uncontrollably; she laughed so much that I was asked to come help out with the situation.

Mrs. Rodriquez told of climbing steps at a Catholic cathedral in Mexico to get forgiveness, but nothing happened. She had wept at many liturgical services, but her sins weren't forgiven. When she learned there was nothing she could do to obtain salvation but believe in Jesus, a great burden was rolled off her back. All she had to do was invite Jesus into her heart. Hearing about grace, she began to laugh with the joy of freedom in Christ.

Were you saved with tears or laughter? Even after salvation, weeping can become a part of prayer. Sometimes we weep over sin in our life. Sometimes tears are natural because of our failures or disappointments, or when circumstances turn against us. We weep over the death of someone close to us, even if it was his or her time to die.

When Mary's brother Lazarus died, "Jesus saw her weeping" (John 11:33). It's only natural to cry when a part of your life is taken away in death. It's both you and the other person who has lost something to death. Jesus also wept (see John 11:35), not only for Lazarus but also for the unbelief of Mary, Martha, His disciples and the Jews. He wept because they rejected Him; no one thought He could conquer death. Don't you feel like crying sometimes when you're rejected?

Perhaps you're praying for a Daniel Fast project, and if your prayers are not answered, it will result in a financial loss, a spiritual defeat or a loss in the eyes of those who knew you were fasting, and also a loss of your spiritual vow to God. When we suffer loss, our hearts should break like a dam where stored-up waters begin to flow.

Sometimes our memory causes us to weep. The Jews who were taken captive to Babylon remembered the good times in the Promised Land and the presence of God in the Temple. Their sin led to God's punishment, and Babylon took them into captivity. They cried, "By the rivers of Babylon, there we sat down, yea, we wept when we remembered Zion" (Ps. 137:1). Their captors asked them to sing their psalms. They answered, "How shall we sing the LORD's song in a foreign land?" (Ps. 137:4). There is a time to put away enjoyment and weep over the memory of what we have lost.

Sometimes you will weep over lost loved ones. Perhaps you have added to your fast prayer for the salvation of lost people who are special to you. Paul felt that way when he prayed for lost Jews: "I have great sorrow and continual grief in my heart. For I could wish that I myself were accursed from Christ for my brethren, my countrymen according to the flesh" (Rom. 9:2-3). His tears were not for what he lost, but for those who were lost. Sometimes you will weep over sins in your life, and probably the greater the sin, the greater the tears.

King David committed adultery with Bathsheba, and, to cover up his sin, he had her husband killed. Are there greater sins than adultery and murder? What makes these sins so terrible? "But the thing that David had done displeased the LORD" (2 Sam. 11:27). Every sin is against God, but when we come to realize our sin has personally hurt God, it's then that we weep.

> David therefore pleaded with God for the child, and David fasted and went in and lay all night on the ground. So the elders of his house arose and went to him, to raise him up

from the ground. But he would not, nor did he eat food with them (2 Sam. 12:16-17).

Out of his deep repentance, David wrote Psalm 51, which reflected his deep repentance with tears before God.

> For I acknowledge my transgressions, And my sin is always before me (Ps. 51:3).

> Against You, You only, have I sinned, and done this evil in Your sight. . . . Hide Your face from my sins, And blot out all my iniquities (Ps. 51:4,9).

It's much easier to search for your sin when you deal with it in a biblical way. If you harden your heart and act as if you have no sin, God will eventually break your heart and He will deal harshly with your sin. If you know anything about God, He'll be more severe on your sin than you will be. So deal with it yourself and save yourself some added pain.

Also, be careful about praying for God to break your heart. He may do it and cause you more pain than if you dealt with the sin immediately and completely.

When God breaks your heart, it may be as severe as when you lost a loved one that you thought you couldn't lose. There may have been a time in the past when the pain was so severe that you thought you couldn't go on living. If God has to break your heart, you may have to go through that pain again, only it will be more severe.

How do you deal with known sin? First, recognize disobedience in your life and call it what God calls it—sin. Don't blame your sin nature that tempts you to sin: "If we say that we have no sin, we deceive ourselves, and the truth is not in us" (1 John 1:8). Also, don't say you never even sinned one time: "If we say that we have not sinned, we make Him a liar, and His word is not in us" (1 John 1:10).

Second, confess your sin to God, which means you recognize your sin for what it is: "If we confess our sins, He is faithful and just to forgive us our sins and to cleanse us from all unrighteousness" (1 John 1:9). Did you notice that God cleanses *after* we confess it to Him?

Next, realize that God forgives all sin, with an emphasis on *all*. "If we walk in the light as He is in the light, we have fellowship with one another, and the blood of Jesus Christ His Son cleanses us from *all* sin" (1 John 1:7, emphasis added).

Fourth, you must forsake your sin and then determine not to do it again. Fast and pray: "And do not lead us into temptation" (Matt. 6:13).

Finally, learn a lesson from the experience so you will be stronger and can live above that particular temptation.

My Time to Pray

Lord, show me the sin that hinders my prayer life;
I'll confess and repent.

Lord, I repent and turn from sin that blocks my
fellowship with You.

Lord, Your forgiveness feels good; I enjoy praying
in Your presence. Amen.

My Answers Today

_____
_____
_____
_____
_____
_____
_____
_____
_____
_____
_____
_____
_____

For suggested recipes, see pages 180-192.

❧ DAY 17 ❧

Introspective Prayer

Even if we wanted to, we could not manipulate God. We fast and pray for results, but the results are in God's hands. One of the greatest spiritual benefits of fasting is becoming more attentive to God—becoming more aware of our own inadequacies and His adequacy, our own contingencies and His self-sufficiency—and listening to what He wants us to be and do. Christian fasting, therefore, is totally antithetical to, say, Hindu fasting. Both seek results; however, Hindu fasting focuses on the self and tries to get something for a perceived sacrifice. Christian fasting focuses on God. The results are spiritual results that glorify God—both in the person who fasts and others for whom we fast and pray.

ELMER L. TOWNS

Have you ever felt like you were wandering in a desert and you didn't know which way to go? The horizon seemed distant, and nothing was familiar. Have you ever felt lost and didn't know which way to turn?

The psalmist also felt lost: "In the day of my trouble I sought the Lord . . . my soul refused to be comforted" (Ps. 77:2). Again he cried, "As for me, my feet had almost stumbled; My steps had nearly slipped" (Ps. 73:2).

And complained: "Do not hide Your face from me in the day of my trouble" (Ps. 102:2). The psalmist felt lost and couldn't find God. Have you ever felt like the ceiling of your room was made of iron, and your prayers bounced back in your face? When you cried out to God, did it seem like He wasn't there?

When that happens, most people retreat into introspective prayer. Fasting can be a dark time in their life and they feel hopeless and helpless. All this leads to depression. They feel they can't begin to fast and pray for a prayer project.

Some people complain to God or they complain about God. Instead of reaching up to God or reaching out to others, they retreat inward. They blame themselves, and as a result, they feel even more hopeless and helpless.

Job's prayers are perhaps the best example in the Bible of introspective prayers. He did nothing wrong; there was no outward sin in his life that he should be judged by God. Yet most people know well that he was the victim of violence, family loss, theft and bankruptcy. Job went through incredible suffering and pain, yet he was godly; and no one could accuse him of transgressions. Job was blameless.

Job's cattle were stolen by raiders; his sheep and employees were killed; lightning burned up his crops; and a tornado or hurricane collapsed a house on his children, killing them all. In a different raid upon his possessions, more camels were stolen and more servants were murdered (see Job 1:13-19).

The day we all dread financially came to Job, yet "he fell to the ground and worshiped" (Job 1:20). Instead of complaining, Job exercised faith in God: "Naked I came from my mother's womb, and naked shall I return there. The LORD gave, and the LORD has taken away; blessed be the name of the LORD" (Job 1:21).

Satan, who had masterminded the first wave of persecution, then attacked Job personally. Job developed terribly painful boils that hurt him so severely that he sat in ashes to dry the mucous and scraped himself with the sharp edges of broken pottery shards to relieve his suffering.

That is the day we all dread physically. Job agreed. "For the thing I greatly feared has come upon me, and what I dreaded has happened to me" (Job 3:25). Introspective prayer is always rooted in fear.

When we can't deal with fear, we end up in hopelessness. We give up like Job seemed to give up. "My days are swifter than a weaver's shuttle, and are spent without hope. Oh, remember that my life is a breath! My eye will never again see good" (Job 7:6-7).

His wife also gave up. She was no support to him in his suffering. She told Job, "Do you still hold fast to your integrity? Curse God and die!" (Job 2:9).

There may be times in your life when you feel abandoned by God. Maybe the prayer project for which you are fasting has you discouraged. Maybe you're doubting that God will answer, and you're about to give up.

Yet the Bible is filled with promises that God will come to us when we completely throw ourselves on His mercy and beg for His presence. "This poor man cried out, and the LORD heard him, and saved him out of all his troubles" (Ps. 34:6).

Then later the psalmist promised, "The LORD is near to those who have a broken heart, and saves such as have a contrite spirit . . . but the LORD delivers him out of them all" (Ps. 34:18-19).

Sometimes it's not sin that has us stranded in the desert. Maybe we've taken a wrong turn on the pathway. We've made the wrong decision and miss God's will. So we didn't commit a sin of rebellion or deliberate transgression. Maybe we ignored God's instructions, or we didn't seek His plan for our life. Maybe that's why the One in heaven is silent.

The Lord sometimes allows us to wander off the straight and narrow way because we need to learn the lesson, "Not My will, but Yours, be done" (Luke 22:42).

Maybe God didn't yell at us to call us back to the straight and narrow because we weren't listening to Him. We probably wouldn't have obeyed if He did yell. When we don't pay attention to the biblical signposts, or the inward Holy Spirit, would we have heeded His yell?

Sometimes we get lost in the desert because we were inattentive. Maybe God was trying to direct our lives, but we were too busy with our own business to do His will. So God let us get lost so we will feel the consequences of a life without God's presence. Then we get scared and begin our own yelling.

When I was five years old, Mother took me to downtown Savannah, Georgia, for Christmas shopping. She had a large multicolored tapestry handbag and told me to hang on to the strap.

Everywhere she went shopping, I hung on to the strap as we mingled in the crowd. I remember it was in Woolworth's five-and-dime store that I let go of the bag to examine a pearl-handled six-shooter I wanted for Christmas.

Then I saw the tapestry bag leave, so I ran to grab the strap. As we were crossing Broughton Street, an elderly African-American lady looked down at me and asked, "Why are you holding on to my bag?"

I let out a blood-curdling scream that attracted a policeman who lifted me into his arms and held me till my mother arrived.

I didn't get lost because I wanted to leave Mother. I just didn't pay attention to what was necessary. Is that you? Now, if you spend time fasting in God's presence, you may find your way back to where you got lost.

When God talks to us and we don't listen, what does He do? He can yell—He can also shout—but usually does something different. God does the opposite; He stops talking. He's silent until we're ready to listen to Him. By seemingly abandoning us for a while, God gets our attention and we desperately search for Him.

There's one great thing we learn from being lost in the desert—we learn self-knowledge. One of the best lessons we can learn in life is what we can't do in life. It's even a better gift than learning what we can do.

Remember, there are only a few things that most of us can do best, and then a few more things we do tolerably well; but there are hundreds of thousands of things we can't do. Blessed is the one who knows the boundaries of his spiritual abilities!

The foundation of self-knowledge is the basis upon which you build the rest of your life. When you know yourself well, you can make additions, subtractions and changes. You build a well-rounded spirituality when you build on a proper understanding of yourself.

However, if you spend the rest of your life in introspective prayer, you'll have a miserable, empty life. You won't just feel defeated; you'll be defeated. Temptations will easily trip you and sin will blind you to the perfect will of God.

How does a blind person walk? Not very knowingly. That person misses a lot that he or she would like to see and trips over things that he or she can't see. A blind person ends up seeing only his or her failures and lives in a world of darkness. Do you like living in darkness?

When you're self-blinded, you end up feeling sorry for yourself and you punish yourself for the wrong decisions of your life or the mistakes you've made.

When we look at our life introspectively, we cry with Paul, "For the good that I will to do, I do not do; but the evil I will not to do, that I practice. Now if I do what I will not to do, it is no longer I who do it, but sin that dwells in me" (Rom. 7:19-20). We should never let our prayer of introspection be our last prayer.

You go to the doctor when you hurt. Yet the thing that is causing your pain may not be the root problem. The doctor makes a complete examination to find out why you are sick. So, to get well, we have to listen to the doctor and follow his instructions.

He may prescribe medicine or an operation or exercise or other forms of therapy. The point is, we must follow medical advice to get well. In the same way, we must follow the Doctor's spiritual advice to get well.

When you take an introspective journey into your innermost being, you must take the Doctor (God) with you to tell you what is really wrong and what you must really do to get well. Make sure that when you're looking at yourself introspectively, you're looking through God's eyes. Why? Because He is truth and He will tell you the truth.

Always read the Bible when praying introspectively. Then pray with David, "Open my eyes, that I may see wondrous things from Your law" (Ps. 119:18). Then claim the promise, "The entrance of Your words gives light; it gives understanding to the simple" (Ps. 119:130).

God will reveal to us the things we need to know about ourselves, and He will hide what we shouldn't see. God will not show you all your wickedness; none of us could take it. Notice Paul's frustration when he really saw himself:

For what I am doing, I do not understand. For what I will to do, that I do not practice; but what I hate, that I do. If, then, I do what I will not to do, I agree with the law that it is good. But now, it is no longer I who do it, but sin that dwells in me (Rom. 7:15-17).

The prayer of introspection should bring us to the place of forgiveness. When we look away from our sins and failure to Jesus Christ, we seek cleansing.

But if we walk in the light as He is in the light, we have fellowship with one another, and the blood of Jesus Christ His Son cleanses us from all sin. If we say that we have no sin, we deceive ourselves, and the truth is not in us. If we confess our sins, He is faithful and just to forgive us our sins and to cleanse us from all unrighteousness. If we say that we have not sinned, we make Him a liar, and His word is not in us (1 John 1:7-10).

So what can you learn from the above verses? You can learn that when you walk in the light, you are automatically cleansed from *all* sin (see v. 7). God loves to forgive you because He knows you can't live a perfect life; you have a sin nature (see v. 8). He knows you will continue to practice sins (both ignorantly and volitionally; see v. 10). He offers forgiveness if you confess your sins (see v. 9).

Forgiveness is a new beginning, because God allows you to start over again. You can't ignore the sin you find from your *prayer of introspection*. Deal with it honestly—in the desert—and it will amaze you how quickly you find yourself out of the desert and back on praying ground.

However, you must turn away from your frustration and failure. You must learn about yourself and seek His will. Everything you learn about yourself in the desert will be a foundation upon which you can build for the future.

My Time to Pray

*Lord, sometimes it feels good when I begin my introspection,
but it feels so frustrating when I stay there.*

*Lord, I know that in myself is no good thing; I look to You in
Scripture to find the perfect will for my life.*

*Lord, I confess my sin of self-pity and ask for Your cleansing
and forgiveness by the blood of Christ.*

*Lord, I will walk the straight and narrow path to fulfill
Your will for my life. Amen.*

My Answers Today

_____
_____
_____
_____
_____
_____
_____
_____
_____
_____
_____
_____
_____
_____
_____

For suggested recipes, see pages 180-192.

❧ DAY 18 ❧

Resting in Prayer

Then Esther told them to reply to Mordecai: "Go, gather all the Jews who are present in Shushan, and fast for me; neither eat nor drink for three days, night or day. My maids and I will fast likewise. And so I will go to the king, which is against the law; and if I perish, I perish!"

ESTHER 4:15-16

There are many different ways to pray. There are desperate prayers, warfare prayers, struggling prayers, bold prayers and "never give up" prayers. But also, there is a time *to rest in prayer*, or silent prayers. Didn't David say, "I wait quietly before God, for my hope is in him" (Ps. 62:5, *NLT*)?

If you are fasting from food, you are letting your body rest. That means your stomach is resting and the heart is not working as hard to digest your food. Don't forget about your soul. It also needs some rest.

You begin your Christian life by getting rest from sin. Jesus invited us, "Come to me, all of you who are weary and carry heavy burdens, and I will give you rest. Take my yoke upon you. Let me teach you, because I am humble and gentle at heart, and you will find rest for your souls" (Matt. 11:28-29, *NLT*). After salvation, you must continue to get stronger spiritually by seeking occasional rest.

Why Silence?

We love noise. Think of all the constant noise within your life. When I was a young man, we had only three channels on TV; now there are hundreds available to us. Every time I walked through an airport, I was looking for a pay phone; now I've got a cell phone in my pocket to talk anytime and almost any place. Some people keep their Bluetooth® headset hanging on their ear for ease and increased conversation. I thought that I was up-to-date when I bought an MP3 for constant music. Now the young people Twitter and carry iPhones and iPods. We can get streaming noise without stop.

What did Paul mean, "Aspire to lead a quiet life" (1 Thess. 4:11)? What did God mean, "In quietness and confidence shall be your strength" (Isa. 30:15)? There is power in silence before God. It's not the absence of words that gives us strength; it's God's presence that empowers us. David wrote, "Truly my soul silently waits for God; From Him comes my salvation" (Ps. 62:1). This probably didn't mean original salvation from sin, but our daily salvation from the domination of sin.

We don't learn as much when we're talking as when we're listening. So we need to kneel quietly in God's presence to learn some of the better lessons in life.

Also, we get strength from being quiet in God's presence. Just as our tired physical muscles need rest to regain their strength, so our tired souls need rest to regain determination and courage to work for God. Your stomach is now resting in this Daniel Fast; what about the rest of your physical body? What about your soul?

You can communicate with God in silence. Most people think silence is wasted time because nothing is happening. But does communication happen only with talking? No! Think of two people in love; they can sit for the longest time, looking into one another's eyes, with no sound from their mouths. Yet they are communicating, even when they don't say a word. Their presence with one another communicates love.

But that type of love has to grow in understanding, acceptance and relationship. There's that word again—prayer is *relationship*. Do you have a relationship with God that allows you to sit silently in His presence without talking? Have you received the strength that comes from wordless prayers?

Rest in God

God considers rest so important that He decreed one day out of every seven was a day of rest. Note the fourth commandment:

> Remember the Sabbath day, to keep it holy. Six days you shall labor and do all your work, but the seventh day is the Sabbath of the LORD your God. In it you shall do no work: you, nor your son, nor your daughter, nor your male servant, nor your female servant, nor your cattle, nor your stranger who is within your gates (Exod. 20:8-10).

Why did God create a Sabbath day? Because He first rested on the first Sabbath. "Thus the heavens and the earth, and all the host of them, were finished. And on the seventh day God ended His work which He had done, and He rested on the seventh day from all His work which He had done" (Gen. 2:1-2).

Did God need to rest from His work because He was tired? No! God is omnipotent, which means He is all-powerful. He created all things without effort. God was not tired, but He rested. The word "rested" means ended or finished. God finished what He intended to do, then took a day off. He invites you to practice the same thing.

Because God finished and then rested, He invites you to finish each week in His presence, on His day, with His assembly of people. You should rest—or finish—the work of each week in His presence. We don't keep Sunday laws to please God as did the Jews in the Old Testament. We finish our normal week of work to do His spiritual work on the Lord's Day.

If you dismiss the Sabbath as mere legalism, you miss an opportunity to rest in the Lord. Most people who go away on a vacation don't cease activity. They golf, swim, hike or do other activities that can be just as strenuous as during the work year. But recreation is a renewing activity and, in the same way, you need renewing in your spiritual activity when you rest in God.

We must sit silently in God's presence to practice the presence of God. When you learn of Him, you can practice His presence while stuck in the traffic gridlock or while waiting in a long check-out line. What do you do while waiting for your computer to boot up? Do you ever steal a few seconds by going to God's presence?

Wordless praying is both an art and skill, and there's a difference between the two. Remember that "art" is that expression of your inner nature that comes naturally from the heart. Skill is developed through training, practice and repetition. Art is what you naturally are; skill is what you acquire.

So *resting in prayer* comes naturally when you quit talking. However, there is a skill to the discipline of silence so that something is happening in the silence between you and God. You're growing, you're getting closer to God, and you're getting your prayers answered.

The Jews observed the Sabbath (the Hebrew word *shabbath* means "rest") as a symbol of their covenant with God. Because they lived in an agricultural world, and the work on a farm is never done, God told them to take a day off so they could rest. But more than physical rest, it was a day of worship, learning and spiritual exercise.

Look at the word "recreation." It means to re-create our emotional determination or our strength or our mental focus. We cease one type of activity—work—to enter another type of activity—play—to re-create ourselves. Do you need spiritual re-creation? You get it when you come into God's presence.

Life is a song. All week long we sing the laborious music of business pressures. Just as music starts and stops, is fast and slow and plays on our emotions, so too our workweek is filled with pressures, deadlines, production problems and just the pressure to do better. Then on Sunday we enter the fellowship of believers to sing God's song. We sing praises to Him; we sing our worship, "You are worthy, O Lord" (Rev. 4:11). We sing joyfully our testimony of salvation and His grace to us.

We not only sing with others, but we also sing with God. Did you see that? The Bible teaches that God sings: "He celebrates and sings because of you, and he will refresh your life with his love" (Zeph. 3:17, *CEV*). Because you rejoice in God, and He rejoices in you, why don't you learn His song and sing together with God?

As you fast, learn to rest and sing with God. It will rejuvenate your spirit and renew your determination.

In this chapter, we've discussed silence before God. But there comes a time for words. Talk to God intimately, but not about your project; talk to God about Himself. Tell God what you enjoy about your fast. Meditate on the great things He did in creation. Then turn your thoughts to the great things God did in salvation. Finally, end up thanking God for the things He has done in your life.

After you've talked to God awhile, stop talking and listen for His voice. You probably won't hear an audible voice, but you will receive a message in your heart. He will tell you what to do. He may even tell you how to pray or what you ought to be praying about. Use the following questions to make you think on God.

- As you read the Scriptures, what is God saying to you?
- As you meditate on Scriptures, what does God want you to do?
- As you wait in God's presence, how does He want you to pray?
- For what should you pray?
- What has God said to you through your successes?
- What has God said to you through your failures?

As you wait, ask God to reveal His presence to you. Remember the illustration used earlier in this book: *If you worship the Father, He will come to receive your praise.* Worship the Father because "the Father seeks worship" (John 4:23, *ELT*).

Accept what you learn, do what you know. Too often we go to God's Word to analyze what is said so we can know what it means. But knowing is never enough. Knowing is never wrong, but if you don't put God's Word into action, you never get God's blessing in your life. The written Word of God must become the living Word of God in your heart.

My Time to Pray

Lord, forgive me when I do all the talking in Your presence;
I will listen and be quiet. I will learn.

Lord, forgive me for making my prayer request more important than
resting in Your presence and enjoying intimacy with You.

Lord, I will come apart to fellowship with You in Your presence at
a certain time each day.

Lord, give me spiritual strength to pray for my prayer project, and help me
continue asking to the end of my fast. Amen.

My Answers Today

For suggested recipes, see pages 180-192.

❧ DAY 19 ❧

Urgent Prayer

*Prayer is reaching out after the unseen; fasting is letting go of
all that is seen and temporal. Fasting helps express, deepen, confirm the resolu-
tion that we are ready to sacrifice anything, even ourselves
to attain what we seek for the kingdom of God.*
ANDREW MURRAY

When you pray urgently, it probably means you're praying with all
your heart, and you keep praying because you really need an answer. When a friend faces cancer surgery, you pray because there's
nothing else you can do.

Urgent prayers come out of a growing need. Urgency of heart
produces urgency in prayer. When you know a bill is due at the
end of the month, and you don't have the money, there is an urgency to do something. As the end of the month approaches, you
feel more and more panic. You ask yourself, *What am I going to do?*
You pray urgently and persistently.

Urgent prayers for lingering problems; Desperate prayers for
a crisis.

There is a picture in Psalm 42 of a young deer being chased by
hunters. The deer is absolutely terrified and is running for its life.
Fear motivates us to cry out for help, and we cry from the bottom
of our hearts. Fear peels away our pride and excuses. The answer
of Psalm 42 is the first step to your urgent prayer. "As the young
deer being chased stays long enough for a drink of water in a

mountain stream, so my soul pants for God" (Ps. 42:1, *ELT*).

What about desperation? You pray desperately when there is an immediate crisis. Peter was walking on the water toward Jesus. His eyes were fixed on Jesus. Isn't that the way we should walk our Christian life? Then, "But when he saw that the wind was boisterous, he was afraid; and beginning to sink he cried out, saying, 'Lord, save me!' " (Matt. 14:30). He prayed desperately:

"Lord, save me!"

What is a desperate prayer? It's when you can't prepare your heart by asking for forgiveness of any ignorant sins in your life. Nor do you have time to reverently enter His presence. You immediately cry out like David:

"Help, O LORD my God! . . . save me" (Ps. 109:26).

What can we say about desperate prayers? You panic, or you're in a hole with no way out. There's no way out of your problem if God doesn't intervene.

Sometimes you've tried everything, but every door is closed. You've worked hard to get out of a jam, but now the tide is coming in and you're running out of time. Nothing has worked, so now you're desperate.

On the other hand, sometimes a desperate situation hits when you didn't expect it. You're peacefully driving along when a truck seems to come out of nowhere and broadsides you. You're hurt, and your loved one is lying on the ground bleeding. It's an emergency . . . a crisis . . . you need immediate help. So, you cry out to God, *"Now, Lord!"*

Does urgency describe your present state of affairs? You've faced a prayer project, and you've prayed about a need, but nothing has happened yet. Now you're at the end of your Daniel Fast; you're desperate; you have entered the Daniel Fast to touch God so He will answer your prayers. Read on because you'll learn how to pray desperately.

Preparing to Pray Urgently or Desperately

First, get mentally prepared for emergencies. You should have been asking God to prepare you for future emergencies, but now you are there. So even in the middle of this emergency, ask God to prepare you for future times of trials and testings.

Technically, you can't prepare for an emergency, but you can ask God to give you the ability to deal with an emergency when it comes. Ask God to give you peace in the emergency, and then ask God to give you wisdom to react properly in times of crisis.

Part of your preparation is knowing that difficulty will come. My pastor says continually, "There are more hard days than there are good days in the life of the saints of God; just as there are more valleys than there are mountaintops."

Second, memorize verses that point you to God in time of trouble. When an emergency comes, you will not have time to look up Bible references to encourage you. But if they are hidden in your heart, God can bring them to your mind.

- Psalm 27:5: "For in the time of trouble He shall hide me in His pavilion; in the secret place of His tabernacle He shall hide me; He shall set me high upon a rock."

- Psalm 34:6: "This poor man cried out, and the Lord heard him, and saved him out of all his troubles."

- Psalm 46:1: "God is our refuge and strength, a very present help in trouble."

- Psalm 56:3: "Whenever I am afraid, I will trust in You."

- Psalm 121:1-2: "I will lift up my eyes to the hills—from whence comes my help? My help comes from the Lord, who made heaven and earth."

- 2 Chronicles 14:11: "Lord, it is nothing for You to help, whether with many or with those who have no power; help us, O Lord our God, for we rest on You, and in Your name we go against this multitude. O Lord, You are our God; do not let man prevail against You!"

Third, know when to move from urgent prayers to desperate prayers. You pray urgently for a project because it is a spiritual need. But then a deadline approaches (the end of a Daniel Fast with no answer in sight). Your prayers move from urgency to desperation. You cry out, *"Lord, do it now!"*

When you're hungry, you sit at a table and eat in a civilized way. You use utensils and chew with your mouth closed. But look at the starving person. It's acceptable to gulp and swallow. A starving appetite trumps decorum and polite manners.

So remember, there is a proper time for desperately crying out to God with tears and deep passion.

Fourth, jump right into your prayers. Don't think about what you are going to pray—just pray. Don't consult your prayer lists; also, don't think about how you will frame your request; just pray. Don't get ready to pray—just pray.

If you were cutting weeds in the backyard and a snake bit you on the leg, you wouldn't ask how the snake got there, nor would you question what people will say. You would yell, "HELP!" and run for help.

If you have a desperate situation, open your heart and yell, "Help, Lord!"

Fifth, keep your scheduled times of prayer. As you approach emergencies, you will cry out instantly and wholeheartedly. When a problem comes, immediately lay the problem at God's feet.

But don't let an emergency rob you of your foundation of continuing prayer. As you continue in your Daniel Fast, don't forget about all the other problems in your life and in the lives of your friends and relatives. Keep bringing those before your Father in heaven.

If you have been missing one or two meals a day to pray, then keep that schedule. Remember, it's in those scheduled times of prayer that you find strength. You will need continuing strength in times of crisis, so be faithful in your committed times of prayer.

It's all right for a starving man to grab any food that's close to him. In the same way, it's all right for a desperate person to cry out in desperate prayers. But there comes a time when the starving person returns to normal life. Then he must eat a balanced diet to keep his strength. He must discipline his meal times and meal intake and eat a balanced diet to remain strong. In the same way, a well-balanced prayer life will keep you strong in Christ. Constant, balanced prayer is the best foundation to get desperate prayers answered.

Sixth, bring God into the crisis. King Asa went into battle with 580,000 of his troops against the Ethiopians who had a million men and 300 chariots. The prospect of victory was slight, and the hope of God's people was dark. Asa prayed for God to be with him.

"Asa cried out . . . 'LORD, it is nothing for You to help, whether with many or with those who have no power; help us, O LORD our God, for we rest on You, and in Your name we go against this multitude. O LORD, You are our God; do not let man prevail against You!'" (2 Chron. 14:11).

Did you see what Asa said in his prayers? The Ethiopians were attacking God's people, but Asa realized they were attacking God. Note that he prayed, "Do not let man prevail against You!"

You are fasting and praying for a spiritual victory. Make sure the fast goal is God's project and not your personal project. Sometimes we try to talk God into blessing the project we do for Him. While doing projects for God is good, there is something better. It's when God assigns you a project. It's His project. When you pray, make sure you and God are on the same side.

The emphasis is not on your begging God to come help you win this battle. No, that's the wrong emphasis. It's not even getting God on your side; it's you getting on God's side.

When the prayer project of this Daniel Fast is God's goal, then you can pray with confidence because God will complete His project, in His way, at His time.

My Time to Pray

Lord, I lay this prayer project at Your feet. This is what You have laid upon my heart. I will fast and pray until the end of my vow.

Lord, I have been praying urgently about the prayer goal. Now I come praying desperately for an answer.

Lord, give me faith to believe You for this prayer goal. "I believe, help Thou my unbelief."

Lord, I need Your help now! Amen.

My Answers Today

_____

_____

_____

_____

_____

_____

_____

_____

_____

_____

_____

_____

_____

_____

For suggested recipes, see pages 180-192.

DAY 20

Spiritual Warfare Prayer

*If you are serious enough about the personal and social tasks before you
as a Christian to take up the discipline of fasting, you can expect resistance,
interference and opposition. Plan for it, insofar as you are able. Do not be
caught unawares. Remember that you are attempting to advance in your spiritual journey and to gain ground for the Kingdom. That necessitates taking
ground away from the enemy—and no great movement of the Holy Spirit goes
unchallenged by the enemy.*

ELMER L. TOWNS

I was in Haiti on New Year's Eve when we celebrated the arrival of
1978. I was sleeping on the back screened porch of missionary Bob
Turnbull. There is a tremendous amount of demonic activity in
Haiti, and New Year's Eve is the high time for satanic manifestation.

I was awakened at midnight when all the church bells in Port-
au-Prince began chiming, and the boat whistles in the harbor began sounding and the automobile horns began honking. I was
told that at midnight on New Year's Eve, evil manifested itself
greater then than at any other time in the year. I shuddered when
I became aware of an evil presence on the porch with me.

When in spiritual warfare—because of an evil presence—I pray
out loud the name of Jesus and claim His blood for protection.
I call on the power of the cross for safety. (Because Satan or demons
can't read your mind, you must pray out loud the things you want
them to hear.) Then in the darkness of midnight, I began singing
out loud songs about the blood of Jesus.

What can wash away my sin?
    Nothing but the blood of Jesus.
What can make me whole again?
    Nothing but the blood of Jesus.

Oh! precious is the flow
    That makes me white as snow;
No other fount I know,
    Nothing but the blood of Jesus.[1]

I got tremendous confidence singing about the blood of Jesus Christ, and it focused me on Jesus, away from any evil that was present. Then I began to ask myself, "What's another song about the blood of Jesus?"

There is a fountain filled with blood
    Drawn from Emmanuel's veins;
And sinners plunged beneath that flood
    Lose all their guilty stains.

Lose all their guilty stains,
    Lose all their guilty stains;
And sinners plunged beneath that flood
    Lose all their guilty stains.[2]

I sang for a long time, forgetting where I was and forgetting my immediate problem. In my mind I went back to the cross where Jesus died for me. In my heart I worshiped the Lord. Then I began to sing again:

When I survey the wondrous cross
    On which the Prince of glory died,
My richest gain I count but loss,
    And pour contempt on all my pride.
Forbid it, Lord, that I should boast,
    Save in the death of Christ my God!

All the vain things that charm me most,
  I sacrifice them to His blood.[3]

There's another place in Scripture where we can learn the principles of spiritual warfare. Moses stood on a high hill to see a battle line unfold before him. God's people were being attacked by Amalek—an evil nation that fought against Israel for 1,000 years.

This was not a battle between two nomadic desert tribes, nor was it sword against sword or brute strength against brute strength. It was God against Satan: the kingdom of light against the kingdom of darkness.

As long as Moses held up his arms in intercession to God, the soldiers of God won the battle. But the battle continued throughout the day. When Moses dropped his arms in fatigue, Amalek prevailed. "And so it was, when Moses held up his hand, that Israel prevailed; and when he let down his hand, Amalek prevailed" (Exod. 17:11).

Of course, upheld arms are not a magical way to get a victory. They are like extended hands today as a symbol of our uplifted hearts to God. When God's people face a spiritual battle, they can claim victory by lifting hands and heart to God.

While you are on a Daniel Fast, you'll be tempted like never before, probably because you're attempting to do something you've never done before. You're fasting and praying for 10 or 21 days for a faith project.

So you may encounter (1) a temptation to quit, or (2) have difficulty keeping your mind on God when you should be praying, or (3) you'll think of a past satisfying sin, or (4) a spirit of discouragement will overcome you, or (5) a besetting sin may return, or (6) other un-Christlike attitudes will manifest themselves.

So, most of your spiritual warfare will not be with extremely evil things such as casting out a demon or dealing with supernatural manifestations of demonic power, or obvious anti-Christian people attacking you or your ministry.[4]

Israel's battle with Amalek was a renewal of hostility. The Jews fought Amalek over water rights in the desert much earlier. When

Moses led the multitude to the oasis at Horeb, the people expected water. But the water had dried up. The thirstier the people became, the angrier they complained. Moses cried to the Lord, "What shall I do with this people?" (Exod. 17:4).

God told Moses, "Behold, I will stand before you there on the rock in Horeb; and you shall strike the rock, and water will come out of it, that the people may drink" (Exod. 17:6).

When Moses obeyed, water gushed from the rock. The people understood this was a supernatural victory: "Is the LORD among us or not?" (Exod. 17:7).

Water is more precious than gold to a person thirsting to death. So the Amalekites attacked Israel to get the water rights. There is a principle here: When we have a great spiritual victory, look out! The enemy may be preparing a counterattack.

Perhaps you experienced a great victory by getting many people to agree on a spiritual challenge to a Daniel Fast and pray for a faith project. But remember, getting a group to begin fasting and praying together is only the beginning. Perhaps you feel a personal victory because you've kept your fast for almost 21 days. Watch out! Evil Amalek may be preparing an attack to stop you from reaching a successful end to the fast.

Practical Helps in Spiritual Warfare

Get strength from your friends. The battle in Exodus 17 was not won by one individual. It took Joshua, the general, and soldiers to fight. It took Moses, the intercessor, and Aaron, his brother, and Hur, his brother-in-law, to support Moses' arms. In the same way, remember that there are others who are interceding with you for the faith project. Call on them to pray for your special need. Share with them your burden. Have them pray *for* you as they pray *with* you. "For we are God's fellow workers" (1 Cor. 3:9).

Actively battle against your distractions/temptation. Perhaps you shouldn't close your eyes when praying. But when you keep them open, be careful not to look at things that will also distract your mind. Write out your prayers as you pray them. Underline or highlight your prayer requests as you pray them.

Pray out loud so you can focus on the target. When you are actively putting words together, your mind will not wander.

Change your prayer posture. Just as Moses got tired (because he was old), so your muscles will not hold up indefinitely. Move from kneeling to standing to walking to lying prostrate before the Lord. Keeping the body active may keep the mind focused.

Know your weakest area. The enemy knows your weaknesses and will attempt to attack you there. So don't let him get you there. Write down what is your weakest area, be aware of it, pray about it and be mindful of it.

Pray against your enemy. Some call this "rebuking Satan, or rebuking the enemy." When you pray against the enemy, do so with caution; for our enemy has great supernatural power. But on the other hand, be encouraged; Jesus said, "All authority has been given to Me in heaven and on earth" (Matt. 28:18). Remember the illustration at the beginning of this chapter? I prayed out loud, claiming the power of the blood of Christ to defeat the enemy.

When Michael the Archangel was in warfare prayer, as recorded in Jude 9, he was careful not to pray in self-confidence or to trust his own ability. His response to evil power was, "The Lord rebuke you!"

Be ready for a counterattack against any success you have in prayer. Paul reminds us, "Pray without ceasing" (1 Thess. 5:17).

Claim the victory that is already yours. God has promised, "He who is in you is greater than he who is in the world" (1 John 4:4).

My Time to Pray

Lord, I want to be strong in Your strength; help my weakness and keep me vigilant.

Lord, the Bible says, "I can do all things through Christ who strengthens me," so I yield my weakness to Your strength.

Lord, thank You for every victory I've had in the past; I learn from them and go forward "from victory to victory." Amen.

My Answers Today

_____

_____

_____

_____

_____

_____

_____

_____

_____

_____

_____

_____

_____

_____

_____

_____

_____

_____

_____

Notes
1. Robert Lowry, "Nothing but the Blood of Jesus." http://www.subversiveinfluence.com/wordpress/?p=1433 (accessed December 11, 2008).
2. William Cowper, "There Is a Fountain Filled with Blood." http://www.cyberhymnal.org/htm/t/f/tfountfb.htm (accessed December 11, 2008).
3. Isaac Watts, "When I Survey the Wondrous Cross." http://www.cyberhymnal.org/htm/w/h/e/whenisur.htm (accessed December 11, 2008).
4. Elmer Towns, "The Esther Fast," _Fasting for Spiritual Breakthrough_ (Ventura, CA: Regal Books, 1996), pp. 157-171.

For suggested recipes, see pages 180-192.

❧ DAY 21 ❧

Stay in the Moment

Fasting is a principle that God intended for everyone to be able to enjoy.
It's not a punishment; it's a privilege! By making fasting a way of life,
you can get closer to God and grow in your spiritual walk like never before.
Fasting is one of the most powerful weapons God has given us for our daily lives.
Through fasting, you can experience a release from the bondage of sin . . .
restoration in your relationships . . . financial blessings . . .
spiritual renewal . . . supernatural healing and so much more!
Another reward of fasting has to do with your future. God has given you
a vision, a divine dream for your life. When you fast, you open up
the blessings and opportunities He has provided for you to pursue that dream.
As you fast, pray for God's direction and guidance. Focus your faith on your
dream and God will show you how you can turn your vision into a reality.
Begin pursuing your divine dream today and make the rewards of
fasting part of your lifestyle.

JENTEZEN FRANKLIN
(HTTP://WWW.JENTEZENFRANKLIN.ORG/FASTING/)

The Israelites and Philistines were involved in continual warfare, but the Philistines had gained the upper hand by controlling the pass at Micmash (see 1 Sam. 14:1-52). Saul was king, but he did nothing about the enemy; he sat on the outskirts of Gibeah, quite a distance away (see 1 Sam. 14:2).

His son Jonathan devised a courageous plan to defeat the enemy. He decided to climb the cliffs near the pass and fight the enemy. His attack was a tipping point in the battle, and eventually gave Israel the victory. Jonathan created a daring plan of attack.

Jonathan began his strategy by putting his trust in God. He told his armor bearer, "Perhaps the LORD will work for us" (1 Sam. 14:6, *NASB*). Why is it that so many do the opposite; they think, *Perhaps God won't work on my behalf* or *I won't do anything foolish.* Why is it that we are afraid to put God on the spot?

Jonathan's strategy eventually became the vision of all the soldiers of Israel, and they won a great battle. So, as you continue to fast—to the last day—your faithfulness and prayers may motivate others to continue to be faithful in prayer. Together, all of you can win a victory. "Now thanks be to God who always leads us in triumph in Christ" (2 Cor. 2:14).

Your fast vow is not just a dream; your fast becomes an *enabler* because it has motivated you to continual prayer. You, in turn, want to motivate God to act in your behalf.

Perhaps you've been thinking, *If I pray long enough and hard enough, God might do something in this matter.* So, apply the words of Jonathan: "Perhaps the LORD will work for us" (1 Sam. 14:6, *NASB*).

Jonathan's eyes were not on his ability, nor on the fact that he was fighting alone. He knew the number of people fighting wasn't the condition of victory when he said, "For nothing restrains the LORD from saving by many or by few" (1 Sam. 14:6). He knew that he could win in God's power, even though he was only one fighting against many. So, it's not your ability to pray, nor is it your ability to fast that will get answers to your prayer. Look to God's ability to perform what you ask.

Can you see Jonathan climbing cliffs, fighting one Philistine soldier after another, coming to the end of the day exhausted yet victorious? It took repeated steps of faith by Jonathan to gain victory, and he gave everything he had to get it.

But where was Jonathan's father, Saul? He was the king. Saul should have been leading the army into battle. Saul was sitting on the outskirts of Gibeah doing nothing. Are you a Jonathan, or a Saul? If you don't do anything, nothing is going to happen.

Sometimes it seems like the victory is too big and the enemy is too large. The Philistines had high ground that is usually necessary in attacking the enemy. The odds were against Jonathan; yet with God on his side (or rather, Jonathan got on God's side), Jonathan led God's people to victory.

I don't know how long Jonathan surveyed the situation, and I don't know how long it took him to develop a battle plan, but there comes a time when you must go beyond vision to action. There comes a time when you have to go public to tell everyone that you are fasting for a faith project.

But look what happened when Jonathan went public. His armor bearer joined Jonathan's plan to climb the cliff and defeat the Philistines. Instead of laughing at Jonathan, or refusing to go, the armor bearer said, "I am with you, according to your heart" (1 Sam. 14:7).

So there are people in your church or friends within your acquaintances who want to do something for God. But perhaps they're waiting on you to be the "Jonathan." Perhaps they are waiting on your vision. Perhaps they are waiting on you to go public with the challenge; therefore, you need to get them involved in fasting and prayer for the faith goal.

So make a faith statement to move the mountain barrier. Don't be afraid to tell others why you are fasting and why you are praying for the faith project.

One more thing: You'll never be completely ready to pray for 10 or 21 days. It may be that praying for 10 or 21 days is more than you've ever done before. Maybe you've never had experience in fasting. Maybe you think you don't have education enough, or spirituality enough, or enough of anything. But one person—like Jonathan—can lead many others to win a victory for God. What was the result? "So the LORD saved Israel that day" (1 Sam. 14:23).

Don't quit your fast when you're almost to the end. Remember, quitters never win and there are no great stories about people who quit. There's nothing like crossing the finish line with the inner confidence that you've done what you set out to do.

Keep true to your original commitment and be focused on the moment. Do one day's assignment at a time—live within the moment—one day at a time and always with focus on the goal.

To get a college education, you do one day's assignment at a time, attend the classes of that day and pass one exam at a time. Being faithful to your daily assignment leads to a successful semester. Then two semesters add up to a year. Stay in the moment for each day of the second year and you'll have two successful years under your belt. You're halfway there. Continue the process and you'll finish four years of college. But the secret is to make each moment successful.

You never win a race with only a fast start from the starting block. A race is one stride at a time, so learn to remain in the moment and be faithful till the goal is reached.

No one writes a whole book in one sitting; he or she writes one page at a time. No one wins the World Series in the first game of the season; it's winning one game at a time throughout the summer. No one wins the golf tournament with one tremendous shot, so they must focus on the present shot. They must stay in the moment.

Victory is a choice; it's the present pitch of the baseball, the present class you must take, the present stride in the race. Today is the twenty-first day of your Daniel Fast, so stay in the moment. Then later today, you'll reach your goal.

Victory is a door; you must open and walk through the door to enter the victor's circle.

My Time to Pray

Lord, I'm almost to the goal; I will keep my eyes focused on the finish line until I get there.

Lord, raise up a hedge of protection (see John 1:9) around me so that no emergencies or attacks from the Evil One can stop me from reaching the finish line.

Lord, I'm still praying for the faith project for which I'm fasting and praying. Give us the thing for which we fast.

Lord, I give You the credit for enabling me to finish this fast. Now I pray You will be glorified when others hear of this fast. Amen.

My Answers Today

_____

_____

_____

_____

_____

_____

_____

_____

_____

_____

_____

_____

_____

_____

_____

_____

For suggested recipes, see pages 180-192.

❧ SECTION 3 ❧

Appendices

It was in 1994 that the Lord really began to deal with me about fasting in a fresh and powerful way, and to give me new insights into the subject. On July 5 of that year, God led me to begin a 40-day fast for a great spiritual awakening in America and for the fulfillment of the Great Commission throughout the world. Also, on the twenty-ninth day of my fast, as I was reading God's Word, I was impressed to send letters to Christian leaders throughout America and to invite them to Orlando, Florida, to fast and pray together for revival and the fulfillment of the Great Commission. Invitations were soon in the mail. I was praying and hoping for at least "Gideon's 300" to respond positively and to join me at the planned December event. More than 600 came! They represented a significant part of the Christian leadership of America from many different denominations, churches and ministries. It was three wonderful days of fasting, prayer, confession and unity. Many of the leaders gave testimony that it was one of the greatest spiritual experiences of their lives. But before God comes in revival power, the Holy Spirit will call millions of Christians to repent, fast and pray in the spirit of 2 Chronicles 7:14. I have been impressed to pray that God will call at least 2 million Christians to fast and pray for 40 days for the coming great revival.

WILLIAM R. BRIGHT

Nine Kinds of Fasts Found in Scripture[1]

To better illustrate and reveal the significance of the nine biblical reasons for fasting, I have chosen nine biblical characters whose lives personified the literal or figurative theme of each of the nine aspects of fasting highlighted in Isaiah 58:6-8. Each fast has a different name, accomplishes a different purpose and follows a different prescription.

I do not want to suggest that the nine fasts are the only kinds of fasts available to the believer, or that they are totally separate from each other. Nor do I want to suggest that there is only one type of fast for a particular problem. These suggested fasts are models to use and adjust to your own particular needs and desires as you seek to grow closer to God. What follows is a brief overview of the nine fasts that are found in *Fasting for Spiritual Breakthrough*.

1. The Disciple's Fast

Purpose: "To loose the bands of wickedness" (Isa. 58:6)—freeing ourselves and others from addictions to sin.

Key Verse: "This kind goeth not out but by prayer and fasting" (Matt. 17:21, *KJV*).

Background: Jesus cast out a demon from a boy whom the disciples had failed to help. Apparently they had not taken seriously enough the way Satan had his claws set in the youth. The implication is that Jesus' disciples could have performed this exorcism had they been willing to undergo the discipline of fasting. Modern disciples also often make light of "besetting sins" that could be cast out if we were serious enough to take part in such a self-denying practice as fasting—hence the term "Disciple's Fast."

2. The Ezra Fast

Purpose: To "undo the heavy burdens" (Isa. 58:6)—to solve problems, inviting the Holy Spirit's aid in lifting loads and overcoming barriers that keep us and our loved ones from walking joyfully with the Lord.

Key Verse: "So we fasted and entreated our God for this, and He answered our prayer" (Ezra 8:23).

Background: Ezra the priest was charged with returning to Jerusalem to restore the Law of Moses among the Jews as they rebuilt the holy city of Jerusalem by permission of Artaxerxes, king of Persia, where God's people had been held captive. Despite this permission, Israel's enemies opposed them. Burdened with embarrassment about having to ask the Persian king for an army to protect them, Ezra fasted and prayed for protection.

3. The Samuel Fast

Purpose: "To let the oppressed [physically and spiritually] go free" (Isa. 58:6)—for revival and soul-winning, to identify with people everywhere enslaved literally or by sin, and to pray to be used of God to bring people out of the kingdom of darkness and into God's marvelous light.

Key Verse: "So they gathered together at Mizpah, drew water, and poured it out before the LORD. And they fasted that day, and said there, 'We have sinned against the LORD' " (1 Sam. 7:6).

Background: Samuel led God's people in a fast to celebrate the return of the Ark of the Covenant from its captivity by the Philistines, and to pray that Israel might be delivered from the sin that allowed the Ark to be captured in the first place.

4. The Elijah Fast

Purpose. "[To] break every yoke" (Isa. 58:6)—conquering the mental and emotional problems or habits that would control our lives.

Key Verse: "He himself went a day's journey into the wilderness. . . . He arose and ate and drank; and he went in the strength of that food forty days and forty nights" (1 Kings 19:4,8).

Background: Although Scripture does not call this a formal "fast," Elijah deliberately went without food when he fled from Queen Jezebel's threat to kill him. After this self-imposed abstinence, God sent an angel to minister to Elijah in the wilderness.

5. The Widow's Fast

Purpose: "To share [our] bread with the hungry" and to care for the poor (Isa. 58:7)—to meet the humanitarian needs of others.

Key Verse: "The jar of flour was not used up and the jug of oil did not run dry, in keeping with the word of the LORD spoken by Elijah" (1 Kings 17:16, *NIV*).

Background: God sent the hungry prophet Elijah to a poor, starving widow—ironically, so the widow could provide food for Elijah. Just as Elijah's presence resulted in food for the widow of Zarephath, so presenting ourselves before God in prayer and fasting can provide for humanitarian needs today.

6. The Saint Paul Fast

Purpose: To allow God's "light [to] break forth like the morning" (Isa. 58:8)—bringing clearer perspective and insight as we make crucial decisions.

Key Verse: "And he [Saul, or Paul] was three days without sight, and neither ate nor drank" (Acts 9:9).

Background: Saul of Tarsus, who became known as Paul after his conversion to Christ, was struck blind by the Lord as he was persecuting Christians. He not only was without literal sight, but he also had no clue about what direction his life was to take. After going without food and praying for three days, Ananias, a Christian, visited Paul, and both Paul's eyesight and his vision of the future were restored.

7. The Daniel Fast

Purpose: So "thine health shall spring forth" (Isa. 58:8, *KJV*)—to gain a healthier life or for healing.

Key Verse: "Daniel purposed in his heart that he would not defile himself with the portion of the king's delicacies, nor with the wine which he drank" (Dan. 1:8).

Background: Daniel and his three fellow Hebrew captives demonstrated in Babylonian captivity that by abstaining themselves from pagan foods, and eating healthy foods, they could become more healthful than others in the king's court.

8. The John the Baptist Fast

Purpose: That "your righteousness shall go before you" (Isa. 58:8)—that our testimonies and influence for Jesus will be enhanced before others.

Key Verse: "He shall be great in the sight of the Lord, and shall drink neither wine nor strong drink" (Luke 1:15, *KJV*).

Background: John the Baptist, the forerunner of Jesus, kept the Nazirite vow that required him to "fast" from, or avoid, wine and strong drink. His fast was part of John's adopted lifestyle that testified to others that he was set apart for a special mission.

9. The Esther Fast

Purpose: That "the glory of the LORD" will protect us from the evil one (see Isa. 58:8).

Key Verse: " 'Fast for me ... [and] my maids and I will fast ... and so I will go to the king' ... [and] she found favor in his sight" (Esther 4:16; 5:2).

Background: Queen Esther, a Jewess in a pagan court, risked her life to save her people from threatened destruction by Haman, the prime minister. Prior to appearing before King Xerxes to petition him to save the Jews, Esther, her attendants and her cousin Mordecai all fasted to appeal to God for His protection.

Note

1. Elmer Towns, *Fasting for Spiritual Breakthrough* (Ventura, CA: Regal Books, 1996), pp. 20-23.

Six Ways to Fast

There are nine biblical fasts described in *Fasting for Spiritual Breakthrough*. There are nine Bible studies that tell the various ways that fasting was done in Scripture, and the various purposes for which people fasted. However, there are probably as many ways to fast in our modern times as there are ways to pray—obviously, there is no set number in either case. The following six ways of fasting are good guidelines for you to follow or modify as God directs.

1. The *normal fast* or *juice fast* is going without food for a definite period during which you ingest only liquids (water and/or juice). The duration can be 1 day, 3 days, 1 week, 1 month or 40 days. Extreme care should be taken with longer fasts, which should only be attempted after medical advice from your physician.

2. The absolute fast allows no food or water at all, and should be short. Moses fasted for 40 days; but this would kill anyone without supernatural intervention and should never be attempted today. No one should attempt an absolute fast for longer than three days. A person will die if they go longer than seven days without water. The average body is 55 percent to 80 percent water, and must be replenished on a regular basis. Be sure to test the spirit that tries to talk you into a 40-day fast that does not include liquids.

3. The *Daniel Fast*, also called a *partial fast*, omits certain foods or is on a schedule that includes limited eating. It may consist of

omitting one meal a day. Eating only fresh vegetables for several days is also a good partial fast. Elijah practiced partial fasts at least twice. John the Baptist, and Daniel with his three friends are other examples of those who participated in partial fasts. People who have hypoglycemia or other diseases might consider this kind of fast.

4. A *rotational fast*, also called a *Mayo Clinic fast*, consists of eating or omitting certain families of foods for designated periods. For example, a person has an absolute fast for one day to cleanse his bodily system. Then for the next week, he eats food from only one food group or food family. The various food families are rotated to determine what illness may be attributed to certain families of food.

5. The *John Wesley Fast* was practiced by Wesley, the founder of Methodism, prior to the Methodist Conference where the ministries gathered for retreat, revival and preparation for continual ministry. Wesley and the other leaders fasted 10 days prior to the conferences with only bread and water to prepare themselves spiritually so they could teach the pastors.

6. *Supernatural fast*. Moses fasted for 40 days: "He [Moses] was there with the LORD forty days and forty nights; he neither ate bread nor drank water" (Exod. 34:28); apparently Moses spent two 40-day fasts on the mountain praying and receiving the Commandments from God. The two fasts were separated by a few days when the people made the golden calf, i.e., a false God (see Deut. 9:9,18,25). God did a supernatural miracle for Moses in these fasts where a person normally dies when they go without water for more than 7 days. No one should attempt a 40-day fast without water.[1]

Note

1. Elmer Towns, *Fasting for Spiritual Breakthrough* (Ventura, CA: Regal Books, 1996), pp. 23-24. .

Recipes to Use During a Daniel Fast

John P. Perkins

Executive Chef and Development Director of the
John M. and Vera Mae Perkins Foundation

When you are focusing on your Daniel Fast and purposing in your heart to give up meat as your sacrifice, you will need to make sure that you are getting enough protein in your diet. You only need 15 percent protein in your diet, and there are a few ways that you can get this necessary amount. One way is by eating legumes, and for this reason eating peas and beans will be important during your fast. In the following section, I will provide you with a few recipes that you can use to infuse the necessary amount of legumes into your diet during your fast.

The Hoppin' John (Black-eyed Peas)
1 lb. dried, soaked or frozen black-eyed peas or field peas
1 large onion, diced small
1 small tomato, diced
½ gallon vegetable stock
½ lb. or 1 cup cut okra, fresh or frozen
salt and pepper, to taste

Bring ½ gallon of vegetable stock to a boil and add peas and onions. Allow it to simmer for 1 hour and 15 minutes. Add tomato after peas have been cooking for 45 minutes. Season with salt and pepper to taste, add a ½ cup of okra, and cook for another 15 minutes. Serve with 1¼ cups white rice (simmer white rice in 4 cups water for 18 to 20 minutes, or cook parboiled rice for 10 to 12 minutes).

Classic Red Beans and Rice

1 lb. dried kidney beans or red beans
1 large onion, diced small
2 bell peppers, diced small
2 tbsp. minced garlic
½ stalk of celery, diced small
¼ cup Worcestershire sauce
¼ cup brown sugar
½ gallon water or vegetable stock
salt and pepper or seasoning salt, to taste

Bring ingredients to a boil and simmer for 1 hour and 20 minutes. Add salt and pepper or seasoning salt to taste and simmer for another 15 minutes. Serve with 1¼ cups white rice (simmer white rice in 4 cups water for 18 to 20 minutes, or cook parboiled rice for 10 to 12 minutes).

Black Bean Soup

1 lb. black beans, dried and soaked
1 small onion, diced small
2 bell peppers, diced small
2 tbsp. minced garlic
½ stalk of celery, diced small
1 tomato, diced small
1 tbsp. olive oil
1 tsp. Italian seasoning
½ tsp. cumin
2½ quarts water or vegetable stock
salt and pepper or seasoning salt, to taste

Sauté the onion, bell peppers, garlic, celery and tomato in a little olive oil until they are translucent. Add mixture to the black beans and water or vegetable stock and your Italian seasoning and cumin. Bring to a boil and then allow the beans to simmer together for 1 hour and 20 minutes. Add salt and pepper or seasoning salt to taste and simmer for another 15 minutes.

Homemade Granola

2½ oz. sesame seeds
2½ oz. sliced almonds or pecans
11 oz. oats
4 oz. cashews
4 oz. honey
3 oz. dried cranberries or raisins

Toast the sesame seeds in a dry skillet until golden brown. Place in a separate bowl. In the same skillet, toast almonds or pecans to a pale golden color. Add the sesame seeds and continue to toast until the nuts are golden brown. Add the oats and cashews to the skillet and continue to toast, stirring until light brown. Add the toasted sesame seeds and honey to the skillet. Heat and toss until all the ingredients are coated with the honey. Remove the pan from the heat and stir in the cranberries or raisins. Spread mixture on a baking pan with a liner of parchment paper at the bottom. Bake in an oven at 350° until golden brown (about 15 minutes). Allow the granola to cool and then break into chucks. Store in a cool dry place. (**Note:** Unlike many other cereals, oats retain the majority of their nutritional elements after the hulling process. If you eat this recipe in moderation, it will be a considerably enjoyable snack—but it is high in fat, so watch your intake.)

Fresh Fruit Parfait with Honey-Vanilla Yogurt

1 qt. nonfat vanilla yogurt
4 oz. honey
8 oz. banana, diced
6 oz. strawberries
5 oz. apples, cooked
8 oz. granola
sprig of mint (if desired)

This recipe is a great compliment to the above granola recipe, and when accompanied with fruit, you can't beat this dish. Begin by stirring the honey into the vanilla yogurt. Place fruit in a separate bowl and toss together; keep refrigerated until needed. Place a small layer of granola in a presentation dish, wine glass or parfait cup. Place a small layer of yogurt over the granola, and then place a small layer of fruit (bananas, strawberries and cooked apples) over the yogurt. Continue this pattern until the dish is filled. Garnish with the granola and add a sprig of mint if desired.

Daniel's Vegetable Fajitas
2 tbsp. olive oil
1 tbsp. garlic
5 oz. red onions
12 oz. red bell pepper
12 oz. yellow bell pepper
12 oz. green bell pepper
1 lb. shredded cabbage
12 oz. cooked kidney beans
5 oz. red chili sauce
18 flour tortillas

Heat the olive oil in a large sauté pan. Add the onions and the garlic. Sweat the onions until they are translucent. Add the peppers and cabbage and sauté until tender (add a teaspoon of water if necessary to sauté the cabbage—the cabbage cooks by steam). Stir in the kidney beans and chili sauce and heat just until warmed. Cover the tortillas with a lightly damp towel in a warm oven at 225°. Wrap vegetable mixture in the warmed tortillas. (**Note:** I often select this recipe because it is healthy, and those who enjoy Mexican cuisine will particularly enjoy it. Bell peppers are a great source of vitamin A, B and C and contain folic acid, which expecting mothers especially need during their pregnancy.)

Grilled Vegetables
12 oz. yellow squash, sliced about a quarter-inch thick on an angle
10 oz. zucchini, sliced a quarter-inch thick on an angle
6 oz. yellow or red onions, sliced a quarter-inch thick
6 oz. green bell pepper, sliced a half-inch thick

6 oz. red bell peppers, sliced a half-inch thick
6 oz. medium mushrooms, sliced in half
5 oz. balsamic vinaigrette

For this recipe, you will need to get out your grill. Grilling is one of my favorite things to do as a chef, and vegetables taste so good when they are grilled. For this recipe, first toss all the vegetables in balsamic vinaigrette (as a marinade) for about 30 minutes. Then grill the vegetables on a gas grill or a flattop grill for 2 minutes on each side (fork tender). You can also add eggplant, tomatoes and other veggies.

Wild Rice Succotash
1 tbsp. extra-virgin olive oil
6 oz. whole corn kernels
5 oz. medium mushrooms, sliced
2 tomatoes, diced
4 oz. butter peas or lima beans
4-6 oz. wild rice or white rice (cooked)
2 oz. vegetable stock
1½ oz. scallions, sliced thin on an angle

Heat the olive oil in a sauté pan. Add the corn and mushrooms and sauté until tender. Add the tomatoes, peas or lima beans, rice, vegetable stock, scallions and salt and pepper to taste. Mix the ingredients and heat thoroughly. (**Note:** Cooking with corn, mushrooms, tomatoes, butter peas or lima beans and wild rice is a great combination. This is a leftover type of dish that can turn corn or rice used in a previous meal into a succotash. Every mother in the world needs this recipe!)

Roasted Corn and Black Beans
1 tsp. of olive oil
1½ oz. red onions, diced
2 garlic cloves, minced
1 lb. roasted corn kernels

6 oz. dried black beans, cooked
1 tomato, diced
1 tbsp. lemon juice
salt and pepper, to taste
2 tbsp. chopped parsley
1 tbsp. chopped cilantro

Heat the olive oil in a large pot. Add the onions and garlic and sauté until translucent. Add the corn, beans, tomato, lemon juice and salt and pepper to taste. Toss over high heat until the mixture is hot. Remove from the heat and stir in the cilantro and parsley. (**Note:** This dish is versatile and makes a great side, but it can also be very filling as an entrée.)

Barley Pilaf

5 oz. onions, diced
1 tbsp. garlic, chopped
1 qt. vegetable stock
11 oz. barley
2 bay leaves
1 tbsp. Italian seasoning

In a saucepan, sweat the onions and garlic in 2 ounces of the vegetable stock until the onions are translucent. Add the barley, bay leaves, Italian seasoning and the rest of the vegetable stock. Bring the liquid to a boil and cover the pot tightly. Cook in an oven at 350° for 45 minutes or on a stove 12 to 15 minutes until the pilaf has absorbed all the liquid and the barley is tender. Stir in herbs just before serving. (**Note:** You can turn this into a Barley Walnut Pilaf by adding 2 ounces of chopped, toasted walnuts to the pilaf before the barley is cooked. After the barley is cooked, add another 2 ounces of chopped nuts.)

Basic Rice Pilaf

6 oz. of yellow onions, diced
4 oz. celery

2 tbsp. vegetable solids (margarine)
16 oz. white rice
30 fl. oz. vegetable stock or water
6 oz. broccoli florets
8 oz. baby carrots
salt and pepper, to taste

Sweat the onions and celery in 1 tablespoon margarine until they become translucent. Add the rice and sauté with the onions and celery. Add the vegetable stock or water to the rice mixture. Cook rice in the oven at 350° for 40 minutes or on top of the stove until rice is tender but not finished cooking (about 12 to 15 minutes). Add the broccoli and carrots and continue to heat until the rice and vegetables are cooked all the way through. Add 1 tablespoon margarine and salt and pepper to taste. (**Note:** This is my southern variation of the classical French dish Rice Pilaf along with the Barley Pilaf recipe that I presented to you earlier. Both are outstanding dishes and deserve to be in your repertoire.)

Stir Fried Barley

4 oz. green bell pepper, diced
2 oz. onion or shallots, diced
2 oz. carrots, diced
2 oz. celery, diced
2½ tbsp. olive oil
16 oz. barley pilaf
½ tsp. dried thyme or 2 tsp. fresh thyme

In a saucepan, sweat the peppers, onions, carrots and celery in the olive oil until tender. Add the barley pilaf and thyme and stir-fry until heated thoroughly. (**Note:** This is my favorite type of recipe for this particular fast. It is a compound from a previous Barley Pilaf recipe. These are the type of recipes that enable you to use leftovers, keep a low-food cost, and save money in the end. Dieting is expensive, and we have to be good stewards of our resources.)

Rosti Potatoes with Celeriac
20 oz. russet potatoes
20 oz. celeriac
1 tbsp. Dijon mustard
½ tsp. Cavenger's Greek Seasoning
1½ tbsp. olive oil

Peel and grate the potatoes and celeriac. Combine the grated potatoes and celeriac, mustard and seasoning. Form the mixture into
20 1½-oz. cakes or 10 3-oz. cakes. Heat enough oil to lightly coat
a nonstick sauté pan. Sauté the cakes until golden brown on each
side. Finish by cooking the cakes in the oven at 475° until thoroughly heated (about five minutes).

Daniel's Four-Grain Waffles
1 qt. nonfat buttermilk
3 whole eggs
2 oz. vegetable oil
8 oz. all-purpose flour
6 oz. whole-wheat flour
6 oz. rolled oats
3 oz. cornmeal
2 tbsp. baking powder
2 oz. sugar
9 egg whites

Combine buttermilk, whole eggs and vegetable oil in a large bowl.
Combine all dry ingredients (flours, rolled oats, cornmeal, baking
powder and sugar) in a separate bowl. Add the dry ingredients to
the liquid ingredients and mix just until incorporated. Whip the
egg whites to a soft peak and fold into the batter. Lightly spray a
hot waffle iron with vegetable oil. Ladle the batter into the waffle
iron and cook until the waffles are golden brown (about 3 minutes). Serve immediately. (**Note:** topped with the fruit salsa below,
this is wonderful treat for the fast.)

Barley and Wheat Berry Pilau (Pilaf)

3 oz. wheat berries
15 oz. vegetable stock
2 tsp. vegetable solids (margarine)
1 oz. leek, diced
2 oz. carrots
½ oz. celeriac, diced
2 tsp. of minced shallots or red onions
2 tsp. minced garlic
6 oz. pearl barley
5 oz. white grape juice
salt and pepper, to taste
6 oz. chopped spinach

Soak the wheat berries for 8 to 10 hours in 3 times their volume in water. Drain the berries and combine with the vegetable stock. Cover and simmer until tender (about 1 hour). Drain any excess stock and reserve. Heat the margarine in a medium saucepan. Add leeks, carrots, celeriac, garlic and shallots or red onions. Sweat until the vegetables are tender. Add the barley, grape juice, salt and pepper and the reserved wheat berry cooking liquid. Bring the liquid to a boil and cover the pot tightly. Cook in an oven at 325° or on the stove until the barley is tender and has absorbed all the liquid (about 45 minutes). Cook the spinach in lightly salted water until tender. Drain well. Combine the wheat berries, barley and spinach and serve.

Vegetable Pot Pie

1 lb. frozen mixed vegetables
6 oz. whole kernel corn
6 oz. broccoli florets
13½ oz. cream of celery soup
2 pie shells (one deep dish)

This recipe has the potential to become a family favorite. Combine the mixed vegetables, corn, broccoli florets and cream of celery soup in a bowl. Mix together and place in the deep-dish pie shell. Invert the other pie shell, place on top of the pie filling, and crimp the sides together. Place slits on the top pie shell, creating vents for the vegetables to steam and the shell to cook properly. Place in the oven at 365° for 50 minutes. Serve with cranberry sauce.

Vegetarian Dirty Rice

3 oz. dried cranberry beans
2 oz. onions, diced
2 garlic cloves, minced
14 oz. vegetable stock
7 oz. long-grain rice
1 tbsp. tomato paste
1 tbsp. vinegar
2 tbsp. minced roasted jalapeño
1 tsp. crushed black peppercorn
1 tsp. Cavenger's Greek Seasoning
1 tsp. pepper
1 tsp. paprika
¼ tsp. cayenne
3 oz. grated cheddar cheese
4 oz. roasted corn kernels

This powerful dish is one for the ages and will go along well with your fast. First, cook the cranberry beans in boiling water until tender. Drain and mash with a fork and keep as reserve. In a medium saucepan, sweat the onions and garlic in 2 tablespoons of the stock until they turn translucent. Add the rice and sauté briefly. Add the remaining stock, tomato paste, vinegar, jalapeño, Cavenger's Greek Seasoning, pepper, paprika and cayenne. Bring the stock to a boil and cover the pot. Cook in an oven at 350° until the rice is tender and has absorbed all the liquid (about 18 minutes). Fold the mashed beans, cheese and corn into the rice.

Vegetable Burgers

1 lb. carrots, grated
2 oz. celery, grated

2 oz. onion, grated
1 oz. red pepper, minced
4 oz. white mushrooms, minced
4 oz. scallions (green onions), minced
4 oz. walnuts, minced
1 egg, beaten
½ tsp. parsley, chopped
½ tsp. thyme, chopped
1 tsp. minced garlic
1 tsp. salt
½ tsp. Tabasco sauce
½ tsp. sesame oil
¼ tsp. ground black pepper
1 oz. crackers, crushed into meal

I couldn't have written the recipes for this fast without our giving you a burger to eat. There are a lot of veggie burgers out there—the only difference is that this one is good! First, place the carrots, celery, onion and pepper into a sieve, and press to release the excess liquid. Place the mixture in a large bowl and add the mushrooms, scallions, walnuts, egg, parsley, thyme, garlic, salt, Tabasco sauce, sesame oil and black pepper. Stir to thoroughly combine. Add enough cracker meal to make a firm mixture, and form into 10 3½-oz. patties. Roll each patty in additional cracker meal if desired. Bake each patty on a sheet pan lined with parchment paper at 475° until thoroughly cooked (about 10 minutes).

Wild Mushroom Chowder

2 tsp. vegetable solids (margarine)
4 oz. onions, diced
2 oz. celery
1 tbs. minced garlic
1 oz. arrowroot or cornstarch
1 qt. vegetable stock
12 oz. russet potatoes, peeled and diced
6 oz. evaporated skim milk

2 tsp. heavy cream
2 oz. grape juice
1 lb. wild mushrooms (without the stems)
5 oz. mushroom stock
salt and pepper, to taste

You can't go wrong with this soup! Begin by heating the margarine in a large soup pot. Add the onions, celery and garlic. Sweat until tender. Combine the arrowroot or cornstarch with enough stock to form a slurry. Add the remaining stock to the vegetables and bring to a simmer. Add the slurry to the stock and bring to a simmer until thickened. Add the potatoes to the thickened stock and simmer until tender (about 15 minutes). Remove the pot from the heat and add the evaporated milk, cream, grape juice, salt and pepper. In a large sauté pan, sweat the mushrooms in the mushroom stock until tender. Gently stir into the soup and enjoy.

Tropical Fruit Salsa

16 oz. mango, trimmed and diced small
8 oz. papaya, trimmed and diced small
4 oz. red bell pepper, diced small
4 oz. red onion, diced small
4 tbsp. cilantro
4 tbsp. lemon juice
1 tbsp. minced jalapeño
2 tsp. olive oil
salt and pepper, to taste

Combine all ingredients and allow to set for one hour before serving (refrigerate if not serving immediately). (**Note:** To prepare this dish for a dessert or brunch item, substitute mint for the cilantro, strawberries for the peppers, and onions and honey for the olive oil. Serve as a filling for crepes or with muffins, pancakes or French toast, or accompany with biscuits. You can also substitute honeydew melon, cantaloupe and pineapple in place of the papaya and mango to create this dish.)

Black Bean and Corn Loaf

2 tbsp. corn oil
6 oz. onions, diced
6 oz. red pepper, diced
2 oz. minced garlic
12 oz. cooked black beans
4 oz. seasoned tomatoes
2½ tbsp. cilantro, chopped
¼ tsp. Tabasco sauce
1 qt. vegetable stock
1 tsp. salt
½ tsp. crushed peppercorns
8 oz. cornmeal
2 oz. all-purpose flour

Heat the corn oil in a large skillet. Add the onions, red pepper and garlic and sweat until the onions are translucent. Remove from the heat and stir in the beans, tomatoes, cilantro, and Tabasco sauce. Heat the vegetable stock, salt and peppercorns in a saucepan. Slowly whisk in the cornmeal. Reduce the heat and simmer, stirring constantly, until the mixture pulls away from the sides of the pot (about 20 minutes). Remove from the heat and fold the beans mixture into the cornmeal. Lightly spray a 1½-quart loaf pan with vegetable oil and place the mixture in the pan. Refrigerate for 8 to 10 hours. When ready, unmold the loaf and slice into 15 equal slices. Slice each piece on the diagonal to make 30 triangles. Lightly dust 2 triangles for each serving and sauté in a hot skillet sprayed with oil until golden brown.